the
Singer
Sisters

the Singer Sisters

SARAH SELTZER

PIATKUS

PIATKUS

First published in the United States in 2024 by Flatiron Books,
An imprint of Macmillan Books
Published in Great Britain in 2024 by Piatkus

1 3 5 7 9 10 8 6 4 2

A CIP catalogue record for this book
is available from the British Library.

Hardback ISBN 978-0-349-43779-8
Trade paperback ISBN 978-0-349-43778-1

Printed and bound in Great Britain by
Clays Ltd, Elcograf S.p.A.

Papers used by Piatkus are from well-managed forests
and other responsible sources.

Piatkus
An imprint of
Little, Brown Book Group
Carmelite House
50 Victoria Embankment
London EC4Y 0DZ

An Hachette UK Company
www.hachette.co.uk

www.littlebrown.co.uk

In loving memory of

Molly Seltzer, Joan Seltzer, Lillian Libman,

and Bernice "Bunny" Lewis.

Thank you for starting the melody.

PART I

PART I

EMMA

When Judie Zingerman and Dave Cantor sat down at the kitchen table and told their children they were splitting up, Emma didn't cry—even though her parents' news made the back of her throat sting and tears collect behind her face.

In a family of performers, you had to fight for the stage. So she decided to counter them with an announcement of her own.

It didn't help that all afternoon she had been in her childhood bedroom with her mother's old acoustic guitar, trying to write a song even half as good as one of her parents'—and failing. And it didn't help that when Judie called them together that evening by playing three notes on a triangle, Emma found it all tedious: the round glass table supporting eight forearms, four tumblers of sherry. An uneaten apple pie in the center of their family circle, forlorn, four plates stacked beside it.

"Separation. Separate tracks. That's how Judie puts it—when she talks about it, it makes sense," said Dave, his ring finger scratching his mustache. "I want to live near the Dharma Center. Your mother has the teaching job in Brooklyn."

The tabletop under Emma's hands was moist with sweat. During so many family arguments, she had stared at her palm under the glass and followed its veins like maps out into a future where she shone, alone. Judie promised that they'd still do Thanksgiving in New Hampshire. Dave said, "Dammit, Judie, if I'm getting one thing from this, it's to avoid that infernal drive."

"Glad that's settled," said Emma's brother, Leon, his tone (and eyes) dry.

Emma succumbed to a hiccuping laugh and squirted sherry from her nose. Judie handed her a paper towel; Emma thanked her.

"Don't worry, Emma-bear," said Judie, her hand on Emma's. "Providence isn't far."

"You mean Portland," said Emma, withdrawing her hand, unable to resist letting a smirk settle on her lips as she twisted the knife.

"What do you mean?" Judie's eyes trained on her daughter, her smile fixed and bright, almost like Aunt Sylvia after her facelift.

Emma noticed their old chandelier, one of its four bulbs blown out. Her parents, one of music's "most enduring" couples (according to *The New York Times*), had decided to no longer endure. They should feel some pain in exchange: their daughter, an Ivy League acceptance and all, had elected instead to spend her foreseeable future with a ska band in the Pacific Northwest.

Judie had done one absurd thing after another in life: Quit music after Leon was born, despite being a genius songwriter. Refused to support Emma's singing career. Taken a part-time job at Windermere's Theater Department. And now, abandoned Emma's father. She had written some of the century's most beloved songs instead of going to college but obsessively demanded that Emma take a different path. She hadn't earned obedience.

"I don't understand," said Judie. "Do you have a record deal?"

"A headlining set?" asked Dave.

"Does Mae have a producing gig?" asked Leon.

"No, no, and no. I'm opening for the same dudes. They got booked on a big tour next year, is all, and Mae and I are going with."

"But Emma, your academic *excellence*," said her mother. "That paper on *Middlemarch* . . . your writing prizes."

When Emma first said that she was deferring Brown for a year, Dave had thrown his hands into the air and said, "Well, she'll be a legal adult." But Judie kept haunting Emma's bedroom with stricken eyes. Judie had *notoriously* pleading eyes. "Don't do what I did," she'd begged. "Don't throw it all away."

Emma was throwing it all away.

Besides, the *Middlemarch* paper her mom kept harping on had won first prize in a contest for a group of four progressive New York City schools, not the state, not even the city. In its pages she had argued, with rhetorical heat, that Dorothea Brooke's choice to marry for love instead of pursuing her own greatness was a Tragedy, capital T.

Emma would be no Dorothea.

⌣

er mother, still lecturing her as though she were twelve: "You just tell those boys you changed your mind. They'll find another singer."

Emma, groaning, saying she'd promised them she'd go to Oregon.

Her mother saying what about her promises to Brown, to her *family*?

"They might be locked in combat for a while, Dad," said Leon as he cut himself and Dave each a slice of pie. They began to eat.

Emma explained to Judie that the undergrad assistant to the Office of Admissions, Jade, hadn't taken Emma's news badly, had even promised to talk to someone she knew at the Office of Student Life about Emma playing a show at Brown next year.

"Jade in admissions is like, a major, major fan," Emma said. Unmentioned: the girl had said her mother was a major fan of Judie's group with Aunt Sylvia, the Singer Sisters.

But who needed to know that detail?

Certainly not her mother, who didn't perform anymore—her mother, whose face was surely crumpling with sadness, then blazing with rage, then crumpling again as disappointment in her wayward child won out over all other emotions.

"What are you trying to prove, Emma?" asked the blazing-crumpling face.

With parents and a brother who were all musical geniuses, Emma felt the answer to that question was too obvious for her mother to miss.

Still, she tried to explain. Tour vans took her from one sedate, cloistered campus to another. "I like my life better than that," she said.

Judie insisted her daughter was scared. Of what? Of being *normal*, said Judie with a snort. "Onstage, anyone can pretend that they're special."

The little girl in Emma wanted to scream that *she was special*! Instead, she sneered.

Judie put her head in her weathered hands, with new calluses from her teaching-with-a-guitar life. Emma could just see her mother smiling tenderly at some fourteen-year-olds in Emma's old classrooms, sounding out chords and lyrics, gently discussing harmony and projecting, and breathing, and all the while shining her Judie light on them, her marvelous Judie light, bestowed so rarely but so coveted by all. Once, a hippie had come right into their apartment without invitation, simply to breathe in Judie's aura.

"You need a fallback plan when this doesn't work," said Judie, now.

"It *will* work."

"That's what people like us always say."

"Mom, I'm *not* like you. I'm not going to flame out, play housewife, and end up being a teacher at my kids' old school, and I'm sure as hell not leaving my husband in his dotage because I don't want to take care of him!"

Three intakes of breath from around the table.

"For Christ's sake," said Dave at the very same time that Leon said:

"Dad has a new lady friend, dummy. From the ashram."

"Oh," said Emma, flaming. "Please tell me she's over forty."

"Forty-three," said Dave defensively.

Judie's head had remained in her arms from the moment Emma said the word "housewife," an occasional shoulder heave breaking her stillness.

"You lied, Emma," she said now. "You said you would defer a year, but you never were planning on going to Brown next year. You let me hold on to this dream. I carried it around!"

Emma hadn't lied—she just hadn't decided.

"What I want to know," Emma asked, "is why Mom wants a separation instead of just hitting Dad with ye old Judie Zingerman silent treatment?"

"What a nasty comment," Judie snapped. Her sherry glass shook. "I guess I earned it—the way I carped at my dad."

～

Once Judie grew taciturn and weepy, Dave always shooed the kids out of the house, saying, "Your mother needs her rest."

Somehow, even now, they obeyed; they scraped chairs back, donned their black peacoats, shoved hands into sleeves and pockets, with Emma's sighs punctuating the process. At the door, Judie handed her daughter a tube of lipstick—"not the drugstore kind"—and told Leon to say hi to the bouncer at Small's and see if the new bassist had any chops.

"Emma, bring home a quart of milk if you remember," she said.

"Okay, Mom."

"Do either of you wear any color but black?" asked Judie as the door closed behind them.

~

The mild winter night opened its arms. They grabbed beers and went to Small's, a tiny jazz club whose long line to enter made for the ideal place to stand and talk.

Leon rolled his eyes at the ink-black sky. "You're hard on Mom," he said. The rings from their six-packs dug into their virtuoso fingers.

Judie was hard on *her*. Emma favored Dave, fumbling, well-meaning Dave. And Leon—more distant from Dave (who never wanted to offend his gay son but was *puzzled* by him)—claimed Judie as his personal tragic heroine.

"Maybe Mom will finally make a record," he said. "I could produce!"

"She'd let you," said Emma. "They actually support *your* music."

"They believe music insulates me from the gay bashing and whatnot," said Leon. "And they think it *exposes* you, wee sis."

"That doesn't make it fair," said Emma, who always liked to have the last word.

~

At the front of the line, the bouncer winked at them. "Long time, Cantors," he said. "How are Judie and Dave?"

"Baffling," said Leon.

"Positively enigmatic," said Emma.

He laughed and let them in.

Inside, the bass player's spindly, deft hands made Emma think about sex, a kite line that got tangled in the thought of her parents splitting up. Her *parents splitting up!* Any magazine article about a divorce would feature one of the two famous photos of Judie and Dave, either the one on the flowered blanket, Emma as a fat baby cuddling up to her mother's cleavage, or the daisy-haired one from their wedding in New Hampshire.

The articles would begin, "After over twenty years of marriage, one of folk-rock's most enduring couples is calling it quits. . . ."

Leon slipped off to the bathroom to snort a few lines. Emma picked at a fingernail, whose metallic-black nail polish had chipped into an island. When Leon came back, he'd be restless. He'd cajole her up to the new family apartment uptown, bought for Leon and Emma with their grandparents' estate, so they could "jam" all night. She opened another beer and chugged the whole thing before it even hissed and settled.

Her brother slid into his seat.

"Hey, sis," he hissed on cue, his eyes newly bright. "Uptown for a jam sesh?"

~

She jammed, she jammed hard. But at three a.m., sloshing with beer and hair perfumed with smoke, Emma arrived back in her childhood bedroom, thinking she ought to move her stuff uptown with Leon already, only to yelp with shock at a dark mass in her bed.

Soft lamplight revealed Judie, curled up in the twin bed's corner, her form almost submerged under a wool blanket. Her beloved Brown course catalog was cradled in one arm, Emma's *Middlemarch* paper with the stick-on medal peeling at the corners lay open beside her.

"Mom, you obsessive snoop," muttered Emma, scooping up the square shoebox that had once held her Doc Martens and now held her sundry papers. The Zingerman women always had a shoebox under the bed.

Judie's face was in the pillow, her slippers still on her feet. Emma moved the blanket away from her mother's nose, yanked a clean T-shirt and underwear from her dresser, and took the box over to Leon's room.

But before she even crossed the threshold, snores reminded her that Dave had been sleeping there for weeks. Maybe more.

Only one place left to go. On the floor of her parents' unused bedroom, she opened the box, if only to avoid dwelling on what she had seen, like it was an image of violence. Her mother, a disheveled heap on her bed. It poisoned her, this weakness in Judie, this cloying need for Emma to take a respectable path. Every cell in Emma's body rebelled, yearned to create something strong enough to lift her out of this game of musical bedrooms, of enmeshed disappointments, of dancing around Judie's feelings but hurting them anyway, so that every step felt like the Little Mermaid walking on swords.

Wide-awake now, she rifled through the box, her hands animated: letters from camp, postcards, an old three-ring planner decorated in stickers, and collages of photos from bars and open mics. She smiled and tossed each item aside until she came upon an envelope with a hand-drawn lily on the cover. She remembered this envelope: she had found it on the kitchen table a decade ago, after that old hippie came to visit unannounced.

Emma read the words inside the letter. Flower had sent these words to them, to her. Emma's heart began to thud, and she realized that what was flowing into her was a song.

1985

Emma was eight and home alone, and she opened the door when the bell rang. She had expected Judie—a brisk forehead kiss, a hand combing her curls, bags slung onto the counter. Instead, a stranger swept into the foyer.

"Where is Judie?" the tall woman with a coiled blond braid asked.

Seeing Emma's surprised face, she softened. "I know her. You're her spitting image."

Emma explained that her mother had gone to do an errand (her father was touring with his band, her brother was at their aunt's house). The stranger's name was Flower. She called the lobby *fancy*, bragged that she'd slipped in behind a lady with ten dogs, and leaned down close.

"So, you're one of the murderers who killed her genius," said Flower. "I *had* to tell Judie what 'Route 95' means, I had to tell her right away."

Emma wanted to ask why, if Flower knew Judie so well, she couldn't call her on the phone. She offered Flower a drink.

"My mom lets me fix drinks when my dad's away," she explained. "He's sober."

Flower called Emma a minx. They moved to the table at the kitchen window where family "discussions" took place.

Flower chose gin, pouring it into her glass and draining it. Clink, it went down. Glug: more gin. Aunt Sylvia drank a lot, but Flower seemed *thirsty*.

"Do you ever wonder about a secret message in your mother's songs?" Flower asked.

"Her songs for *me* are the best," Emma said. "One is called 'Saucy Cat.' My brother and me sing on it. I know seven chords."

Emma didn't mention that *Dave* had sat down and taught her those chords, not Judie.

Flower shook out her braid; her hair unfurled like Rapunzel's. She glided from room to room until she reached the den, with its thick Moroccan rug, its couches where Emma and Leon were not welcome to horse around.

Her hands lingered on Emma's most cherished photo, framed in silver: Dave and Judie in New Hampshire, holding up their wedding bands as they kissed in front of the town hall.

Emma grabbed the picture, held it to her chest. "Don't touch that!" she said, protecting the daisy chains in their hair, the ceiling of white clouds, the romance in their eyes. The picture had been propped up near the one platinum record (for "Sweet Camellia Wine," the song the family knew as "Dave's Hit").

"Eternal," said Flower, prying Emma's hand away to stare. "But . . . the end for Judie. I traveled here to tell her that."

"I thought you traveled here to say that 'Route 95' was the best." Emma wished that Flower would leave, or her mother would come home, or at least they'd go back to the kitchen.

"Are you actually her friend?" Emma whispered.

"Your mother—she's a *prophet*."

At first Emma had pegged Flower as young like her teacher, Ms. Bell, but from up close she wasn't young or pretty.

"Tell me, sweetheart, why did she leave you here *alone*?" asked Flower, her face inches away, her gin breath hot. She put her glass down, hard, on the glossy coffee table. "You look just like her, really. Maybe I should take you back to Michigan with me as proof."

"Hey," Emma said. "You're supposed to use a coaster on that table." And that's when she started to cry.

PROVIDENCE, RHODE ISLAND, 1996

It began the way so many mornings on tour did: with the clang of hammers on a stage, the shuffle of a few fans arriving for sound check, and the low chatter of Emma and Mae themselves as they plotted to become more famous than Emma's parents.

At only ten a.m., dozens of kids in jeans and black fleeces had claimed spots on the dew-drenched lawn. And as they lit up their cigarettes and sneak-a-tokes, Emma marveled. These kids might have been her classmates. But instead, they were her audience, killing time waiting for *her* to take the stage.

Okay, they were waiting for the main acts, but the early birds were here to catch the whole show, and the whole show started with Emma.

Today, she and Mae were sound-checking at Brown's legendarily debauched Spring Weekend, where they'd open for ska act Less Than Jake and noise rock group Dinosaur Jr.

A simple setup: Emma on guitar, Mae on drums. They'd toss in some harmonies, the kind her mom and her aunt had been known for in the sixties and seventies. Maybe the Singer Sisters themselves would be in the audience. No, they wouldn't. Recently, Emma had been craning fruitlessly to find her mother at every show. The road crew massaged her neck a lot.

As far as Emma was concerned—and she had some authority as the daughter of two semi-famous musicians and the niece of a third—becoming a bona fide rock star required three elements. The look, the presence, and yes, the songs, the sock-you-in-the-gut, break-your-heart kinds of songs Judie Zingerman had scribbled with ease, even at Emma's age.

On two of the three, Emma felt solid. She kept her curly black hair short, which her friends said looked "hot" and "androgynous." *Check.* In performances, she snarled while strumming the guitar with one foot forward, a power stance she hoped would become her trademark. Her steel-toe boots kicked beer cans back into the crowd with the soaring arc of a soccer star and elicited screams of delight. *Check, check.*

But as for the third element, well, students reviewing her shows in college papers called Emma's songwriting "simplistic." Not going to cut it, if she hoped to be a star. Her brother, Leon, who those same writers said showed Judie's "raw talent," wrote compositions that burst at the seams with rich melodies and strange, ethereal accents.

Emma needed a change in fortune. Her dad had gone full crunchy and left town, her mom was teaching theater classes, her brother was always traveling. She had been fueled by bluster and rage recently, not the confidence that had launched her out on this tour. If this coming summer of gigs didn't lead to something bigger, a "breakout," she sensed, she would be a loser. Judie would be proved right, and Emma would fail and slink home, hat in hand.

Yet the clock hadn't run out. She had *it*—the *mojo*, the *vibe*, the *whatever* that ran through their family. Not yet twenty, she had steady work, more than she needed. Sometimes, when she was playing solo at festivals, acts like Joan Osborne or the Indigo Girls brought her out onstage for a final sing-along and embraced her as one of them.

The late-morning sun began to burn the dew off the grass. Emma strummed her acoustic guitar and did vocal warm-ups while the sound technician turned his knobs up and down and asked Mae to play notes on Emma's Stratocaster. Eyes closed, she let the damp New England breeze kiss her forehead. Sylvia and her mom were probably bickering on the deck right now, as mist hovered on the lake just a few hours north.

Her family wouldn't come today, but her devotees would: the girls who loved her shows best, their dark lipstick making them into a sea of vampires. They crowded up front, in flared sailor jeans that skimmed their chunky boots. Strands of green, pink, or red hair fell over their faces, chokers circled their necks; they had nose piercings, eyebrow piercings, lip piercings.

They were primed for Emma, thanks to Alanis, thanks to Jewel. Emma was close to catching this wave. But pressure was mounting, too. Waves always receded; her family had taught her that.

She yodeled, chased the stiffness from her fingers. This gigging life murdered the body. Some musicians used drugs to push through long days. Emma used grit. Well, drugs sometimes. But mostly grit, which her father said she had "in spades."

Grit was not the same as talent.

"Going to try 'Flower' today?" asked Mae. Mae, her drummer/manager/bestie, had ditched a cello for a drum kit at age thirteen and had goals of being a "feminist Korean version of Puff Daddy, but for rock." ("So . . . not like Puffy at all," Emma said. "Smart-ass," Mae replied.)

Flower. If she played it and it flopped, nothing remained in her arsenal. No other secret compositions. On the other hand, "You nail it, you could go Top Forty," Mae told her, as she so often did. "Have you heard the new Jewel single?"

Emma was alive and breathing, so she'd heard the song. It dug its claws in. Jewel had lived in a van in Alaska—no journalist forgot to mention *that* tidbit. The apocryphal tale made Emma's childhood in a seven-room apartment in Greenwich Village look plush. Her dad's affair, his sobriety, her mom's youth as a revered folkie—none of their dramas could live up to Jewel's origins.

"They're all *copying* my mom," she told Mae about Jewel and her ilk. "And yeah, I *have* been working on that tune . . . ," she added, almost in a whisper. "I think it's as good as like, a B-plus Dave Canticle song."

"Well, that's not bad! His songs were certainly better than his corny stage name. How's Dave doing?"

"Dave *is* still sober, unlike everyone on this lawn," Emma said, smiling. "His neighbor upstate raises goats."

"Any more talk of the big D?"

"No divorce talk. Not much talk at all with either of them."

What Emma didn't say: with Judie, it still felt like walking on swords.

~

When Judie did come home, that night of Flower's visit, they rushed her—Emma with Flower at her tail. Emma's wild arms had flung themselves around her mother's waist, a gesture usually reserved for her father or her aunt.

"Judith Zingerman . . ." Flower dropped into an honest-to-goodness curtsy. "What an honor. My name is Flower Robinson, and I traveled two days to tell you that your music has been the most meaningful I have con-sumed as a woman in this messed-up world."

"How did you sneak by downstairs?" asked Judie. She didn't wait for answers, nor did she ask about Emma's tear-streaked face.

"Wait . . . two days . . . for *me*?" Judie continued. "I used to hear from fans right and left. Now, Dave's fans are another thing—we always catch them trying to figure out if it's him, with the belly and the kids. Right, Em?"

She asked Emma to fix her a drink, then, saying she'd had *a day*.

"Flower drank your gin!" Emma shouted, but Judie held up her hand. This whole night was *wrong*, and Judie didn't notice it, and Emma felt tiny and alone.

When Emma trotted back with the cocktail, her mother and Flower were huddled in the foyer. Judie signed a piece of paper, ushered Flower out, and double-locked the door.

"For God's sake, Emma, ask who it is when someone knocks," said Judie. "Forget the drink. I have a headache."

A week passed. Flower sent her letter.

I call myself Flower because I am a flower, but my petals had curled up and dried—until I heard your songs.

In the 60s we had a vision about rainbows and light. I believed it, but the man I lived with didn't see it the same, which is to say he saw himself as entitled to more of the rainbows than I could get, and he hurt me for it.

I saw in your words a great secret and I think I know it because so many women do—somewhere in the past, a terror. A melancholy that spoke to our being trapped, not by other people, but by our own choices. When I look at myself in the water, I will also see your face, and that of your girl.

After Judie scanned the letter, snorted, "Overwrought hippies," and tossed it on the table, Emma swiped it. She was learning how to hide things. Judie was her teacher.

~

As Emma tuned her guitar for the opening notes of "Flower," three Brown students in pajama bottoms walked by the stage. Emma could appreciate the way college kids got cozy: on a stone bench in a corner of campus, in the library, in bed with each other. But she preferred them adoring her. At the choruses, they jumped, slamming their small, soft bodies against each other. "Chill out, I'm acoustic," she joked. This display proved she was meant to have more: a backing band. A laser show. Dozens of amplifiers. Magazine covers. Still, she needed one thing: "A killer song," as Leon told her. "Dig deep for one."

And she had. She hummed a few chords to Mae. "I am a great *flower*," she sang, barely above a whisper. She played the bridge on her guitar.

"Freaky," said Mae, exactly the word Leon had used. "Release it, Emma!"

When "Flower" entered the world, finished, it could explode. But when to send it flying? Today, for these potheads? Next week? Next *year*? Emma longed to call her mother for advice, to hear Judie's chuckle. But Judie had been weighing down their phone calls with long, uncomfortable pauses, as though waiting for Emma to relent. Emma didn't know how to puncture the discomfort to tell her mother about her own creative urges and fears.

Emma pranced around backstage with her guitar, trying to inflate herself into significance. Maybe she could ditch the black cutoff shorts she'd been pairing with combat boots, try a floaty Victorian dress. But she'd keep the boots on, use them to march into the pipeline of crooning women flowing up, up, and onto the airwaves.

"Easy on the frets," said the soundboard guy as Emma tried out a chord. "Why is every girl so angry now?"

"Get bent," said Emma with a grin, cheerfully living up to the stereotype.

"Bitch," he muttered, either humor or hatred in his tone. Before Emma could feel the sting, Mae hugged her, hard, the same fierce way Emma hugged Mae when people asked her where she was *from* (the answer was East Sixty-Fifth Street). They had an unspoken agreement: tight squeezes only. Girls who rocked didn't cry in public.

As they tried out a few notes of her new song, a humming started in Emma's chest, what her mother dubbed *the moths*. Judie meant it pejoratively, but Emma couldn't live without it.

When sound check ended, Mae tapped her on the shoulder. "Got invited to play with this Spanish Korean music troupe. College life, man. Come?"

"I'm going to shop," Emma said. "For a flowing dress, witchy and divine."

Mae approved. "The Singer Sisters would like that."

They would have, once upon a time. "The Singer Sisters are dead." Emma laughed. "Long live the Singer Sisters."

~

E mma's friends typically viewed childhood as innocent and adolescence an awakening. But for her it had reversed, because of her mom. Judie made an odd mom to little kids; she had no job, yet she didn't do stuff like fix crustless sandwiches for lunch, tucked next to apple slices.

But Judie, the mom of teens who had pizza delivery numbers posted by the kitchen phone and a credit account at the deli, who had stories about seedy hotels in London and drinking too much whiskey before shows—*that* felt natural. Judie, not necessarily by design, treated her family like a wild-flower garden.

Emma missed the mom of her early gigging era, a Judie of midnight popcorn and gossip, a mom who'd present her with a talisman of luck before a show or party: a silk scarf or sparkly earrings, even an embroidered jacket.

Later than she should have, Emma returned to campus, one vintage jew-eled belt buckle tucked under her arm. As she charged toward the backstage area, she practically tripped over a woman on the narrow steps. Elegant and leggy, like her aunt Sylvia.

This stranger, oblivious, blocked Emma's path, her wrist swirling a lemon-ade. "Excuse me!" said Emma. The woman hoisted herself up with effort, and as she did her silver jewelry caught the late-morning sun—hoops in her ears, a thick bangle on her wrist, and a chain with a crystal pendant disappearing into the scoop of her shirt. She wore loose slacks and an earth-brown blazer and had thick-rimmed glasses. Her sandy hair was as short as Emma's own. She looked up at Emma and her dark eyes widened in recognition.

"Sorry!" the stranger said, waving fingers positively stacked with rings. A musician couldn't adorn her hands that way and still play. The woman leaned back as if to take Emma in from head to toe: appraisingly—almost intimately.

"Emma Cantor. It *is* you." The woman's accent rolled like the hills of Scotland, or Ireland, or maybe Wales.

"You a fan?" Emma's cheeks glowed and her heart skipped.

"Yes! But I know you. Though it's a decade, isn't it—"

Emma scratched her head. A bunch of her new "fans" these days were actually old friends from the Washington Square Park playground, or camp, or once, even, an abortive Hebrew school attempt. But none of them were Irish.

"—since the lake house?"

"Oh. My. Freaking. God," said Emma, her voice squeaking. It was Rose, her Irish au pair. A slightly fuller face, more lines, shorter hair, but her old nanny was unaltered otherwise. "Poor Rose, chased away by my speedboat devilry?"

A flame tongue of embarrassment hit Emma as they bantered. Couldn't Rose have waited until *after* the show to remind Emma of that shameful summer, the way Emma had tried to drive away her jumpy babysitter, so out of place she couldn't even swim?

Emma tried to access the deep breathing Dave taught her to do before a show: two long breaths in, filling the belly, the lungs—then four out.

No use. She smelled lake water and spicy pines. The *gnawing* of that summer—of that era. Her mother's trip to Ireland, the summer of Rose, Rose disappearing to California, the intense family recording sessions for *Chant and Sing* interspersed with grudges and recriminations between mother, father, aunt—and then later that year, Flower at their door.

The phantom pain of these memories, of being a child in a clan of singers, where feelings stayed unseen if they couldn't rise to musical magnificence.

About the speedboat incident, Rose had mostly felt sorry for Emma, she now said, young and needing attention. She murmured about *connecting* to Emma's music. Mae wiggled into sight, shaking her hips, trying to get Emma to laugh—and hurry up.

"I've gotta go play," Emma said. And that should have been it: an awkward reunion, a show. But Rose had begun praising Emma's music, and Emma adored praise. So she tossed out a "Beer afterwards?" as she began to walk toward the stage entrance, preparing to brandish her plastic backstage pass.

Rose trailed her, the way she followed Sylvia and Judie around that summer long ago, like a dog. "Sure! Well, soda." She pointed to her stomach, where a mound could just be discerned beneath the well-tailored blouse.

Emma hadn't noticed. She forced a smile—pregnancy struck her as boring, gross. But Rose had unnerved her. "Stick around," Emma said. "You might hear something special."

After leaping the stairs two at a time, Emma found Mae backstage with a bottle of Coke. They sipped, squatted, and stretched. They were on in twenty. An astounding thundercloud of smoke now hovered above the audience.

Halfway through her breathing exercises, a pool of steely resolve began to radiate within Emma. Dig into childhood, Leon said. Dig *deep*. That summer, her mother and Sylvia patiently stood waist-deep in the freezing lake, teaching Rose to swim.

Why did the Singer Sisters take so much care with someone they barely knew, instead of teaching Emma to play guitar like her brother? Why, when Flower showed up, did Judie happily receive her flattery instead of checking on Emma? Why, oh why, was Judie acting so frosty at Emma for skipping college when she had done the same thing?

Emma heard hoots from the students assembled on the lawn. She breathed in the skunky undergraduate pot. That perfect breeze from earlier encored, cooling her hot skin. She licked the soda off her lips, closed her eyes, debating whether to play the song. That night long ago, Flower called Judie a *prophet* and "Route 95" the song of the century.

Emma shook her head, now flooded with her mother's most famous lyrics: *begin to begin*.

"Okay, Mom, I will," she whispered, and stepped out onstage.

JUDIE

When another aspiring folk musician sat down at her family's Shabbat table, Judie Zingerman narrowed her eyes. Taking off his newsboy cap and washing his hands, Dave Cantor resembled a Beatle, like most boys. But a Beatle-haired boy who knew how to bless the candles, who washed his hands and sucked up to her mother? *That* was unique.

Judie and her older sister, Sylvia, stared at Dave over their vegetable soup. His face made an appealing sight, framed by a silver tea samovar on one side and their parents' portrait of Eleanor Roosevelt on the other. Their cat, Adlai, lounged on the chair beside him.

What might a wandering musician on a winter evening make of their home, the tendrils of smoke from the candles, the twisted roses on the dark wallpaper? And the smells: yeasty challah and salty soup? The room could be interpreted as warm—or suffocating. Ornate, or overdone. Judie's braids, tied with lavender ribbons, probably looked childish. Meanwhile, a silver pin pulled Sylvia's short curls aside, accentuating her startling gray eyes.

Judie had to act fast to capture his attention.

"Where do you live, David?" asked her mother, Anna, after they had broken the challah.

"I live in Greenwich Village," said Dave. "Thompson Street. In the thick of it."

Judie needed no more invitation to launch herself into the conversation. "A bohemian! He needs *two* helpings of soup," she said, affecting a knowing tone.

"Who taught her to speak that way?" her father, Hyman, demanded of his wife.

"Watch your tone, Judie," said Anna with the rote weariness of a toddler's mother. As open-minded as the Zingermans claimed to be, their acceptance stopped at the threshold to their house. Raising accomplished musicians was second to raising *good girls*.

But the Singer Sisters, as Sylvia and Judie planned to name their folk-singing duo, had their own plans.

~

Sylvia and Judie spent the afternoons of their early lives at music lessons. Sylvia would walk beside Anna, regal, her portfolio of sheet music snug in her arms. Judie darted ahead or dawdled until, inevitably, their mother rebuked her with, "I'll tell your father."

And that got her to comply, because Hyman had told them his story again and again. Long ago, he had set aside his flair for piano to join the family business, but he yearned for music. After he came home from the war, married, and made a small fortune building houses in the suburbs, he returned to "his passion," constructing and running a recording studio near Central Square and squiring Sylvia and Judie to recitals.

The Jewish community called them homegrown prodigies. At synagogue concerts, they sang duets. Sylvia was lithe, bird-voiced, and destined for the stage; therefore Judie, though not without a voice, harmonized. Judie's teachers and relatives assured her this made sense. Every orchestra needed its second-string. Besides, adults called her "smart" and said she'd make an excellent teacher herself, before she married.

Without realizing it, however, Hyman had given his girls ideas. Nowadays, the spare room in their Cambridge home regularly housed musicians traversing the New England circuit. The girls dubbed these visitors "Papa's troubadours," emissaries from a new, wild world mere steps away, one of smoky coffeehouses, raunchy jokes, and young people making eyes at each other over instruments.

Sylvia, a college girl at Wellesley, instructed her younger sister to look and listen: the troubadours' visits offered a chance to study the airs of *real* performers, so they'd know how to act when they got their own big break.

Judie tried, she did, but she tripped on her own restlessness. She envied the men who sauntered in and out, who spoke without being told to lower their voices, who walked through the world with dirt on their jeans and un-combed hair. Her own inability to fasten her cardigan straight caused Anna's eyes to turn to heaven for assistance.

To make matters worse, every man who stepped into the house fell for Sylvia—blinking when Judie made a clever remark, as if to say, "Oh, right, the other one can talk too."

Judie craved their company, anyway. While the singers slept downstairs, she would lie awake, tapping her legs against the wall and scribbling in her notebook. She would close her eyes and imagine buying a train ticket, skip-ping town with a banjo—in the shadow of night, in pursuit of the kind of music that could change the world. Yes, she was "book smart," but with the adults being so grim about civil rights and war and social unrest, the idea of years of study made her quake. Sylvia urged patience, practice, but Judie didn't want to wait.

She could vocalize her desire in one way only: with pert sarcasm. Last week, she had weaponized an Elvis song: "Like the river flows / Surely to the sea / Papa, you must go . . . / Downstairs, away from *me*!" After the tenth time she sang it at top volume, her parents confiscated her guitar in retaliation; it lasted a whole day.

Dave was regaling her parents about friends who were part of Freedom Summer.

"Do you weigh enough to survive jail?" Judie asked, and Sylvia laughed too loudly. Dave guffawed; Anna clicked her tongue. Hyman poured himself more wine, sighing.

As Anna voiced disapproval about unmarried young men and women traveling together, and Dave responded with words like "equal relations" and "freedom," Judie blurted out that marriage was hardly a guarantee, given that some men *mistreated* their wives.

"Anna, control her," said Hyman, and Judie felt their threat. She had been dismissed from dinner three times in the last week.

Sylvia rose to help Anna clear the plates, giving both Dave and Judie a chance to admire her figure: willowy, graceful. Judie suspected that a whole-some Shabbat wasn't what lured Sylvia home on weekends. Instead, her ulterior motive for the weekly return was Bella Bernstein, living at home and taking classes at UMass. Sylvia would slip away on Saturday afternoons and wander Cambridge with Bella, and Judie stewed in jealousy. Beautiful boys—no, men—salivated over her sister. But Sylvia, her head tilted toward Bella's, didn't care.

And that left an opening. Judie may have been the smaller, plumper one, her sharp features more Jewish. But lately, in her mirror, she'd assessed herself and decided that her wide dark eyes and perky figure were *fine*.

Rather than rising to help with the clearing—why bother when her mother was already cross?—Judie sat next to Dave, putting the cat on her lap, and brought up the Voting Rights Act.

"The franchise, Judie, is the hinge of democracy," he opined.

"But don't you think if the vote is extended by law, the powerful will find a way to manipulate it, so it doesn't matter as much?" she pressed, watching his eyebrows fly upward as people's often did when she tried to engage in actual conversation.

A plate clattered in the sink. Anna summoned Judie.

After the girls cleaned up, the topic turned, inevitably, to Bob Dylan. Anna made strong coffee, and Sylvia began strumming her guitar and humming scales, as fiendish for performing as Judie was for talking. They discussed the way his stage name hid the Jewishness of Zimmerman, and Dave admitted that he was toying with using "Canticle" as his surname while performing.

"Brilliant," said Sylvia.

"I don't love it," said Hyman. "But you have to do what you have to do."

"Dylan plays on MacDougal Street at the café where my girlfriend Valerie waitresses," Dave said. At the word "girlfriend," Judie grew fascinated with the curve of the samovar handle, its teardrop shadow on the wall.

"I'm trying to write a song for Valerie, actually," he said. "But I keep re-writing Dylan. He gets in my head."

Judie had been running up against the same problem. Despite the silent vow to shut up she'd made a minute ago, she chimed in again: "My songs are derivative of his, too. But his are copies of others!" Valerie inspired misery and curiosity, both: How did a woman end up working in the same space as *Dylan*? Did Valerie sing, too?

From her corner, Sylvia piped up. "Judie's songs," she said, "could rival Dylan's. We could be a popular folk group *right now* if our dad let us play the hootenannies."

"I'm all for it," said Hyman. "Sylvia as the face of the group, and Judie harmonizing. But college first. And besides, those hootenannies get wild."

Judie noted her father's inability to discuss her songwriting. "I can merely harmonize, Sylvia," she said.

"She takes it as an insult," said Hyman to Anna. "I like how they sound together, that's all. We spent enough money training them."

Judie registered Dave taking a deep breath before he spoke next.

"I'd love to see what you've written," he said. "Men from the labels swarm around clubs in the Village like bees to honey. Having original songs helps you stand out."

"You should play a tune of Judie's at your next performance," said Sylvia.

"Oh, for heaven's sake, forget *Judie's* songs, let's sing something *good*," said Anna.

They moved to the piano, which sat right under the bay window, the pride of the house, framed by lace curtains and tree branches from outside. Hyman played: the girls began a duet of "Blowin' in the Wind." Sylvia sang lead with the voice that wowed: clear but rough, with a warble all her own.

Judie, as promised, harmonized. Dave bopped his head, mouthed the lyrics; she flamed up inside. Then he rose and walked toward them the way her father did when she'd made a mistake. Judie's fingers shook. Was he going to laugh at her? Correct her? Her voice faltered. She broke off her part and scooted back to the couch.

Sylvia gracefully finished with Dave, but everyone turned to Judie.

"I was thinking about how each verse of the song," Judie said, "has two questions—but it's the *third* that jumps out at you and keeps the composition from being trite."

"I think I see," said Dave, looking right into her eyes. Judie began to speak, but Anna clapped her hands again.

"Let's play one that doesn't make Judie think too much," she said. Sylvia began "Goodnight, Irene," and Anna and Hyman joined in. Dave's smile, as he added his voice to the mix, made Judie forget to oppose her parents.

She sang, too.

On Fridays, when Sylvia returned for Shabbat, the sisters shared Judie's attic room under the eaves so they could talk unsupervised across a sea of scattered sheet music, scarves and ribbons, bobby pins and guitar cases.

Tonight, as they put on their nightgowns, Sylvia began to criticize Judie for "monopolizing" Dave and defying their parents, to explain that being a girl had its advantages, because no one noticed you, so you could get away with murder, like how "me and Bella bummed cigarettes off these beatniks. . . ."

Judie plugged up her ears. Sylvia meant well, but someone who moved through the world like a ballet dancer couldn't have much to teach *her*, Judie of the wrongly buttoned sweaters and loud opinions. She turned off the light.

"In our group, we need to sing about the urgency of the—the social situation, like Dave said," Judie said into the darkness. "And the terror of war and all that."

"Well, no one will buy a record without a message," Sylvia agreed.

Judie laughed. "We haven't even made an album and you're worried about sales."

Judie lay awake, shifting from side to side, buzzing like a radio: Dylan and MacDougal Street; the vote; record company men.

She rolled out of bed and crept downstairs. Her self-stated mission was to drink some tea and think, but on the way, she stationed herself near Dave's door and scrunched her face. She heard him tinkering with his guitar and warbling some chords. A night owl, like her.

She drew her breath and knocked, pleased at her own impulse.

"Hungry?" she asked as he opened the door a fraction of a second later and grinned at her. "I'm worried about your health."

"Starving," he replied.

Boiling tea and preparing a plate for him, she found herself shy; she piled up cold chicken and cabbage, challah, and pastries without a word. As she bustled, he tried small talk.

"Your sister is as talented as your dad said," he began. "That voice. That face! She ought to come down to the Village and make a go of it. She could be the next Joanie Baez."

His words struck Judie like stones. She picked up the plate she'd prepared and tilted it over the sink, her whisper turning savage.

"Are you just going to slobber over my sister?" she asked, wishing she could keep her mouth shut.

"Don't take your temper out on the food. I need fattening up, remember?"

He called her prickly, and she muttered that her parents' insults probably made him feel entitled to put her down.

"No one is insulting you by praising her . . . not me, not them," said Dave. "I'm not trying to make it with her, anyway. I have a girl. How about you show me your songs?"

She frowned, torn. Vanity won. The plate and napkin were released to Dave, and she skipped upstairs to fetch her notebook. She might be bashful and awkward about her looks and her behavior. But she was not shy about her songs.

He wiped his fingers before thumbing her pages. He said he couldn't believe that they were all her songs. All of them! They had been pouring out of her like frustration bubbling over. He told her they got better as the notebook went on.

"*I'm* the one who should be in the Village," she said, scooting over to sit next to him. "Even if my father doesn't like my music."

"Don't be hard on him," said Dave, his voice taking on a paternal air himself. "He encourages you. My parents escaped Hitler. They barely speak to me—you think your parents' 'college first' rule is bad, but they told me to quit guitar, or they'd cut me off."

He explained this—that he'd tried to follow their wishes and focus on school, but he felt almost possessed by a desire to sing, and now he was without any allowance—while eating his chicken leg, looking half miserable, half proud.

"But I'm a girl," she said. "I'm their puppet. I don't even care about music like they do."

"Nonsense! These are *songs* you wrote, aren't they?" he asked.

"Music, art, politics," she said. "I don't care how; I just want to be part of a bigger life. I wrote about it right here, on page ten. See—'The Big River of Life.'"

He scanned the lyrics.

> *I'm tired of waiting on the shore*
> *Don't you know I want something more?*
> *Bring your boat to my feet and let me ride*
> *The big river of life to the other side*

He pointed out a cliché here, a repetition there, and she snatched the notebook. "It's a first draft."

Dave swiped the notebook right back. "You say it's all the same to you—politics or music or art—but you filled this whole notebook. It's a gift."

Judie paused. Everyone nattered on about Sylvia's "gift," her golden voice. Of Judie, people said "smart cookie," praise that sliced backward.

She pressed her case for her own residency in Greenwich Village: staying with Valerie (she said it without wincing), backing up other acts, helping Dave write his first record.

He sat back, wiping the crumbs from the stubble over his lips, and regarded her. Needing a task for her fingers, she began to untwist her braids. His hand darted and tugged a ribbon, letting it cascade onto the table.

She looked back at his lips, now crumb-free, and wondered what it would be like to be kissed by them. His mind was, she hoped, similarly occupied, as he leaned in closer and pulled a final strand of hair from her braid. "You won't join Sylvia as the 'face of the group' if you don't practice in public," he said, his voice teasing. "Without stage fright."

"That's exactly it," she said, her cheeks flaming. In her mind, she was already spiriting down to New York City to join the meetings and folk sing-alongs in the park. With *him*.

"If you come, it's temporary," he said. "Before college in the fall."

She nodded but made no promises and conjured up tasks as they talked: Pack a bag. Save allowance. Ask for directions to the Planned Parenthood clinic on Commonwealth Avenue, "for a friend," so she could get on the famous pill.

Her thoughts grew grander and stretched further into the future as the clock in the hallway ticked down the hours and she and Dave talked about music.

The songs in that notebook were her ticket. She would move to the Village and write for all the leading men in the folk world. She would lose her virginity, and go to protest marches, and turn it all into music.

～

Too much fun with Dave last night?" asked Sylvia the next morning. Judie whipped around to see her sister peeking over the kitchen counter.

"I asked Dave if he had slept well and he told me about your summer plans," said Sylvia, beginning to wipe down the silverware in the rack. "I wonder, who will dry the spoons with me when you're smoking hashish in New York?"

She handed Judie the forks and knives, and Judie opened the drawer and slid them in place.

"Careful," said Sylvia. "Mama likes them stacked neatly."

Judie looked sidelong at her sister. What had Dave told her about their talk?

"Dave thinks I should run away, too," said Sylvia. Judie thrust a knife into the drawer, hitting the back.

"You should. We can start the Singer Sisters . . . pass the hat, find a manager, make an album without Dad's help."

Sylvia thrust a hand in the drawer to correct the position of the knife. Judie tugged her sister's sleeve, her sister's bracelet. Alone together, they found their discourse reverting to childish gestures, faces, ways of communication that predated sentences.

"No," said Sylvia, her tone cross and face ashen. She turned her back on Judie and reached for the next batch of utensils. "I like school, I have . . . friends. Why would I run away?" She seemed to be asking herself as much as Judie, and her voice grew heavy.

"Because you're desperate to be famous?" asked Judie. Her sister didn't show fear, not while waving spoons in the air and talking about future adventures. "What's the matter?"

Sylvia sighed with extra volume in the breath. "You wouldn't understand," she said. "You see things simply. Don't go to New York. Something terrible could happen. . . ."

"Just try to stop me."

"I could! With one word to Dad." Sylvia smirked, and Judie felt her blood rise. They were squaring off now, armed with a ladle and a spatula, respectively.

"If you did, I'd tell them about *you*," said Judie, a rock of an idea coalescing in her mind—Sylvia barely acknowledging the appreciative looks of men, compared with her gushing joy when Bella swung by—plus her recent withdrawal from their sisterly huddles.

"I'll tell them about Bella," Judie said. "I'll tell them you're not the perfect young woman they think, that you two get up to . . . whatever you get up to."

She had overplayed her hand—her sister's face collapsed. Sylvia moaned and took both of Judie's hands in hers, no longer aloof.

"*Please*, Judie—if I had to spend more time apart from her than I already do, I would die." What was this? Collected, chic Sylvia begging for mercy?

Judie swore she wouldn't tell. "I mean, what exactly would I be telling them, anyway?"

Sylvia dried her eyes. "Sometimes I think she feels the same—the same way towards me," she whispered. "And sometimes I'm not sure. She knows she has power over me. It's *agony*, I swear."

"And you feel for her—like you would die apart?"

Sylvia nodded, unable to meet her eyes.

Judie began her next question, then stopped. No point in prying when one already knew the answer. They sat for a long time, until the floor made Judie's legs cramp and she hoisted herself up with the counter.

"We have to become famous singers," Judie said. "Then we can both be free to do whatever we want."

EMMA

Backstage, Emma and Mae put their hands on each other's shoulders and whispered their "silly affirmations": "To the goddess, to the moon, to going electric at Newport."

Judie loved to recount that even though she couldn't attend the festival in '65 and see Dylan plug in, *Bringing It All Back Home* was the album of the year. She used to say, "I studied it like a college textbook, Leon. Like a college textbook."

Emma and Mae broke their two-person circle. Electric: she felt electric today.

"I might go in a different direction with the set list and call some audibles," Emma said as they stretched their shoulders and swigged some water. "Can you keep up with me?"

Mae was excited. "Let's get wild."

Emma watched a cloud obscure the sun, then keep moving along. "Do you, um, know my mom's big song?" she asked.

"'Route 95'? Duh, Emma. It's kind of a classic of the form."

They stuck their tongues out at each other, but their eyes twinkled in unison.

It was time. Emma stepped out onto the stage, lifted her arm with the guitar, felt the wind on her armpits, smelled the sweat and pot and booze. Smelled the spring.

"What's up, kids?" she said, jocular. She *belonged* here, not in a lecture hall; no one could stop her, least of all her mother.

"So. Spring break is coming. Are you psyched? Who's inviting me to

Cancún?" She began to ramble. "Going to try some new stuff today. This first song was written by my mom, actually, and, you know, she came up with this tune many years ago, when she was starting out. And since then, it's been important if you give any kind of shit about, like, *music*? I don't play it much, so this is special for you. I hope you assholes appreciate it."

Mae squealed. And a few music nerds in the audience screamed, knowing what was about to happen.

Emma stepped up to the mic, put a hand over her eyes to shield the sun, and began to sing the first bars of "Route 95" a cappella, her guitar behind her back.

"Sinners by the window, wheels below," she sang, making them strain to hear her. "I had to make a change / So I left the life I know."

Good lines, Mom, she thought. Good lines. She repeated the lines twice, until she could feel the crowd hush. Now. Now she had them. Then she shouted, "One, two, three, four!" and Mae began to add a beat, and Emma swung her guitar around and attacked it.

"He sees me looking, and your eyes on me / I see us rolling far away from the sea."

A few cries of "woo-woo" began to emerge from the audience, and some-one yelled, "*Damn,* girl!" Emma felt herself filling with a rolling current of emotion as they hit the chorus and Mae introduced it with a vicious drumroll.

> *I'm on Route 95*
> *I'm coming alive*

Kids were clapping, actually *clapping,* to a spare, angry version of her mom's old standard, as the first song of the first opener of a free show.

A group of tiny girls wound their way to the front of the stage, fresh-men by their looks. They held hands. The first girl in the chain, heavier and more lipsticked than the others, carried a big red cup. A joint dangled out of her mouth. Emma sang to her, the bad girl of the group, and urged her guitar through the bridge. She loved this stupid song. She'd learned it by heart in the weeks after Flower told her about it. When she was done, the clique had arrived inches from her feet. They were waiting, counting, and when she sang the final "begin to begin," they shouted in unison, *"We love you, Emma Cantor!"*

Cheers came from the area around them.

"I love you bitches too," she said with a swagger as the applause died down.

She signaled to Mae, kicked her Coke can toward their faces, and launched into her regular set, but with gusto and a kind of flair one couldn't predict. The music connected; more kids pressed up against the stage, and others piled in behind them.

Emma played to them. At a hint of flagging, she remembered what had spawned her manic verve: the babysitter on the steps, who was there, and her mother—who wasn't.

"We're off script already," she said a few songs in. "And this secondhand smoke is *strong*. You guys are amazing today, so I'm going to give you something that almost no one has ever heard. Once upon a time, a strange woman showed up in my apartment, and you guys, she scared the crap out of me. Then she sent my mom a letter, and I kept that letter, and I turned that letter into a song. I'm going to sing it by myself because my insanely awesome drummer, Mae, has never even heard it." Mae, who had in fact heard the song, hammed it up, shrugged her shoulders, a drumstick in each hand.

Solitary before the hundreds of fans, Emma channeled her thoughts to the five girls in the audience who loved her the most—and to Rose on the steps, and the hippie at her door, and her mother and aunt all the way in New Hampshire.

And then she played a few chords to introduce the new song, which she'd considered unfinished until approximately thirty minutes ago.

> *I am a great flower*
> *But my petals have curled up and dried*
> *I used to have a vision*
> *But thanks to them, that vision died*
>
> *I saw in your eyes a secret*
> *I know it because women do*
> *Somewhere in the past, a terror*
> *Somewhere in your words a clue*
>
> *Ohhh, ohhh, ohhh*

I dreamed of so many rainbows
But he wanted them all for himself
I dreamed of holding hands together
The world it dreamed of wealth

Now I'm back here by my own riverside
It reminds me of your still waters
I see your reflection in the tide
Yours and your little daughter's

Ohhh, ohhh, ohhh

I am a great flower
And you are the sun
I am a great flower
And you are the rain
I am a great flower
And you are the pain. . . .

Somewhere in the second verse, Mae had joined in with a beat and a harmony, and it worked. It worked.

A reverent millisecond or two of quiet followed the final chord of the song, and then rapturous applause. In the front row, one of the "we love you" girls pushed away tears. More "woo-woo" shrieks emerged from the back. Howls. Someone hurled a beach ball to her feet, and she tossed it back out.

During the process of wringing "Flower" out of the old letter in the drawer, Emma had imagined the song accentuated by a thudding bass and some new age sounds that Leon could layer in. But the song had just proved itself solid, unpolished, without his help.

Her mom at age eighteen could reach down her own throat, take out her heart and guts, and put them in music, but Emma couldn't do that. What could she do? Imagine someone else's story. That's why "Flower" succeeded. She had done it. Take that, Singer Sisters.

She could cry from relief. These kids might even start telling their friends about today. After the clapping and the shrieks and the lighters, she got hustled off, because she had only half an hour to play, and she'd gone over by three minutes.

Standing in the wings, she toweled the sweat off and reapplied her black eyeliner, listening to people come up to her and remark on her "killer set" and "gorgeous new tune." Emma's wild confidence began to wobble over into hysteria.

"Oh. My. God," said Mae. "What happened to you?" She laughed and Emma laughed. "I wish your mom and aunt could have seen that."

Emma shook her head. Her stomach growled. After the high of a killer performance, she deflated, wanting to dissolve and wake up at home, in her childhood bedroom, with Judie and Dave together and bickering in the kitchen over drinks: kombucha for him, espresso for her.

But those mornings were gone.

~

Emma roamed backstage between sets, telling herself to cool down and behave. A loyal bandmate would stick with Mae until they departed for Boston. A comradely musician would chill out backstage, waiting to shake hands and share beers with the friendly dudes from Less Than Jake, who would bask in her attention and help her in the industry. A serious singer might save her voice, or her body, by finding a shady spot to hydrate.

A single, awkward drink with Rose wouldn't atone for her shenanigans at age eight.

But Rose had a need in her eyes that mirrored Emma's endless desire, and it compelled Emma back to the lawn to seek her out. Was it masochism, or guilt, or a thirst for novelty, or all of the above? Emma didn't stop long to ruminate; her stride was sure. Over her shoulder to Mae and the roadies she called, "Meet you at the van!"

Sure enough, Rose remained a few yards from where she'd been before: sitting on the hillside behind the stage, not far from two girls who were lying on the grass moaning.

"The universe is *spinning*," one recumbent beauty said.

"This is the best music I've ever heard," said the other. No music was playing.

"Penny freaking Trosterman," said the first, sitting up and pointing at her friend on the ground. "I haven't seen you since *prom night*. I am *sooo* high right now."

Their babble touched Emma, evoking the untraveled road.

Rose saw her and scrambled to her feet, clapping and cheering. And then Penny and Penny's pal, through their haze, saw her and began whooping, too. Emma bowed, feeling the smile rise to her face. She strutted over to Rose.

"That beer?" asked Emma. "I mean, soda? Are you okay, out in the sun?"

"It's fine. Might as well make hay. . . . Soon I'm going to get so bloated I can't wear my shoes, or my rings." Rose patted Emma on the arm.

Emma's eyes drifted down to the rings, sought the engagement stone, the wedding band, that would tell her more about what kind of woman Rose the old au pair had become. Was she bohemian (as she seemed to be) or high maintenance?

While performing this inspection, Emma noticed an unexpected bauble. She stepped back with a jerk: glinting on Rose's left pinkie finger sat Grandma Anna's old enamel ring, a black-and-white oval with two small white gemstones, one on each side. A shiver traveled up Emma's sides.

It had flitted into her mind, now and then, the question of where this ring or that pendant had ended up. But why investigate? All the baubles had been scooped up by Sylvia and Judie and would wind their way to her—Leon wasn't about to marry a woman.

Emma scrutinized the ring, the hand, for a moment without end, her breath caught in her chest—and Rose, seeing her gaze, took her exposed hand and covered it with her other one.

"Holy shit. Is that . . . ?"

"Yes, it is. It *is* Anna's. I can explain," Rose said. "I *want* to. That's why I stuck around."

"Well, you stuck around because my show was fabulous," said Emma. How pathetic that Rose had stolen this ring—or been given it out of pity, admiring it in front of Judie that summer. Or wait—had Grandma Anna given Judie her ring at that point, or was she still around, wearing it herself back then? Emma found herself massaging her forehead between two hands, trying to sift through the years. She had no brainpower. *It's all onstage.*

Rose touched her arm.

Emma looked up again, blinking into the late-spring sun, to find her old babysitter sitting down again on the steps, eyes wet with emotion.

The power that surged through Emma then. To think that Judie renounced this life, this ability to draw tears out of people like witchcraft.

"Why are you crying?" asked Emma, but she knew it was because of her music.

JUDIE

The bus smelled like pee and smoke, and Judie fought off nausea. Her heart bumped along with the wheels. For her entire life thus far, she had used her (formidable, people said) mind to take flight from the comfortable, claustrophobic house in Cambridge, writing, singing, sometimes arguing. Now, she had the chance to take her body along, to make her way unfettered. Smells, danger, fear. She closed her eyes to feel it, then opened them to observe.

She had chosen a seat next to an older woman who wore her hair in a knot, with a small crucifix nestled below her throat, avoiding the spots next to men, who looked at her. Although when they turned away, she looked at them, too. Male arms and shoulders and thighs, all crammed together in the seats.

Two days ago, Judie had received her high school diploma from Girls' Latin School with honors. She wore her lavender hair ribbons but kept Dave's address in her pocket, where it had remained almost constantly since that winter night when he visited.

Tomorrow, she was due to start a summer job as a guitar teacher for the twin daughters of a state senator her father knew. But instead of starting the job, she'd left home, newly procured birth control pills in her guitar case, leaving a note on the table and catching a Greyhound bus down to New York City.

At her age, did it count as running away? Judging by her feeling of stepping into a chasm, by the white-knuckled, tense vigil of the night before, it at least felt *daring*. She had slept perhaps two hours, the rest of the time thinking about the only trips she had ever taken alone: to Newburyport with Sylvia to walk by the shore, to New Hampshire with cousins.

"I see what you're doing, you know," her seatmate said in a low voice as Judie craned her head to take in the scene on the bus. "Jesus sees your sin, too."

Judie was alarmed but undaunted. She looked right at her seatmate's face and said, "Then he sees you, too, judging me." The intake of breath she heard seemed louder than the bus backfiring. She trembled with the force of it but was pleased with her newfound courage.

"Perhaps you'll give me the window seat to shield me from these people and their tainted ways," she offered to her companion. "If you'd be so kind."

Now, nestled next to a view of the trees and factories, Judie opened a notebook and began to write a new song, an ode to the traffic-clogged highway that was taking her to freedom.

"Sinners by the window, wheels below" had a nice ring to it. "I had to make a change, so I left the life I know" wasn't bad either. But the next lines that she summoned grew opaque.

This was the strangest song Judie had written, and she couldn't *wait* to show it to Dave.

Valerie stood at the bus station as promised in Dave's letter, and although only Sylvia's age, she looked a decade older. Her jeans were weathered, with a high, tight waist and loose pant legs, and she completed the look with a man's oxford shirt, probably Dave's.

She saw Judie, asked, "Dave's little friend?" and at the resultant nod grabbed her guitar case and steered them with a firm grip down a stairwell to the subway below, loud and sooty.

Judie scrambled to keep up, her heavy duffel bumping against her legs (thank goodness Valerie had condescended to take Judie's guitar). Two minutes in New York City, and she had to learn to carry her own luggage while being a cool observer.

"Dave says you're a runaway."

"Of a sort. I graduated school—"

"Listen, there are so many runaways downtown now, we're getting to be out of room. Tourists too, packing MacDougal. You can't walk to the corner for a smoke. Don't be one who turns back in a week, I've seen plenty. Dave says you've got talent and you're hell-bent on being here. But he's been wrong before."

As Valerie hustled her up the subway stairs and down the street, the sounds, the sirens, were musical—freedom and abandon in beats, screeches, and calls. And the odors overpowered her: rank, and sweet, coming one after another. Incense and garbage and smoke.

She had arrived in Greenwich Village.

~

At the apartment, the girls got wind of Judie's pills. She had carried the precious cargo in a brown bag at the bottom of her guitar case on the Greyhound, having taken three pills in a row before she left for New York.

"You're not with a man," Valerie said greedily when she saw the package. "Consider it rent. Besides, if you take it every other day, everyone knows it still works."

Judie couldn't exactly say no to the women who were putting her up for a pittance scraped from her allowance and guitar lesson money. Besides, sharing pills seemed pragmatic and in keeping with the spirit of the place, a cluttered but clean two-bedroom on the third floor, with a fire escape, a claw-foot tub, and two cats named Lead Belly and Hank, who kept the roaches at bay. The girls rotated between single beds in each room, a plastic-covered couch in the living room, and a mattress on the floor of the larger bedroom. Valerie's weary hospitality reminded her, in a way, of her mother's.

When men joined them for parties and meals, the energy shifted. Someone leapt up from her book or her sewing or chatter to open the fridge and put things out on a plate—potato chips or bagels, sliced bologna or celery. Often as not, the girls were called on not only to feed but to flirt. They soothed, entertained, hosted, and cleaned up afterward.

Judie learned the rules. And as June heated up into July, the apartment's denizens acknowledged it. Some of their crowd split for San Francisco, and new cousins and hometown friends showed up to crash on the floor. They moved Judie up from the mattress to the couch.

Her new status also rose when she began to play gigs with Dave, backing his vocals and adding a touch of whatever was needed—accordion, guitar, harmony, or an assist with writing, smoothing out a bridge, or finishing a lyric.

"You blow me away, kid," he told her when she did the latter, although he generally kept their communication clinical. When Judie sat on the floor to help Dave write, Valerie perched on the arm of the couch and watched. So far, no one had heard "Route 95," but Judie kept polishing it up in her head.

～

One late night after a gig at the Lantern Pub, her favorite place because of its arched ceiling and brighter lights, Valerie made a rare nonappearance.

Dave asked Judie to stay for a whiskey on the house, and her heart soared toward the ceiling. They had been playing music together constantly, writing it, too, yet hadn't talked this intimately since their midnight chicken assignation in Cambridge.

"So, kid, how are you liking old New Yawk?" he asked.

"Okay," she replied, watching the bartender pour out the brown stuff. Dave was the most regular drop-in at their apartment—to see Valerie, but also to run through material with Judie or give her what he thought was a generous cut of the last show's earnings, which she immediately turned over to Valerie for rent or food. At some point, he and Valerie would slip off into a room together and turn up the radio.

Judie struggled to keep her eyes from fixating on the molding over the doorway where they were, to stop herself from imagining them together and wishing Dave were in there with her instead.

"Cat got your tongue?" Dave said. How could she ask: Did he ever think of her like she thought of him? Would he take an interest in her songs again? Judie burned to play him "Route 95" but hesitated to let go of it yet, her secret work of art.

"Listen, kid. It's August already, and I've had a letter from your father. It scared the hell out of me, to be honest. All sorts of threats if you got in trouble."

She took in about a gallon of air, tried not to let him see the tears that sprang up without her consent, threatening to expose her as the runaway princess the girls teased her for being.

"I said you were telling the truth in your letters, living with Valerie and playing music and handing out leaflets, and that we'd send you back in time for college in the fall. . . ."

He took her whiskey, which she'd barely touched, and finished it.

"Give that back!" she demanded, grabbing the glass, sucking at the dregs.

"Judie, parents are *important*. Take it from someone who can't really talk to his."

"That's your problem."

Their faces were only about two inches apart. He put his hand over hers and her insides scrambled up just like they did when, about to sing, she lost her nerve.

"You're my boss," she said. "Are you firing me?"

"No, I'm giving you advice. As a friend." They regarded each other warily. All the musicians around them wanted to have fun, cause trouble, make things fairer in the world, but Dave wanted to bend the world in his direction. And so did she, now that he'd convinced her that music was her destiny. Their peers wanted to touch the shirtsleeves of Joan Baez and Bob Dylan. Judie and Dave wanted to *replace* them.

She had come far this summer. The small, loud, smoky clubs brought a new urgency to her stage jitters. The smell of sweat and beer, even at the dry clubs. The eyes—male eyes—on her. At their first gigs, she zeroed in on Dave's bootlaces as if they contained the sheet music. Only after four shows had she been able to look at the audience during a show. But she'd persisted. She played for her keep. She wasn't leaving, not for home or college.

"I'll walk you home, kid," he said gently.

The day had been humid and thick, but once they started across Washington Square Park a fine rain materialized and cooled the air. Judie put out her palms, then let out a whoop of unbridled joy.

"Summer rain!" she shouted, then hummed an impromptu melody. "Summer rain. It washes us clean." She repeated it, twice.

The rain pounded. Thunder rumbled in the distance. They dashed to the arch to take shelter, laughing. Was this love? This loamy smell, this sense of danger and safety at the same time? She shot out from under the arch, the rain pouring onto her hair, and began to yodel her ridiculous tune, but he was right behind her, and he caught her waist and dragged her back into shelter. She protested, laughing. Their giggles clashed like cymbals, the stormy sounds a bass. He pulled her closer, rubbed her shoulders.

"This reminds me. I wanted to tell you," he said. And she waited, all her breath trapped inside, waited for his answer to the questions in her heart.

"Someone important is coming to town, and Steve at the Lantern says he wants to get a drink with *me*! *Can you imagine? Me!*"

"Sure," she said, looking away so he wouldn't see the pesky tears that were pushing against her eyelids.

Shoulder to shoulder they surveyed the park. "He's a wonderful singer, Judie. His name is Eamon Foley."

"Oh? I've never heard his record," she said, looking up at the arch and the velvety purple-gold sky above it. The view was a dream. But the moment had collapsed, like all the others she fantasized into being.

"Come by and I'll play some for you. You can meet Eamon, too—in fact, I'll bring him round to Val's place for a party."

The rain stopped, and what had seemed like a change wasn't one at all; the air was just as hot and humid as before.

～

At the party Dave threw to welcome Eamon Foley, he played a brand-new song for Valerie, who sat cross-legged on the floor at his feet. The song was called "Summer Rain" and it included the line "it washes us clean."

He had stolen Judie's words. True, the *melody* wasn't hers, and true, his composition worked with the lyrics. But the theft was galling.

"This is the best song you've written!" Valerie cried, jumping onto Dave's lap, wrapping her arms around him, and kissing his head.

Judie put her hand on the doorframe to steady herself. Her heart had been bruised before. But coming after their magical walk home in the rain, his theft, on Valerie's *behalf*—this was a sharper stab.

Standing on the outskirts of the crowd, she swallowed the lump in her throat. What would Sylvia do?

She walked purposefully to the drink table, poured herself a glass of something clear, downed it in one gulp, and smiled at the wall. A sob—short, quick—threatened to escape. She gave up on being stoic and fled to the bathroom to cry in silence. Sitting on the edge of the bathtub, she touched her neck with one hand, as if it would soothe her burning throat.

She had been hanging around Dave all summer, waiting for what? For him to ditch Valerie and declare love?

Such faith was absurd. He'd called her "kid" repeatedly the last time they talked, at the bar; he kept their conversations limited to music. Why, the night they'd huddled together back home, he'd even praised her sister's looks first.

He advised her to go home to her parents.

These weeks with their songs and heat and dizzy joy had been the best of her life—but how much of her pleasure had come from the anticipation of a crowning moment of romance? Men didn't even see her: their eyes roamed past her to Sylvia or Valerie.

In the toilet bowl, six cigarette butts floated around like dead fish. She heard a rumble in her stomach like an approaching train. Well, she hadn't had a proper meal beyond spaghetti or eggs in weeks. The bathroom began to tip back and forth; it felt fine to ride the waves. A distorted face laughed in the mirror. When a harsh knock insisted on her exit, she meandered back into the room, sitting on a low stool and letting the sounds of the party float and hover on the border of her consciousness.

Was it an hour or a minute before a tall man ambled over and sat down right beside her, smiling? His clear blue eyes and crooked mouth shocked her out of her fog.

"The thing is," she said to him as though they'd been talking for hours, "no one has taught me how to properly smoke a cigarette, and I've been here over a month!"

"As a smoker since childhood, practically, might I volunteer?" he asked in a velvety, Irish-accented voice.

Even her feet and her ears were blushing. This man whom she'd flirted with was Eamon Foley himself.

She froze up in her old style, stammering, "Oh, uh . . ." But her shyness didn't stop him from suggesting that they have a lesson out on the fire escape, so she wouldn't be embarrassed when she coughed the first time. They opened the window and slid out.

"I find it easier," he said, "to practice a new skill *without* an audience. The ego should be uninvolved."

He lit her cigarette, and she puffed for him, five or six times—a few coughs and laughs and a hand bump or two. She looked in through the window, smiling, knowing that the loud bang of the sash being raised had probably caught Dave's and Valerie's attention.

Eamon guided her through the entire cigarette. She liked his gentleness and laughing eyes, and in his presence, she conquered smoking like learning a new chord—bringing the cigarette to her lips until she could guarantee mastery.

As she practiced, he told her all about himself. He had come to America at eighteen—"Just like me, at least to New York!" she cried. He had worked construction at first. "Just like my father!" she enthused.

"Why did you come?" she asked.

"I fell in love with Elvis Presley," he said. "Or with the screaming girls around the lad."

"My sister loves Elvis," said Judie wistfully, and his eyes widened, and she wanted to scream like one of those girls, because they were light and fine and made the rest of his face turn from interesting to marvelous.

"I have four sisters, but one is special," Eamon said. "Mary. She sees me as her own child, like. Wept right along with the rain when I left home." Rain in Ireland, apparently, fell even while the sun glistened on the water.

Luck, he told Judie, sent him to a bar on Jerome Avenue in the Bronx on a blustery December day, where a socialist folk fanatic named Ira Dersh held court. In exchange for Eamon's company at a few concerts and some more drinks, Ira gave him a guitar.

"That was the beginning," he said.

"Already writing your own legend, I see," she joked, remembering what Dave had explained to her and Valerie last night as they'd spun Eamon's record, about how Eamon had graduated from singing Irish classics in Bronx bars to writing his own songs, to making the kind of impression on the downtown scene that led to a coveted recording contract.

"You've got a mouth on you for such an innocent," he said, laughing. Unable to look above the stubble on his chin, she heard his songs in her head, thrilling to his deep voice and spare, clever lyrics. "Golden-Haired Girl," which wove together the myth of Apollo and Daphne and the story of an affair with a woman on the road, was a new favorite among sophisticates in the city, according to Dave.

Judie looked out on Grove Street, empty save for a few young men hooting and kicking a garbage can lid. The moon cut a small bright sliver in the sky.

"I've heard your songs," Judie said. "'Golden-Haired Girl' is your most accomplished composition, although the bridge is flat."

He let out a loud, barking laugh, not an angry one. "Are you a critic?" he asked.

"I write songs, too. In fact, people *steal my lines*."

"A songwriter who can't smoke."

"They call me 'princess' here," she said. The building tipped about ten degrees, on account of the gin. She grabbed the railing to steady herself. "Because of the whole innocent thing. I suppose your song is about sex.... With the pillow image—how could it not be?"

He inspected her in a different way, now, that made her feel, not exactly like a curiosity but like an object of study.

"I suppose I won't be able to make it in songwriting until I gain experience in that arena. You know, if I *did* write songs about sex, it would be the end with my parents. I can feel their anger all the way from Boston, like a heat wave."

"You want to try a lot of new things at once," he said, looking out into the trees. "Like a man might."

"Is that wrong?" she said. "I'm j—"

He kissed her, sounding a note through her that eclipsed the few kisses she'd shared at camp dances. She kissed back. "You taste like smoke," he said after a few minutes.

She was definitely drunk. "Now that I think about it," she said, running her knuckles across her lips. "Since my parents are already angry at me ..."

～

At least, she reflected much later that night at the apartment, after an impressed roommate let her back in, it didn't happen in an alleyway or a car. Properly, they had slipped off to his room at the Washington Square Hotel, where the label had put him.

"We're leaving," she said to Valerie and Dave at the door. "Don't steal any songs while I'm gone."

Dave put a restraining hand on her shoulder. "Hey, wait a second, kid, are you ... *drunk*?" he asked. "You shouldn't—"

She put one palm to his chest, pushed, and left.

She and Eamon walked hand in hand, like two shy kids at a dance, and Judie put one foot before the other with care. She wished she had learned to drink whiskey with more confidence when he offered her another drink back at the hotel. He turned the lights off; he was gentle when he kissed her again and gathered her hair in his hands, sending static down to her toes. He asked, Was she all right?

What was she going to say when he asked that kind of question, when she had been the instigator? "I'm on the pill," she said proudly.

He was determined, but not hasty. He told her that he loved staying at the hotel, because six years ago, when he first came over to America, they wouldn't even have spared a glance at him—they would have assumed he was there to fix a boiler.

"Are you going to be famous?" she asked him. He combed out a curl of her hair with his guitar-calloused fingers.

"I want to be, yes," he said, baring her shoulder and touching it with his lips. "I love the attention, *especially* from women."

She paused his hand. "Lots and lots of them?"

"A gentleman won't say," he said. "But I'm not a going-steady kind of guy at the moment? Or any moment? But you're something else, little St. Augustine—don't renounce your quest for experience."

"Of course," she said, *not a going-steady kind of guy*—it hurt to hear him confess his intentions, or lack of them, but in a sweet way that made her long for her guitar, for a window to open, for space away from all the roommates. He drew her to him; she had a moment's hesitation, what with all her mother's warnings. Sylvia's, too.

But she took a deep breath. "Okay," she said as he leaned over her, planted a kiss beneath her ear, and tugged at his own belt. "I think I can handle two lessons in one night."

Slowly, he took off her clothes; he asked again if she was all right, which was generous. After all, she was not a child.

~

At three in the morning or thereabouts, Judie discovered that the bathroom in Valerie's apartment was irrefutably free. The cigarette butts were gone, but the smell lingered, even when she opened the tiny, barred window and ran herself a bath, cringing when the faucet squeaked. She leaned her head back in the warm water, then submerged her body. Now that she'd become a

woman of the world, she had to write about it. She hummed a tune, began
to fill in the lyrics.

> *He came into my life at half-past ten*
> *And somehow, I knew already then*
> *Behind the curtains, behind the smoke*
> *Behind the pretty words he spoke . . .*

The tub had gotten cold, but she couldn't risk the noise of another attempt
at the hot-water tap. The next line of the song eluded her. What *did* she know
when she met Eamon? Besides the fact that she had a chance to lose her
virginity and make Dave jealous?

The song lacked a vital piece, but she was too sleepy to figure it out. She
drained the tub, mopped herself with a thin towel, let her mind flit to the
fluffy towels at home, the pajamas she would have helped her mother fold.
She shook out her hair, dressed herself in the nightgown she'd been sleeping
in all week, and curled up on the couch for a few fitful hours, lines of her new
song moving through her dreams.

～

At seven o'clock on a humid August night, as Anna and Hyman Zing-
erman pulled up downstairs in their sedan, Eamon and Dave were at
Judie's feet on the fire escape, listening to her play the opening chords of
"Route 95." It had been three days since she lost her virginity to Eamon,
and she had slept with him again, the previous night, and let herself enjoy it.
"You're a quick study," he'd said.

Her new companions saw her in a changed light, Dave in particular.
He stared at her more but talked to her less, as though to avoid treading
on Eamon's territory. Now, when she met his eyes, he hastily looked elsewhere.

But their musical collaboration continued. The previous night, she'd
backed Dave up at his biggest gig yet, opening for Eamon, and instead of
just sitting on the stool, she'd *shimmied*. Looking right at the audience, she'd
smiled, closed her eyes, and tried to move as Sylvia did, like soft gray silk.
Eamon had been in the crowd, listening, and soon he'd come up to her and

said, "Not bad. Play me a song of *yours* sometime soon?" And then he'd leaned down and whispered that she ought to come back to the hotel.

Eamon, not the going-steady type, was leaving town soon. Contemplating this made her brain go haywire. She chose instead to present "Route 95" to Dave and Eamon, a parting gift in the midst of yet another "hip" gathering.

In this heady frame of mind, on her fire escape perch, about to unveil her creation, she saw them—her parents—disembarking. Her father, ever the gentleman, helped her mother out of the car.

She turned her head to capture the scene: to hear city noise, in distinct individuality and in symphony—a siren, a shout, a tree shifting in the wind—and the plucking of a Folkways compilation on the phonograph.

A few nights earlier, her parents would have intercepted Judie before she met Eamon. A few nights later, they might have discovered her reading a book alone with a cat and a few sober friends. As it was, they were about to discover her in a crowning cloud of marijuana smoke, wearing borrowed trousers and cheap lace-up sandals, flanked by both Dave and Eamon.

Judie heard her own voice go flat, then croak, and then stop. The men asked if she was going to faint, if she felt sick.

"No," she said. "It's just that my father is here."

Moments later, she heard her father berating Valerie's guests with phrases like "innocent girl," "marijuana," and "shame on you."

She pushed out between the partygoers sitting around in their buttoned shirts and blue dresses, their clouds of smoke and thick-rimmed glasses.

"Hello," she said calmly. "I assume you're looking for me."

The room hushed itself for a performance, drinks paused mid-sip. Judie's eyes sought a picture on the wall, a cheap poster of a purple-blue Barnett Newman painting from the MoMA, a silver-gray zip slicing the colors in half.

"Fun's over," said Hyman. "Wellesley sent your packing list, Judie."

All she had gained, all the respect and experience, evaporated at her father's tone. Eamon whispered not to cry and called her "little saint."

Valerie stepped to her side, facing her parents.

"She's going to give you hell if you take her home," Valerie said.

"Dear, put some shoes on," said Anna, glaring at Valerie's bare feet, a smudge of dirt on one big toe.

Judie's shoulders slumped. Her parents, in the flesh, were disgusted, and she was a fraud, a rebel child who had told them she wanted to change the world but only ended up flirting at smoke-soaked parties. She was equally a fraud to her new companions—who now saw what a soft mattress she had to land on. A father in tweed, a mother in a silk skirt.

"I don't want a scene," Judie said, faking strength. "Let me collect my things."

EMMA

The enamel ring on Rose's finger drew Emma's gaze until she asked to hold it. Rose agreed too quickly.

"Oh, memories," said Emma, slipping it on her own forefinger, bringing it to her lips. Daring Rose to claim it back. But Rose sat, placid hands in lap, looking at the clouds. Big, seventies-style sunglasses hid her eyes. Her blazer somehow both hid and accentuated her bump.

Rose said again that Emma's set had been *amazing*. "Especially . . . that spin on 'Route 95.' Like nothing I've heard before."

Grinning, Emma explained her choice to "call an audible." A crashing cheer arose from the lawn for the next act. Penny Trosterman and her friend, summoned by the noise, wandered away, grass stains on their jeans and dirt on their black polar fleeces.

Emma eased down onto the grass next to Rose, letting her legs stretch out before her. She uncapped a Gatorade that a roadie had given her. A long swig. They stayed that way while the music onstage carried over.

When Emma said, "Well, I don't want to linger on campus because even though I have few fans, they are devoted and about half of them go to Brown," Rose reacted with such pebbly giggles that Emma relaxed. She couldn't loathe someone who laughed at her jokes.

Rose knew a place without undergrads. A dive bar, nondescript, hidden. They took back streets until they heard soft music from a basement. Down in the nearly empty bar, they sat and ordered a beer and a soda, respectively. Their eyes latched on to the shining rows of bottles behind the bar, neither speaking first.

"Rose, what happened after the lake house?" Emma asked after exhausting labels to read.

"The short answer is, I took a bus to California, had a torrid affair, it ended and left me a wreck. And then ... I needed help. And Judie helped. Sylvia too. I owed them, and they felt responsible for me."

Rose changed the subject to Emma's music. She wanted to know what happened *inside* a person, performing like Emma had?

Without cliché, how could Emma explain the magic of it, the way the stage swallowed her resentment and doubt and the wobbles in her, smoothed her out and turned her into a siren, and how the music—even when it was cymbal-crashing dissonance—morphed into molten beauty, just pouring into her and out of her? Only sometimes. When it ended, you chased it again.

Judie, with her stage fright, had an ambivalent relationship to the stage. But Emma was like her father and Sylvia, she explained. A vamp. A card. A *singer*.

Emma tumbled forward with what she realized was *the story*. The Brown story. How she had gotten in early, with a handwritten application, how her parents had rejoiced, toasted her. Juilliard and Brown, their genius kids. But then she'd been invited by friends of Leon's to do backing guitar and vocals on their tour in the Northeast, so she had deferred Brown, then hardened her resolve to avoid a fate of four years looking out the window, waiting to escape.

Rose said she herself hadn't been convinced that Emma made the right choice. But now she had seen her perform, she got it.

"Have you, like, *discussed* this with my mother?"

Rose made an ambiguous circle with her head, a nod and then a shake, and Emma didn't care. The heat had built inside her.

"If my mother had stayed in school, the world wouldn't have *Singer Sisters I*, which has a perfect first side, blah blah. Mae, bless her heart, won't hear a word against my mother, even though Judie is effectively boycotting our shows. Mae wants Judie to make music again."

Well, Rose wished Judie would make music again.

Well, of course, Emma did, too.

The smell in the bar was warm and woodsy. Emma had been in her share of glossy restaurants: mirrored walls and long banquettes, decor that made you feel decadent. Sylvia's kinds of places. But Dave had reverted to a pref-erence for dingy places where you could hide, and Emma was her father's daughter.

"Well, if you know her so well, why do you think she didn't start playing music again after we grew up?" Emma wanted to know. "We were floating around town like ruffians with our artsy-fartsy friends. Why not then?"

Rose said she got the impression from Judie that the thought of perform-ing, of the studio, all of it, seemed *tiring*.

"You act like you talk to her all the time."

Rose jumped up and ran to the bathroom, holding her stomach, groaning about a phase of pregnancy that was supposed to be over. After a pause to look around the bar, Emma followed her, standing outside a stall and hearing groans and retching notes.

The door opened.

"I don't know how to tell you this, but someone out there has a box of newly hatched chicks. For sale," said Emma.

"Only in Providence," said Rose.

"It's the most backwater city, no offense," said Emma. She stepped out of the way while Rose flushed her toilet and took a damp paper towel to her face.

Because she hadn't eaten, Emma felt about fifty times as drunk as she should. They found the woman with the chicks, craned their necks to look over her shoulder at the box, which was filled with stringy pieces of brown paper and its bundle of tiny, fuzzy goodness. The woman sported overalls and a crop top and gestured with a big glass of beer. The patrons gawked at her cargo. "I'm selling," she explained to Rose. "Keep a chicken coop in your backyard, get fresh eggs!"

Rose wanted a favor, she whispered. Emma leaned in close. "Order me a Guinness? It's the only thing that settles the sickness. Just a few sips."

Emma shrugged. "Your body, your choice."

Emma ordered two and took them to a corner booth. A sip or two in, Rose asked Emma if she'd ever regretted the college thing, and Emma ad-mitted that she pondered it daily but didn't want to spend her time arguing about whether women should be spelled with a *y*, and Rose giggled and Emma thought, again: This nanny is good for my ego.

Her turn: "Do you miss Ireland, with your pregnant Guinness and all?"

And Rose said, "Yes, terribly, but no one singles me out for my brown eyes here. Or my ambition. I fit in." One more sip and Rose handed the pint back to Emma, who tipped it back and finished it, wiping off the foam mustache with a flourish. Rose wondered if she could show Emma something at her place, right nearby.

They got up, and things spun. Rose patted her stomach and said, "The baby loved the beer."

While they'd been sitting in the bar, the soft spring rain that threatened all day had come and gone. The streets of Providence were strewn with damp petals, their fragrant scent filling the air.

Around them, in the frat houses and the dorms, parties would be heating up—or maybe, so blasted today, the students would be hungover by nine p.m. The surroundings surrendered few clues, just dashes of thudding music, a cheap strobe light now and then, scurrying kids in fleeces.

Rose kept a swift pace until they stopped at a wall with a bulletin board advertising the day's concert, and Rose touched Emma's name at the bottom.

"I saw this and that's why I showed," she said.

"Hey," said a voice. "Are you Emma Cantor?"

Three girls, swaying from drink, approached. Possibly the front-row girls.

"We were wondering if you could sign our Planned Parenthood brochures," they said, holding out the leaflets that had been following Emma on her tour—with dedicated volunteers giving them out before her concerts. She signed each one of them, and the girls nudged each other and giggled as she asked if they were already hungover.

"I mean, it's Spring Weekend, so *yes*," said the girl with the eyebrow ring, the chubbier, braver one. "Your show was *epic*. That new song, especially."

"It's dope, raising money for Planned Parenthood," a second said.

Emma thanked them. They gushed. No, thank *you*, for the show, for your work. The girls wandered off.

"Aunt Sylvia took me to Planned Parenthood," said Emma. Which was technically true, although it had been for a friend of Emma's, not Emma herself.

"She took me, too," said Rose. "That's what happened that year, actually—the year I was with you in New Hampshire."

"Does it change your feeling now . . . that you have a pregnancy you want?" Emma asked.

"I'm pragmatic," Rose said. "Life is chance. You wouldn't have been born if your parents fucked five seconds later," she added, her voice changing tone.

"Dude," said Emma. "Harsh way to put it."

"Sorry for the language."

Hilarious, the idea that Emma might be offended by the word "fuck," and Rose laughed as she said it.

"I've come to the conclusion," said Emma, "that I should not have tried to kill you that summer."

Rose had something to show Emma. From Judie. "You should see it. She didn't *give* it—she told me to look for it. I found it." Rose was tripping over her own words—trying to explain. "Emma, your music. Seeing you perform that song . . . I need to show you this."

They came up to a nondescript Victorian house, shrouded by three or four elms. It had bay windows, like her grandparents' place. Rose stopped and patted her pockets for her keys.

The house was furnished with what Emma thought of as generic semi-bohemian: a big brown corduroy couch, a cracking leather recliner with orange stuffing peeking out, and a low, unfinished wood coffee table. Books piled themselves on all horizontal surfaces. Ziggurats of papers made appearances, too—neatly constructed but fundamentally unruly, threatening the room with a takeover.

A life nestled itself here, a family of two—and Emma felt shy, stepping inside. A slim, medium-height guy with a goatee stepped out of the kitchen.

"Felix," he said, putting out his hand.

"Emma," she said, hesitating a few seconds before shaking it.

"I take it you found her," he said to Rose. "I'll head upstairs and give you two a minute." He turned around and she saw he had a butterfly tattoo on his calf.

"Nice ink," she said impulsively. She'd gotten tattooed at sixteen and been screamed at by her grandmother about Auschwitz. Anna, whose ring now sat on her finger, not Rose's.

"Thanks," he said, stopping. "This one is for Rose." He pulled up his sleeve and showed the outline of a rose on his lower forearm.

"Bony spots—you're a sucker for pain?"

He snorted. "I'm soft, actually." Emma sat on the couch and then leaned down until her head touched her knee, dizzy. She noticed a silver samovar, like the one at Grandma Anna's. Where had that old samovar gone, anyway?

"Emma, are you all right?" asked Rose, who was holding a rosary in one hand and a manila folder in the other. "Oh, yes—the samovar."

"Is that . . . also Anna's?"

"It's a loan. Judie loaned it to us because Felix wrote a paper about *tea*—"

"I used to play with Anna's samovar as a child," said Emma, walking toward the thing. "The tap squeaked."

All night, Rose had watched Emma with drill-like eyes. Asked endless questions, with such an intimate air. Emma turned the knob, heard the familiar loud squeak.

"What the hell?" Emma asked. "Why do you have all my grandma's things?"

The room, windows open, was damp. And quiet. Rose's eyes had gone wide and dark—wide and dark and *familiar*.

And unbearable.

As though she had charged into a barbed-wire fence, Emma spun toward the door. Wordless, she pushed her way out, let it fall shut behind her.

The gathering mist caught her in its arms, pulled her close. She ran.

"Wait!" she heard Rose calling, but she kept running around the corner. "Emma, *please!*"

Emma ran. One block, then two, three; outrunning a pregnant woman was a piece of cake.

Pausing on the street, she closed her eyes and tried her dad's yoga breathing but gave up after the third inhale. It occurred to her that she had been due to meet up with Mae at seven so they could sleep on a friend's pullout couch in Boston. The dark sky told her she had missed their rendezvous.

She got lost twice on the walk back. When she found the spot in the parking lot where the van had been, she saw a note affixed to the "Guest Parking" sign with Scotch tape: "E, looked for you—hope you're having fun. Here's our # in Boston." Emma pocketed the scrawled digits.

Clouds kept massing above Providence, ominous olive green and gray, the spaces between them dark voids with a single star or two in each. She would do what Sylvia did when in a "muddle"—let the pavement burn off her thoughts.

Walking, she was free—more than free, obligated—to remember that long-ago summer. How she couldn't wait to go up to the lake, to show off her swimming skills, to stay up late catching fireflies. Even the mosquito bites wouldn't bother her. She'd loved it when her mom rubbed calamine on her, pink and gooey with a funny smell. Her dad and aunt would be there, too, and said they'd let Emma and Leon play and sing on the album they were planning to "cut" with Judie's songs, and Rose would be there, too—Rose, not a babysitter but an "oh, pear."

Dave drove alone to the airport to pick her up, so when Emma and Leon careened into the apartment after park time with Judie, they found their au pair at the kitchen table sipping water from Emma's favorite glass, the blue one that her parents never let her use for fear she'd break it. The au pair jumped up from her seat when the three of them entered.

"Welcome," said Judie, holding out both her hands and taking Rose's. Her mom was a cheek presser or a hair ruffler. Not a double-hand-holder.

"Thank you for having me," said Rose in a formal tone.

"Do you want to see my new drum kit?" asked Leon. He led Rose into the other room. Emma trailed behind.

They left for New Hampshire the next morning. Dave drove Rose and Leon in a rental car. Emma, Sylvia, and Judie took the train to Boston to get a car from her grandparents' house.

On the train, her mother and aunt smoked and talked between the cars. Emma sat with *Little House on the Prairie*, reading it for the third time. She despised how older, blonder sister Mary was favored over mischievous Laura. But then Mary went blind, and she felt guilty.

It was *definitely* not the summer Emma had hoped for. When her family was in the studio it all slid together, clean as a jigsaw puzzle—her mom and dad and aunt bent over sheet music or instruments, arguing, happily so. And Rose stayed outside. The songs themselves made Emma dizzy with pride. They were for *her*—well, most of them were about Leon, but a lot about her, too. The jangly tambourines and tinkly triangles chimed out happy times: sing-alongs, story sessions, games of dress-up, and theatrical productions rigged up on rainy days.

Outside the studio the family was "a mess," in Sylvia's words. Her father kept going to the city for the weekends, though her mom said, "Stay for once." Aunt Sylvia hung off her chair with the phone cord wrapped around her wrists "talking to people" all day. Judie asked Rose the au pair if she "needed anything" fifty times a day. Rose spent a lot of time alone on the dock, her feet in the lake, or following Judie around as she gardened and did chores.

Rose the au pair couldn't swim. Imagine spending the summer at a lake and not being able to swim. Yet she waded waist-deep, and sometimes even chest-deep, and said, "Oh Mother of God, it's cold!" daily, and they all laughed. Emma was learning to dive off the dock, but no one cared.

Judie tried to teach Rose, putting her hands beneath her stomach as she lay on the water's surface, saying, "Kick, kick." Emma crossed her arms and stalked away. She had learned to do this years ago! Her mother acted frustratingly euphoric during these lessons, patient, saying, "Kick, dear," and laughing when Rose swallowed water. Soon enough Rose could doggie paddle and tread water. But she ended the lessons without learning a crawl.

"That's enough for me," she said. "I can save my own life now—no need to go out for the Olympics."

The days got hotter, and they spent more time in the lake. Emma mastered diving. She rode the motorboat while Dave was teaching Leon to drive it. She learned by watching: how to put the key in the ignition, kicking out a tsunami of spray, how to steer, how to loop around the entire lake.

The grown-ups, even Judie, were down in the studio one day and Emma was dying to go out onto the boat for a trip.

"Will you go with me, Leon? Please?"

"I'm reading," said Leon from the hammock.

"I'll go by myself! I can drive the boat!"

Rose unfolded her long legs. "I'll go with you, love," she said. "But I don't know how to steer."

"Emma can do it," said Leon. "She's been practicing with me."

The clouds hung low and cottony. You could reach out and snuggle them. They trapped the heat; that's what made them all so cranky, her mom said.

Emma's fingers ached, as if she needed to play the guitar. Rose was typically lost in reverie. Emma steered the boat out to the middle of the lake with no problems at all, and they cut the motor.

"Do you miss Ireland?" asked Emma, and Rose gazed at the sky. It seemed unfair that Rose got to act all *gloomy* despite getting all of Judie's attention. Emma stiffened.

Rose grew animated. "Let's swim!" she said. She slipped over the side and cried out with delight, kicking her legs and floating on her back. "Brrr!"

Emma stayed back in the boat, fixated on the image of Judie's hand on Rose's back, supporting her as she learned to swim.

Suddenly, she turned the key in the ignition and sped away. The kick of the boat on the water was so fast. She giggled; what a trick.

"Emma! Emma, come back!" Rose started yelling. Emma felt sorry, but she didn't know how to turn the boat that well and panicked, making a much wider circle than she planned.

"Come on, darling," Rose said. "Come back!" Emma turned the boat around, but the circle grew wider and wider—almost at the other side now.

And then the screaming stopped. After a minute of fast breathing, Emma was able to remember Dave's lesson and bring the boat back around, but she didn't see or hear Rose.

Oh God. She had *drowned* her babysitter like an evil child; her mother would murder her alive. Sweat poured from the area behind her neck and in front of her chest, too. Her eyes a lawn sprinkler of tears, she circled the area again. She cut the motor.

"Hey!" a voice squeaked over the water. "I'm here."

Rose was holding on to a canoe on the side of a neighbor's dock, about fifty feet away from the shore. She bobbed up and down with the boat, the lapping lake.

"Thank God in heaven," said Rose as Emma steered to her.

"You scared me!" Emma said. "I couldn't turn the boat that fast."

"I scared *you?*" Rose shouted.

"I was playing a joke," Emma insisted.

"You know I can't swim well, little shit," said Rose.

"You jumped off the boat!" said Emma in a grown-up tone. "You swam fine. *Relax.*"

Rose climbed into the boat with arms completely shaking, so badly that she fell back out and splashed into the water. Emma had to give her both arms and help pull her up.

"I didn't know you'd spaz out," she said.

Rose, waterlogged, tilted her head each way. "Surely you did," she said. She lay on the bottom for a while, the towel around her shoulder. "A family of liars," she spat out. The boat chugged to shore.

~

Emma walked up and down the slanted streets of College Hill, breathing in the blossoms until after midnight, when she started to feel a friction on her heel—even her worn-in boots couldn't withstand a day of performing and a night of walking on what felt like concrete mountain. She yawned. Maybe she should clomp down to the bus or train station, grab a ticket to Boston, and sleep in her seat.

Her thoughts pursued her. Judie meeting with Rose on the sly, giving her precious heirlooms. Emma clutched her hand and felt the outline of Anna's ring. She could remember her grandmother's smell: Ivory soap and the yellow Chiclets she chewed constantly. Emma associated those smells with a mix of disapproval (for Judie's parenting and her kids' manners, for the state of the apartment, for their catered meals) and grandmotherly indulgence: dolls, and keyboards, and music books, and cookies.

While trying to figure out where downtown was, she ran into a group of undergraduates smoking on a corner.

"Yo, guys, it's Emma Cantor! Emma, you were dope today, will you smoke a j with us?" they asked.

Emma laughed, pretending not to be temporarily homeless. "Sure," she said. "Sure, why not?"

"Rock on!" said someone. They peppered her with questions, mostly about what other stars she had met and known, rather than her own work or even her family.

They trooped back inside a house built like Rose's, sat cross-legged on the floor. A hookah, a lava lamp, a rainbow pride flag, and a bunch of stuffed animals piled on each other constituted the decor. With deep seriousness, they solicited her opinions on nag champa vs. sandalwood incense.

She learned as they sat in a circle that the house was rented by six people, three guys and three girls. The girls, who lived upstairs, were ethnic studies majors and self-described radical activists who were involved in ending sweatshops (they kept saying the acronym for their movement, USAS, which sounded like *You, sass!*). They went to shows in Boston, mostly, at half a dozen venues where Emma's father, her mother, or her aunt had played memorable dates, all too big for her to fill herself yet.

Their bad white wine ran out and someone mentioned a vodka bottle in the freezer. Emma wrinkled her nose and contemplated the pathway to the door and to Boston.

"Wait, you know what I have on CD?" one of the girls shouted. "*Chant and Sing*! You were on it, as a kid, right? Oh my God. We *so* have to play it."

Emma crossed her arms before her face, groaning.

"No, no," she said, "not that."

The schwag that the kids called "weed" fogged her up. The album—the album they made that summer, before Rose left, then after Rose left—was procured from a flip-the-pages CD case and put on the player. Emma tightened her eyes, wishing she could shut out the sound.

~

When they trooped in from the lake that summer day, the grown-ups had been busy overdubbing tracks on *Chant and Sing*. After Judie rang the triangle for dinner, Rose inspected her food, head bent low over the table.

"Are you all right?" asked Judie. "You look pale, honey."

"I'm fine," said Rose. "Too much fresh air. I think I'll go lie down."

Judie made a clucking sound but let Rose climb the stairs. That night, Emma heard someone moving around, then boxes shifting, even some noise in the attic. Unable to stand it, she crept down the hallway and saw Rose downstairs with a bag, half-packed, sitting on the floor.

"I'm leaving early tomorrow," Rose said.

"Because of me?" asked Emma.

Rose walked up the stairs toward Emma, a few steps. "I don't hate you," she said after a minute. "I have to find my own way."

"What do you mean?" asked Emma. "Your own way to *what?*"

"I dunno. Don't kill anyone with that boat, so. Little devil."

Rose's absence was the topic for days. Sylvia kept saying, "I'm befuddled, I thought she was happy."

Emma pursed her lips into the fish shape, wrinkling her nose. "She said we were a family of liars," she confessed.

"Oh dear," said Sylvia. "I mean it's *true*! But oh dear."

A day of phone calls followed. The ringing got so persistent that Sylvia took Emma and Leon out to the porch and tried to do a puppet show with them. They ended up trying to stuff all the puppets into the biggest puppet to create what Leon dubbed a "mega-puppet." At one point, Judie banged on the table from inside the house. Emma jumped out of her seat.

"Sean, honey, I don't know where she's gone," Emma heard her mother on the phone, both annoyed and sad. "She's fully grown," continued Judie. "I left home at that age. . . . Sure, I mean yes, I know—but it's different. And she's worldly. . . ."

Emma stayed up late. She heard her mother and Sylvia talking into the night, and noises that sounded like tears and like laughter.

Days later a postcard slid into their mailbox. Emma saw it first: it had lemons on it and the word "CALIFORNIA" in all capital letters with blocks and shadows.

"Mom!" she said, holding it up, and Judie, sitting on the staircase with the phone next to her feet, picked it up and read it and laughed—and sprinted across the lawn in her bare feet, down to where Sylvia hid behind a magazine, smoking.

Emma followed behind, happy to hear them laugh. "She's in San Francisco!" she heard her mom tell Sylvia. "What does she think it is, 1968?"

Sylvia was looking at the postcard over Judie's shoulder. "Well done, kid!" she said. "You know, she must've planned this from the beginning. When did you last pay her?"

"She probably did," said Judie with a sigh. "She wanted to see America."

Sylvia hugged Judie. "You worry too much."

"Let me look at that again. Is there a return address?"

Emma did a cartwheel on the lawn. She ran back into the house and grabbed Leon and said, "I have a candy stash. Want to share it?"

He looked out the window at the sisters and said, "Ah, I see, the return of joy." Another postcard followed, with redwood trees all over it.

In the fall, a new babysitter arrived from the city, a girl named Liz who worked for Dave's record label as an assistant, getting coffee, and was basically "loaned out to them," according to Leon.

Liz wore big gold earrings and spoke with a funny accent, but different from Rose, all "cawfee" and "shew stowah." She told Emma all about sex and menstruation—in detail—and informed her that her brother was "queer as a three-dollar bill" and Aunt Sylvia "swung both ways."

She taught Emma how to do the diamond and box stitches with lanyard, and she had boyfriends, and she made dinner, and she must have had the night off when Flower came.

⁓

Chant and Sing was still on the goddamn CD player. Emma's new friends sang along, arms draped around each other's shoulders—what was it with college kids and public touching?—and clearly wanted her to join. To oblige, she mouthed some words before scooting her way to a corner by a couch where she could huddle, unobserved, too wiped out to make an exit.

One song on the album featured Judie Zingerman as co-lead vocalist, uncredited. Dave had written it for Emma; it was not a standout Judie composition. This one was called "Sad Bear." And while they recorded it, Rose had been hovering around.

> *Sad Bear, Sad Bear, Little Bear don't be blue*
> *Sad Bear, Sad Bear, Little Bear there's a cave for you*
> *A cave for you*
> *A cave for you!*

As the sound of her parents' crooning voices intensified, sleepiness overwhelmed Emma. She was being chloroformed by her own personal lullaby. The undergrads began scattering. She pulled a pillow off the couch. Before oblivion set in she had a half dream, as the music from the party blended with the music of her memory. She let go. She dreamed.

At a dream lake house that was different from the *real* lake house— here, the woods surrounded the house thickly, the lawn didn't exist, and the lake was smaller, greener, more of a mysterious pool beneath the canopy— she roamed around, looking for Leon. But she couldn't find him, and she yelled for her family to help. A canoe was missing. She looked out across the murky surface to find her brother, scanning, scanning the edge of the water.

Emma woke up in sunlight, with a flimsy, scratchy blanket on her. Someone had taken off her shoes, left them neatly lined up against the wall, with her smelly socks tucked into them and her miniature backpack wedged between them. She opened her wallet—totally intact. As she put her boots back on, she considered this stacking of possessions. A stranger had taken care of her. A fan, who felt connected to her. This almost made up for the humiliation of having dozens of adolescent eyes on her while she heard her parents' voices and dozed off. Almost.

Her mouth craved water, her eyes were crusted over with mascara. Disgusting, but not unfamiliar.

College life was maybe not as different from tour life as she'd thought. She caught a scent of her own armpit and felt chagrined—so much for rock star mystique. She washed her face using someone's Noxzema, goopy, white, and medicinal. A dab of toothpaste on her finger squished over her teeth. She gargled. Some guy's spray deodorant was useful: aerosols killed the ozone layer, but a necessity was a necessity. One quick spritz under each arm and his crappy cologne on her inner thighs and behind her neck. Great. She smelled like a college boy. One stop at the fridge—ahh, perfect, a Diet Coke—and she was out of there.

In front of the house, the girl who had rolled the joint the previous night lounged on the steps, smoking, wearing a black bra covered by a sheer top and a pair of big bell-bottoms that were ragged at the hem. Her jet-black hair remained distressingly glossy. She had an eyebrow ring.

"You conked out to your father's lullaby," said the girl as Emma sat beside her holding her Diet Coke. "Deep."

"Accurate," said Emma with a dry laugh. The girl stubbed out her cigarette and introduced herself as Alicia. "Thanks for taking care of me," Emma said. The day was duller than the previous one; it still smelled wet and muddy.

Alicia thanked her for the show and offered to send her a bootleg tape of the whole day at Brown that a friend of hers made. Emma scrawled her AOL email on Alicia's wrist and felt a frisson of excitement, imagining what it would be like to sign girls' wrists all in a row.

"I feel like I learned from you . . . that a person can be like, this electric rock presence, but then be a mess. Like, wow. I mean we all should have realized it from Kurt blowing himself away, right, but I learned it from *you*."

Emma tried not to spit out her Diet Coke in horror. She sank lower into the stoop and bullshitted about the universality of suffering, and Alicia continued talking about Emma's parents being a "musical dynasty" opening doors for her.

"I mean you're good. You're *way* good. But most people never get a chance to prove it?" Alicia added that she loved Emma's song "about your stalker."

A few students wandered by in their baggy pajama bottoms, and Emma took her leave, wincing from the hot spots on the backs of her heels. Her thoughts curdled. Alicia was tucked away on this bucolic campus with a family who probably loved her lots and had no secrets. Alicia didn't meet random people who flashed her grandma's ring at her. Rose had the samovar. Rose had the ring—no, Emma still had the ring.

Food would help. She slid a few bucks into a vending machine to get another Coke and then changed her mind at the last minute and got her money back and went to a corner store for orange juice and a muffin. She shoved aside the inner voices of Judie and Anna and their exhortations against pastries (Sylvia agreed but made an exception for chocolate) and told herself she needed a layer to line her stomach. Munching, she went into a pay phone at the bus station and called collect overseas.

"Hullo? Yes, I accept the charges."

"Oh, thank God you're home, Ned," she said. "I am sorry for this, but I'm in a bus station in Providence."

"Providence—do you mean you're in *heaven*? My goodness, what a turn of events." Ned, Leon's new love, must have been witty even in his dreams.

He fetched Leon, who drawled hello. "*Collect*? Are you in jail?"

"Providence, Rhode Island. Bus station."

"Even worse." Leon yawned over the line as Emma began to talk. "Rose the Irish nanny? What about her?" he asked.

"She nosed me out at Brown," she began. "Wearing Grandma Anna's ring. . . ."

"*Intriguing.* Mom and Sylvia have their secrets, as we know."

"We do?" Emma held the phone away from her ear. Her brother continued to react to her confusion with what sounded suspiciously like *glee*. The phone booth bench was cutting into her tailbone and her feet still hurt.

"Why don't we tell each other stuff in this family?" Emma asked, her voice breaking. "I'm tired of it."

"Oh, Em, dry those eyes."

He let her sniff and complain, humming "Early Morning Rain" while she gurgled long-distance. Then he asked if she wanted an answer to her question.

"It's in the songs, Emma—I mean the first *Singer Sisters* record? It's about trauma. Or what about that song Mom wrote for Sylvia, about her marriage to Dave? You have to listen. But that has never been your thing. You're a shouter."

A family shuffled through the station, each parent holding a big duffel bag under one arm and tugging on a kid's hand with the other.

"They're calling my bus," she lied to her brother. "I have to go. . . . Should I call Mom? Dad? I don't know where to go with this."

He breathed heavily. She heard beeping in the background that she recognized as London sirens, their pitch higher and lighter than New York's.

"Let me think on it. Call when you're better situated?"

She boarded a bus about twenty minutes later and rested her head against the hard plastic back of the seat in front of her. She missed Leon. They hadn't even talked about her new song that she wanted him to produce. How it might be a hit. *That* would be worth his delight and fascination.

"*Listen* to the songs," her brother had said. She closed her eyes and pictured the track listing for her mom and aunt's debut album.

"Route 95," the song she'd sung yesterday onstage, was obviously about leaving home. "The House by the Lake" *did* have super-dark themes, like Leon said.

One more song seemed important: "Long-Legged Man." But as though her consciousness simply couldn't absorb her thoughts anymore, her head jerked forward against the seat ahead of her and she dozed.

⁓

She's here!" When Emma schlepped up to the door of Mae's friend's house, a surprise awaited her inside: champagne and roses. Mae had made an ample pot of coffee and was pouring cup after cup into porcelain teacups and handing them around like shot glasses.

Emma scratched her head, fuzzy and full of the final song on the album that she'd been thinking of as she fell asleep. Emma had assumed "Long-Legged Man" expressed a twisted yearning for Dave.

But her father had muscular legs of average length. She should know—she'd *inherited* them.

Rose, on the other hand, even pregnant, had pins that went on for days.

"Emma, snap out of it. I've been on the phone all day," Mae said. "Some Brown kid whose dad is in the industry made a call last night and wheels started turning. Emma, you're going to be a star."

JUDIE

S itting in a lecture about John Milton and the use of free verse, Judie knew she was going to throw up. Indecorously, she got up and fled the auditorium, resting in the hallway in a semi-swoon until the class poured out. A friend fetched her abandoned notebook and a glass of water as terror rose in her chest.

How could this have escaped her? She had been so focused on scheming about how to run away from Wellesley and get back to New York that she hadn't registered a missed period: one month or two? *Shit*. Now, as she retched in her room, she recollected the sanitary pads in her trunk, still unopened.

She sheltered on her bed chewing on a piece of bread, and though shedding a tear or two would have made her feel better, nothing emerged save ragged, dry breaths. What would the girls here say in whispers to each other? That the unfriendly classmate who played her guitar alone was a *bad girl*? Judie had avoided befriending her dorm-mates because she saw them as naïfs who didn't know how to live with ten others in an apartment, subsist on scrambled eggs, follow men back to hotels—or stare at an audience through a scrim of smoke.

In an hour of agony, she forced herself to reconsider her entire chain of decision-making. Why had she told Eamon she was on the pill? Why had Valerie assured her it would work if she shared it? Why had she been convinced that going to the Village was her only chance to chase a dream, when the person whom she'd followed there didn't even care for her?

All of Sylvia's and Dave's patronizing—even her parents' concerns—had been *right*. She had ruined her life.

Yet even in her panic, Judie couldn't shake the indignant sense that she was *also* right. Sleeping with women hadn't ruined Eamon's life, or Dave's, and she had to bear the cost of Eamon's freedom. A tiny, rebellious thought poked through her self-remonstrance: in addition to failing herself, she had been failed by them. By all of them.

But no one would ever see that.

Whom to call for help? Valerie? She'd been the one to siphon away those pills, after all. No. Valerie looked down on her—and how could she impose herself on a girl with no resources, a waitress and a typist who had helped Judie out too much already?

Maybe it would happen by itself; sometimes women bled late. But until then, Sylvia was her recourse. Sylvia, the queen of the school, who had made more peace efforts than a Quaker, who'd invited her kid sister to come play the spontaneous concerts she organized in dorms and dining halls, who had been fretting about Judie's well-being—with reason, it turned out.

Through a message passed to a friend from home, Judie told Sylvia to meet her by the lake. The whole campus was afire with autumn, leaves littering the walkways and a few bare branches poking the sky. Judie wore old jeans, faded ones that had belonged to a male cousin. Pants were a campus no-no, pants with the top button unfastened unthinkable. She huddled on a stone bench, tucking her legs up, and put her head down when her sister arrived.

"How many weeks ago did the parents snatch me from New York?" Judie asked.

Sylvia puzzled out the math.

"Sylvia, I'm in for it," said Judie. She opened her mouth to explain but retched instead, leaning over and kneeling on the ground.

"What's the matter?" asked Sylvia. "Are you sick?"

"I'm pregnant, dammit. How is that possible after only one—well, after nearly one—after just a handful of times?"

Sylvia let out a gurgling noise.

"Don't make sick-cat sounds," said Judie. "Did you expect I'd come back from New York a virgin? I almost did—that's the funny thing. Oh God, I suppose I'll have to have an operation, and it will be costly and secret and awfully scary."

To their surprise, Sylvia began to cry. Big, weeping sobs that had her so shaky she put her head on Judie's shoulder. Judie hushed her but felt the fear rise in her like a volcano. If Sylvia had lost control, she was in big trouble.

"*Don't* do that," Sylvia said. "A girl from my class at school who played tennis . . . she . . . Judie—isn't there another way?"

"May MacGregor." Judie shivered. The rumors had reached her, of the fair-haired, wispy girl who died trying to get rid of a baby, who returned to the dorms at Simmons and bled and bled. She had been nice, too, with a kind word for the younger girls at school.

"Do something else."

"Get an itinerant folk singer to marry me? Raise a baby?"

"Folk singer—Dave?!"

"If only . . . it's an older one from Ireland. Eamon—"

"*Foley?* And *you?* That song about the golden hair is out of sight . . . Jill Cohen and I have been listening to nothing but."

Jill Cohen had recently replaced Bella Bernstein as Sylvia's most special friend. Naturally they were listening to that infernal song.

"He's a goy," said Sylvia.

Judie began to laugh, and then to shiver more, and Sylvia took off her own sweater and put it around her sister's shoulders. She scrutinized Judie's body. "You seem different," she said. "Oh Judie, why did you skip town when you could have been here with me, impressing the girls? They follow me along like ducklings! And they love your songs, especially 'Route 95.'"

"Who said you had the right to play my songs, anyway?" Judie was being petulant, but her head spun as though from a million whiskeys and no water to chase them.

"We've got to tell someone!" said Sylvia, adopting her sister's tucked-knees position on the bench. Sylvia ticked off the months on her hand: Judie would be showing by winter.

They planned to reconvene the next day. Judie walked away, grinding an occasional pile of dead leaves with her boot heel and relishing the way the crunch turned soft.

A baby would come in the spring. Instead of regret, Judie burned with restlessness. Outside the bucolic prison of campus, the world moved swiftly. What if her friends downtown had begun experimenting with new music, without her? What if Dave made a record, and got famous, and forgot her? Though she was due in astronomy lab, she snuck into town to have a slice of cherry pie. *You destroyed your life*, one voice said, but another shut it down: *You had a lovely time. You did. And it was all so interesting.*

Now that she had told Sylvia, her parents would find out. There would be a family inquisition. And then what? No Wellesley, no running back to New York.

A rush of affection for Sylvia overtook her, maybe not love so much as raw need.

On her way back to the dorms, she scribbled some words in a notebook, then let herself into Sylvia's room and left the notebook on her sister's bed. The new song she had begun that night she slept with Eamon: now it had an ending.

> *He slipped into my life at half-past ten*
> *And somehow I knew already then*
> *Behind the curtains, behind the smoke*
> *Behind the pretty words he spoke*
> *That the long-legged man would murder me.*
> *That the long-legged man would murder me.*

LACONIA, NEW HAMPSHIRE

A few times during Judie's confinement in New Hampshire, Sylvia drove up to look in on her. Their chats stalled—as they had since Sylvia told their parents about Eamon, and the pregnancy, and then used Dave to track him down—but they still listened to music together, albums Sylvia brought: Joan Baez and Phil Ochs and Donovan, and *One Day*, the new album by Dave Cantor, singing as Dave Canticle.

The needle went down, the record spun: the opening song, "Little Brown Sparrow," began, a loving tribute to a stalwart bird-woman. Judie clutched her hands over her heart.

"It's for Valerie," she said. "She has that brown skin and hair."

"Is it?" Sylvia asked, pulling her sister's chestnut curl. Judie thawed.

"After this is over, let's make our record," said Sylvia, clearly encouraged by a single sisterly smile. "We'll use Dad's studio. I know you've been writing music—'Route 95' is perfection. So is 'Long-Legged'—I mean, um, so is the other song."

"You're dreaming," said Judie, even as the dream enveloped her, too. "I won't set foot in Dad's studio, after how he's treated me."

Judie turned the record off. The absence of melody assaulted the room. A lone branch creaking in the wind grew louder and louder.

"I hope that branch falls already," said Judie. "Maybe I'll be lucky, and under it."

Their mother's family's decision to buy a house by a cold mountain lake, instead of on the sunny Cape Cod shore, or even up in Maine, bespoke the streak of flintiness that their father loved to complain about in his in-laws.

The house sat on the outskirts of a small town, a mile's walk from Main Street—with a vast lake down the hill. They kept a boat and a small dock, but mostly what the place boasted was the grand lawn that sloped down to the shore and the view of the lake from the house.

Anna enjoyed the feeling of gentility she got from sitting atop the hill. "My parents traveled steerage for what? For this hill," she told the girls when they were young, and then they rolled down it and got obscenely bright green grass stains on their dresses.

⌐

When Eamon had come to the Zingerman house for a reckoning earlier that winter, they had squared off in the parlor, where Sylvia and Judie had once played "Blowin' in the Wind" for Dave. The bay windows behind Eamon's colossal head, with their trim of lace, showed skeletal trees, a few with a jumble of curled leaves clinging to them, their days numbered.

"I will marry Judith if that's asked of me," he said to them. His face was pinched.

The week before, Judie had wrapped herself in an old dressing gown of Anna's and gone on strike. Her belly had popped, and in response to Sylvia's remark that she couldn't show up to synagogue like *that*, she'd responded that she wouldn't show up *anywhere* and had driven them crazy with her refusal to move. But Eamon's arrival—after Sylvia, through Dave, had tracked him down, weeks of letters and phone calls that didn't involve her—drew her out. That morning, she carefully dressed in an oversize sweater of Hyman's that allowed her to keep her jeans unbuttoned, and descended.

Eamon's guitar rode on his back when he knocked at the door, but the smart wool coat he was wearing, with two rows of brass buttons, belied his humble pose. Clearly, his fortunes had continued to improve since the summer, however much this development with *her* had worried him. This thought—of him eating well and traveling while she locked herself upstairs—made her fists curl up in rage, as they had the previous year when the troubadours clomped around downstairs every weekend.

"You look well," she said to him.

"As do you—" He coughed a few times, unable to finish. Shocking them all, she let out a caustic laugh. And so did he. And then she laughed again, and then he laughed, harder and more genuine.

"What is *wrong* with you two?" Hyman barked; she had to look at her feet to prevent another peal of laughter. Eamon coughed. She snuck a glance at him—not handsome, but craggy, with eyes like a September sky. She had found him beautiful, yes. She wished they *could* whisk themselves off together, make music and a family. If only she could reconcile that vision with his offer, currently being debated by her parents in the parlor, parleying a treaty.

"You're . . . a Catholic?" asked Anna.

He coughed.

"I'm sorry I didn't get the, you know, operation," Judie said. "Eamon, I am."

She hadn't said his name out loud yet. "I was scared, I didn't want to be butchered—I'm a coward, and I know it, and now you're here."

Her voice was measured, but underneath a tremor heaved. His eyes were opaque, but she was no fool. He saw her as a trap: a career trap, a life trap, one he'd never *actually* submit to—he was too much like her. What had his words been before he fell upon her body like a gift to unwrap? "I'm not a going-steady kind of guy"?

He felt sympathy, maybe attraction, too—but he didn't want her as a burden, and she didn't blame him. She identified with him: saw herself as cooped up and bloated and felt his disgust for her take root and spread on her skin.

Anna's mouth was a slim dash of disapproval. Judie imagined her mother's thoughts: not long ago she had chided her daughters for talking about conflict in marriage at the table, and now they were negotiating unspeakable things in her own parlor. The carpet between Judie's crossed feet and her mother's stretched on, beige and endless.

"Ahem . . ." Eamon shifted in his chair as though the thing couldn't contain his bulk.

"If you wanted me to take your religion, too, I'd do it. I would. I'm an honorable person. And . . . I like Judith, you know. I do like you," he said to her. "Though I don't know you well."

"Judie," she said. "It's Judie."

Hyman had been interlacing his fingers, in and out. He raised his head at his daughter.

"Nu, it's settled?"

"No," she said simply. "No. I won't make him do this."

"You won't raise a bastard—" said Hyman.

"Don't use that word," said Judie. "It's archaic." Three pairs of eyes rested on her, expectant, waiting for the whore to speak. "I won't marry someone who doesn't love me, doesn't *know* me, like he said. I want to keep living. I want to make music . . . to go back to New York." She paused. "We'll have to find someone to take it, that's all, to raise it. I'll go away until it's settled."

Eamon cleared his throat and leaned forward.

"I didn't want to bring this up so soon," he said, "but I have a sister. From Dublin, but in London for her man's job. She never had a wee one of her own and it breaks her heart. I think . . . I haven't gone so far as to ask, exactly, but I *know* she would raise the child. She raised me."

Judie swore that she saw the sun poke through on the street out the window at that instant, and that the future revealed itself. And she saw now why Eamon had looked pained but not terrified when he arrived. He had this ace up his sleeve the whole time. A man like him probably saw the whole thing as a blessing: appease the girl, the sister, the disapproving family, in one fell swoop. How convenient for him.

She didn't care.

"Yes," she said. "Yes. Give it to someone who needs one. Yes, that's what we'll do."

Anna and Hyman exchanged looks, then Hyman nodded, barely.

"Where will you go before . . . before the birth?" Eamon asked.

"We have somewhere quiet," said Anna.

⌒

The idea was that Judie would stay in the house, with visits from her mother and sister when they could, minded by a local woman who could move in for the duration.

"We'll pay whoever we find extra for her discretion, and if she tells the entire town, it's New Hampshire," said Anna. "Thank God no one lives here."

Hyman dropped her off before Christmas. He checked that the heat worked and that the housekeeper, a stout local from two towns over named Beattie, was there before he turned the car around.

"She'll be all right," said Beattie, shaking Hyman's hand as Judie shivered in the doorway. "Same thing happened to my niece; gave one up at sixteen, now she's married with four."

That was the longest sentence Beattie ever uttered. Since then, Judie had haunted the house, hearing only Beattie's one-word commands to eat and the occasional shot of birdsong. She watched ice form and melt on the surface of the water. She began feeling kicks against the inside of her belly, which made her curious and afraid.

The newspapers let her know that the world marched on, and music marched on: new albums, concerts, arguments about Bob Dylan. Throughout January, not much snow fell. So each afternoon Judie put on thick boots and walked the twenty minutes to the town's only diner. After a week, the staff left her to contemplate her usual order (bacon, lettuce, and tomato, to spite her parents), stretching time until it lost meaning.

At home, once she thawed, she would sit down at Hyman's desk, which he'd built himself: broad and oak with no adornment save three slim drawers. Her guitar sat beside it. Almost the minute she put pen to paper, the words began to flow. Then she'd pick out a tune on the guitar.

The songs she wrote shocked her as they emerged, laced with pain, songs that took the form of folk and bent it back to obey her caged fury. When she sat at the long, eggshell-white kitchen table, composing letters to the only people she could—her sister, Dave, and twice to Eamon—the correspondence was witty. But at Hyman's desk, in her notebooks, the sentences she scrawled came from someone else.

"The cold ground calls me," one song began. "I will always be alone," said another. Invective about her father, her mother, her family, pushed itself into her lyrics. Minor chords sprang up, spreading like weeds.

One night in Cambridge she'd perched on the stairwell, hearing her parents arguing as the top stair dug into her back.

"She'll bring shame on all of us," Anna said, sobbing.

"Shame," Judie wrote at the top of her page, frowning and digging the pen into her cheek. Later, in bed, she wrote and wrote and wrote until she passed out, the ink from the pen staining her fingers, smudging the pillow she clutched in her sleep.

~

I n late February, it snowed for days on end. Judie was homebound, with a belly that could be contained only by a flannel nightgown of her grandmother's, topped off by Hyman's old coat. The nightgown began to smell, and she had to wash it frequently, while wearing a shirtwaist of her mother's that didn't provide any warmth, her feet losing feeling. She would wrap herself in a wool blanket that made her sneeze and her skin turn pink. She hung the nightgown by the woodstove to dry, and sometimes it got singed, a small streak of brown and yellow at the edges. One night she dreamed that she was in the old apartment in the Village, and it had extra rooms. She ran from one to another looking, until she found Eamon and Valerie in bed together, laughing. They turned to look at her.

Judie woke up to find a wet spot on the bedsheets. It took her a while to grasp that her body had made milk for the baby, weeks early.

The stain spread, oblong and damp. She bolted up and frantically tried to blot the sheet, filled with revulsion.

The trilling, wild woman sitting on the fire escape in New York was dead—before she'd lived. Impossible now to creditably write about soaring flight as she had with her bite-size masterpiece, "Route 95." Going forward, her tunes would be requiems. She wouldn't recover from this, and she shouldn't. Being bold had destroyed her. One of her new lines rat-a-tatted in her head: "The cold ground calls me. The cold ground calls."

The phone rang. She shuffled downstairs, picking up on the sixth or seventh ring. When Sylvia couldn't make it north, she called her on the phone for a weekly pep talk, to encourage Judie to keep writing music, saying that after this ended, they'd make their album.

Today, Judie didn't play along. "*You'll* make the album," she said. "You and Dave. My music is too sad to record. Sylvia, I *don't* want to do this anymore." She hung up without saying goodbye, feeling desperately that she couldn't chat one minute longer—burn down the house or kick a wall. The thought had lodged inside her: No matter what turns my life takes now, *this will have happened.* This humiliating, lonely, bitter vigil.

A swift, stern kick landed in her left abdomen as she heaved downstairs.

"Yes, I know," she said. She paced back and forth on the upstairs landing, waiting the hours until Beattie departed for her errands.

Once the door shut, the house went silent, the winter sun making the dust particles shine. She shoved into the front closet to get what she'd need: her boots, Hyman's coat.

Then, the last step: back upstairs for her notebook. Taking care, she tore out six full pages containing her best songs, the ones she couldn't bear to give up, and set them down on the desk under her father's paperweight. With the rest of the notebook in hand, she set out on a familiar walk through the woods to the far side of the lake. She hadn't felt strong enough to go there for a month at least.

The week-old snow with a half-melted crunch on top was formidably slippery; she stumbled and then, remembering to stomp with heels first, steadied. Her hands were sweating.

She could lie down in the woods, look up at the winter sun through the iron gate of the branches, and allow herself to sleep like an animal in the day's growing warmth.

But that was not her plan.

She trekked and trudged, ignoring the occasional whip of a tree branch against Hyman's coat or, once, her cheek. Her hands dampened as the sun rose in the sky, then chilled as the perspiration settled. Shuffling through the drifts of white turned her feet wet and soggy. Her lungs hurt from the exertion; they had no room in her chest, crowded out by the fitful, kicking contents of her belly.

When she reached the edge of the lake, the sun hurled itself onto the crystalline world. From the log where she sat, Judie recognized her location—a clearing she and Sylvia often hiked or boated to, a vantage point for looking back at their lawn. A dusting of snow coated the lake, but patches of ice, by the shore, were robin's-egg blue.

This warmth recalled the beach in summer. She lifted her face to the sky, then turned to the lake, where sunbeams danced on the ice. The kicking began again, aimed at her left ribs, insistent. She was hungry again; she had to pee again. She looked at her notebook and shrugged.

"Be brave," she said. She took a step out onto the ice; it felt solid. Her steps grew more confident; she would leave her notebook in the middle, and when the days grew warmer, the lake would take her words. This was an offering to the gods; for what? For another chance at life? For an end to uncertainty and pain? Maybe, maybe.

She moved farther out, resting her notebook on a windswept spot, and turned around on her heels, walking back quickly to safety.

⌒

The ice cracking was a gunshot in her ears. Instinctively, her hand went to her belly. She saw a fissure spreading from her foot like a train speeding away, and her eyesight fogged. She found herself dropping to her knees and sliding, with her belly skimming the ice, one inch, then two. Tiny white threads darted away from her body when it moved.

She didn't have to make it all the way to shore, only to the shallows. Still, she had walked too far. Her breath felt hot, disjointed.

The shore, with its graceful trees, seemed agonizingly far, but over *there* a long tree branch stuck out; she aimed her crawl there. Her knees hurt; the kicking inside her grew frantic.

"I'm sorry," she said to her stomach. "I'm so sorry."

She shuffled, the sound of cracks reverberating in the bowl around the lake. She would faint from cold and fear; she would die here and be swallowed up along with her baby and her songs, and the songs had been *beautiful*, why had she chosen to abandon them? Judie turned around to see the notebook where she'd dropped it, but the sun on the ice obscured her view.

She felt a wetness creeping up her pant leg. She couldn't look. Her heavy clothes would weigh her down; she would sink fast.

But even as she faced the worst, the thought asserted itself: she wasn't dead, and it *hadn't* been her fault, what happened with Eamon.

⌒

Judie!" She heard her sister's voice echoing toward her; she must already be dying if Sylvia was calling.

"Judie, this way." Judie looked up and saw a flash of movement in the woods. A hand waved. A figure gesticulated on the shore. One of the locals, maybe. She opened her mouth to scream but squeaked instead.

Then a thwack: a stick landed yards away, tied onto a long, gray wool scarf with a single violet stripe up its length. Reality arrived with it: Sylvia's favorite scarf, the Isadora Duncan scarf that the family told her would kill her someday.

The figure *was* Sylvia. A few dogged minutes of slithering, and Judie had grabbed on to the stick with her aching fingers; holding the wool, she crawled as Sylvia pulled, until she reached the edge of the water.

Sylvia had ventured onto the ice herself, onto its blue edge. She grabbed Judie's shoulders and pulled her to shore. There were shouts and exhortations and cries of "What were you thinking?" and "Where did you come from?" But their yells faded as a melodic sound began to fill the air.

The day had brought such an unusual, sharp thaw that the ice was *singing*.

"Oh, Judie," said Sylvia. The sisters leaned together on their log. A slim hole about the size of a young child opened along the pathway that Judie had crawled.

~

S ylvia had picked up the ominous thread in Judie's tone. She'd borrowed a friend's car and driven straight up *like a madwoman*. When she got to the house and Judie wasn't there, she had seen the footprints in the snow in the woods. "A bad feeling" led her to run straight down the grassy hill to the lake, bypassing the long route.

They didn't discuss Sylvia's instincts. Judie felt overwhelmed by gratitude, with an edge of resentment. She so often required rescuing, and her sister so often played the rescuer.

"Were you trying to kill yourself?" Sylvia asked Judie after a warm bath and tea.

Judie curled up in bed. Sylvia roosted on the covers, her weight pulling the blankets too tight over Judie's legs.

"I don't know," said Judie, weeping true tears for the first time since she had discovered her pregnancy. The old wooden bed now shook with her sobs, her big voluptuous body that was fine, alive, and warm again. The covers rubbed against the bruises forming on her knees, but she remained otherwise unscathed.

"I just—I felt *horrified*, and I thought dropping my book of songs through the ice would . . . get rid of the bad feelings."

"A stunt like that is not the sign of a right mind," said Sylvia, leaning forward and taking her by the shoulders. "Promise you'll do what I say from now on."

Judie began crying again. "I'll do whatever you tell me."

"Did you think you were going to die?"

"Yes," said Judie. Then a flicker of her old defiance. "I would have made it back without you, though, don't you think?"

Judie took one of her sister's hands, ran her own fingers across it. She couldn't tell Sylvia how she had felt pity for the baby, and then a new sensation: that she was unworthy of the life in her body—but also that she had to save it. Fierce. Animal.

Sylvia crossed her arms and turned away. "You're so crazy, it's aging me," she said. "God, I hate you sometimes."

Judie laughed. "I know," she said. "Me too." She meant that she hated herself, and also Sylvia, so sure she had saved Judie's life in the first place by convincing her not to have an operation. Judie wished she'd had the operation.

"Do you think my heart hasn't been broken, too?" asked Sylvia, her voice soft now. "Do you think I haven't wanted to do drastic things—run away, sleep with strangers, jump on the ice?"

Judie held Sylvia's hand and listened as her sister began to lecture her about growing up and being a woman. Sylvia continued to move through the world with grace, stronger than Judie. The wallpaper flowers swam in the air; focusing felt difficult. Her head drooped.

"Sylvia," she asked, her voice a whisper, "why do I have to give it up *or* marry Eamon? What if I find a way? What if you and I live here and take care of the baby and write music and make an album? Who's to say we can't—"

Her sister's eyes flared out into circles, then narrowed.

"Sleep," said Sylvia. "You're delirious."

She did. All afternoon, lifting her head only when she heard her sister's car pull away, before sleeping more, torpor lasting through the darkening evening and the night.

The next day when she woke up, the sun had gone behind a bank of low clouds and the house turned purple and gray. Yesterday's merry dust particles had merged into shadows.

Judie didn't leave the bed, even when she heard an engine idle for a few minutes, the creak of the front door. She stayed even when her mother's voice called to her from the foot of the stairwell and grew closer.

"I'll be with you until it's time," said Anna, standing at the doorway.

Judie turned away so her mother wouldn't see the tears that ran down her cheeks. Her mother. Thank God. He didn't exist, but thank God.

Anna drew a hot bath; she cooked; she combed out Judie's hair and arranged pillows on the bed. Judie began to sleep at night and be awake during the day, and she stopped writing. The songs she'd saved from the notebook lay untouched in a drawer.

"Your father gave you bad ideas," said Anna one day, close to the end.

"They were your ideas, too," Judie replied coolly. "Freedom. And music."

"Not freedom to get taken advantage of. . . ." Anna shook her head.

Judie frowned. "Freedom that is limited is *not* freedom," she said. But she feared her mother was right.

"When did you become so obstinate?" asked Anna.

"When did you decide . . . that I am an embarrassment to you rather than a person with feelings?" Judie spat it out.

She watched her mother's face waver as a hand came up to touch Judie's brittle hair.

"It's right," Anna said. "This plan is the best. Far away, a loving home, an eager mother . . . You will start over." She rubbed Judie's swollen foot. "Do better." A plea, a command, a wish all at once.

"Women don't have much choice in life," Anna said. "We do the best we can, but nature is strong," she continued. "Women are idiots to try to outrun it. But Judie, you can make something beautiful of the mess. You can."

Judie straightened up, wanting to voice her secret wish.

"What if I don't give up the baby?" she asked. "*Or* marry Eamon? What if I . . . take care of it? Raise it alone?"

Anna looked at her shrewdly. "Not a real question," she said. "Motherhood is a behemoth, Judie. If you think you'll be able to do the things you love, music or poetry or just being young, you're wrong. It just eats away at you—I don't know how else to put it."

Her drawn face testified to her words.

The time slipped perilously on; early contractions came, a hardening of her belly. A poking sensation beneath her ribs made it hard for Judie to sleep, sit, walk. Anna boiled hot-water bottles and made a vat of stew with root vegetables and kosher beef she'd packed on ice from Boston. Judie ate it ravenously, without complaint.

CAMBRIDGE, MASSACHUSETTS

The backyard in Cambridge met Judie's gaze when she returned: the stump where an apple tree had been removed. A new shoot of green poked out near its roots.

Sitting gingerly in the back seat, Judie had come home to a street clothed in soft green, a signal that her stubborn city had accepted spring. At night she sweated buckets, the ache in her breasts only now subsiding, even with the cold cabbages she applied. Only a few things fit, so she shuttled from the laundry room to her bedroom, where she looked out the window, an endless solitary circuit.

Part of her longed to go out into the world, to hear the shouts of boys and the chimes of glasses and silverware at cafés, to smell smoke, and most of all to hear music. But the determination that had pushed her out onto the ice with her notebooks had been scooped out of her by the doctors at the hospital. She sometimes touched her stomach, expecting to hear an echo. Any time a new instinct flickered inside her, she dutifully swept it away. Impulses led you astray. She had turned out to be a terrible steward of herself.

~

Two days after her conversation with Anna in New Hampshire, Judie had woken up screaming as her labor began. They drove to the hospital in the nearest town, only thirty minutes away, and her water broke on the floor. The doctors barked at her to shave and get dressed in a gown. They injected a long needle in her arm, and she remembered thinking it had grown pale and flabby that winter. She recollected nothing after that, though later the nurse told her she had screamed "quite a lot." She heard a small wail from somewhere in the room and turned to the nurse with horror.

"What did I scream?" Judie asked. "Please, what?"

The nurse clucked. "It wouldn't be right to say."

She fell asleep again, woozy, overwhelmed by the lights. When she awoke, Eamon was settled in the chair beside her. Hours had passed; their plan, that he would take the baby to his sister waiting in Boston, had whirred along.

"We can still do this together, Judie," he said as she assumed Hyman had commanded him to in some smoky meeting in the waiting room. "Get hitched."

Judie imagined setting up house with this stranger, yet again. Sitting alone with a baby while crowds applauded him, women circled him at parties and smiled, slowly, invitingly, as she had. Her mother said a baby took from you, ate you up inside.

"Could I do it and still be a singer?" said Judie.

Eamon's face looked wan; it had been winter for him, too.

He tried again. "Times have changed—we don't have to live like your parents."

"That's the point—you'll never be faithful—you'll never be home. You told me that night. And I'd be stuck in the nursery."

He changed the subject, then, to Dave's "Little Brown Sparrow" climbing the charts, and a nurse bustled in, holding a small bundle wrapped tightly in a white blanket.

She brought it over to them. Eamon motioned her to look.

Judie looked. In the white bundle lay a pink and miniature face, lids closed, face scrunched. The baby was totally bald, and she—it *was* a she—began to squirm, to scream. A phantom kick pulsed in Judie's stomach. She leaned closer, though it hurt.

"Rose," she said. They'd agreed on Rose: Jewish, Irish, and beautiful. "They'll love her, over there?" she asked.

"Very much," he said, a catch in his voice. "My sister, she's a good sort. She's on the airplane now. I'll be driving down to Boston tonight to meet her."

The baby next to her was destined to leave America; its mother—its future mother—now soared over the cold Atlantic. Judie wanted to fly like that, too.

The baby wailed. "Should we do something?" she asked, and with effort scooped the bundle up.

The tears and squealing stopped as the small head nestled against her chest. Eamon produced a bottle the nurse had given them and began to feed Rose.

They stayed that way, the three of them, as a strong cramp pulsed through Judie's abdomen. She gritted her teeth against the vision that arose: she and her sister, happy in New Hampshire with the baby. Eamon visiting when he could.

Eamon touched his eye with a single finger.

"Are you getting sentimental, Eamon?"

"I write songs. I'm sentimental by trade."

"So do I, write songs I mean, but my latest notebook is in the mud," Judie began. And then she stopped talking. It cost too much to speak.

He blinked a few times and patted her hand.

"Make it worthwhile," he told her before he took the baby, before she drifted off again. "Make music."

~

N ow she wondered about Rose, but "wonder" was too active a phrase. She simply shuttered operations and let Rose float, ghostlike, around her empty cavity, a phantom of pain. She closed her eyes to the world and its charms. She didn't listen to music, or write letters, or talk to Sylvia.

The world had nothing to say to her. A few weeks into her "white vigil," as Sylvia called it, Hyman took Judie's guitar and harmonica and left them outside her room. He uncovered the piano and played scales, hoping his daughter would hear. It registered like a faint tapping. The blossoms returned to the trees, and the grass to the lawn, and Judie, upstairs, cocooned herself in white noise.

A dream one night: Sylvia in the bed in New Hampshire and herself, sitting over her, shaking her sister to wake up. "Wake up, you dolt!" And then her hands, reaching for Sylvia, turning into ice, and cracking. She woke up, flexing her hand.

~

A nd then, somehow, it was summer, and roses were blooming, and she was curled up beside the Blue Door soundboard, listening to Sylvia run chord progressions, clear her throat and gargle like a professional, imitating the more famous folks who had passed through the studios and clubs in town.

Without crookedness or dimples, Sylvia's face improved on Judie's. Symmetrical, clean: her voice, too, sounded like Judy Collins's, but more birdlike. A sliver of roughness to the vibrato, Judie believed, was the manifestation of herself in her sister, pebbles in a crystal river.

"I need you to practice your harmonies," Sylvia exhorted. This refrain now made up one part of her daily campaign, Sylvia's fevered attempt to pull Judie from the icy valley.

How had she ended up at a studio? She had gotten dressed, presumably, gotten into a car. Only now, as she ran over the notes, did her mind sharpen. She saw things again, heard them again. She could even sing.

A smear of dust caked the Blue Door window. The garbage pail overflowed with coffee cups, and a small bottle of whiskey, opened, sat in the corner by the soundboard. Judie held it to her nose: it smelled like the night she had talked with Dave and he'd told her to go home to her family. More wise advice she didn't heed. The green-flowered couch, faded, was covered with an old knit blanket. Judie's blanket, which had wound around her shoulders for weeks, until an hour ago.

~

H er return to life had begun when May gave way to June and Sylvia, now a Wellesley graduate, bounded upstairs. At Judie's bedside Sylvia begged her sister to play her the songs she'd written over the winter, the six she'd saved from the notebook. Judie felt too listless to pick up the guitar, but she did allow Sylvia to open her drawer, remove the yellow pages, and play them herself. She opened her ears to her own creations as Sylvia sprawled on the floor and worked them out, and the sound grew louder and louder.

As Sylvia tooled around in her room, Judie sat up straight. "Wait, play the bridge higher," she said. "No—not like that. . . . Yes, like that."

She'd said not much more than "Whatever you say" in weeks.

"These *nasty* songs won't work," said Sylvia. "'Father Fascist'? Lock them up. But 'The House by the Lake,' my God, Judie. This may be your best one yet."

Judie leaned over to inspect the pages with her. "Cross your heart?" she asked.

"Yes," said Sylvia. "I'm not trying to buck you up here."

Judie lowered herself to the floor, keeping the blanket around her as Sylvia played on. After Sylvia completed her survey of all the songs, Judie tapped her sister's shoulder.

"I'm too hungry to focus," said Judie. "Let's go fix ourselves a sandwich before we work on this some more."

Her sister's slate eyes registered the change. Quietly, she led Judie toward the landing.

~

Hyman's construction and carpentry business had specialized in the last decade, focusing on high-end needs—theaters, ballrooms, hotel lobby fixtures—and he'd done quite well. But his studio on a side street between Central Square and MIT was his pride and joy. The space was small, but Hyman had worked with a master engineer from his shop to make it acoustically pure. Books of sheet music fought for shelf space, and photos of singers like Woody Guthrie and Paul Robeson were carefully grouped in the hallway. For years it had been used for chamber music or jazz and an occasional folk record, but during Judie's confinement, he'd partnered with Alfred Davies, a local impresario, who had a tiny label known as Pathways. Pathways had begun bringing folk acts in from other cities to cut records at Blue Door Recording.

Knowing this, Sylvia made her application. That explained why, by the end of June, Judie was nestled in this building she'd forsworn entering. A goateed sound technician named Al, who clearly wanted to sleep with Sylvia, brought them each a lemonade. Hyman had made a deal with Pathways to split the cost of recording the Singer Sisters' album and the proceeds, should it sell. Thus the arrival of Al and a second technician, as well as friends of Sylvia's who played and sang and some classical musicians Hyman knew.

Al told Judie that Sylvia was a "natural." The lemonade tasted tart, and it influenced Judie's tongue, as after a few sips she turned to him and said, "You'd need the purest voice in the world to do justice to these songs."

For the next song, Judie stepped up to the microphone and adjusted the headphones, and Sylvia slipped in beside her. Judie looked at her sister, while Sylvia looked at the guys in the booth and smiled. Then she turned to Judie and offered her a small nod. "Go on, Judie," she whispered. "Go on."

Judie began to sing her lower part, and Sylvia began the main melody. This song was going to be the most painful to get through: "Rose of Winter."

> *Underneath the snow, a rose does grow*
> *Across the sea the rose will go*

As she sang, Judie willed her own heart not to seize up; if the album was going to be a success, she would have to grow accustomed to a workman-like approach to her heartbreak, her ode to the warm bundle sent across the ocean. Sylvia's early listeners had thought the "rose" in the song was a symbol of a new world order—peace, love, and harmony.

"I'm alone with the weary moon," Sylvia sang, and Judie let a tear slither out from her eye. Damn it; the whole singing enterprise meant nothing to her without the emotion. She had to feel the thing to her core. Sylvia drilled into her eyes and coaxed the tears out. Her sister, the producer of her life. They nailed the harmonies after four takes.

The Singer Sisters sessions that they'd dreamed aloud for years had begun.

"It's like honey laced with arsenic," Al said after the two girls clustered around the microphone—their voices climbing heavenward, or at least to the snug rafters that made the place so acoustically sound—had come out for a break. "You fit together like pieces of a puzzle. Your dad trained you well."

"For some things," said Judie with a snort.

"She takes her coffee bitter," said Sylvia with a sigh. "Like her lyrics, and her life. That sounded nice, though, didn't it, Al?" she asked. "We should do 'Route 95' next. I have the bridge solos worked out."

One of the things that perked Judie up the most was determining the order of the songs for their album. The idea that each one would follow from the other, that each side would have a beginning, an end, a story. She and Sylvia put each song name on a note card and switched them around endlessly, settling on her best originals like "Route 95," "The House by the

Lake," "Rose of Winter," "Long-Legged Man," "Let's Be Thunderbolts," and "Gentle People," interspersed with a few covers. "Barbara Allen" closed out the album, at Hyman's absolute insistence.

Judie accepted his interference, agreeing with Sylvia that if they succeeded with this, they'd never need him again. The album had an aura around it that no one could sully. Busying herself with arranging the vocals and the track list made the time go faster. Sometimes they listened to the radio, where Dave Canticle's "Little Brown Sparrow," lingering at a respectable number sixty-two on the *Cash Box* singles chart, might be heard.

Dave was primed for a national tour, starting with the Newport Folk Festival—after this weekend, he wouldn't be back on the East Coast for months.

"Hello," said Judie, standing in the entrance when he arrived at Blue Door to say hello and goodbye. "What makes you think you're welcome here?"

In truth, she'd invited him. She had written him a scorcher of a letter from New Hampshire, about her predicament and his and Eamon's growing fame, and he'd responded, saying he was "sorry for the mess."

He told her he'd beat up Eamon Foley if he ever saw the bastard again, which was a lie but pleased her enough. "Don't do that," she'd written back. "But come around if you're in Boston again. You owe me."

"I heard some cute girls were cutting an album in here," Dave said.

Cute girls. Judie couldn't help herself: she brought Dave coffee as he liked it—strong with a splash of cream—and Sylvia joined with her guitar. They sat around singing standards, while Sylvia's gray eyes blazed. After Sylvia went back to talk with Al about a flautist, Judie whispered to Dave, "Wait, stay." As in New York, their collaboration felt established, intimate.

On the couch, close together, she showed him two unused songs: "Father Fascist" and "Shame," the most furious outtakes from the notebook at the bottom of the lake.

Dave scanned the lines, shook his head, and thrust the papers back at her as though they scorched him. "I didn't know a woman could get so pissed off," he said.

She said that was why they weren't on the album. He bored into her with his gaze. She narrowed her eyes at him. "Play them with me."

As she sang, he strummed, until beads of sweat popped up on his temples.

He stared at her again for a long time when they finished, until her face turned hot.

"Your songs are the real thing, kid," he said. "You should probably burn these two."

She didn't. She took them home in an envelope and hid them in her desk. The Singer Sisters sessions ended, and all eyes turned to Newport and Dave's debut. His star rising fast, Dave gave an interview to *The Village Voice*, mostly about the festival. But he made sure to mention seeing the Singer Sisters in their studio outside Boston and anticipating their album: "Judie is as first-rate a songwriter as they come, and Sylvia has the voice of an angel."

It helped. Store owners and critics read the paper and saw Dave's excited quote. They called the studio, clamoring for Hyman to send them copies when the album was pressed. Sylvia seemed to be walking on air, but Judie felt a quieter satisfaction at their dream coming true.

Because even as she exulted, her mind turned to the songs she'd omitted from the album, those primal screams of rage—as though they were a slice of her heart, locked away.

EMMA

Another summer of sweating, performing, sleeping with strangers, and snorting substances in sporadic moderation drew to an end, much like last summer before it.

Except for the bidding wars over her album. Notable change number one: her plan had worked. Her career had hardened into a definite thing now, an album contract drafted and waiting for her signature. She'd record the following spring. Momentous change number two: Rose. Rose, Rose, Rose. When exactly she'd let the truth fully sink in, who knew—somewhere between Northampton and Santa Cruz. On the highway, in her stomach.

The van, driven by a roadie she'd shared with another band for the last few weeks, pulled up outside the building on West 101st Street, where her friends put her duffel bag on the sidewalk and helped take her guitars upstairs. Half of the group was heading downtown, half to Philadelphia.

Leon, who owned the apartment with her, kept postponing his return from London. Love was grand. Dust coated the shelves; the plants were brown around the edges and the air stale. Traffic noise sounded below—horns and the sigh of city buses.

Emma opened all the windows, flicked on fans, and considered going out to a bodega for a beer. She weighed getting on the subway and going to her mom's place. They'd have a drink at the kitchen table, but then they'd have to talk about Rose.

Their only conversation about it had not gone well. Judie had insisted they wait to discuss it in person.

"We've waited my whole life, so what's a few more weeks?" Emma had snorted.

"Listen to the album again in the meantime."

Singer Sisters had always been held up as a platonic ideal of a folk album. Now, allegedly, it would contain the key to the mysteries of not just all life, but *her* life specifically.

The fan hummed. Nestled on the couch, she put on MTV, before opening the door to her neighbor Pam, in a bathrobe. "I heard the TV and thought I'd give you your insane pile of mail," she said.

Emma held the stack of mail in her arms and pretended to stagger from its weight. In the stack of mail was the promised tape from Alicia with her Brown performance and a box from Leon in London. "Ooh, I think these are shoes!" she said, delighted.

Two manila envelopes nestled among the catalogs. One bore the return address of the record label, another from an address in Providence. She pushed them aside and tore open the box to marvel at the boots, lace-up platform boots embossed with flowers. Spice Girls chic.

The last time she'd brought up Rose with Leon, he'd said, "Pass the pie, Jerry Springer, it's going to be *the best Thanksgiving ever.*"

They all dodged her requests for conversation. Her dad offered zen mumbo jumbo, her mother vague promises to "talk in person."

She ended up restacking the mail and ordering delivery. She should open the Providence package, but she needed a burger first.

~

Sylvia arrived the next day in a floor-length flowered dress and big sunglasses and took Emma to the Mill luncheonette, where they had iceberg wedges and lime rickeys.

"Are you going to go on a diet now that you're back from the tour?" her aunt asked. "You've probably been eating crap and it's going to go right to your face."

She went on for a while about face creams and lemon-water fasts before Emma told her about Rose.

"Waiting for you outside the show? How *Fatal Attraction*!"

In response to Emma's plaintive demand for information about Rose and the ordeals she and Judie must have each gone through, Sylvia blew air out her lips and played with her lettuce.

"That was a tough time, honey," she said. "Excruciating. I thought your mother might—well, harm herself." Emma tried to close her eyes and imagine her mother's pain, but the pity soured. "I'm not sure Judie ever forgave me for telling Anna and Hyman to go get her in New York."

Sylvia began a long, meandering monologue from which Emma mostly learned about her aunt's unrequited love for a Cambridge beauty named Bella. As they paid the check, Emma asked her aunt to play a women's festival with her, at an arena outside New York City.

"I am supposed to be in London that week," said Sylvia, who had one standing gig now, at a cabaret club downtown.

"For what?"

"I've met someone . . . or I'm committing to someone I've known a long time, through your mother. And she has a big album release in London."

"So, you can't come?" asked Emma.

"Don't you want to ask about my girlfriend?" said Sylvia. "I'll be in London for months. You're more like Judith than you think."

n the middle of her second night home, Emma woke up as if she'd slept long and deeply, thinking about the brown envelope that contained whatever Rose had tried to give her that night in Providence.

Though tempted to trash it unopened, Emma tore the flap. She slid out ancient, lined sheets bearing her mother's handwriting, accompanied by a scrawled note on yellow legal paper:

Dear Emma,

Judie gave these to me that summer at the house—and in a sense they're mine. But you ought to sing them yourself, it will help you understand. Also, they're made for your sound. Seriously, I'm a fan. I'm sorry our visit ended the way it did, and I know I ambushed you.

I'll be giving birth around Labor Day, so I'll be busy—but if you ever want to be in touch, I'm here.

Rose

The tone of these scant lines mixed passive-aggression and generosity. But the package was priceless. Words, chords: these were *songs*. The first appeared to be about Emma's grandparents:

> Father or fascist
> Mother or warden?
> Should I beg your forgiveness
> Should I beg for your pardon?
>
> Should every girl be locked away
> Should every girl be patient
> I'm waiting for a new day
> I'm waiting for liberation
>
> Should every girl be silent
> And walk on her tiptoes
> Should every girl be innocent
> Until her secret grows?
> And grows, and grows?

The second song, on a sheet torn up the side, was in the voice of Anna, or Hyman, or both.

> **"Shame"**
>
> She wanted to fly
> Down the highway of the world
> Shame upon us all
> Shame upon this girl
>
> Shame on this household
> And shame on this town
> Shame on this weight
> That's making us drown
>
> Shame in my fingers
> And shame in my heart

Shame in this secret
That tears us apart

She wanted to roam
So we let her leave
Now she's back from the garden
And we grieve
And we grieve

She'll bring shame on us
All, shame on us all
Shame on us all
Shame on us all

Judie had been *pissed*. And lonely. And raw. On these pages, her voice sounded exactly the way Emma wanted to sound right now.

In the deepest hours of the night, Emma's CD player circled round and round, playing her mother's first album. Rose had sent her its missing songs.

A lilac sky said morning was coming. Emma found her bicycle in the front hall. It had a flat. Down a steep hill near the river, she went to a gas station to blow up the tires. She pedaled south again, pumping her legs until the pain slivered through muscles she didn't realize existed. All the while, her mother's song played through her mind: "Father Fascist, Father Fascist."

She laid the bike on the grass, stretched out, and closed her eyes. Over the river the sky burst into clear blue, and she shone with an answering light.

"You have to understand," Sylvia had said earlier, the lime rickey in her hand. "You guys *saved* your mom's *life*—and she wanted to protect you both, in different ways."

"My whole adolescence, she was sneaking off to have coffee with Rose, apparently."

"She broke down in the seventies, Emma. She was on painkillers for her knee, she was walking offstage, forgetting lyrics—like, full-on rock stuff. I had to kick her out of the band."

"Yes, I've heard all this. What's the point?"

"*Why* do you think she was so messed up, Emma?"

⌒

Emma had listened to her mother's most iconic songs rarely as a child, constantly as a teenager, occasionally as an adult. Until she met Rose, it hadn't occurred to her that these songs were not simply extensions of her own feelings: loneliness, horniness, longing for love and a nameless escape. This had endeared Judie to her even when she had the urge to kick in the walls of the apartment. Her mom's music spoke like Bruce Springsteen spoke to her, like Hole spoke to her, like Prince: a desire for freedom, and belonging.

But Judie had been a documentarian. "Route 95" was literally about her mom leaving home and taking that highway to New York City, where she'd meet the "Long-Legged Man" who knocked her up. "The House by the Lake" was a specific snapshot of New Hampshire when Judie was pregnant; "Rose of Winter"—that was obvious, too.

Emma played the Singer Sisters album six times back to front, standing and beating out a rhythm on the windowsill, imagining Mae's drums and herself on an electric guitar.

Yes, it could work. She stopped the CD and rushed to her couch to grab the sheets of paper Rose had sent her. She clutched them to her chest.

JUDIE

J udie looked up to see Dave standing up and walking toward her, a guitar slung across his back. He'd had a haircut and maybe something done to his teeth—his smile seemed whiter, or wider. A young woman shuffled behind him. He handed his groupie the guitar so he could embrace Judie with both arms.

"Little Brown Sparrow" played on the radio every so often; the Singer Sisters had added their own version of it to the encore of their residency at Club 47.

As they chatted and gossiped, Judie kept looking around to see whom he was smiling at. "Can you take this guitar back to the hotel, honey?" he asked the girl, whose name was Simone. Despite her wariness of Simone, Judie felt light enough to fly. Dave knew about Eamon and her parents, and the shame of it, and had heard the songs she'd written in her darkest moments, and he wasn't bothered. As though seeing her meant good times, he touched his forehead to hers. They sauntered to an old Spanish coffee shop to sit under a yellow umbrella and sip strong tea.

"Val's out of the picture—she took up with a guy who makes ugly sculptures. I have girls throwing themselves at me now, I mean it's crazy—like that chick Simone who took my guitar, she's been hanging around since she stayed over last night. But it's not for me. I'm a romantic. I'm not like—like, certain others."

Dave wanted to hear that she was okay, Judie realized as they spoke, plus he was nosing out whether she still held a torch for Eamon. He stirred his tea with a spoon in a way that suggested a new sophistication, even since July.

"You know my song was about you?" he asked her. She almost spit out her drink—saving herself and swallowing it. She coughed, and he got her a napkin.

"I'm the sparrow? But—I thought you wrote it for Valerie. She was so brown and thin."

"It's about her too, but the part about flying the nest was inspired by your journey from Boston."

"So, it's your version of 'Route 95.'"

"No, 'Route 95' is your version of this," he said roguishly.

His soft face had grown more rugged and handsome but maintained an endearing, babyish quality. Dave said he was pleased to find Judie so animated. Was it due to her good press? "Sylvia Zingerman's voice is like butter, with a twist of lemon," one critic wrote in Boston. "But her sister's songwriting makes the album, and performances, unique. A girl speaking so directly through song is a real thrill. Naturally, it doesn't reach the global and poetic significance of a Dylan or even an Eamon Foley, but it's stirring to hear."

"Aren't you mad?" asked Sylvia when they read it. "He makes such a fuss out of us being girls!"

"I'm *not* as good as Dylan . . . as for that other personage, I admire his . . . talent. I do! That's what got me into this mess," Judie said.

Sylvia was so taken aback to hear Judie joke about her *mess*, she had no retort.

~

Dave placed himself in the front row as they played that night, and when, in the encore, Judie played the opening of "Little Brown Sparrow" on the harmonica, as she had that handful of times in the Village, they locked eyes. A buzzing shot through her, "the moths" when a performance began to leave her control, to whirl itself either into the territory of a triumph or a bomb, to be guided by forces bigger than her. Her voice unleashed itself; she strummed with abandon. This hit song was for *her*, for that Village idyll that had mattered to him, too.

That night the applause was so friendly, she bathed in it, like diving into the lake on a hot day. It bit you at first and then you could swim forever.

When she finished, Dave jumped to his feet and clapped, and a murmur began to spread through the crowd: Dave Canticle was *here*, celebrating the sisters' cover of his song! More rapturous applause followed, and in the intimacy of the club, it echoed.

The girls tried one more song, but the general attention moved to the back of Dave's head. He was "somebody" now; and even if purists saw his modest success as selling out, most were drawn to this brush with fame.

So, an ecstatic night of performance petered out, one song away from sheer triumph.

Judie couldn't be sore about the ending, because of the bridge that went up when she played the song to him that he had written for her. An inch of air spread out between her feet and the ground as she walked home, by herself, leaving Sylvia chatting with Dave and a group of admirers. She threw her jacket over her shoulders and walked down to the river, smoking cigarette after cigarette, humming. The Charles in its evening purple looked dressy and elegant.

She chose a spot near the Weeks Bridge where the grass met the water. Seven months ago, she had thought about walking out into the ice in New Hampshire, sinking to the bottom, letting go. Now she might be able to flit right across the river. Maybe, maybe, she could construct a new life, moving like this river itself, full of rich colors and murky depths. She positively danced back to the apartment, thinking about the beauty of each lamppost in the mist, picturing Gene Kelly twirling in the rain.

After this residency, there'd be a tour—and festivals, and maybe New York, or San Francisco, and she would get serious about writing. She could collaborate with Sylvia and Dave, learn a new instrument. Maybe she would even lead a demonstration against the war like Joan Baez, who was so fearless, with that enviably flat hair.

At the steps to the building, she fumbled for her keys; a hand brushed her arm and she screamed and then laughed. Dave smelled of whiskey and smoke.

"Where did you go?" he asked plaintively, almost pathetically. "I thought we had a moment during your song."

"And then you ruined it," she said, laughing. "Stole all the attention." She shook her box of cigarettes at him and he caught it, letting their fingers touch, and took one out.

He asked for her forgiveness, and she gave it. "I'd forgive anyone right now, you know."

"Remember that night we had whiskey and walked under the arch? It got hot, and then it rained? I have wanted to do this ever since then," he said. "Before then, probably. Since we broke your mother's challah. I know it sounds like a line, but it's true."

"Do what?" she said, but she knew he was going to kiss her.

As soon as his lips touched hers and the wind ruffled her hair and his arms closed around her, she wanted to sleep with him, and she began to reach under his jacket. "Not yet, with both of us drunk," he said, though she was sober, "and all you've been through. Let me stay, and then we can see, in the morning."

He had compassion. Her limbs ached with it. When Judie woke up to Dave beside her in bed, it reminded her of being a young girl on a holiday, snuggling beneath the blanket, inhaling early cooking smells, and hearing her parents talking in the kitchen.

Who knew how things would go? She didn't speculate. Dave gave her two sensations at once: a homey comfort and a taste of adventure. He could help her navigate.

"What I told myself I wanted last night," he said over coffee, "was to invite you and Sylvia to tour with me, next year. I'll be going out starting in January, playing a mix of big and small places. And then, you know, we could be together, write together—more, if you want."

He cleared his throat, and took her two hands between his, and lunged for her with a hunger that made her body respond again, after so long—and as he kissed the area where her curls began to form behind her ear, she let out a single, anguished sob, like the ice cracking on the lake, but less frightening.

EMMA

I'm making things happen, Emma." Mae said that a lot these days as they prepared to record their album. The studio that Emma's grandfather Hy had built in Cambridge was currently run by some recent grads of Wesleyan; Mae had called around. Those kids were eager to attract talent (it was Boston, after all) and cleared a month for Emma and her team to come record. She wanted the whole family on it: Dave, Leon, Sylvia, and Judie.

"Heck, Rose can hold the goddamn tambourine if she wants," she joked, even though they hadn't spoken since Providence.

The Goddess of Rock had taken up permanent residence inside Emma's psyche, seized hold of her destiny. She and Mae had become fully obsessed with their project, trying to book session musicians and demoing drum parts and writing bass lines and fills for other instruments.

"Do we want Pat Smear from Foo Fighters for a song? Or what about Johnny Rzeznik from the Goo Goo Dolls? Foo, Goo—why do male bands sound like baby talk?"

"I'm going to call the album *Female Troubles*, or do you think I should call it *Female Singer*?" Emma asked Leon when he arrived.

"I think you should give Mom a heads-up you're using her long-lost work," said Leon with an exaggerated drawl that masked disapproval. "Like, *now*."

"I'm going to surprise her!" said Emma. "Besides, I have three of my own and two I wrote with Mae, and I want you to work on one with me too."

Leon had agreed to produce "Flower" and had been sending her tapes in the mail with ideas for instrumentation. The way he was able to hear music and respond with notes, sounds, production—that was beyond her. But he didn't have this: her idea, her zeitgeist-seizing, chart-topping potential of an album idea. They rented an apartment near her grandparents' old place in Inman Square so she could channel the whole gestalt.

Once she recorded her first passes at "Father Fascist" and "Shame," she called Judie, who was up in New Hampshire, asking her to come visit and hear out "a few special tracks."

To Emma's surprise, Judie said she would come.

⌒

When Judie arrived at the studio, which hadn't been called Blue Door in years, her face was tight. She moved through the door with caution. Memories lived here. Emma twitched with anticipation.

At first, it felt wonderful. Judie clasped her daughter's hands. "So now you finally see," Judie said. "About my life. Why I encouraged you to go to school instead of . . . *this*."

Emma dropped her mother's hands.

"Mom, we're not rehashing that. I have a huge record deal."

Right, Judie said, but that was *now*. Emma might do so much more, later.

Emma squired her mother to an armchair with cracks in the leather and fetched her water. She took a deep breath as she entered the control booth and rolled the demo tapes, and watched her mother's face, as note after note sounded, as her mother's eyes began to swim.

Her mother had begun to panic, horrified at the sound. Those hands that Emma knew so well rose from her lap and cradled her cheeks. Judie's eyes threatened to take over her face.

The tape stopped and the studio became a box of silence.

"You did a solid job," Judie tried, before lowering her voice and ranting about having *to leave this old place before long*, about it *all being too much*. She moved to the doorway, looking around the studio with a mixture of contempt and curiosity. Maybe only contempt.

"*Rose* gave you my music?" she asked Emma, turning back.

"And encouraged me to play it."

"I see." Judie sat—or collapsed—back on the old couch, her finger following the blue stripes. "This was once an awful couch with big green flowers on it," she said.

Emma scooted to her mother's feet; her jaw clenched so tight she was sure she'd get a migraine.

"Do you like it for my album?" she asked. "*Please*, Mom?"

"Emma," said Judie. "Those songs are private. They're *private*. Delete the tracks."

"That's a problem to take up with Rose," said Emma sharply. She was being petulant, but she couldn't stop. The songs were a perfect fit. She couldn't give them up. Every note on the demo was hers. "She *explicitly* told me to record them." Emma's face was hot.

"They're her songs, I suppose," said Judie more thoughtfully. "But no. I can't." She shook her head like she was trying to get water out of her ear.

"Mom," said Emma. She began to feel like she had been possessed by someone else, someone shaky and tear filled and angry and bloody determined—and heartless.

"You've got to see how much this means to me. I'm planning to give you songwriting credit, needless to say—*royalties*. It will get your name back out in the press."

Judie said she didn't care—money, credit, press. Didn't Emma remember she'd been uncredited on *Chant and Sing*?

Emma asked why she couldn't go ahead with the plan, then, if Judie didn't care?

Judie's eyes flashed hot. "I could sue you."

"Sue me, Mom. I look forward to the subpoena. Meanwhile, I am going to make the hit record you never had the balls to make yourself."

"I was busy raising you, Emma."

With her hands up in fake quotation marks, Emma parried the blow.

"Raising," she said. "Raising. Remember that psycho woman you let roam around the apartment? She scared me so much I wrote my single about her, so maybe you should have been raising me harder."

Judie protested that Flower was a harmless hippie. "Have you written any other songs like that? No! I sheltered you, so you have no other material. That's why you had to steal my songs, my pain."

"Your pain is my pain, you idiot." Emma, now standing, held her guitar like a shield, hearing her own rants about her art being *hers*, about the versions of the songs she'd recorded being hers now.

Her mother said no, no, and began apologizing about Rose, about the lies, about it all, saying that the secret nestled in, and she didn't want to upset her kids. Emma felt this to be a dirty move, using a long-desired apology and explanation to reclaim the songs from Emma.

"It's never been my story," said Emma, choking. "My whole life *hasn't* been my story. You never fucking told me the truth."

They planted themselves, Judie red-faced and white-lipped, Emma actively crying, big oily tears bringing the mascara down her cheeks, asking why Judie wouldn't just let Emma have this.

"Everyone always wants my songs," said Judie. "I'm a person, too."

Leon breezed in from a coffee run and stopped in his tracks, seeing them.

"Well, this is going about as well as I imagined," he said, but his sarcasm fell flat. He slumped on a bench, telling Judie sorrowfully that they should have told her, they should have warned her. Apologizing. Selling Emma out.

Judie's tone turned from angry to mournful as she gathered her things. "Let her steal the damn songs, like her father and aunt do. Have a nice *career*, Emma."

The panic rose all around Emma, inside her now. She shouted at her mother's back about the bidding war, about why she'd done the album, about restoring Judie's legacy.

"Legacy?" Judie traced her own eyebrows with her forefingers. "Not my word, not my idea."

———

The door behind Judie closed quickly, and they braced themselves for a slamming noise, but someone had oiled it, or their grandfather's construction was timeless. It merely clicked. Emma paced the room, refusing to look at Leon, then dashed for the door herself.

Circling the block, she found her mother on the corner, shaking.

"Don't do this," Judie said. "It will open a rift between us. You have lots of other songs."

"The 'rift' is already there," said Emma, choking out the words. "You left Dad—you turned cold on me when I pursued music, and you kept this . . . *enormous* secret from me, your songs, the samovar—the ring. My *sister*. My sister. My *sister*."

Judie shrank away from the accusation, turned back to the songs, *her* songs.

"Are you actually going to sue me?" Emma asked, her voice small.

"You're my daughter," said Judie, as if that answered the question decisively. Did she mean "Never, you're my daughter" or "You're my daughter and you've betrayed me, and I will sue you"?

Emma couldn't be sure, and so she kept going, and so did Judie. Two decades of anger boiling over, volcanic and endless.

Emma called her mother a lazy artist who used kids as an excuse to leave music and abandoned Dave to shirk caring for him in his old age.

"You don't have a nurturing bone in your body," she concluded. "Imagine wasting your musical gift to be such a mediocre mom."

Judie shot back: Emma was an idiot for refusing college, since she had half the talent Leon did and no backup plan, and she was just like Dave—leaning on others' songs, *all style and nothing true in her work.*

"How can you say that?" Emma asked. It was not true. None of it was true, what they were saying now—but the words etched into her. Judie, wild haired and more uncontrolled than she'd been at Anna's deathbed or Grandpa Hy's funeral.

Judie wiped her eyes and looked away. No traffic drove by, save an old blue station wagon. A ropy, tan woman with gray hair in a braid began to untie a bicycle from the rack, casting a single glance at them as they faced off on the sidewalk. Just two women howling epithets.

"I can—I *can* be nurturing," said Judie. "I've been taking care of my granddaughter."

"Go be a mother to Rose, then," said Emma. "Go. You loved me sideways because of her, why not admit it?"

This last revelation thinned her own anger into bilious gruel. Her mother *could* be generous when she put her mind to it. Rose and Judie would make a pretty pair bending over some earthy bassinet, passing the infant girl back and forth, cooing in harmony.

"I *tried* to love you," Judie said. "You hated me from birth."

That ended it.

As Emma shuffled back inside, she pictured Judie walking on, likely to get the T and go somewhere else. Back to Providence? To New Hampshire? Away from Emma, closer to Rose.

Emma ran into the studio and began to slam her hands against the wall until Leon rushed to her and grabbed them and said, "You need these for guitar."

Emma let him hold her as she wept.

"You two will be okay," he said. She wasn't sure. Trembling, she picked up every piece of garbage in the studio and threw it out. She went to the apartment on Inman Square and tried not to act out by shoving her body at various pieces of furniture.

Instead, she walked back and forth to Harvard five times until her legs gave out and she sat on the sidewalk and cried, yet again. The only option that appealed to her, as she stretched out on the curb, was sleep.

But she had an alarm set each morning, because she was on the verge of making a record that the brass at the label thought was going to be "big." And they wanted one song above all, after "Flower"—"Father Fascist."

Caffeinated and exfoliated and just the tiniest bit stoned, she showed up at the studio again the next day, ready to work.

"Being a wreck brings out the best in you," her brother said, watching her slam on the drums to show Mae how a song should sound.

She had taken to wearing Anna's ring, moving it from finger to finger.

"Give us primal, give us raw," said one of the guys in suits who flew up to Boston for the day to hang out in the studio. "Think more Meredith Brooks than Alanis—edgy, but not too weird. Like, a bitch but also like, empowered, and sexy, you know."

She agreed with whatever they told her, eager to please. "We want it to be a good pop song—like your daddy's tunes. But womanly, like your mom," another told her. "So, I guess be like them, but also, act like you hate them? Ha!"

The guy clapped her on the back. She flashed a smile, sunny and decorative and exactly what he wanted.

JUDIE

J udie was looking for a pay phone as her feet sped away from the studio, as block after block unfolded between her and her children, between her body and the insults that had hurled themselves out of her daughter's fat lips.

For years now, Judie had been ticking off a mental tally of wounds caused by Emma. She recited them to herself as she walked—talking to herself or murmuring, looking like a fool old lady gone over the edge.

Emma openly disparaged the teaching job, an unexpected joy in Judie's life. (Emma, who had been her teachers' delight, despite her pot smoking and cutting class to play guitar on the front steps of school.) Windermere kids shyly showed up at "Ms. Judie's" office door during free periods. The questions they asked her, about the old days—even about Emma—she had answers! She barely had to lesson plan. They got a kick out of her unruly hair, her mismatched buttons, her bulky notebooks. Emma saw her as a loser.

Emma, deceiving them about college, tossing her own fierce intellect on the slag heap so she could hang out with mediocre male entities, making mediocre music.

Emma, casting aspersions on Judie's mothering, tallying all the take-out containers, the flights of reverie and depression, the mistakes (oh, the mistakes). Well-fed Emma, passing herself off as a waif with a sob story about Flower, painting Judie as absentee.

Blaming Judie for Dave moving out, when Judie had stayed with him all those years *for Emma*!

And this final indignity, this grand larceny. Emma, recording *her songs*, the most uniquely Judie Zingerman creations in the world—more than her offspring! Primal cries of melody from *that winter*—she shook her head on the street. She still couldn't allow herself to directly recollect those months.

Songs saved from the lake. Emma had opened an ancient wound right back up, right now, not an hour ago, and it stung.

Why be surprised—after all, of the three, only Emma's birth created a thick, tingling vertical scar that for months Judie worried would split open again and let all her insides spill out. Did that count? Should it be added to the tally?

~

J udie felt an uptick in the wind, a new smell, and she looked up and around. A long time ago, she had stood in front of this wide, brackish river and decided to embrace life, which at the time meant Dave and a kiss at her apartment door.

On that night, jolts of life force had entered her body. She had begun looking forward once more. *Begin to begin.* Now she was beset by aches that came from looking back.

A few weeks after that, she and Dave and friends had come out here to see a meteor shower. They had sat in a circle in the middle of the footbridge at two in the morning, all in their wide sleeves and bell-bottoms, passing a pipe around. How the boys' eyes had roved to her, the girls' to Dave, evidence of the friction their coupledom had brought into their "scene"—the power it had given them.

From that, they had created this mess of a family: anger and schisms.

Who said maternal love is unconditional, anyway? Her own parents, subjects of those cursed songs, proved what happened when love was too tied up in pride. Judie intended to raise Emma differently, to let her explore and be free.

She had failed. So much so that she was running away from her children, as she'd wanted to do so many times, so many nights of tears and tantrums and loneliness.

Still, she could be of use to Rose and Dolores. Dolores's smiles would come often, her fingers would curl around Judie's—she'd cry but not talk back. And Rose needed her help, because Mary had once again gone back to

Ireland. "I think she's having a harder time than she lets on," Felix had said on the phone before summoning Judie. Dolores would be waiting, chubby wrists and eyes like a creature in the wild, a milky smell. Needs that made sense.

She had to tell someone about Emma and those songs, to confide her anguish. Whom to call? Dave had heard those compositions and joked about burning them. And Dave knew how Emma could take and take. But Rae, the girlfriend, was at the house, keeping watch.

The pay phone she sought was two corners away. She went over to it, dropped a quarter in, and rang the number for Dave's red ranch house in Phoenicia.

"Judie, my love," said Rae, always preternaturally affectionate when hearing from her predecessor. "He's really worn out after our Ayurveda workshop. Sleeping it off. He was crushing herbs in a stone pot, Judie, you would have died seeing it. Should he call you back—"

"I'll try another time."

She called Sylvia next, knowing already what she would say, ultimately: *Judie-Jude. Let it go.*

"Are the demos good?" asked Sylvia, cutting to the chase.

Judie sniffed into the phone. Emma's interpretation had been perfect. (With Leon's help and Mae's help.) Her vocals so anguished and fierce, almost hoarse. As though she understood what it felt like to be buried under snow and isolation.

"They're okay," Judie lied. "For such primitive songs. I'll go to Providence early and call you from there."

"Let's let Emma chase fame," said Sylvia. "We did."

She'll suffer for it, thought Judie. *We did.*

She returned the phone to its hook, heard the click, walked up and away toward the traffic of Memorial Drive.

PART II

PART II

SYLVIA

NEW YORK CITY AND LONDON, 1974

B ecause people saw Sylvia as Judie's manager, they had started to warn her that Judie was "all nerves" and needed help. "A lot of us are like that these days," Sylvia shot back.

Even if she didn't admit it to those idiots, Sylvia worried. Judie hadn't been herself for a month or two. She had been sleeping all day, drinking before shows, ranting about politics while the band warmed up onstage. And Sylvia had seen Judith Zingerman go dark. Those silent days in Boston, the desperate winter at the lake. Even thinking that Judie might head back in that direction brought a choke to Sylvia's throat. But this time was different. She was *fine*. She had Sylvia and Dave looking out for her.

Apparently, a friend of Judie's told her to go to a women's lib meeting and "shake out her blues." Since Judie knew her sister was "involved in all that" (by which she meant *Sylvia, you sleep with women*), they went together.

"You have to try *something* to cheer up," said Sylvia. Burnout was general among their set: the new thing was to find some elixir beyond drugs. Judie's pal Angela Darwin had gotten into tarot, Dave did yoga now, and three roadies were macrobiotic. But for Sylvia, the fix was their life itself: the magnificent curve of a secondary road on the way to a gig, hot pine smell coming through the window, the vibration of planes taking off ("see the silver bird on high," she hummed), the hush before the Singer Sisters stepped out of the wings onstage.

She needed nothing extra. But she *did* need Judie to pull herself together.

I 'm glad I'm taking you along," Judie said as they walked down East Eleventh Street, arms linked. "You need your consciousness raised." Sylvia laughed, the question between them perennial—who was chaperoning whom?

They schlepped up a few stories in the East Village. A narrow hallway led to a high-ceilinged living room where a group of women sat around a case of beer. The women had thick glasses, for the most part, were white, for the most part, and young, for the most part. In the corner of the room, Sylvia saw a girl she had spent a few nights with on their 1970 tour, before Judie and Dave got hitched. This old fling had gotten pudgy and militant looking in overalls; Sylvia avoided eye contact.

A whisper welcomed them into the room.

Dave, Judie, and Sylvia had been folk-rock royalty (a lower rung, but a rung) since 1968, when *Singer Sisters II* came out. The group had begun attracting a cult of wide-eyed girls who felt Judie's songs spoke directly to them; lucky for Sylvia, a few of them were inclined her way, and bold. Usually, she didn't have to sneak down to certain clubs or take any risks to find lovers.

Fine years had followed; the group went into the studio to back up Dave on his second record, *Morning Crickets*, which experimented with drums, and flutes, and electric guitar. Then more touring, more winsome girl fans with halos of frizzy hair and wide eyes. They would turn to Judie and ask her what her songs were *about*.

"Your songs mean so much to me as a woman," one girl said in Manhattan, near Bloomie's. "Especially 'Route 95.' I feel like you are *ours*."

Judie, on edge: "I am here to buy linens."

The girl shook her finger in the air. "Sister, why do we tear ourselves down? What are we looking for, male approval?"

"I am looking for lilac sheets for the guest room," said Judie, sighing. She autographed the girl's paper and walked on.

Sylvia stepped back, tilting her head as if to say, "I'm the sane one. And the beauty." And that worked. Their eyes turned to her; she shone back on them.

Such was their life, whether on tour or in New York, where Judie and Dave bought a place on Sullivan Street in the Village and Sylvia found a spot farther uptown by the East River, each purchased with a mix of album sales and Hyman assistance.

The idea had been to take a break from the whiskey and living out of vans, the horror on the news each night, to get creative in the studio. But the news followed them. The war followed them. They were waking up daily feeling that the world was on fire; thinking, *It can't get worse*—but then it did.

In May 1970, Anna was preparing for a two-month trip to Europe. She called up Judie, which was rare; they usually communicated through Sylvia. Anyway, Sylvia was already there, smoking at Judie's kitchen table. "Why don't you come up to the house, so we don't have to hire a caretaker?" Anna asked Judie. "Work on whatever. Music. But promise two things: don't damage the place, and marry Dave already."

Judie, who had a joint in her hand, which she insisted on bogarting even while she talked on the phone, laughed and told Dave the proposition.

"Let's do it! It's a piece of paper," he said, pulling a strand of her hair. "If it gets you peace and quiet to write."

Sylvia stood maid of honor. They braided flowers in their hair. The justice of the peace had never witnessed anything like the carnival they brought into the town hall.

During the daytime their crowd was brown and buzzed and half-naked, dancing on the lawn to each other's guitars, cannonballing off the dock like kids, making tureens of pasta salads with canned tuna and herbs from the garden and eating it for meal after meal, with endless beer and cold white wine, climbing nearby mountains even when all you could see was mist and their hair got matted and their necks drenched in sweat. Judie and Dave were so disgustingly, sweetly together, sitting on the deck at night to watch the stars. Yet Judie found no peace and quiet to write, and they couldn't forget the world. Each morning (or afternoon, depending on when they woke) Sylvia and Judie burned sage by the lake, hoping as the smoke curled up to the New Hampshire clouds, thick and low and tangible, that the war would be over soon.

~

Sylvia watched her sister watch women at the meeting. Judie's two hands cupped her face; her eyes were roving spotlights.

The first testimony came from a woman with a pert nose and legs like an antelope: she told a tale of a secret abortion, bleeding and pain and rushing to the hospital. She had been scared and young, shamed by the doctors. She needed about ten tissues. The next woman, in a blue dress that clung to her bosom, spoke about a shotgun wedding at a church out on Long Island—a husband who pinned her arms back to beat her, a divorce, ignominy in town. Handed the same tissues, she finished the box, leaving a ball of them smeared with pink lipstick. Sniffles joined together, filling the room.

The organizers exchanged looks: this was *heavy*.

"Judie and Sylvia, the Singer Sisters," said a petite woman with a halo of salt-and-pepper hair whom Sylvia had begun to think of as the *maestro*. "I saw you nodding along, Judie—do you want to share *your* truth with us?"

Judie peeked out with those big doe eyes, the ones Sylvia knew got her in trouble with Eamon, then with Dave. Sylvia's palm on Judie's back nudged her out. This was meant to be a cure.

Judie stepped into the circle. Sylvia's leg buzzed from the hard floor; she shook it. Judie reached out a hand for a guitar, a microphone—finding none, her fingers fell to her side.

"My story is like yours," she began. "Ten years ago, almost—I ran away to New York. In a sense."

Sylvia fidgeted—Sylvia, who hadn't wanted to her sister to leave but hadn't stopped her. Now Judie would tell them—as those other women had. She'd exorcise the demons hiding under her lyrics and her melodies, scratching their way out, for so long. Maybe she'd start with their parents saying she had the ugly voice compared to Sylvia's, or with the forced performances of girlhood. She could explain what animated all the songs she'd written, the tunes these bespectacled girls hummed while throwing their girdles in trash cans or wolf-whistling guys on Wall Street or whatever they did in the name of liberation.

Judie began again: "I was young for my age. I left home—crashed with a bunch of women near here. And then I met—" She looked around.

"I met a singer . . . ," she continued.

The last time they'd seen Eamon was at a concert in a park in some city in the Midwest, gin flowing backstage, all the acts loaded. They'd had about ten seconds in the dusk backstage for Judie to ask, "How is she?" and for him to say, as he had before, "Doing fine, walking," or, "They've moved back to Dublin, and are all right." But this time he was cold. Sylvia saw from five feet away. "You *chose*, honey," he said. "Stop glancing over your shoulder." He'd touched her with a lone, condemning finger, then had the nerve to strut off, guitar case tucked beneath his arm as though the kindness he'd once shown her was packed up in it.

Tell them the truth, Judie. "We lived in an apartment like this," she told the women. "We hung out on the fire escape."

"Oh God, I'm not used to talking about me," Judie confessed, putting her hands on her knees and leaning forward. "I'm used to *singing*."

A funny mood took hold then. The girls in the room began to clap for her apology. They called out requests, like she was a jukebox. Most of them wanted "Route 95."

Judie's eyes implored Sylvia. Onstage, they'd learned to communicate with eyes, nods. Sylvia telegraphed what her sister ought to do: *Tell them, Judie. No cop-outs. No songs.* Judie unlocked her gaze from Sylvia's. Her shoulders dipped. She pointed at the first girl who had made a song request, and the girl squealed, predictably.

"Back to that group of women—they changed my life. So, I guess—this song is for them, and for you," Judie lied. "Sylvia? Join me on a chorus?"

With no choice but to obey, Sylvia rose, put one hand on Judie's shoulder, and sang with her. Loyalty had downsides, like when you helped each other hide from the truth.

~

Sylvia suspected that Judie wanted out. Not when she first woke up in the morning; she seemed fine, even happy, ordering strong coffee from whatever hotel they awoke in and opening the curtains to push on the windowpanes and let the air circulate. But by bedtime she'd coil up like a dying insect, cursing the songs, the life she'd chosen. She blamed Nixon; she blamed napalm; she blamed album sales and a bad review in *The Voice*; she blamed Dave and Sylvia and Anna and Hy. *Maybe Judie was right*, thought Sylvia, and it was all shit, but if Judie stopped singing, if Sylvia was left alone, *she* would be the lost one.

Being a Singer Sister gave Sylvia the chance to be Stage Sylvia, beautiful and slender and strong voiced and vivid, funneling her feelings into notes. But also, when Judie was with her up there, she could live a life unobserved; she could be free, or free enough.

Judie had no clue how much Sylvia needed her; she never had. She hummed a note, and with all those women, they sang "Route 95" a cappella.

As they harmonized on the bridge, Sylvia enumerated to herself what they needed to do before the tour started up again: select guitars and buy the best lozenges at the pharmacy on West Tenth Street. What, Sylvia wondered, was Judie thinking about instead of obligations? Maybe her mind was tripping down the long dark stairway of the Gaslight that summer long ago. Sylvia wished the women at the meeting could have helped Judie more.

"That wasn't angry enough," Judie complained as they sat in a bar down the street, later. "I don't want to whine. I want to wage war on nasty male critics."

She meant the essay that had appeared last year in *The Village Voice*, "Enough with the Prim Folkie Solipsism." In it, a writer named Zachary Jones had inveighed against their third album, *Window Tree* (after the Frost poem)—an album Judie had composed after a long and tortured writer's block. He leveled a brutal assessment:

Enough Emily Dickinson–style interiors, enough women gazing out of them and lamenting their heartbreak, enough sad stories about the raped and mistreated heroines that populate too much of folk music, enough navel-gazing about female confinement.

The liberation of women is here, and sure, we should celebrate it. . . . But it's 1973. We're about to get an Equal Rights Amendment, they're burning undergarments, so can't girls' music reflect that? Look at Miranda Steel! She does what she wants, her stories about her latest lay are why she's the female Dylan, and that makes her refreshingly different from the other girls writing today. Even Joan Baez, who's prudish for my taste, has a word or two to say about social issues. In between these two is a no-man's-land (pun intended), where Judie Zingerman's once promising songwriting has landed, and languished, to be frank. There's not a metaphor in her lyrics that a third grader couldn't figure out, for example. Now her sister Sylvia's voice remains celestial as ever, but it may be time for her to find some new material. I hear Bob Dylan writes good tunes.

Dave and Sylvia had been apoplectic at the time, while Judie had laughed and tossed the thing away. But it had been gnawing away at her, she admitted now, sipping a seltzer and vodka.

Songwriting was for her what singing was for Sylvia—a refuge—and to have it torn down in public like that was a splinter that she couldn't remove.

They ran into Judie's friend Angela Darwin at their second, and final, women's lib meeting, a discussion on housework. Angela was an in-demand session singer with a wicked alto and a notable Afro. She was also a downtown art scene fixture; she and Judie had palled around ever since a party at the Chelsea Hotel. Sylvia had lost Judie for hours and then discovered her with Angela, on a back stairway with a Moroccan hash pipe between them, quoting Shakespeare rowdily and pondering whether the best lyrics qualified as poetry.

"The Singer Sisters in the flesh!" cried Angela. They kissed cheeks as the meeting let out, then eased themselves down on the stoop next door with cigarettes and a few hangers-on.

"These white women act like a maid will solve their problems," said Angela, whom Judie had described to Sylvia with glee as "a Panther in spirit." "But what about the maid? *She's* a woman. Probably an immigrant. You can't send shit downhill forever. Someone has to scrub toilets."

"*Men* should scrub the toilets," said another young woman standing three feet from them on the sidewalk. A bushel of tawny curls that she wore free and unadorned sat on her head like a crown. It recalled Eamon Foley's first song; Sylvia swooned at the thought of those perfect notes.

"Men will *never* scrub toilets," said Angela. "They'll take care of you in bed, maybe cook a chili. They will never scrub shit stains off toilets."

Their shoulders together, Judie and Sylvia chuckled. Judie's hands were twitching, a recent tic.

Angela, enjoying her rapt audience, told the girl all about the sexist record industry, and it sounded familiar: "They beg you to sing but only pay for the session—no residuals. Plus they try to sleep with you every damn time, even when you're on the rag and you'd rather go home for a sandwich. They're just as bad as certain men in the church used to be when I was a girl."

Angela's forthrightness recalled Judie's, she had a sense of humor, and she was stylish and smart. Why did Judie, who left all the business dealings to her sister, get to make friendships like this, while Sylvia confided mostly in Dave?

"I just wanted to say," the young woman said, now turning to Judie, "your songs mean the universe to me." Judie, eyes blank, blew smoke onto the sidewalk.

"Hey," the girl said. "You seem bummed. Hang the critics. We need a new Singer Sisters album!"

Judie offered a tight smile and pulled at Sylvia's sleeve ruffles, pestering for an escape.

"Those radical girls sure love the Singer Sisters," said Angela. They had walked a mile or two and were now having cottage cheese at a diner on Waverly Place and reading personals in *The Village Voice*. "Judie's their Dylan. That's basically what Curly Sue back there said."

"No one important hears you unless your music speaks to men," Judie said with a melodramatic sigh.

Angela wore an amethyst geode on a piece of twine that caught the light in the diner, nestled perfectly beneath her collarbone. It gleamed at Sylvia, who stayed quiet. It hurt how Judie pushed away the praises of friends and strangers alike. Angela shared a quick commiserating look with Sylvia and then started describing her two-week meditation retreat in Santa Fe earlier that year with a couple of famous guitarists and a ton of mescaline, and they dropped the subject.

～

But other people couldn't drop the subject. Two weeks later and thousands of miles away, after their second show in London, the two Singer Sisters sat at the legendarily cramped 100 Club on either side of Dean Banks, a coked-out executive. His brazen, thick fingers were crawling their way up both sisters' knees.

"You know, I can handle two talented women at the same time," he said. Judie, in jeans, recoiled as if struck by lightning. Sylvia stayed put. Dean controlled the label purse strings. She crossed her legs, fluttered her eyes. Someone had trimmed the man's beard too neatly, and the effect was unctuous.

"We've never heard that line before!" Sylvia joked, papering over her annoyance with a smooth voice. "Do you fancy yourself the first man who's propositioned us?" She let her fingertips slide over his shoulder, placating him.

"Worth a try," he said with a shrug and a look at Judie's chest, which was at his eye level. "One of you has the legs, and the other has the tits, so why not?"

"Now, now," Sylvia said gently, oh-so-gently. "My sister is a married women and I'm a committed spinster."

"That's not what I've heard," he said, leering. (Sylvia did have a slight reputation.) But he seemed more interested in Judie, which was rare.

"If you want to write a better record and not be called a washed-up has-been in *The Voice*, you need to live the *life*, Miss Prim-Married Judith. You need a jolt. I like a challenge. I'll see you back at the hotel if you're looking for a party. I know your room number."

Sylvia sent Judie a pointed look—reminding her of her duties—and Judie glared and gave him a shoulder pat.

Then they tried to watch the end of the set.

Dave had gone back to New York the week before to rerecord a track or two. Maybe he was jumpy; maybe he was cheating on Judie. So much back and forth, so much running around, it could be hard to keep track of your own brother-in-law, who was also, maybe, your closest industry friend.

"Go, go," Judie told Dave, trying to be a liberated woman. But without him around, the freezing up that took hold of her—opening her mouth expecting true music to ascend to the heavens and finding a croak instead—was spreading like a virus to the stage.

Sylvia didn't know how to inoculate against it. Judie would start to sing or play, and her lips would begin working unusually hard to make words, her face vacant. She'd flutter her finger so Sylvia saw what was happening: her symbol for the *moths*. Usually, she pushed through it okay. Vintage Judie, bringing her *issues* to the stage.

If she wobbled, Sylvia would dig in and shake out her hair and look at the audience and give them a strut and try to win them harder. She made her fingers dart showily across the frets, strummed until blood came, hit the high notes, to convince them to look at her first. They adored Sylvia. Sylvia gave herself to them. Judie saw it.

A quiet menace settled between them. Judie called Sylvia the taskmaster, but Sylvia saw herself as the caretaker. It tired her, managing Judie's *mishegas*, as Hyman would call it.

Sylvia had complaints, too, private miseries and neglected desires. She looked in the mirror and saw triangles cut into her face. She was thin. She was alone.

~

The encore started and Dean got up to piss, and they slipped away in the dark.

"Why do men do that?" Judie said, brushing her hand against her jeans with venom. "It's disgusting. They don't own us. Why is he saying 'rock and roll' when we're folk singers?"

They had heard it before, all year, after *The Voice* opened the floodgates: that their sound was too soft, that Judie's songwriting hadn't changed enough from the folk café days.

"What did those jeans ever do to you?" Sylvia said, stopping her hand. "They technically own us, Dean and them. Our music."

Judie brushed Sylvia's hand away. "I miss Dave."

Sylvia returned her silver-bangled hand to Judie's waist, needing to touch her so she would understand.

"You, a damsel in distress?" she asked. Maybe Sylvia was too sensitive. In New York, she'd had a long affair with a suit from another label, a married man named Kevin who dressed not dissimilarly to Dean, overly manicured beard and all. Her true heartbreak was Lily, a redhead encountered backstage at a festival. After a few months living in Sylvia's apartment, eating the deli sandwiches Sylvia ordered her, kissing in the mornings, Lily was now following the Grateful Dead like an idiot, somewhere in the Midwest. All Sylvia had of hers was a ring she had worn, with an enamel lily on it. Lily asked for it back when she left, but Sylvia claimed she'd misplaced it.

"Check the laundromat, babe," she said.

Maybe Sylvia would never have another ring. Was it possible that, on occasion, she toyed with and discarded the men she was with, to avenge what women did to her?

On occasion, it was possible. Hence her reputation.

In the bathroom mirror, Sylvia regarded Judie's heart-shaped face, reflected against the collage of lipstick, graffiti stickers, and soot, and saw her own face soften with love. Sometimes Sylvia worried that her secrets would get the better of her, but Judie's hadn't killed her yet.

"You're right. It *is* a drag," Sylvia said.

Judie turned her palms in, then out, then in. "I wish I were as tough as you. I have deeper feelings."

"Screw that," said Sylvia, her response whenever Judie pulled that line. "You're too wrapped up in your own blues to see mine, but I have them."

Judie did her wide-eyed thing, then turned away. Sylvia grabbed her arm, but she slipped out, skipped down the stairs. Wrapped in the shroud of her sorrow, Judie had never asked Sylvia about the summer she ran away, about what had kept Sylvia in Cambridge—or who. Judie never wondered aloud why Bella stopped coming around, so Sylvia never told her about the Saturday, the Shabbat, when Bella had kissed her lips and said, "You taste like challah," and Sylvia pulled away, surprised by her own desire, and how the next week she begged off after shul and planned to tell Bella her feelings. Oh, they'd planned a magical end-of-summer day—they called it that, a magical day—getting afternoon tea at the museum, with such fanfare. That morning Sylvia's lips were so dry, she kept drinking water and peeing like a baby doll.

Judie didn't know how her big sister lingered on the white museum steps, how Bella was late and the sun got high and her face began to sweat. And then Bella ran up and didn't hug like usual but kissed the air near her cheek and said, "I invited my new friend Sandra from class!" and smirked at Sylvia in a sharp manner that telegraphed a new wall between them.

Sylvia had had to spend the whole day with the two and watch Sandra treat Bella's elbow as though it were a kitten she was trying to catch.

That was the first of a series of letdowns, ending with Lily. Sure, each one had calcified her heart, but not enough, not enough for Judie to act like it wasn't a heart anymore. On the steep back stairs, their hands braced against a brick wall for stability.

"Sis," Judie said, addressing the door, "I didn't mean it that way—"

Judie tugged at Sylvia's arms, pleading, like they were kids. This perpetual war.

"Did you see the way his necklace was swinging on his chest?" Sylvia asked, offering a truce. "So distracting."

"Freud would have a field day with *that*," said Judie with a snort.

"Is it Freud, or your own mind?" Sylvia teased her. Judie stammered; the critic was right. She had a prim streak.

"You're the one with too many lovers for me to count; I've given up," she shot back. "I'm married, yet Mom and Dad think I'm the whore of Babylon and you're virtuous."

Sylvia snickered. "Yes, it works out nicely for me."

Judie punched Sylvia in the shoulder. They took new air into their lungs. Drizzle streaked the night, London in its own low cloud. Judie pulled a pack of cigarettes out of her back pocket. Sylvia had an urge to deposit her at the hotel and ditch out for Soho, find someone to spend the night with, maybe do some lines. But Judie radiated a need to be accompanied. Sylvia imagined, not for the first time, how Eamon had seen her as a big innocent target.

"You have it easy thanks to Dave and me," Sylvia said. "You know that, right?"

Judie huddled up against the wall of the club, trying to strike a match.

"No one asked you to protect me," she said. Sylvia reached over to help her spark the thing; it sputtered, died, sparked. "It's not my fault, what I've been through," she went on.

"You can't throw your one rotten break up at me for the rest of our lives!" Sylvia said. "If it hadn't been for me . . ." Sylvia, calling their parents to say she was knocked up. Calling Dave, using him to track down Eamon, coming up with the New Hampshire scheme, saving her damn neck on the lake, sparing her life by telling her not to go to some back-alley abortionist.

Judie choked on her first puff, then handed the cigarette off while she coughed it out.

"If it hadn't been for you, I would have gotten rid of the baby before— before it *was* one. You *begged* me to keep it." Her face turned orange and white in the glare of the changing streetlights. "I thought I would come back to myself; I thought I had, but I never did."

Sylvia shook her head as their mother might. She made a habit to never think about this part, about what she had asked Judie to do by asking her to spare herself.

"Way too heavy, darling," she said. "You're having a bad spell, is all."

Judie was making a habit of being *heavy*—she had put on ten pounds, and she yammered about weighty subjects, Cambodia and the big abortion case the previous year. She had a particular hang-up about Vietnamese orphans, some of whom she said were airlifted without their parents understanding the separation was permanent. She cut out the headlines about that and kept them in a folder, Dave told Sylvia.

They walked on.

"She could be here," Judie hissed in the lamplight. She affected an accent: "We could be passing my baby right 'ere in bloomin' 'yde Park." They knew for a fact the girl had moved to Dublin.

Their path meandered toward their hotel, down a burned-out block, empty of late-night partyers or tourists. Sylvia was in a mood to lecture.

"Judie, you bring up the worst things to make yourself *feel* worse. Why? The girl is with a loving family."

"How do you know?"

Sylvia tried another tack. "So why not get in touch?" she asked. "It's the 1970s—things have changed. You can talk to her mother. I mean—I don't mean—I mean Eamon's sister."

Mulish Judie knew she could call. She *should* call—they were here in the British Isles for a month. She could even *visit*. But she now moved on to her second-favorite theme (behind self-pity): complaining.

"Do we have to be on the bill with Melanie next week? She's so . . . anodyne."

They trudged on, wet leaves and pavement under their boots. Sylvia ignored her own wisdom and speculated. Rose might not live here anymore, but she once had; the girl *could* be visiting friends, on this street, in the park, off this Tube stop.

The night concierge buzzed them into the hotel. Europe smelled like tobacco and urine; Judie talked about the Greyhound bus smell and the Village, how exciting those kinds of dissipated odors had been when they were kids. Now, she made gagging noises.

Judie in the lead, they climbed another narrow staircase, its thick carpet marked by unmentionable dark splotches. Sylvia's back hurt: too much carrying, too much hunching. They reached the door to their shared room, but somehow Dean had beat them there, and in the same hour as their walk-and-talk, he'd lost his tie, jacket, and coherency.

Judie gently tried to get around him into their room, and he made several poor attempts to lunge at her. His fixation had not faded but been heightened by booze or whatever he was on, and it turned him into a creature. Sylvia's heart sped up.

She stepped in front of her sister, spoke sweetly to him, led him to his room, Judie trailing.

Shut the door on Judie, got him to his bed.

And nothing happened, not really, in those minutes in the room. Except she bruised her shoulder hard on the doorway out, and as the door clicked shut behind her, she discovered she was shaking like a kitten.

"Darling, what's the matter? Did he try funny stuff with you?" Her sister's arms were around her, and Sylvia thought: *Just in time. No, too late.*

"Oh, he tried to paw me and then passed out," Sylvia lied. "It's nothing."

"That's not nothing!" shouted Judie. "I told you not to go in there, Sylvia!"

Judie wrapped Sylvia tightly with her arms, and Sylvia allowed her head to drop low to Judie's shoulder. How restful, to be the one leaning. And Judie was so soft, so broad shouldered, and so sturdy.

But after a mere sob or three escaped she put the brakes on, because if she fell apart, the world would collapse. The world she'd built: the group, their life, Stage Sylvia. Self-pity poisoned a person; she would end up like Judie, alone in bed for weeks on end, staring out the window with dead eyes. And she'd never get up again. Sylvia wouldn't have what Judie did: a sister who spilled sunshine on her, cajoling her out of depression.

"Don't you see?" Sylvia said, wiping her eyes. "He'll say I was 'nice'; he'll help with the next record. . . ."

Judie's face remained pale. Her eyes in the dim hall lighting showed fear, and guilt, and—was it possible?—genuine pity. Well, they had something in common. They had both been rescued by Sylvia, so many times.

Sylvia hoped the door never opened again but knew it would, and she would toss flowers when it did. The hallway allowed two abreast; so, at some point one of them struggled up and tugged the other up behind her. In the dark of their room, she whispered, "It was his palm covering my mouth that spooked me, sis, his paws got nowhere," and she didn't hear a response, but when she woke up, Judie had moved into her bed, her arm across Sylvia's pillow.

Sylvia flung it away and got up to wash her face.

⌣

For their inaugural show back in New York City, they played the Bottom Line on a night of terrific thunderstorms. The evening began with a feeling of dread. Judie lurched around with a bottle of Scotch in her hand, but Sylvia had seen that before. Judie kept swigging, and Sylvia hadn't seen that. They stepped out onstage and began to play. But halfway through "The House on the Lake," Judie stopped.

"I can't go on this way," she said, her lips so close to the microphone she could kiss it. "Moaning about my private sorrows when the world is on fire. Nixon is only the beginning, isn't he? Kent State still feels like yesterday," she said. "Those kids shot in broad daylight and they didn't do anything about it. Someone should be in jail for murder, but kids get arrested for stealing junk instead. And in Southeast Asia . . . Did you ever hear about the orphan airlift? Did you know . . . ? Their parents didn't know. They didn't *know* their children were permanently being taken from them." And then she started crying too hard to continue.

~

This whole mess started when they returned from London. They were jet-lagged as hell, so Judie and Sylvia began to get up early to walk. Sylvia learned again, as she had before, that one can survive on minimal sleep. She didn't tell Judie, but she got two locks added to her door, and that helped, though she still checked on them around four in the morning, and usually that was it—if the sun rose, Sylvia didn't sleep.

She kept busy taking voice lessons with an opera singer from the Met and doing guitar work with Dave; he was teaching her how to string her own instrument, and she was teaching herself to do bluegrass-style picking. She wanted to tour as soon as possible and started calling up bookers, asking about summer festivals.

When she picked up Judie in the mornings, Sylvia sensed that they each wanted to talk about things that they didn't talk about, instead gossiping about who was *shtupping* whom in the music world and whose songs made them jealous, maybe kvetching about their mother.

One morning, after Sylvia finally made it back to sleep around five and slept like a log, Judie took their walk alone—and tripped on a cobblestone and hurt her tailbone walking across the small triangle near Carmine Street.

The injury happened to women who had had children, apparently. A week in bed, mostly alone, reading the newspaper, Judie's dark mood like quicksand. Dave decided she needed to see this doctor all his friends had told him about—he helped showbiz people with nerves and pain. They went downtown together, half-drunk—Judie said they'd been watching the Watergate House impeachment hearings all morning and drinking coffee with whiskey in it.

"Yes, she has a nasty bruise—but it's causing her anxiety," the doctor said after the briefest of visits in which Judie told him about her shaking hands, her drowsiness, her lethargy. "Take these every day," he said.

The early doses perked her up. The Singer Sisters played a show in Great Barrington, and Judie was as cheerful as she'd been onstage for months, shaking her hips and never looking at her boots. *Perhaps they'd avoided a sinkhole*, Sylvia thought (like an idiot). Maybe they could stay the Singer Sisters forever. Traveling past neat colonial houses with green shutters, the curve of the mountains behind them, shadowed by thick woods.

In the car ride home, Sylvia was so happy she dared ask Judie if she was writing. Judie, with an arch look, said, "Things are brewing."

Within a week, though, the pills turned her jittery.

"Who's languishing?" she yelled as she paced her apartment, shaking a tambourine that she'd grown attached to and snapping at Dave for leaving his pipes and half-opened books and nutshells on the table—and for his indifference to the political situation.

"Terrible things are *still* happening in Southeast Asia," she told Sylvia as she poured a mimosa at a brunch they were hosting. "I wish I'd gone off to change the world instead of just writing songs, you know?"

"Songs change the world," Sylvia said. Judie responded by glumly reciting what she'd learned just that week about Agent Orange—she could see their attention slipping, so she got louder, angrier.

"Chill, babe," Dave told her—he was in a quaaludes phase himself. She started drinking more to calm down.

~

At the Bottom Line, a bearded man in the front row jeered at Judie in a way she didn't like. "Do you have a problem with a woman speaking her mind?" she asked.

"Shut your piehole, bitch!" he shouted.

"You shut up!" said a girl next to him.

Judie wasn't a rock musician; she didn't have the bravado that the Janis Joplins and Grace Slicks did, their sexy shimmies and moans and drama. But Sylvia of all people knew that sometimes her sister had chutzpah.

"Let's pray for the children of Cambodia and Vietnam," she said as Sylvia approached her, panic in her chest, her throat, her entire body. "I want them to know I'm thinking of them."

And then her sister knelt on the stage and put her hands up in the air in prayer, and that might have worked, but then she began to teeter from the whiskey and allowed herself to fall over like a theatrical pratfall and hit the floor with a thud.

Images of burning monks entered Sylvia's head, the way they keeled over before being consumed. Judie wasn't the only person who cared about the dying world. People yelled from the pit in front of them. The "bitch" guy reached over the lip of the stage to touch Judie's leg, and she kicked him, hard.

It erupted through Sylvia, from the floor where Judie lay. "Enough," she said. She stepped in front of her sister, blocking her from the crowd.

The stage floor cradled Judie's body. The vibrations from the audience coursed through Sylvia's feet: their sweat, their movements, their anger.

Looking backstage, Sylvia signaled Bert, their roadie, to come. Judie swore she was fine.

"Get off my stage," said Sylvia. Bert helped Judie up, she staggered out, threw her fingers up in a peace sign, and at least some of the crowd got behind her with cheers.

"Oh for Christ's sake," Sylvia muttered at her back. "It's 1974, not Wood-stock." The mix of sounds: a smattering of boos, cries of "We love you!" as well as a single, loud "Peace and love, bitch!" The leerer.

As she pivoted to face them, she became Stage Sylvia. Cheerful. Funny. Mean.

"My sister might have tried the brown acid, folks," she said. "Don't worry, I've seen Judie weather much worse. She's a tough broad and these are tough times."

She strummed a few chords and dialed the charm to top volume. "So, anyway, welcome to the Sylvia Zingerman acoustic solo portion of the evening—planned or unplanned, I will entertain."

The voice of an angel—that's what the critics said of Sylvia. She began to sing a quiet version of "Barbara Allen," with no accompaniment. The crowd hushed beneath her spell. She was singing them a lullaby. She was singing to get them to forget Judie.

A folk song, the kind people sang on their porches on summer nights. What Sylvia was created to do. She was onstage. She was home.

~

Judie had parked at her kitchen table with a cup of tea and an empty aspirin packet when Sylvia arrived the next day, feeling as grim and cold as she had on the day she was twelve and a ten-year-old Judie had broken her favorite Elvis record.

Judie's thick, sensual mouth was almost invisible, she had drawn it so tight. Her apology was rote: "I don't know what's gotten into me. I'm acting like Jim Morrison."

Sylvia said she didn't know what had gotten into her either.

"Such a small theater! No one saw," said Judie. *You are languishing*, Sylvia thought. Judie blew hard on her tea and took a sip—then winced.

"This tea is *rude*," she said.

"Word travels, Judie," Sylvia said.

"Who isn't an imbecile onstage sometimes?" Judie said before licking her lips.

As Sylvia inhaled, she allowed herself to tick off the items that had been running through her brain all night: Judie in that graffiti-strewn loo, saying Sylvia's feelings weren't *like* hers. Judie sitting on the rug of the hotel hallway while Sylvia managed things with cokehead Dean. Judie praying like a nun onstage and keeling over while men pawed at her feet.

"If this keeps happening your reputation is shot, and so is mine. You're out of the band, Judie." Sylvia felt positively feline. "Take a break."

"You can't kick me out of an equal partnership, sister dearest," said Judie, letting her voice go cold to match Sylvia's metallic timbre. "I've been telling you for months I didn't want to do this anymore—to perform. And no one listened, not you, not Dave—you saw dollar signs. There are children dying—children—little children. Did you know about the Vietnamese orphans? Their mothers didn't know they were giving them up."

Sylvia knew. She threw her scarf around her shoulders on her way out.

"You and your royal ways," said Judie.

"Yes, we were making money," Sylvia said. "But that's not the point. It's the best thing I can do . . . it's the *only* thing. I will never have a husband to mooch off of, so I have to work!"

"Don't give me that 'woman of the people' crap!" snapped Judie, pushing her own chair back, scraping it on her nice parquet floors, following Sylvia to the door. "Good, honest work? Who are you, Hemingway? As if you're so decent, jetting around with married men even though you *don't* prefer their company."

Sylvia turned back to her and dropped into empty space. Her sister's crumpled, teary face was so *known*—a reflection in a fun house mirror, with all the disapproval of Anna and Hy flashing in her dark eyes.

"You think you have a monopoly on suffering," Sylvia said, pressing her hand to her heart.

The door slammed behind her. The hallway smelled its musty New York smell, and the elevator took forever to ding and usher her down to the street. As girls, she and Judie used to push hard against both sides of a doorway until it hurt, and then their arms would lift up as if by magic.

That was how her entire being felt now. She wondered: Where were the Grateful Dead doing their next festival—and could a solo Sylvia Zingerman act get on the bill? She greeted the neighbors like she might on a normal night. It *was* a normal night. Who would blink these days if the Singer Sisters took a break?

Downstairs the cold air numbed her cheeks, and she meant to turn around and make amends, but she looked up at the sky and saw a constellation, Orion, peeking through the clouds. In New York City, despite it all, the lights had let it through.

JUDIE

A summer evening settled onto the stoops of Sullivan Street. Baby Emma, fussy, expelled buckets of drool and tears and used her mother's arms, breasts, fingers, as a teething toy, leaving red welts on Judie's skin. Mother and baby were restless, so they went to the stoop across the street, to sit with Shirley and Gina, the two nicest winos on the block.

Judie's apartment was missing most of its regulars: Dave touring behind the unstoppable force of "Sweet Camellia Wine," America's number-two single; Sylvia opening for Richie Havens in Sweden; Leon staying the night with Anna and Hy in Sylvia's empty apartment.

Judie's friendship with her neighbors was easy. After the fiftieth time, Judie, with Emma in the buggy, passed them sitting there, they peeked in and cooed and got to exchanging names. They reminded her of Valerie and the girls from the summer of 1965. Now in the evenings when Dave was gone, Judie brought the baby and they sat together in the glow of sunset, and the women quietly passed a bottle back and forth in a paper bag. Sometimes Judie had a sip.

She wasn't supposed to drink much because she was breastfeeding, but she reasoned that she needed a sip to take the edge off the long days and the nights that stayed so hot.

Dave had sent her a telegram from Chicago: "GOOD SHOW, SO TIRED."

Him, tired.

"Wonderful," she sent back. She missed him, but not the part where she woke up at a whisper from the nursery and he snapped, "Stay still, Judie, for Christ's sake."

"Dada," said Emma, looking up. "Bababababa. Dadadadad."

"Getting big," Gina said.

"She gained a pound at her last checkup," said Judie. *Her* body had done that.

Gina and Shirley saw, even with glassy eyes. They noticed if Emma's hat was at a cute angle or if the bags under Judie's eyes were too dark. They leaned in and smelled Emma's hair and gave Leon marbles, and sticks—his favorite. They didn't discuss the fact that Judie had been a Singer Sister. They didn't care. They had lived in San Francisco for a long time and then out in the desert, they said. But it had turned out to be *no good*, so now they were here.

⁓

Recently, with Dave gone, she had been having a perverse daydream fantasy. She liked to imagine that she was a Jewish girl in World War II France, forced to be a concubine to a cruel Nazi. After hate-fueled sex on his orderly desk, she dreamed of reaching into his drawer, finding his letter opener, and stabbing him to death. Then she would leap from the balcony, martyred.

He would be discovered when the blood soaked through the ceiling of the room below. Like *Tess of the d'Urbervilles*, when Tess finally kills Alec.

She wasn't sure what it meant, except that she'd read *Tess* for the fifth time and that after engineering a family reconciliation when Leon was born, she'd been helping Dave take care of his aging father, who had left Europe in 1939 and told stories. Actually, she knew what it meant: a fantasy about coming through when you've been counted out. A dream of redemption, even at the price of death. Making the world better with your sacrifice.

She was so lost in her reverie on the stoop that she didn't notice the smell from Emma's diaper. Gina did.

"Do you have Pampers?" Shirley asked Judie. "Bring her in and change her on my kitchen table—why schlep back?"

Judie, who had burp cloths and diapers in her purse, gratefully trooped inside. The apartment was shabby and smelled sour, but it wasn't dirty. A clean space on the rug seemed homey enough, anyway.

Across the street seemed far to walk. Plus, they helped her change Emma, and got another bottle of wine from the shelf, and threw the dirty diaper in the garbage—which was full to overflowing—laughing and talking all the while.

It reminded Judie of what she still loved about motherhood: The tenderness. The clucking. It reminded her of when Leon was a baby.

Judie had been so happy the first year of parenthood and most of the second and even part of the third when she was pregnant with Emma. As her belly grew, Leon, with a budding beauty and wit, was toddling around like the king of the house.

God, she had been so relieved—convinced she was done with all the creative angst, the performing. Who needed that aggravation, when she could spend time writing ditties for Leon, telling him stories about a series of woodland creatures she invented: Charlie the Chipmunk, Robin the Robin, and Danny the Deer?

She had thrown herself into teaching Leon his words and numbers, and playing funny games, and dressing him sweetly, and walking him out to the park to meet other toddlers.

How could one describe the particular bliss of that interlude in retrospect, to put words to a love so powerful it allowed her to stop narrating her life? She and Leon were best friends. They completed each other. What was broken in her had fixed itself. The months floated by in a dream of hormones and heaven. She missed her closeness with her sister, and she missed her friends—but she was *glowing*.

Her father had once given her a lecture over BLTs. Judie was in exile from the Singer Sisters. Dave was miserable working at an advertising firm, only a few months in, the bald spot growing on the back of his head and increasing his irritability. Even their drinking and smoking pot, the occasional line of coke, had become rote; their hearts didn't quicken before a party; they worried they would be held up at gunpoint. A half-filled pipe could sit on Dave's bedside table for weeks before they finished it.

When Judie met her father at a diner on West Fourth Street, Hyman searched her face and said, "You look older than your years, honey."

"Dave is in the dumps—and I can't write," she admitted. "Or sing. Or make money."

The money they did have owed itself to a smash hit toothpaste song ("Mentofresh makes you smile!"), ghostwritten by Dave for an ad guy he met at a party. That had led to a job that he took because the pay was good, but instead of creating another jingle, he spent days twiddling his thumbs, passing off mediocre tunes from old notebooks as new. And the hours were killing him—the dress code, the office politics, the meetings behind closed doors.

"Have a BLT," her father said as she explained Dave's predicament. "It's your favorite."

She ordered the sandwich. He cleared his throat. "Judie, you're sad because you're not fulfilled as a woman," he said. She jerked back. "You've been married for a good handful of years. And Dave has a job—but he needs a *reason* to go in. A family."

She focused on the plate, pushed food around.

"You're scared," he said. "After what happened. . . ." He paused. She sipped her vanilla Coke.

The salty, sweet meal delighted her. Even though she hadn't intentionally dieted in a few years, the lifestyle had stayed with her: astringent grapefruits and wilted iceberg lettuce and coffee and cigarettes.

They attacked their food—Judie remembering the Howard Johnson's where they'd stopped on the way back to Boston after they'd retrieved her from Valerie's place. She had the roots of Rose in her body and didn't know it, but she'd been starving. They'd let her order the *traif* without comment, her parents, as her father did now. They'd rather see her fed than hungry.

"Maybe," she said to Dave that night, "we should have a kid."

His glum face brightened. "You're ready?"

"I think so."

He jumped out of bed and rushed to her side and knelt on the floor and kissed her hand.

"Gosh," she said. "If I'd known it was this easy to make you smile."

They were pregnant after three months of trying. And then, halfway into her pregnancy, a friend of Dave's from the folk-singing days who had a big job at a label called and told him, "I've got a song for you."

The song, "Sweet Camellia Wine," had been written by a singer named Miranda Steel, a pixie in short-shorts and knee socks who told the label that "it didn't fit her image" and passed it on.

"It's nonsense," said Judie when she heard the tape. She sucked air into her lungs, fighting a wave of nausea. "Treacle—and exactly like what's all over the radio."

"They want to put a jazzy saxophone hook right here," he told her, pointing at the sheet music. "It would go like this—dooo, dooo, doo. I thought we could do guitar instead."

"Oh, that's terrible," she said. "That won't leave my head for *days*."

"Isn't that what we *want* in music?"

"I prefer when it *won't* let you in at first, and you have to knock on the door. But once you go inside, the house is endless."

"So this song is what? A flophouse?"

"No—it shows up, slips in, and then refuses to leave. A bad guest." His laugh at her joke sounded rote.

"Call my sister," said Judie.

Sylvia blew in through the door as promised, wearing a gray dress with bell sleeves—on the way to a party downtown. She patted her sister's stomach gently.

"I suppose the baby can't come get high," Sylvia said with a sigh. "I'm in the mood to stay up all night and look at the moon."

"I'll be up all night with gas," replied Judie, and Dave made a face.

"Sexy," he said.

"Don't go all June Cleaver on me," Sylvia said.

"Hardly possible."

"Have you written anything, Judie?"

Dave shook his head at the same time as Judie.

"My creativity is going to *him*. I know it's a boy, by the way. I can feel the energy."

Dave took Sylvia into the den to play her the demo—putting the cassette in the player. Judie hung back as her sister listened with eyes closed, nodding at the first bridge, the chorus.

"It's a tad much," he said. "The line 'Sweet Camellia wine / You make me feel so fine' makes me want to throw up, but I also, Syl, think I might die if I have to go to an office again."

Sylvia helped herself to the Scotch on their side table.

"So if you cut the single they'll fund an album," she said. "Back in the thing."

"They played this jazz riff they want in the middle there, before the second bridge." He hummed it again.

"That's smooth," said Sylvia. "Maybe make it a guitar solo instead? Davey, hon, there's no choice, is there? You have to be out there, the hands clapping for you. I'm the same, we need it like water, or we wither like . . ."

"*Sour* Camellia wine?" he asked.

Judie bellowed and Sylvia spat out her drink into the glass.

"Go get your hit," Judie said.

"Judie's cranky because you knocked her up," said Sylvia.

~

Dave's song had indeed been a hit, and Leon a jolly baby. They had called Dave's parents and brokered a tentative peace. And once they were flush with money again, and Dave was cutting another album, with Miranda Steel cowriting songs and Sylvia doing backup vocals, Judie and Dave began to try for a second child.

Maybe Hyman had nailed it: maybe her destiny was to make chubby, musical babies.

But Emma's birth, ending in a cesarean section after hours of labor, had torn her body apart. Judie's recovery proceeded millimeter by painful millimeter, as Emma's fretful infancy surprised her daily, after Leon's relative placidity.

It didn't take Freud to see how Emma opened an abyss in Judie, too, by looping her back to the past: "This is what Rose never had" accompanied diaper changes, kisses on Emma's head, waves of love chased by revulsion toward this scrawny girl, a desire to see the face of the pink bundle of a decade ago. Assaulted by memories, Judie wanted madly to write it out of her system but found her time sucked away by the kids.

Judie hid her discontent from Dave. He'd flip his lid if he saw into her mind, remembering her terrible year. So she folded miniature white shirts and hung them up to dry.

Inside she was screaming and pounding on the walls. Chugging whiskey. Perhaps that's why Gina and Shirley were such good company.

~

Back out on the stoop after the diaper change, she rested a hand lightly on Emma's back. The baby's fists clenched a guitar-shaped rattle Dave had gotten her.

Obscured under the shade of its awning, their own doorway across the street yawned like the mouth of a cave. And under it Angela roamed, hand shading her eyes, looking around.

"*Angie!*" Judie hollered.

"Jude, Jude a Judie-Jude," said Angela, jogging across the street. "I was looking for you. Patti Smith is playing on the Bowery tonight and it's going to shake you up."

"How can I? Leon's off my hands but I have Emma."

"I didn't think about that," said Angela, frowning.

"*We'll* watch Emma," said Gina.

"Sure will," said Shirley.

Angela hugged them. She had to go find her friend Caleb, whom Judie would love. But Judie worried about Dave's reaction.

"You doth protest too much," said Angela. "You never come out . . . you deserve it, working so hard to raise that man's kids." She winked.

"You *have* to do it," said Shirley. "We'll watch the babe . . . leave us a bottle or two. We'll put her to sleep right on the blanket here . . . then you come home and scoop her up."

"Put some lipstick on," they told her. "Change your shirt. Go, go."

She looked down: spit-up or yogurt stained her shirt's right breast diagonally toward her waist, a twisted pageant sash.

Within the hour she was walking across Washington Square Park, laughing with Angela, on Caleb's arm. Her royal-blue scarf fluttered in the breeze like a banner.

~

In the cavern-dark club, bodies pressed against her; smoke smells made her woozy, like early pregnancy. The same folk-fever she remembered had taken a new form. Caleb's elbow hurt. Judie was squeezing it. She apologized, her words engulfed by the noise.

Different kinds of touch were so *different*: her children's small, warm bodies clinging to her, Dave's overtures at night when he was home, now these strangers fighting for room with her but also sharing it, comrades and competitors.

Angela got her a rum and cola, which she vowed to sip slowly, and they shared a cigarette. She tried not to think about Emma at Gina's, about the clock and the coming of night. What was she doing here? What kind of mother was she? Another drink.

Patti Smith stepped out almost unnoticeably, slim and neutrally clad. But then she moved across the stage, lithe and dirty and raw, and began reciting her strange, angry music in a low voice. She was both mannish and womanly, and in control.

Judie hated it. She hated it with a sick envy-hate. She missed melody, and sweetness, and not fearing a stampede on the Bowery. Her eyes grew hot. The beat moved through her, a subway train of sound.

She leaned on Angela, who handed her a small white pill and said, "This will help," and nursing be damned, it did, if turning into spaghetti counted as help.

This was what Dave's life must be like—pulsing and midnight blue and full of pills and booze. And women. She'd known it, to be sure, but it hit hard to step inside it herself, that feeling of heart rush, a dark room of bodies and music. At least she had found a pair of sandals, the sturdy platform kind. They matched and fit. Her feet glowed green.

After a while, she had to pee. She descended a narrow stairway and passed a woman who belonged there, young and slender in a striking black top with a gash across the shoulders. "These stairs are so *tight*!" the girl said, three times, as Judie squeezed herself against the wall. The man behind her stepped aside, too. "Oh, *you* don't have to do that," the young girl said to him. *"We're both thin."*

It took Judie a minute to feel crushed. She hadn't gotten *that* fat—had she? She could hear Anna and Sylvia kvetching about how a woman could not eat pastries after the age of thirty-five, and she groaned.

Judie rocked and keened. She davened, like Hyman at synagogue. The show stretched on. People moved and she moved. Someone stomped on her toe and brought her down-to-earth.

They staggered out into a night now plunged into unexpected cool. The baby was at Gina's without a change of clothes. As though they'd been waiting, images of harm to children began to crowd into her head: tortured, ripped from mothers' arms.

"Where are you going?" asked her friends, but Judie, aware of time again, raced home, feeling the booze slosh around inside her, a blister under her sandal strap, crossing the park diagonally, not looking at the arch, the sky. She ran up the steps to Gina's door, still cracked open.

Judie let out a small but primal yell: Emma, exposed to the elements of this city. Any manner of lowlife could walk in and snatch a child. Dave had been held up at knifepoint last summer! What had she done? Hot panic enveloped her.

She pushed inside the apartment, greeted by silence, and found herself on her knees on the floor, crawling toward the living room.

Gina lay asleep on the couch with a half-empty glass lying on the floor and a stain on the rug. Emma slumbered on the selfsame rug, on a neatly spread sprigged sheet, in her tiny dress. She breathed regularly as Judie watched, but as Judie approached a whimper escaped her lips.

Emma couldn't yet crawl, but she could wiggle. And there was booze on hand right here. What if she had consumed some already? Judie kissed her daughter's sweet lips to see if they tasted like alcohol, but her own lips were too rum soaked. She heard a scratching sound from somewhere nearby: A mouse? A rat? A feral cat?

She had to get the baby home right away. Shirley was nowhere to be found. Judie tapped Gina on the shoulder and the woman let out a belch and shifted in her sleep.

"I'm taking the baby home," she said.

Emma woke up and began to wail. "Ummaa!"

Gina said, "Sure, honey," and went back to sleep.

The kitchen clock read two o'clock when she brought Emma into their own apartment. The phone was ringing and ringing; she had heard it from downstairs.

"Hello?" she said, jiggling Emma with the other arm.

"Goddammit, Judie, where have you been?"

"Darling, I went to see the most interesting concert—I don't know if I liked it but it *dislodged* me."

"A concert? Who was watching the kids?"

"Leon was with my parents, and Gina and Shirley watched Emma."

"Who?"

"Our neighbors."

"The *drunks*??"

"Dave, I have to tell you about Patti Smith and CBGB—"

"Who is Patti? A junkie you found, who's babysitting Leon?"

"I had a revelation. I want to write again—"

"I don't have time for this; I'm playing Milwaukee tomorrow and it's a schlep," said Dave. "Call Anna. Anna needs to come stay with you for a while. You can't do this by yourself."

"Maybe not," said Judie. Emma was gnawing on her shoulder contentedly, leaving a string of iridescent drool where Judie's bra strap had dug in.

"Next time you want to go out, hire a girl. I'm selling out theaters—you can afford it." He coughed a few times. "Talk soon, babe."

She stared at the window as the dial tone droned. In the dark, a smeared version of her face, with Emma's fuzzy head on her shoulder, stared back.

A light sleep found her soon enough, but she was awoken again at six by Emma, soaked in her own pee.

"How much can one person pee in a day?"

"Um, Umma, Umma," said Emma. It sounded like "Mama." Her voice trembled.

"Mama's here," said Judie as her head rang. Shirt off, diaper off, clean diaper, clean shirt, a wipe with a towel, shh, shh. A head kiss, a whisper, and they were on the chair, rocking.

For lullabies, Judie had a catalog: "Don't Think Twice, It's All Right." "Suzanne." But as Emma quieted, Judie subbed out her usual finale, Dave's "Little Brown Sparrow," for something new. She decided to sing "Golden-Haired Girl," even though Emma's hair was black.

By the second chorus, she heard Emma's breathing slow, the chubby hands relax. Judie kissed her again, as though it could erase her transgression.

～

A few days later, she wrote her freshest song in years. She sent the lyrics, with chords scribbled on top of them as she always did it, to Sylvia's hotel in a thick envelope.

Dear Sylvie,

I'm awash in diapers and xylophones; Leon is banging tunes all the time, I'm afraid he's got the family disposition, or indisposition. But I do have exciting news! I smoked hash with Angela last night and I rattled on about that summer at the lake. I was thinking about the hammock where you and I used to sit and laugh, and Dave walking back and forth to check on us, the sage we burned for peace, Dave and I on the deck watching the fireflies all night. How we talked—about the war, about music, about our parents. Oh Sylvia, having kids robs you of the innocence of having time ahead of you.

I told her ironically, the summer I got married was the summer I felt freest, and she said, "That sounds like a song," so I wrote one, Sylvie. I wrote it, from start to finish! Maybe because it's so silly, but I scribbled it easily. Is it possible that New Hampshire is my muse?

I'm enclosing it here, a few notes—I leave it to you to perfect it on the road. You can try it out on some of your European audiences.

The summer I got married
was the summer I felt most free
We lay all day in the hammock
beneath an old oak tree
We sat out late by the water
We sunned ourselves on the dock
And I was nature's daughter
I never once watched the clock

We danced our way to the old town hall
with ribbons and tambourines playing
We swore we'd never let each other fall
We didn't know what we were saying

The summer we got married
was many years now flown
And around our youthful palace
the briars of time have grown
But the summer we got married
was the summer I felt most free
So bring back that golden summer
Oh bring it back to me

Well, it's not exactly subtle. I don't see the critics asking, "What does it mean?" But . . . What do you think?

Judie

When the letter reached its recipient (she sent it to the hotel Sylvia would be staying at, weeks ahead), the phone on the kitchen wall would surely ring. And when it did, the sisters' words poured out loose and playful.

Sylvia had sung the song to an audience in Germany, and they *loved* it.

"Maybe you should be on this tour. We could surprise people and reunite!" said Sylvia. "It's *not* too late—fly out, Mom can watch the kids."

Emma crawled between Judie's legs, pulling on her skirt hem, and Leon was tumbling off the couch.

"I can't," Judie said.

She called Dave to tell him about Sylvia's offer. But laughter gurgled through the receiver—a giggle, and then loud, fuzzy feedback, then some music, maybe the Stones.

"Dave, is there a party?"

"No one, no one," he said too quickly, too emphatically.

"I hear people."

"Oh, a few folks unwinding after the show. You know how it is. . . ."

She did know. And he hadn't even begun the leg of the tour featuring the lissome Miranda Steel, who had the irritating ability to scribble the type of song that entered your brain and stayed without permission.

"Dave, you're breaking my heart a smidge," Judie said. And she almost heard her heart crack as she said it.

⁓

Judie heard reports about Miranda. "She wears makeup like a clown," said Angela. "And *very* skimpy halter tops."

Miranda had gotten a write-up in *The Times* as an "up-and-coming singer, with the gift for a big hook you don't expect in such a small person. Her work will satisfy those with a hankering for the folkies of the sixties, those chanteuses of yesteryear, but in a pleasing young package."

That Judie and her peers were categorized as "yesteryear" added to her envy, which visited in quiet moments, a snake on a sunny garden path. It slithered in when Judie turned on the radio and heard an advertisement for a concert. A day before she might have been blithely tending her life, and now she was digging at her cuticles, wondering, *Are her songs better than mine or just catchier?*

When she played "The Summer I Got Married" for Angela, proudly announcing the end of her slump, they planned to pen a song together, to capitalize on Judie's reacquaintance with the muse.

"I want to make a rock and roll record," her friend said. "To get Mick and all the guys who use my voice to show up for an hour each and get a small paycheck, back me up, lay down some tasty guitar solos—and then be dismissed."

"Is that revolution?" asked Judie. "A switcheroo?"

"No revolution. Just a record," said Angela, holding her spliff in Judie's face. They were smoking out the kitchen window.

"I'll write a song for it, okay? I'll write you ten," Judie promised.

"When I have time. They're flying me to London tomorrow to do more vocals for this band that sounds like second-rate Kinks," Angela said. "So much glamour, no cash. Still, over there they get that I don't just want to do R & B."

"Come home soon."

Maybe to break through again, Judie needed a partner: someone to hold her accountable who wasn't her husband or her sister—who didn't have intimate knowledge of her idiocy but admired her work. They heard Emma kicking the wall in the bedroom and stubbed out the joint.

"Hey," said Angela quickly, leaning in close. "Your sister. Is she . . . does she still like girls? You know, not a full-on lesbian, but like me? A little . . . flexible?"

Judie froze, ignoring Emma's yowls. Angela's usually frank face was shadowed by uncertainty. She wouldn't meet Judie's eyes. Was this *possible*? Like everybody who had come to their house from the age of fifteen on, Angela claimed to admire Judie's songs but really wanted to get Sylvia into bed?

"Maybe," said Judie, drawing out the word, "but . . . they end up with broken hearts."

Sylvia owned the heart that got smashed up. Her sister tried damn well to hide it, like they both concealed their undereye circles with goopy makeup.

Sylvia slept with men and girls, but oh yes, Judie knew, she had known since that infernal Bella Bernstein, Sylvia wanted a woman to love, maybe even with some pets and Mexico vacations. And Angela, Angela had a *crush*. Judie should be generous. She shouldn't hoard her for herself, this friend, this potential songwriting partner.

Selfish, stupid Judie.

"I didn't mean to discourage you about Sylvia," said Judie, her voice sounding like a squeak. "I just . . ."

"No, it's okay," said Angela. "I appreciate the warning."

"Well, people *can* change," said Judie. "I used to be fun, for instance."

"Please, you were born a pill," teased Angela.

With Emma now babbling in the stroller, Judie and Angela loitered at the intersection where they usually parted, a dust of pollen from the trees falling in the wind and glowing in the traffic lights. "I'll send you a postcard from London town," said Angela.

"Angie," said Judie to her back, "don't settle down. Like Dylan said, paint your masterpiece. Use any songs of mine you want."

Angela lifted an arm; her bracelets clinked in the wind. A sinkhole opened in Judie. Angela off to fly the world: like Sylvia, like Dave, like her old self. But the thought of waking up early as her friends did and getting in a cab to the airport—no. The bags under your eyes and the dry skin, drugs they gave you to make you feel alert when you landed, and the hangover. No.

Though she drank too much coffee at home, too, and wasn't sleeping here. So, what was the difference? Easy. Angela hadn't made her masterpiece yet, and Judie had made it at twenty.

Back home she considered the mirror, her lilac bathrobe matching purple undereye circles that no makeup could hide. She tried to hum a new tune about the shadows under streetlights and the joy of talking to a friend. She realized she was rewriting Bob Dylan's "Fare Thee Well" yet again.

～

By the time Dave's endless tour finished the next year, with a show at the Hammerstein Ballroom, Judie was even more on edge. Daffodils did their best to pierce the grimy film of winter, but a spate of muggings and stabbings in the news convinced her: she needed a man around the house.

He asked her to unpack his five huge suitcases, but she didn't—not the first day and not the second. When she did unpack the bags they were full of stupid costumes—fur jackets and gold-threaded shirts, even a turban, a studded cowboy hat, red leather jackets, and a white bandit mask with some woman's lipstick kisses all over it.

The third morning he was back, she found him in their room.

"Who are the girls?" she asked. "Are they throwing themselves at you or do you sniff them out?"

Sitting at the edge of the bed, he ran his hands through his hair, moaned, dropped his head back down onto the pillows.

"I was so happy to be home, to be with you all, and have some peace and maybe your scrambled eggs."

"I've pierced your dream."

"You've never been particularly successful at sarcasm, Judie."

She let out a noise between a harrumph and a sob.

He rolled over onto his stomach. "I love you like crazy, but things have been different since Emma—you know it. Evolution, baby, we've been together over a decade."

The flowered bedspread from her grandmother was rumpled on the bed; reflexively, Judie pulled a corner of it straight.

"You've done a fine job with the kids," he continued.

"Fine? Don't dodge the subject. Are any—do you have feelings for anyone?"

He sat up to face her slowly, as if doing so were admitting defeat.

"I used to believe I was purer than other men. I'm not. I want to be with *you*—it's impossible when I'm gone for so long. But baby, I'm home now."

The curtains had faded, the blinds' slats were askew. Superficial cleanliness pervaded the apartment, a bright lemon smell even, but its deeper soul had been overtaken by neglect.

"Will you promise to cool it on the next tour?"

"Will you stop sending songs about our marriage for Sylvia to perform on the sly?"

"Oh—"

"I'm not the only one with my own thing going on, apparently. How could you do that?" he asked. "What am I, your muse?"

He reached down to the space next to the bed and pulled up an old Barbie doll, disrobed from the waist up, matted hair and her face dirty. Her plastic curves caught the light. Judie didn't tell him that the doll was Leon's.

"I never asked you to quit singing," he said, holding up the doll. "For this."

Judie curled up on the bed, her knees by her chest, and closed her eyes.

He flopped beside her. "I'll cut a new album, we'll do press—I'll take Leon to the park to play ball and teach him guitar. We can do this, Judie."

She had her head in her hands, and he grabbed her shoulders and pulled her to him, and she let her body sink onto his and rest there, for now.

When Sylvia had called, inviting her back on tour, she hadn't told her sister the truth: she *wanted* to go, to leave the kids with Anna. But some acts were unforgivable. She had abandoned a child before. And if she left now, she would never come back.

SYLVIA

S ylvia was recording her second solo album at a Twelfth Street studio when she heard the strains of a Miranda Steel record coming from an office down the hall. The album was being made with Dancing Tides Records, a smaller label whose people treated her like a star, so she poked her head in to see a couple of the engineers in their faded jeans, sitting around bullshitting.

"*Such* a good song," she said. Maybe she thought of Miranda as part of her world; maybe she wanted to impress them. "I'll never forget her 'Sweet Camellia Wine' demo for Dave."

"That song ain't all she's given him," someone said with a snicker.

"That girl is *wild*," said another. "Your sister ought to give her a slap . . . or ten."

More laughs, a whistle. "Now, I would buy tickets for *that*."

Sometimes the things men said about women were a crime, not for the substance but because they were *so* unoriginal. Sylvia flounced from the studio without uttering her observation. She had no desire to encourage them or to learn what they'd heard about *her*.

Her previous LP, *Sylvia Sings the Sixties*, a stripped-down collection of Singer Sisters songs retooled, along with some Dylan, Ochs, and Canticle, sold well, grabbed up by thirty- and forty-somethings wistful about the glory days.

This nostalgia filled her with contempt. She preferred the present day with its colors and cocaine. People indulged themselves as they had, but without pretending they were enlightened.

Judie had never given Sylvia a review of the album. Most likely she thought it a retreat, artistically.

This time, Sylvia sought edgier sounds, with "The Summer I Got Married" as a centerpiece and two songs of her own. Yes, Sylvia Zingerman, interpretess of others' work, had *written* songs, maybe not single-worthy—but not terrible. She felt satisfied with the track list. She felt satisfied in general. She kept her hair in an easy, short cut and favored boxy jackets like Diane Keaton's in *Annie Hall*. Life post–Singer Sisters tripped along, though she did miss singing with Judie.

Especially since her sister's drama hadn't exited with the band. Never in a million years did Sylvia think of Judie as the type to gloss over infidelities, but Judie had surrendered after Dave's *Sweet Camellia Wine* tour and all the road partying.

It was for the kids. Sylvia got it. When he was around, he was *around*. He let Judie lie in the park, resting her sore head, while he romped in the grass with Emma and Leon, and they adorned their immobile mound of Mommy with mushed-up dandelions.

Emma worshipped her father, toddling after him and calling him "Day." Freudian, but Judie wasn't jealous, at least not in front of Sylvia: Emma could be a handful; he unburdened her.

Sylvia didn't want kids. She didn't want to put them first.

⌒

Her hands jammed in the pockets of her trench coat as she left the studio, fury building in her chest, throat, shoulders: Why worry about her sister's marriage? Judie had chosen: quit music, popped out kids, now channeling her genius into writing animal songs and training Leon to be a prodigy—as Hyman had done with her.

Sylvia once had an analyst opine that she felt responsible for Judie getting knocked up. She let her sister go to New York and kept their parents from going to get her. From behind his pince-nez glasses, he elucidated: her "rescues" of Judie had given her a delusion of being a protector. He advised Sylvia to stop calling Judie for a set period—not an angry break, like when the band broke up, but a "conscious cooling."

Sylvia stopped paying him her hard-earned dough after *that* session.

What would he say today? Maybe Sylvia had her own Freudian invest-ment in being the third member of the Cantor-Zingerman marriage. One way or another, he'd scribble down on his pad what was wrong with Sylvia, and she'd roll off the couch without changing a damn thing.

~

The next time Sylvia visited, Judie admitted she'd traded Dave a "yes" to a family photo shoot with *Rolling Stone* for a promise not to tour for a year. "Trading favors blatantly," she said. "Like lawyers."

Did Judie suspect Miranda? Or care? Dave zipped out to shows and parties and asked her to come—but she pleaded a headache or moaned about a six a.m. wake-up or one of the kids being feverish.

And Miranda was a dervish, jumping around like a grasshopper, smoking and giggling. But more than that, she was writing songs for and with Dave. *Good* songs. Dave was sweeter than most men, but he was still a man. Sylvia couldn't look her sister in the eyes.

Rolling Stone crowded into the apartment to photograph the whole family. Judie wore a white peasant blouse that bared her shoulders and upper chest. Dave had chosen it. Sylvia curled her hair with a hot iron. They lay on a flowered blanket with the kids and made eyes at each other. Everyone had some wine with the photographer; at the bottom of Sylvia's glass were wings. They fluttered into her mouth and nested in her throat.

~

Sylvia wrapped her album a week after the shoot, booked club dates around the city, rehearsed her show.

But Dave's new album swallowed him whole. He had a sizable budget, maybe thirty times Sylvia's, and hauled in session musicians: horns and flutes and singers who traipsed through the studio running up bills and leaving pills and powder on every surface. His laugh boomed but ended in a cough. He was snappish with Judie, expecting breakfast at noon on Saturdays even though the kids would be antsy by then.

One night Sylvia was at a party all the way uptown near Columbia, sit-ting by the window with a fire escape. The sash opened and Angela Darwin,

Judie's old pal, climbed in, smelling like grass and Chanel No. 5. Angela, who was supposed to be in London.

"Sylvia, Sylvia," she said as though they'd been talking all evening. "A little bird tells me that our mutual pal Dave Canticle and *his* pal Miranda Steel are drinking near here. Shall we scope things out, us two?"

"I might scream at her," Sylvia told Angela. The previous night she'd woken up like a bolt had gone through her, sitting up in bed. Shuffling the cards of her mind, Sylvia drew Miranda. Self-loathing followed: she'd gone to the window and waited for the traffic on the highway to speed up, lulling her back to sleep. It didn't. She walked the perimeter of her apartment; the gleaming view compensated for the one bedroom. Mostly, she could see clouds, moving lazily up and down the East River. On perfect days, she saw only sky, broken up by the occasional swoop of a bird or a plane heading out over the island.

Sylvia must have been biting her lip, because Angela asked if it was tasty.

"I wonder what's up with his album," Angela said, sliding onto the couch until they touched. "Word is, it's out of hand . . . he's wasting cash recording things twenty times." She told Sylvia she thought Miranda had "fire," but she was going to "burn it right up her nose." Angela's own project was "stalled" in London, so she was here on a break.

Elbows linked, Sylvia and Angela ditched the party and walked up a windswept side street over to Broadway. Angela dished more: Judie had called her the night before, crying softly, saying Leon sensed it. "Are you and Dad going to get divorced?" he had asked matter-of-factly. Three kids in his class had parents getting divorced.

Sylvia pictured his round face, thick bangs, and big Zingerman eyes, Judie's shape but Sylvia's color, filled with frightened tears. She took out a baggie of pot to roll a joint on the corner, willing her hands not to stiffen while making the old motions. She had sworn off drugs recently, but pot wasn't a drug.

Angela took the task from her halfway through, folding and licking the thing and helping herself to the first puff. They polished off the j before going into the bar, shoving through the college kids. Miranda and Dave had curled up on a hard wooden booth, looking as much like father and daughter as lovers, four or five people crowded around them, and a small city of empty glasses across the table. Seeing them, Miranda pooled her tiny body far into a corner.

"He's someone's husband," Sylvia told her, trying to sound like silver-tipped daggers.

"He's not her property," Miranda said, venom in her voice. Then she simpered. "You know what's funny? Your sister is an Aquarius and David is a *Virgo*! Terrible combination." She began laughing until she coughed. "How did they get so far? Now Eamon Foley, he's a better match for her—oh yes, I heard all about *that*."

The men at the studio had said Judie should slap this girl. They had a point.

Miranda yawned. "He says Judie has given up and stopped singing, and the kids latched on to her tits so long it ruined her figure and possibly her brain." Her words were thick, her dry tongue talking on and on. Dave, not hearing them, was holding court with Angela and a few others: "... backstage at the Rolling Thunder tour ..." Gossip. *Old* gossip.

"It's *funny* you're here," Miranda continued, her thin fingers on Sylvia's forearm. "I bought my first guitar after I heard *Singer Sisters II.* . . . You and Judie inspired me when I was a teeny thing, and now I am making music with Dave while Judie raises his kids. It's *funny*."

"*Kurveh*," Sylvia said in Yiddish, making a hissing sound like her grandma did. She yanked Dave off the bench and clamped on so tight she pinched his arm. She dragged him to the area by the restrooms, hearing, "Ooh, Davey, you're in trouble," echo behind then.

"David Cantor, you'd better watch out!" Sylvia said to him. "Fooling around with groupies is one thing, but this—"

He surprised her by throwing his arm around her and resting his head on her shoulder. "You're too late," he said. "Judie knows."

He began to cry, not tears but dry hiccups. Sylvia patted his neck. "She ... she kicked me out of the house *yesterday*, Sylvia. I miss my kids already."

"Oh," Sylvia said. What had happened after Judie called Angela?

"Miranda will ditch me if I give in to Judie," he replied. "And I need Miranda's songs, Syl, or I'll lose my way again. Want a drink? I'm closing this place down like I used to before I dropped out of school."

Sylvia wished he were stronger, and Judie, too.

~

Papa was right about him," said Judie in her living room the next day, as the whole sordid spiel tumbled out. The kids watched cartoons; Sylvia sat cross-legged on the floor, and Judie lay on the couch with her feet up, complaining of a pain flare-up.

Miranda was an evil bitch, Sylvia assured her, neither sexy nor talented. But she fretted; the evil bitch's words about Judie *giving up* had a ring of truth. Sylvia had been pissed at Judie, too; Sylvia had left Judie, too.

"I'm not telling you what to do, but maybe it would help to go out in the world more?" Sylvia asked.

"You don't see," Judie said. "I thought an artist's life would elevate me. It didn't."

"You're happier this way?"

"No, but up until Dave got ideas, I wasn't *unhappy*. I was floating along."

She sounded miserable. Sylvia assured her this was a phase. She believed it. After all, she had returned to sit at Judie's feet, literally. Still, her sister looked tired. Not dissipated like a few years ago; not tragic like the sixties. Tired.

"Before Dave left, I couldn't rest," Judie said. "I'll be able to, if he takes the kids on weekends."

"He won't until he sobers up." Sylvia tried again. "Fine, no parties, but maybe by being a partner to him, music-wise, you could fix things? She's no Yoko. He misses you."

Judie picked up a photo off the shelf, of her and Dave with their wedding rings glinting, and turned it on its side.

"Darling, Dave was never my partner that way," she said. "*You* were."

A bang and a crash emanated from the TV behind the kitchen, then a long meow. The kids cackled wildly. Sylvia strode up to the shelf so Judie wouldn't see her face, poured a sherry from Dave's decanter, turned the picture back up, facing out. She raised a glass to the heartbreak she shared with Dave and downed the booze.

"Well, look at us now," Sylvia said. "You never even told me whether you liked my album."

"Oh, Sylvia," Judie said, coming up behind her and pushing the picture back down again. "I couldn't listen to it more than once through before the memories obliterated me."

At least she listened, once.

~

It wasn't their year. Within two weeks, Anna called, telling Sylvia that Hyman was sick. Cancer. The sisters switched off visiting Boston—the hospital, the house. Weeks passed; the view from Sylvia's window grew too bright, and she had to close her curtains. The kids spent hours under the sprinklers in the park. Sylvia watched them so Judie could rest; she slept best knowing someone had eyes on the kids.

Dave moved out of Miranda's and into a producer's "coke and whiskey" pad on Thirty-Fifth Street. Hyman took a turn for the worse. It might be months, the doctors said, but there wasn't more to do. Sylvia planned to move to Boston, but before she did, she called Angela.

At the Subway Inn, Angela slid in beside her, and Sylvia smelled patchouli and Chanel and felt safe. Angela put an arm around her even though they'd met a mere handful of times. A gesture for Hyman. The feeling reminded her of being a girl in Boston, stupid and small, walking into the front door after a snowball fight, smelling popcorn on the stove.

It ambushed her, the feeling. Judie had withheld important information about Angela, she felt in her marrow. Angela loved women.

"Are you . . . ?"

"An Aquarius like Judie," said Angela, pointing to her amethyst geode charm. "*February* Aquarius. Hence, my tardiness."

They ordered beers. Angela tapped the table with two forefingers, drumming a beat. "I know you, Sylvia," she said. "My new guru believes in auras, and yours is on a different spectrum from Judie's."

Sylvia didn't blink. Everyone had a spiritual path these days: a few years back, Dave discovered Buddhism while Sylvia tried Freudian analysis. Yet the way Judie talked about "Angie"—being clued in to the art scene, nosing out new acts, and critical of the music industry. Not a guru-following lesbian.

"Do you believe? Higher power?" Angela asked. "I shook the doctrine of my youth, but not the spirit. Your sister's a skeptic." Sylvia blushed into her beer.

The answer, she admitted, was *yes*. She didn't know how to describe it except to say that she pictured a hand, a silvery Torah pointer, on her shoulder. She tried to explain to Angela, who listened with vigor. She wanted to know more about the Torah pointer, and the Torah itself.

"My dad is dying," Sylvia said. "My sister's a mess. I want to go back to my own, stupid, queer life. I want the road, which *is* my real life."

Angela's eyes shone. "My life is waiting for me, too. After I make my album."

She put her hands on Sylvia's forearms and they agreed to try an affirmation she'd just learned.

"Breathing in, I hear your suffering," Angela said, looking at the bottles behind the bar. "Breathing out, I offer you my assistance."

"Um, thanks?" Sylvia said.

Then Angela started laughing and laughing.

"I can't pretend it doesn't sound dumb as bricks," she said. "Damn."

She took a long, long swig of beer while Sylvia coughed some beer down her own throat and tried to regain composure.

"Breathing in," Angela said, "I am ready to murder Miranda Steel. Breathing out, I want to move to the beach and give up."

They clinked glasses. Sylvia noticed a small series of scars resting in a row on Angela's forearm—circular burn marks—and wanted to kiss them.

Instead, she suggested dinner, and they went to the Silver Star diner and ordered cottage cheese and grapefruit, for their figures. Then they shared a side order of fries and a cream soda, anyway.

Their tête-à-tête continued. By some miracle, Dave's delayed, overbudget, and troubled double album, *Violets on My Mind*, had come out in September. One or two critics called it a baroque masterpiece, but the majority said Dave had morphed into a pompous soft-rock has-been. *Violets* sold, but not enough to justify the expense of making it. Dave needed a world tour to make the dough back.

Sylvia had kept tabs on him, swinging by the producer's place, asking friends for tidbits. Dave was hanging out with people whose lives were marked by the rhythm of the next party, the next hit. But he visited Emma and Leon on Sundays. He was late sometimes, but he came, and Judie said they each grabbed a leg and wrestled, and he kissed them and they squealed.

Over their fries, Sylvia and Angela moved on to their own music. Sylvia said her album had been *good*, but without a tour it hadn't outsold *Sylvia Sings the Sixties* and she was itching to go out and play. In turn, Angela lamented a song she'd recorded in the UK that had gotten tied up in a legal battle between two labels.

She finished the fries. "I'm sorry your family is going through this, but it's nice to have a friend in this world," said Angela.

"Yes," Sylvia said. "Let's do this again. When I come back from Boston."

~

I think I'm going to divorce Dave," Judie told their father on her last visit in the heat of August. Sylvia sat up with a start.

"*Ach*. Wait for him to come home—he will," Hyman said. "You'll never find another man."

"I'd like to start a new chapter," Judie said.

"Then get a good lawyer," he continued. "Want me to call around?"

And then, his tired eyes more piercing than they'd been in weeks, he said, "Wait until Emma grows up and leaves the house."

"She's a baby!" Judie cried.

"You can wait," he said.

After he died, they sat shiva and cried, and helped Anna pack up his belongings. Judie enrolled Emma in nursery school and Leon in music lessons. The kids got strep, the flu, ear infections, lice, and chicken pox in one winter.

Dave showed up at the funeral, then went incommunicado. Emma's questions about him got more urgent as Judie's lies expanded: he was on tour and called only after their bedtimes. Angela and Sylvia kept up their spying, gathering of gossip, talking on the phone, meeting for a drink, not telling Judie.

~

Sylvia knew she had fallen for Angela when Angie announced she was off for California to record a solo album, for real this time, while smoking outside a bar on the East Side. Exultant was Angela, back on the idea of covering the Singer Sisters, of hiring male rockers she'd backed to lay down a single guitar solo, then ushering them out. She must have seen Sylvia's face turn to ash when she described her plan, how once she toured, she would leave the "United States of Bullshit" forever.

"Hey," she said. "I owe this journey to myself, Sylvia. But I *will* be in touch. I want to record 'Window Tree' on this."

"What about your guru?" Sylvia asked. Angela dropped him months before, after he made a pass at her.

"I don't owe him *shit*," Angela said, and they shrieked with laughter.

Sylvia surprised herself by leaning forward and kissing Angela on the mouth. Angela put her hand behind Sylvia's head and kissed back, hard, before turning toward home, and as Sylvia made her way back up First Avenue against the strong river winds, she fought back the thoughts that she'd promised herself she would never have: of reading magazines, feet up, with someone at home, but of taking planes with that someone, too, when the mood struck.

Angela called the same evening, and Sylvia answered in a buttery purr, but she had news, not endearments.

"Sylvia, babe," she said. "Miranda Steel followed the bassist in Steve Winwood's band to Australia. She left Dave. He'll be at your sister's door in no time. And you—you can be done with babysitting and spying—you can go on the road, which is where you belong, and find me out there."

"A *bassist*?"

"You know they have good hands, my love."

My love. Sylvia went to the bathroom and stripped. Would she have the courage to go find Angela again? She let the shower flow over her back and murmured wordless things. She was supposed to be saying thank you for Dave's return, but it sounded like kaddish.

EMMA

In the attic of the apartment Emma and Mae rented in Inman Square, a hexagonal window peered out onto the avenue. Following Dave Cantor's advice, they dragged a beanbag chair up the stairs and settled it below the window to make what they called "Creativity Corner," where Emma did her best to meet the demands of her label overlords.

With Judie incommunicado, Emma had pestered Dave while finishing the album. "They want me to write one more song a certain way," she said. He told her to "create a hallowed space" and "let the memories in."

Emma had spent a week alone with Dave only once, when her mother went to Ireland—a trip whose meaning she now understood. Her understanding rendered the memories bittersweet but didn't eliminate the joy: an adventure to Central Park, where Dave tried flying a kite and it fell, *whomp*, in the grass. A walk to Zabar's, where she picked out pickles to eat on the way home. That night, Emma toted Leon's guitar to the den and said, "Daddy, I can play a C and D chord, but could you show me the others?"

He whistled. "You're one of us, kiddo," he said. And their lessons started. By the time her mom was at the airport coming home, she'd mastered four more chords. Her fingers hurt.

～

Creativity Corner bore witness to late-night songwriting sessions, jams, and a few bitter vigils. Emma did what she needed to do, recording a song she'd scribbled with help from Mae called "Childhood"—exactly as requested of her: angry, but vulnerable.

> *I look outside the cradle, I look underneath the bed*
> *I crawl behind the table, I slip inside my head*
> *Mother where are you*
> *Mother where are you*
> *I crept into the closet, I climbed into the attic*
> *I don't know how to stop this train, I think I'm gonna panic*
> *Mother where are you, Mother where are you*
> *They told me you were frightened, they told me you were wild*
> *They said to get enlightened, but I was just a child*

"Childhood" was derivative—John Lennon, meet Tori Amos—but the label *adored* it to round out the album and congratulated Emma for rising to the moment. It wasn't *total* bullshit. The song tried to fill the place in Emma's insides drained by her fight with Judie, as their feud stretched out for weeks. Emma had become like a balloon she and Dave had let go in Central Park that week, floating skyward—but unmoored.

No longer relegated to the bus, she took the Amtrak home when the sessions wrapped. Flat gray light danced on Long Island Sound through the train window, a backdrop for the last burst of silent anonymity she might know for a long time.

Her time in New York, her window to see Judie and patch things up, was cut off by success. In fact, a reporter called about her album while she was already packing for Los Angeles to shoot her lead music video. This guy, from *Billboard*, couldn't stop bloviating about "Childhood." "It's like Jakob Dylan writing 'Fuck My Dad,'" he said.

"Are you comparing my mom's songwriting to Bob Dylan's?" Emma teased. "It's a *song*," she added, ignoring a clammy wave of shame.

Meanwhile, she hammered out instant messages to Leon.

How's Mom? she asked.

Okay, he said. And then sent her about a million ellipses.

> What r u not telling me?
> Rose's baby, Dolores.

She's v v cute.

Would u hate me if I visited while ur in LA?

Nah, she typed. She left the computer and flopped on the sheets, trying not to get nauseated by the image of her family gathered around saintly Rose, baby in her arms.

"I've been replaced by Rose," she typed to Leon ten minutes later.

He signed off.

～

When Emma was younger, Aunt Sylvia would take her to Rumpelmayer's tearoom for a taste of the good life and some advice about her mother. She ordered a hot chocolate for Emma and a hot chocolate with peppermint schnapps for herself, an "off menu" item. The waiters knew.

Emma didn't understand all of what her aunt tried to tell her at these occasions, like the time she cleared her throat as soon as they ordered and told her about Leon being a boy who liked boys and herself being a woman who preferred women.

"Men are convenient; they're *around* and susceptible to flattery," was the kind of wisdom she relayed as she took Emma's hands and was kind enough not to mention their clamminess. Emma studied her aunt's mascara-fringed lashes, the small but not insignificant set of wrinkles gathered around her gray eyes. "Look after Leon. Take what you want and don't make a big stink with your mom. An argument needn't be a final stand. Judie never learned."

A waiter arrived and topped off Sylvia's schnapps. "I wish I could take you around the world, but Judie would never give you up," she said.

"She doesn't care where I go." Emma must have been ten by then. "She prefers Leon."

"No, her love just looks different for him."

Sylvia got up to go to the bathroom, and without missing a beat, Emma reached over, grabbed her cup, and took a hearty sip. It tasted minty and slightly tangy.

Leon liked to play dress-up as much as Emma did. They used both their mother's and their father's clothes—cowboy boots, capes, hats. They raided a stash of old shirts with bell sleeves and lace trim that fell to their thighs, ran around in the finery, and ripped it. No one got upset.

"Do you want something else delicious and decadent?" asked her aunt upon returning, and Emma gave a hungry assent before Sylvia signaled the waiter over. They ordered a sponge layer cake, one big wedge for the two of them, and parceled it out with tiny silver forks. Each bite of the soft cake caressed Emma's mouth. A secret, schnappsy satisfaction set in.

She couldn't wait to grow up.

Later that night, Sylvia and Judie were having a drink and Emma sat at the doorway, listening intently.

"I told her about people who love people of the same sex," said Sylvia.

Judie sniffed. "That *again*."

Had their lunch at Rumpelmayer's been for Emma's sake or because Sylvia needed someone to listen? She'd tiptoed across the hall to Leon's room—locked, music blaring—and jiggled the knob. He opened the door, his fawn-like eyes tired but awake, and she begged him to let her play. Music was far less perplexing than life.

~

This fact remained true now. Discussing her album, she kept her tone even, her gaze forthright—she'd earned a reputation as drama-free "talent." But when she thought about her family, everything mushed up inside her and she craved distraction and noise. She spent her final nights in New York at lounges in the East Village. Whether she was gossiping with old school friends or with new music-world friends, the atmosphere stayed the same. Glow sticks and smoke moved in the dark, while everyone huddled together, angling for something.

One night, her new agent took her up to a huge restaurant in Gramercy, with floor-to-ceiling windows, and ordered a bottle of champagne.

"Kids of rock stars are having a moment," the woman said. "Just ask Bitsy Calhoun over there." She pointed to a blond girl who resembled a praying mantis, in a lacy black bra and leather pants. "She's been hooking up with . . ." The noise engulfed her, and Emma never knew whether Sean Lennon, Harper Simon, or someone else had received the lady's attentions.

As the night spooled on, Bitsy climbed into their booth. Emma and a producer who had also been at Windermere were playing a vigorous game of Which Windermere Alums Work in Music Now?

Bitsy broke in.

"Wait, your dad is Dave Canticle, but you went to *one* school, like, K through twelfth?"

Emma nodded.

"Your mom *works there* now?"

Emma squeaked out a "yes."

"How *unbearably* wholesome." Bitsy blew smoke above her head. Emma sighed. What she dubbed the Jewel problem had arisen again. If she wanted, Emma could whip out her credentials for the basket-case club: she was currently estranged from Judie due to poaching songs about Judie's secret pregnancy, and her father's musical tutelage had come on the heels of the Miranda Steel affair.

She pretended to be bored.

"Did you do, like, a summer of rehab?" the girl asked, again, perplexed.

"Nope."

"A year in Switzerland?"

"No."

"Jesus. How provincial."

"Okay, *Bitsy*. My family is a mess like all the others," Emma said, feeling like every word betrayed Judie, who deserved reproach but not from *Bitsy*. "Purchase my forthcoming CD to find out about it."

Bitsy's glassy eyes registered appreciation.

"Feisty," she said. "There's something you're hiding, though. Oh, hold on, I have to give that dude something special in the bathroom."

She twirled off.

"Who *was* that?" asked Emma. "What just happened?"

"Get used to it," said the agent, draining her glass. "You're going to LA."

~

"When Mom comes home from Ireland," Dave said one afternoon on that stolen week years ago, holding Emma's sore fingers, "let's be kind. An old friend of hers is dying." He had just taught her "This Land Is Your Land," her first full song on guitar.

"What happens when you die?"

Dave began to sing. "When I die . . . and I lay me to rest . . . I'm gonna go to the place that's the best. . . ." He kept singing: "Gonna lift me up to that spirit in the sky!"

After he started in on the Jesus part, Emma tugged his sleeves. "Daddy, stop! We're Jewish!"

"So was the guy who wrote that song, actually," he said through laughter.

She knew now, as she hadn't then, about her father's cheating and boozing and long tours leaving her mother stuck with the kids. But he had led Emma to her music, and look at where it got her: champagne, and ditzy blondes named Bitsy, and soon Los Angeles and MTV, and then what?

She had never really pondered what came next. She guessed it was whatever the fuck she wanted.

PART III

PART III

JUDIE

Leon at nine was perfect: a curious, creative, and odd child whose battery of questions and jokes kept Judie occupied throughout the flight. Then they slept for two hours, he on her shoulder, her head against the closed window. Toward morning, she opened the shade and looked down at the black waves. Pink clouds veiled Ireland, which appeared, through their lace, like a patch of moss in the water. A rare song was coming to her: Your green shores? Too cliché. Your green hills—no. Your green walls.

"Let's try to write a song called 'Green Walls,'" she said as the lights went on for the plane to land. Leon handed her some Wrigley's.

"Green walls keep growing," he sang.

They chewed. She hummed along, added a line. "They cast a shadow over me."

They drank Evian at the airport and again in the hotel lobby, which had an air of shabby grandeur. They ate shortbread cookies in plastic wrap.

"I'm afraid we have to pay this visit to Mommy's old friend," she said, ruffling his hair. "You know, darling, it's going to be sad, like with Grandpa Hyman. . . ."

"Will there be bagels and lox?" he asked, clearly recalling sitting shiva.

"They probably do scones here, not bagels."

On the phone, Sean, Eamon's brother-in-law, suggested that Judie be introduced as an "old friend of the family"—a signal that no secrets were to be revealed. She wasn't sure how soon, if at all, she'd meet Eamon's sister, or Rose, but they *would* be around.

Sure enough, the instant she walked into the hospital visitors' room at the appointed hour, she came across her counterpart, Mary. She knew Mary had seen her—her breath whooshed in—but Judie couldn't look her in the eye.

She thrust Leon in front of her, a shield: "Hello. This is Leon," she said. "My son. My daughter is home. With my husband. Who . . . I married."

⁓

After Miranda, their marriage held. For weeks after he begged her to take him back, Judie held Dave in bed and massaged his shoulders and let him rub her feet, too, and made endless glasses of seltzer and lemon, to help with his detox.

They laughed at Emma as she tramped around, exulted at Leon's musical abilities, and agreed that his talent might shield him from the pain of being teased for his eccentricities.

They ordered Chinese food and ate it in the kitchen at two a.m., standing in their underwear with chopsticks, two tree branches that were still entwined. They squabbled because Dave's whims were still the ruling order of the household: because it just so happened they made love when he wanted to, and he attended to the kids when he wanted to—which was fine, yes, but still—and he rested when he wanted to, and with gravel in his voice he said, "I don't deserve you," whenever Judie got frustrated with him, and she gave in.

They cared for each other—and on one level Dave was forgiven, as though a year of semi-estrangement was the equivalent of a smear of lipstick or whiff of perfume.

She let him come back because she had hated asking him a question early in the morning, half-asleep—reaching for him in bed and finding only pillows. But mostly she let him come back because of Emma, asking which month her father would "come back" from his tour and looking at her mother with fury, as though she were hiding Dave.

Emma deserved Dave. Still, someday she'd live for herself.

In the mornings, setting out school lunch (that she bought at the deli) and chasing Emma, who had hidden in her room and declared *no way was she going to school*, Judie imagined her life as a march through a battlefield, dodging cannon fire with Dave, for better or worse, her comrade.

⁓

Y ou married your own husband? Generally, that's how it works," said the
stocky man huddled with Mary in the waiting room. Laughing at his
joke made Judie feel twenty years younger, but not in a carefree way, in an
out-of-her-depth way.

"I'm Sean," he said. "We spoke. I'm, erm, Rose's—Eamon's brother-in-
law. He's in a bad way and asked particularly for you—as I said."

He lowered his voice so Leon wouldn't hear. "Wants to make amends or
settle things. It's been concerning him."

"I'm here." Her fingers trembled.

"Mom!" Leon called. "Can I break into my comic stash now? You promised."

"May we speak privately?" asked Mary. She ushered Judie over to a corner
while Sean set Leon up on a chair to read his stack of *X-Men*.

"The girl shouldna know more than she needs," said Mary. "She's had a
bad year. Eamon seemed to want it aired out, but this is an impressionable
girl . . . with a tendency to get too deep. We can fulfill a dying wish for himself, but shield her."

"You're her mother," said Judie firmly, proud of herself for being so firm.
"You set the rules. . . ." She paused. Rose was eighteen, wasn't she? Mary
talked about her like she was twelve.

"You okay, Mom?" called Leon across the room, his voice uncertain. Her
observant child.

"Have you had Irish candy?" Sean asked. He produced a barley-sugar
cone, and Leon took it greedily, and the room settled to the sound of his
crunching and page turning.

Judie questioned why Eamon, with what must be some wealth, had come
to this putrid green hospital—but it turned out he'd taken a religious turn
and donated almost all his money to an orphanage in Africa. The rest, Mary
said, was for Rose.

He'd also become reattached to Dublin—even as half the country emi-
grated out—and lived a (somewhat) monastic life in a refurbished Georgian
house. When he fell ill, no one had known at first, and then he had grown
too sick to be moved.

"We'll be taking him home, after this last treatment," said Mary. Her hair
was the color of a broom and she wore a gray dress and a soft blue jacket,
not dowdy, but simple. Her face was a rounder version of Eamon's, with a

straighter nose. She might have been gorgeous, at least striking, with a fringe of hair across her forehead and some lipstick.

"We bought a hospital bed and hired a nurse. They say it's a matter of weeks," said Sean.

Mary kissed a small cross on her neck.

"Eamon told me you *weren't* religious," Judie found herself saying, her tone sharper than intended.

"I was positively heathen when I was younger," said Mary with a smile. "But like Eamon, I've come back to the old ways. We were brought up in the church, you know."

"I don't know many details about you," said Judie—not that she hadn't wondered and guessed. Mary's downcast eyes made Judie ashamed of her caustic tone. She changed tacks. "But the call of childhood traditions strengthens once you have children—I mean, once you're further on in life. I take my kids home for the holidays now . . . to my mom's. My dad died last year. . . ." She paused. Every mention of her kids hurt. "Sorry to be nattering on."

She admonished Leon not to put on an oxygen mask dangling from a nurse's cart.

Mary's face continued to contort, and Judie imagined her conflicting impulses: charity and protectiveness. "Ach, don't you want to know about Rose?" she blurted out, as though it had been inside her the whole time.

Judie mouthed it: "Yes."

"She's a bright girl, does all her schoolwork, but trouble-prone like her uncle—her—like Eamon. Obsessed with the hunger strikers in the North, thinks she's a revolutionary, gives her food away to street children," she said.

"I blame ourselves for taking her to those marches," said Sean.

"You took her to marches?" asked Judie.

"Civil rights demonstrations, before it got violent."

"So you're political?" Judie asked, embarrassed to not be more aware. The words and phrases were familiar, sure: hunger strikers and violence in places called Belfast and Derry, but in a glancing way. She rarely read the paper now. It made her too depressed.

"Not particularly," said Mary as Sean said, "Yes, in a way," and they chuckled.

"Rose fancies herself a radical . . . and she's secretive with Barry, her lad. . . ." Mary sounded pleading. Judie batted around the words—a radical? a lad? She cleared her throat.

"He requested to see you the moment you came," said Mary.

Judie wanted to hug Mary, to thank her—to apologize for showing up, and to shake her all at once. Eamon was right, at least, in this: his sister had a fundamental kindness. She had begun stiff, but she almost couldn't help herself in reaching out to Judie.

"Thank you . . . I can't even begin."

"I'm thankful he didn't go at the end of a needle in some godforsaken place," said Mary.

Judie needed to sit, but there was nowhere to do so. "I didn't realize it got that bad," she said.

Mary blew air out through her lips. "Go on, now."

Judie's pace down the hall was glacial, with Leon staying behind and reading his third comic book. She rounded a corner to the farthest, presumably biggest room.

She had prepared herself—but still it winded her to see Eamon half his old size. To her he was a strapping giant with a direct glance that had made her quiver. And when she'd seen him across the stage at festivals over the years, exchanging a nod, a grim smile, or in the final days a clipped greeting—his height rendered him painfully impossible to ignore.

He seemed frail and childlike now, there in the bed, propped up on about thirty pillows with a soft, blue-gray knit blanket across his knees—like the baby blankets she'd used for her kids. He lifted his drooping head and offered her a wicked grin.

"Herself, in the flesh," he said. "I should die more often."

She had heard he was sick a mere week ago. The day started out fine; the kids were dropped off at school, safe. Judie boarded the subway and contemplated the free hours ahead. How happy she'd felt that morning—basking in sunny September, its burning light with an undercurrent of delicious chill, and the kids in matching moods. They'd dressed without rancor. Leon had held Emma's hand crossing the street and spent the walk whispering to her.

Late-season flowers on the corner drew their notice; a monarch butterfly alighted on one, a pink chrysanthemum, and fluttered. With faces like toddlers, they had watched him, and as Emma leaned on Leon, Judie had felt a coal light inside her. She burned to write in the notebook that contained her tunes for the kids: the "Zippy Zoo, Tie My Shoe" song, "Saucy Cat" for Emma, and "Silver Spoon Moon" and "Wee Lion, Roar" for Leon. The songs could be made sophisticated. The thing to do was to flesh out the pieces: add bridges, choruses, verses.

Lunches were duly deposited in each kid's hand, goodbyes were said. Leaving, she'd been waylaid by Timothy Bucknell's mom, who wanted to know where Leon got his hair cut and whether Judie ever thought of doing Jane Fonda's workout, and Judie yakked back at her, all pleasant enough. But as they talked, the golden moment ebbed.

She had wanted to write something about the butterflies, with a line in mind, but by the time she left, it had flown away, so she got on the subway up to Sylvia's place. She settled back in the hard subway seat and breathed out of her lips like Dave had been teaching her recently.

"Slow down, heart," she whispered, thinking of a mantra. It sounded like a song title. Because that was what these feelings and rumblings were. They were songs that didn't have anywhere to go, so they rattled around inside her.

Sylvia was out, so Judie turned around and went home, too tired to write but still hoping to squeeze something into the notebook. Breezing in, she saw Dave sitting there, a glass of wine on the table in front of him.

"Davey, no!" she cried, grabbing it away. "It's too early."

He looked up at her with red-rimmed eyes.

"It's just wine," he said.

She rushed to him, knelt beside him, took his hands.

"Eamon Foley is dying—lung cancer. He . . . wants to see you before he goes."

~

Are you here to learn how to slough off this mortal coil?" Eamon's grin— with its eternally louche suggestiveness—revived Judie. Her wariness fell away.

"You certainly taught me *some* things," Judie said.

"Little Judie, all the way across the sea," he said. A cough or two followed this sentence, then a shake of the head, but he seemed gratified when Judie let out a hearty laugh.

"Where can I get a cup of coffee around here, anyway?" she asked.

"I wouldn't get coffee anywhere in this dirty old town, love," Eamon said. "But try the tea, it'll straighten your spine."

"Is it true you've gone pious?" Judie asked. She perched on the side of his bed and let the questions flow out with something girlish emerging from inside her. "I thought your temple was more flesh oriented—plus all that Eastern stuff in the seventies. Dave's into that now."

"I haven't embraced the teachings of the bitch nuns from school," he said with effort. She propped him up as he continued: "If that's what you mean. Sorry for my language."

"Apologizing for salty language doesn't sound like the Eamon Foley I know."

"All right, you. Yes, I've grown, spiritual, you might say. 'All the Eastern stuff' too as you call it. Don't tell my sister but I've got a small Buddha stashed behind the pillow, to balance out the cross. But never mind. I wanted to give *you* something."

"So you summoned me / Across the sea," she sang, quoting his song "Garden Bloom."

"I did," he said slowly. "Because I wanted to say this. . . ." He paused, a few more Dickensian coughs.

"Take your time."

He drew himself up.

"I'm sorry for what you went through because of me. And I'm—grieved you're not making music or writing—that's why I told you not to think of her that day at the festival, but I shouldna have said it. I wanted to tell you . . . you should get to know Rose—I've done so too late, but she's a rare one."

Judie's eyes flew open—her underarms began to seep with sweat, like they had when she'd been pregnant, all three times.

"She doesn't suspect the truth?" Judie wanted her daughter to know for selfish reasons, but a more altruistic side hoped Rose stayed in the dark.

"She guesses the truth about me. A suspicious sort," he said. "Reminds me of you."

"Do you know me well enough to say that?" she asked.

He turned his thin mouth upward. "See? *Suspicious.*"

Judie let her head hang low. "Do you still sing, Eamon, or are your lungs not able to?"

"It's taken that from me. I wanted to give you something. Bring your son in?"

She poked her head into the hallway and called for Leon, who arrived with comic books in hand, and she found herself steering him in by the shoulders as her father had steered her onstage. Eamon summoned her and Leon forward and put his hand on each of their heads, arranged his fingers so they were spread apart like Mr. Spock's on *Star Trek*.

"Listen to this," he said. *"Yevarechecha Adonai, V'Yishmerecha."* That's a Hebrew blessing, a priestly blessing, I learned it from a friend of mine. A rabbi, in Dublin. It's for you, and your family, from me."

"You're acting far too beatific right now. I *am* suspicious."

"A deathbed will do that to you. That, and pissing into a tube."

She gave him a chiding look. A marvelous fact: they'd passed less than three full days in each other's company, out of their entire lives. She didn't know him and she never would, but they'd been together at a conception, a birth, and now a deathbed. She inhaled slowly through her nose, like Dave told her to: she was in Eamon's inner circle, his Holy of Holies, as her father put it.

It wasn't comfortable, to share this sacred space with Eamon, but something numinous dwelt there. Not love, exactly, but she would find the right word in time.

"You can't have only wanted to *bless* me," she said.

He coughed until Judie stood up to get a nurse, but he put his palm out.

"No," he said. "One of these days I'll cough myself right out of this life, but not yet."

"Leon, can you go find some juice or something? Ask one of the nurses."

Leon left, and Eamon pulled her hand toward his.

"Why?" he asked. "Why did you stop doing music?"

She bowed her head, lowered her shoulders, deflected him. "Oh, I don't know. I wish I still had it in me."

"Wasn't that the point of this?" he asked with tears in his eyes. "This scheme with Rose? So you could *sing*?"

Judie lifted her head an inch or two. "I don't know how to answer," she said. "I made records, you know, for years. But life has gotten in my way . . . two kids, a family, sick parents . . ." She trailed off. "Anyway, you wanted a life, too."

His eyebrows drew close toward each other, and her throat caught. He was going to revoke his blessing, or curse her.

"And I had one. Ahh, it was a sin," he said, but without anger in his voice.

"A sin. But, Judie, you know, I still think—" He held her gaze for ten, twenty, thirty seconds. And then he drooped forward, eyes closed, voice stilled. She brought her chair closer, took a bold hand to his chin, moved his head back. He breathed, ragged and slow.

"What—*what* was a sin?" she asked. "What were you going to say?" No response. Leon tiptoed back with a plastic cup of juice, disappointed that Eamon was asleep.

"Can we go now, Mom?" he said, his eyes catlike and dilated. "I've had enough."

Leon's long lashes, beautiful like Dave's, fluttered on his cheeks, unmarred by puberty. She'd shown him something dark here, and she ought to protect him, take him for an ice cream.

"Okay," she said, gathering herself slowly, still hoping for Eamon to respond.

As they exited, a young woman breezed into the room. She wore a soft beige scarf and had the shortest, curliest ash-blond hair Judie had ever seen, like a man's. Her complexion was fair, with rosy cheeks that immediately suggested her name—and the boxy brown sweater and man's pants she wore couldn't hide her beauty.

Her features mimicked Eamon and his sister except for the eyes, because where one expected blue, one saw charcoal-brown depths.

The family eyes. Judie's own eyes.

Surely Judie wouldn't survive the moment—the monitors in the entire hospital would start going haywire, beeping and beeping, as her vital signs spun out of orbit, her breath stopped, her body broke down.

The air stilled. Rose lined up bottles in a row. Judie ought to leave. She ought to go.

"Were you leaving?" said Rose, still not looking at Judie, but taking Eamon's hand and massaging it with her own. "We have so many people going in and out, I can't keep track."

Eamon coughed and then snored. Rose made a humming noise.

"Is it normal for him to stop talking midsentence?" asked Judie.

"He drops off, yeah—morphine."

"I didn't get to hear the end of his thought," said Judie, sounding whiny, like Emma back home complaining about a bottle of juice.

She clung to the doorway, drank in the girl puttering around the room, tucking in the sheet corners, and clearing clutter off the table. She had the posture of the industrious and headstrong, but her reluctance to make eye contact suggested slyness, maybe the kind of young person who would leave home at a moment's notice, like her own mother once had. Judie drank it in. She turned to go, again, then stayed.

"I hope he sleeps long," Rose said, looking up at last, speaking in the beautiful, mellifluous accent of her country. "I'm due at a meeting. Then I'll drop back—he likes a midnight visit."

Judie stayed.

"You're . . . from America, Mum said?" Rose asked.

Judie's old muzzle returned: she found herself blinking, mute. At last, in response to Rose's quizzical stare, she explained her plans in a hoarse voice: they would be going back to their hotel soon and flying to London the next day, where they would meet Anna, who had been in Israel for a month, and all fly back together.

"Hey," said Leon, coming back down the hall. "Can we go rest?"

Judie turned to Rose, hoping to make a profound maternal statement without coming off as odd or spilling any beans. "I'm glad to meet you, circumstances aside," she settled on. "You're so attentive to your . . . towards Eamon."

"We got thick when he came back for keeps," said Rose. "He's a good sort."

"So long, farewell, auf Wiedersehen, good night," said Leon seriously, and Rose laughed.

"I like you," she said. "Adieu to you too. And you, and you."

Leon led the way out, but Judie clutched the doorframe, drinking them in, her might-have-been family, hoping Eamon's eyes would pop open and he'd say, *What I meant was . . . it was a sin to . . .*

But Rose's back accused her, and Eamon's lids, almost purple, stayed shut.

ROSE

Rose saw through them all, the song and dance about old friends, the whispery greetings and headshakes. She'd figured it out years ago, when Eamon was off finding God in India and Mary was scared stiff that he'd never return so she took to praying again, down on her knees. Their flat was so small and her parents' conversations so heated—they drew her ears to the doorway like the pub drew men after church on Sunday afternoons.

"I wish he'd come home and be a father and brother," Mary would say.

"He's not her father—I am," said Sean. That made Rose take notice.

Another time, Sean asked if Eamon knew that "the woman" had a family now? To which his wife snorted and replied: "Naturally, since the man wasn't Eamon."

Sitting on the floor and hearing their words was a divine epiphany. It explained the pitying looks she got at church or walking down the town— and on her birthday, as if a birthday were a thing to mourn—and above all a sense of herself as a round peg in a square hole, as Mary sometimes put it.

She was Eamon's cast-off daughter. Abandoned by her mother. She'd cried bitterly, had rages where she threw her old dolls across the room (she was getting on in age, they were easy targets). But she soldiered on, and when Eamon did come home and Mary called him "Uncle" with a lilt to her voice, Rose looked her right in the eye and said, "Yes, *Uncle*," and they let it rest there between them, both knowing and not-knowing together.

S tupid girl, she had been so far up her own arse when she bumped into Judith, with her father/uncle so rarely lucid—but later that night a jolt hit her while lying in bed next to her Barry, he of the sideburns and tremendous, crushing kisses.

"A friend dropped in—" she said as she told him about her day. "Or a relative? From New York. Staring like I was in the circus, wasn't she?" And then her entire body went stiff as a board, and she began to laugh hysterically.

"Oh Christ. Oh Christ."

"What is it?" asked Barry.

"Oh Christ. My mam. At the hospital."

"What did Mary do at the hospital?"

She paused. She hadn't told him. If you didn't give a boy your virginity, you didn't give him your secrets.

O nce she'd asked her schoolmate Sarah's mother, a notorious gossip, for the truth.

"Do you know about my real mam?"

Sarah humphed.

"Some girl your uncle met in the States, willing to give you to Mary straightaway, and that's what Eamon wanted, too."

At that point she had met Eamon a handful of times, and she remembered the thick red beard, the breath that smelled smoky, his beautiful voice.

"Eamon isn't my *real* da," said young Rose. "Just my *blood* da."

"Brazen thing to say," said Sarah's mother.

"Aren't your parents the ones who raise you and love you?" asked Rose. "I don't see why it matters who *made* you."

"It matters to God," said Sarah's mom, a statement that increased Rose's determination not to whinge about her origins.

A t Barry's, she put her clothes back on, stole a few cigarettes, and took one of her usual long strolls—perambulations, she called them—through the streets Leopold Bloom might have walked in *Ulysses*. This Judith had watched her like a detective as the numbers bleeped and burbled, and that boy with the comics stack she was mad to borrow but too proud to ask.

She found herself outside a pub as it let out; men loafed around, smoking and smelling sour. An opportunity presented. She would shout her secret, as it were, to the wind.

"I met my real mother today," she said to one fellow.

"Good for you, beautiful," she received back. It resembled the confession ritual, but no codger of a priest was judging you and no Hail Marys at all.

The men she chatted with outside of pubs had an unspoken code to not talk about any of the things that interested Rose the most: the situation up North, the one with women right here. Rose liked taboo subjects; why, she spent half her life running up and down stairs to meetings. Airing things out, that appealed to a girl whose life was a secret. And meetings, along with Barry, and caring for Eamon, and her schoolwork—it sufficed to keep her from wanting to fling herself down the well.

Rose wanted and wanted and wanted—the kind of body-wanting that came while fooling about with Barry, the wanting when she gave her food away to hungry children on the street but kept some back for herself. She wanted revolution, a place in history like Maud Gonne so that when she died the people would line the streets to salute her casket. She wanted travel, because while she was spinning dreams and desires, the rain on the harbor at Dún Laoghaire danced before her eyes, the bellowing horn of a boat pulling away and crossing the sea. She wanted the emotions she got when Barry played a new cassette tape and they listened, eyes closed, to the sounds of their desires made into poetry and song.

"Should I tell Judith I know who she is?" she asked the man, in exchange for a cigarette. "Why should I be the one to tell *her*? She might have come to see me before, if she knew I was here, so maybe she's hateful and cold. But what if they never told her either, I wouldn't put it past them to keep it *mum*. Pun intended. Should I hold it close, as I do with all this Eamon business? It's wearing me down, pretending he's my uncle."

"What, you must say *something*," said the man in the cap. "You do seem inclined to the talking."

"Thanks," she said. He was right, her stout-soaked oracle. She bade him farewell; now a light up ahead came from a scattershot assemblage of stars.

In the deep night and only then, Rose allowed herself to feel desolate, to send her tears for Eamon and for her own two-mothered, two-fathered self up to the heavens, as no one could hear her, and even God himself was too preoccupied with life-and-death matters to notice a girl weeping on the midnight streets.

At home Mary lay asleep with her head on the sofa, a book open beside her. Keeping watch—for Rose's arrival, or maybe for Eamon taking the turn that was coming as sure as tomorrow.

⁓

The next morning, Rose walked down O'Connell Street, entering the grand but dingy hotel lobby where Judith would come down. She sat and waited for the woman who had birthed her to step out of the splendid brass elevator, feeling more nervous than she had since the day she moved here from London, at age five. By then, loneliness was as much a part of her as the unruly curls that no one knew how to brush. (Nights she heard Mary sigh and say, "There isn't a comb in Ireland with the strength.") She had gotten teased: "Mick" and "Bog-Trotter" in London, "Coal-Eyes" and "Crumpet-Sucker" when she arrived in Dublin as a child.

For months in Dublin she resorted to using an old bent comb as a pretend phone and "talking" to her English classmates, or imagining that her shabby teddy bear could come alive. Eventually she found outsiders like her—Michael, who lived alone with his father as his mother worked in London; tiny Mira, whose mother was Indian and whose father was a doctor. They had in common being cherished at home but disliked at school. They played on the drab rugs of their apartments, did their homework, and once tried to run away to Glendalough because they heard a fairy there could grant wishes and they wanted Michael's mother to come home. It had seemed so important to Rose that they accomplish this task, and when they didn't even reach the end of Michael's road before getting caught, she sobbed and refused to eat her porridge, even when Mary put butter in it. It made for a rare occasion, as she loved to eat.

Time passed, and Michael's family returned to London, and Mira's to Dalkey, where Mira went to a new school. At twelve, alone again, Rose embarked on her long and virtually seamless series of be-all and end-all love affairs. Something about her—the striking combination of light hair and dark eyes, or the way she held her shoulders like a shield against the world, attracted and challenged men. And she, full of craving, invited them in.

Her first boyfriend, Liam, had been one of her primary school tormentors. Their relationship consisted of kissing, holding hands, and trading comics, until he went off to the big school and found a new girl there. Mary called Pat "the danger"—he was eighteen when Rose was fourteen and wanted her to run away with him to Belfast to fight the British. By then she hung about with radicals and punks and was running her mouth at the nuns. From Pat she learned nothing virtuous—cigarette smoking and everything about sex save the act itself.

He got her blaming the British, those "imperialist cocksuckers." Her heart was torn up by the hunger on the streets of Dublin and he left her with a rudimentary comprehension that a global system had been designed to hurt people from the top down. He taught her to listen to music beyond what was on the charts ("Disco is bull," though she loved to dance).

After his instructive year, Pat ran for the hills (he ended up as a barman in London) and Rose found Barry, sweet, loping, but surprisingly sharp Barry—Barry, who would have spent his entire life spread out on the floor listening to records and talking about the shows he would see someday when he had the cash, who despised injustice but also violence, who wept—only Rose knew—when his dog was hit by a truck on the Galway road.

Around the same time as she started seeing Barry, her "uncle" Eamon bought his mansion, and she began to want to go to America, a want that swallowed all others.

She had come up with an idea in the middle of the night: Judie might be her ticket to a bigger life, to New York, skyscrapers, people marching for justice and dancing like they did in the movies.

The elevator opened, and Judie, looking gray-faced and tired, stepped out, Leon leading her with that stack of *X-Men* comics.

"Hello again," Rose said.

"Oh, hello," said Judith. Her face went white as an old sheet.

"Hello, Judith," Rose said for the second time.

"It's Judie," the lady, her mother, said and stammered out an invitation to breakfast, to share "yummy" scones.

"I must drop down to the hospital," Rose said. She brushed invisible lint off her slacks. "To see my . . . to see Eamon gets moved today. Home. So he can die in peace."

Judith pulled on one of her thick strands of hair, her eyebrows sky-high in puzzlement.

"Well, goodbye, Judith," Rose began.

Judith waved a hand, but as Rose turned away, she said, in a voice like a mouse, "It's *Judie*. Rose. Dear. Is there something—I can do for you?"

Leon was now talking to the bellhop, whom he'd befriended.

Rose supposed she would have breakfast after all. They sat down. Judith—no, Judie—ordered a basket of scones. She asked if Rose was hungry. She said tending to the dying made her hungry.

Rose was famished. She put the scone in her mouth and ogled the spreads: cream and jelly and butter, tea and bread. Obscene, wasn't it, for people to eat this way when others didn't even have a scrap?

"So, do you like U2?" asked Judie. "My husband says they're getting big."

"Do I like them? What, because I'm Irish I must like the Irish band? I think they're sellouts. I think they're *boring*," said Rose, although she had played "New Year's Day" twenty times one night last year.

"Well, maybe you like new wave?" asked Judie, again. "Do you go dancing?"

Rose snorted. "Can you only talk about music?" she asked. "Have you seen Dublin?"

"Mostly the walk to the hospital."

"So you don't see what it's like for people here—the bad lot they're given while you eat scones?"

"I live in New York," said Judie, her voice dry. "I know from bad lots."

Rose flamed. She must seem like a backwater person to someone from New York. Judie leaned forward. "But does Eamon *also* talk about music—or just God?"

Judie's comment nailed Eamon, and Rose was about to laugh but remembered: this was to be no friendly chat. She had a mission.

"You don't know him at all, he's been back years. Even being—old friends, is it?" Rose asked, careful now, but lifting her eyes.

The woman, her mother, examined her butter knife, buttered her scone with slow strokes, looked over at Leon, absorbed in reading the guest registry across the room.

Rose let the truth rip out. "Last night when I saw you I didn't realize but later I did . . . the truth about you . . . and me. And *him*. I've known for a while. Sean is my father, and Mary—but I also knew from years back that Eamon . . . and he came home, and I did come to know him and found him *wonderful*." She stopped.

Judie looked different now, immediately—less tight. Her dark eyes seemed wise, not unsure. She swallowed her bite and said she supposed Rose had lots of questions.

Rose took a deep breath. Now was her moment. "I have a request. I want to see America. You owe it to me to get me over there, don't you think?"

Judie, her mam, her mother, turned whiter but didn't shrink away.

"I'd have to work details out with your—with Mary. And my husband."

"We don't have to make a big thing over it, a drama. You can tell your wee ones a story—the old family friend nonsense, or some such. I'm not after a piece of *your* life, I just need to get over there and start my own."

"I get it," said Judie. "And . . . Eamon would want it?"

This was a question, but Rose didn't answer.

"In fact, I hope it does happen," said Judie quickly, and they flashed a look at each other that was so brief it might not have existed at all, except for the fireworks explosion in Rose's heart. Unruly things, hearts.

"My mother thinks I'm getting too wild," she said. "Maybe you won't want me at all. You didn't want me the first time, did you?"

Judie flushed, moving her lips as though engaging herself in conversation. It had been a different time, she said, she was young, but then cleared her throat: "Rose, we're music people. Believe me, we've seen wild."

Leon returned and helped himself to a scone. "Someone stayed here named Toggle-berry!" he shouted with glee. He sat with Rose while Judie went to the restroom.

"Are you sad about Mr. Eamon?" he asked her, sitting down beside her, like a coconspirator. "Everyone is acting weird."

"People get weird when they're near the dying," said Rose.

He seemed to agree. "My mom gets weird. Sometimes with my dad and my aunt—a lot with my sister. Emma is a *needy* child. Mom said that once. Kids at school say I'm weird too. I'm writing a libretto about a princess in medieval times." Rose suppressed a laugh of surprise. "Six knights want her hand in marriage. It's based on *Turandot*—the opera?"

"That's quite a premise."

"Each knight has an aria."

"I didn't realize you had words in you. You were mute yesterday."

Leon rolled his eyes. "We were near a *dying man* yesterday," he said. "Plus, he and my mom are *estranged*. They are settling things before he dies. It's about money. They feuded about someone's *inheritance* long, long ago."

"Is that so?"

"It happens. My aunt kicked my mother out of their band once, then my mom kicked my dad out of the house. But he's back. And my mom and aunt talk fifty times a day."

He picked up a comic and began to read.

"I like comics," she told Leon.

"I don't," he said. "But my dad sent them with me and I'm *trying* with that man."

She wanted to talk more, but time pressed: Eamon's move home, Leon's flight. It might be nice to confide in this elf who wrote arias.

⌣

She had never taken her coat off, so now she wrapped it tighter around herself to signal her intention to leave. Judie returned, with an envelope: "My number." She handed it to Rose and watched her tuck it into her coat pocket.

Rose hovered at the revolving door, trying to figure out how to get through it without getting caught, when Judie spun her around by the shoulders.

"Honey," she said, "I must know. Have you been *damaged* by all this mess? You seem so . . . normal."

"Everyone has troubles."

"Aren't you angry?"

"Oh, *furious*—all the bloody time. And I want things, different things—"

"That means you're alive." They idled, for what seemed a year or two. "I'll be talking to you soon—if you want," Judie said.

After she'd deposited her tired self on the street corner, Rose saw the bare facts: her *brother* wrote arias. She had a brother. Whose eyes were his, so bright and oval shaped, like glass marbles? She observed her own self in the glass window of a shop: her eyes were all right, but not luminous like that. What had been going on in her mind that she could talk to them for an hour and not even scan their features to see whether they shared any with her?

Three tears, maybe four, spilled out on the walk toward the river. But the morning wind blew cold, too—and her eyes did tear up in the cold.

One must keep busy. Off to hospital straightaway to help supervise the transportation of her dying father/uncle to his home. Late that night, she left the house to go to a meeting, and to be held by Barry.

"Help me find a record. An American group, the Singer Sisters," she said to him.

"You've got that," he said. "Eamon dropped it by months ago—you never listened?"

She threw her clothes on and sprinted home, stopping to count three stars burn low in the west. The west, where her life had begun.

The kitchen clock read twelve twenty-five when she tiptoed upstairs again after listening to *Singer Sisters* four times in the basement, her hand so trembly she could barely move the needle back and forth. She repeated the mantra in her head galloping up the stairs: *My mother was sad about giving me up! It's in her songs! She called me a* Rose of Winter! *She cared! It can't have been her fault!*

But when she barreled through the doorway to her room, she ran straight into Mary, who sat with her back to the door. Her hands rifled through Rose's box of political pamphlets and the comics and punk records, all laid out in a row. Mary interrogated her: "Have you had an abortion?" "Have you held a gun?" "Do you want to run to Belfast to help the cause?" "Have you given money to the IRA?" These were, she swore, the questions she was asking *before* she got Sean involved.

"Those filthy things," Mary said, holding up her cigarette stash. "They murdered your uncle."

"You mean my father?" asked Rose, grabbing one and tucking it behind an ear. "What's with this charade, anyway? Kevin O'Brien from school still calls me a bastard."

"Damn that Kevin," said Mary without addressing the substance.

Mary and Sean were a soft, cozy breed of parent. But they feared Rose traveling, meeting strangers, reading things they hadn't heard of, and music— they wouldn't let her sing even in church. Unspoken was the fear she'd turn out like Eamon, a part of Mary's prayers: "For my brother, sick with drink and drugs," she'd say. "For my brother, who has mercifully been saved from the drink but is away on another continent." And then: "For my brother, coming home to his people at last."

Eamon had detoxed in India, then on an island off the coast of Greece. He stopped touring, bought the house near St. Stephen's Green, and went out to the park to look at the ducks and meditate, sitting cross-legged on the grass. He took an interest in Rose, and his charm melted her wariness. He encouraged her drawing, writing, learning, told her not to fear being whimsical or strange.

"A nice line right there," he'd say, flipping through the sketch pads he bought her. "Good shading."

Neither verbalized their relationship. They behaved like teacher and pupil. He told her about the mantras and meditation that saved him and urged her to look for God everywhere, but not at the bottom of a bottle or the end of a needle. He said that last bit each time he saw her.

He brought her a phonograph player and a pile of his records. Some songs on his final LP appeared to draw from their time together, although the lyrics meandered into the symbolic: "Look for God" and especially "Follow the Line."

> Follow the line, young one
> Follow the line
> But not too close, young one
> And take your time
>
> Let the line stray, young one
> All over the land
> Follow the line from your heart
> And you'll understand

Critics deemed the album saccharine, but it sold well; people *liked* saccharine. Rose played the record in the basement at low volume so Sean wouldn't know that she was wearing such deep grooves into Eamon's recording. She played it for Barry, sitting together, knees touching, jaws clenched as they listened.

A change took hold of her. Barry accompanied her to meetings and demonstrations, and they went out together afterward or met at his dad's laundromat after work. She befriended the women at meetings and became known for hardheaded advice about sex: don't do it without a condom, she said. But condoms were illegal. "So don't do it," she said. "There are other ways to please a man."

She was the first to hear Eamon's cough, and notice how slim he was, and tell Mary, "He's hiding it, but he's sick."

"Secrets till the end," said Sarah's mother when she met Rose on the way to the hospital one day. "I heard he didn't tell anyone till too late."

"We Foleys have our ways," Rose said and swept past her.

~

Now, in Rose's room, Mary deflected Rose's comment about Eamon and held out her arms. "Remember, Rose, a wild journey is what *men* have the freedom to do," she said. "Women must find salvation in laundry loads."

Rose leaned into Mary and tried to memorize the smell of clean towels and strong shampoo. It would hurt when they parted.

~

They mourned Eamon in a Catholic mass, at which nothing personal was said. A public funeral was held two weeks later, where Eamon's last girlfriend, a tall-faced French model known as Marie-Therese (who had dumped him as soon as he got sick), sang "Golden-Haired Girl" dressed in black with charcoal around her eyes.

Hate was a sin, but Rose felt it anyway.

A priest from the church spoke about Eamon's generosity to orphanages in the later years. Was it for her, for penance, that he had done this? Why hadn't she asked him more questions about her birth, about his lost years wandering the world, about his *songs*? About the way he said "tongue" in the song "I Long for You" (which Barry thought was about communion but was obviously about something dirtier)?

Eamon's old friend Ira read a letter from Eamon himself, begging his old pals to get off drugs and booze and rededicate to God, Allah, Buddha, Hashem, Krishna, Adonai, and Jesus, of course. The priest in attendance looked uncomfortable, and Rose smirked.

Later she floated through the reception off the Temple Bar, a strange, dry affair—not a whiskey in sight. She sipped soda water and found herself talking to a man with a short beard and a small skullcap who observed the scene from a corner. He must have been Eamon's rabbi friend.

"His daughter-niece," the rabbi said after she introduced herself.

"Daughter-niece?" Rose looked around—someone would hear, surely. "That's a marvelous thing. I always called him my father-uncle. But not to anyone but myself."

"You were connected deeply," the man said.

She needn't have feared being observed. Clusters had formed around the few celebrities there, and the man spoke on, unnoticed.

"Toward the end he studied Torah with me. . . . Do you know that you are Jewish, because your biological mother is?" the man asked.

"Like Leo Bloom Jewish! That's daft. Oh gosh, I'm sorry. I guess I should be apologizing to myself too if I am one of you. Half of you. Oh God, I'm making it worse, bumbling on."

"Eamon Foley was a seeker," said the rabbi, as if she were in the pew and he were lecturing. "He believed all roads led up the same mountain and that God was on top."

"Yes, I know, he told me that," she said. "People don't know that the song 'All the Roads' is about religion."

"Yes," said the man, tapping his own chest a few times. "I believe it's based on a conversation we had in my office."

"Schoolchildren ought to learn it," Rose said. "He was a genius."

She inspected this new face, wanting to trust him—aching to unburden herself. The old Rose ravenousness. *Did he talk much about me and my story?* she wanted to ask. *Did he use the word "love"? Was he glad we were close? It felt so tenuous, like if I made a move toward him he'd break.*

"He was impressed by the woman you are becoming," said the rabbi lightly, as though he were reading her thoughts. "Come down to the synagogue if you want to talk."

"Thank you for your kindness, but I don't want to go to a synagogue to find out about myself, my life," said Rose. "It started in America, so I want to go there."

SAN FRANCISCO, 1985

She met Leroy in San Francisco standing under the marquee of the Fillmore, arms aloft, taking a picture with careful aim. She had just dropped a postcard in the mail when she looked up and saw him. As he seemed to know his way around a camera, and as she had traveled across the entire country alone, she asked him to shoot a picture of her beneath the sign, hoping it could prove that she had set foot here, that her cross-country bus ride had been worthwhile.

"I'm a tourist," she told him. "But I'm finding my roots, you see—there were singers in my family, and they played here."

"What kind of music?" he asked. She uncoiled because he hadn't asked, *Where are you from?* when he heard her voice, the query that every person large or small in America had offered, thinking themselves original. It didn't hurt that his simple blue jeans and navy sweatshirt seemed as if they were made for his body.

"Folk, I guess, folk-rock?" she said. "I'm still learning."

"Wild times out here in the sixties," he said. "I know stories."

"I'd love to hear them," she said and then blushed because it sounded like a come-on, now that her fair skin was pink as a good dress. But he didn't react as other men might've, only raised his eyebrows and said he had an appointment later that afternoon, but might he walk her to her next spot on the grand tour?

"If it's all about the sixties for you, the Haight is that way." He gestured.

"So I don't have to consult my map anymore?"

He laughed. "I can be your map."

~

Rose sorely needed a map. In her short stay at the family house in New Hampshire, she had felt like a six-legged creature walking up and down the lawn, but one that was invisible during certain hours. Occasionally, Dave or Sylvia or Judie, a drink or a cigarette in hand, would sit down beside her, probe her face with their eyes, and badger her with sharp-edged questions she wasn't sure how to answer.

Most times, though, the atmosphere among the three singers was thick with professional and personal tangles, whether they were huddling in the studio, harmonizing on the dock, or reciting headlines to each other across the table, each with a section of the newspaper in front of their faces. Then, Rose was left to her own devices. She was meant to be minding the kids, but the kids were in their feral place. They didn't need or want her for much besides pouring glasses of milk and pinning wet swimsuits to the line.

And her identity went unmentioned, even by Judie. Cascades of silence. Yet this family seemed a-religious and didn't socialize with their neighbors, so Rose began to see that other kinds of shame existed, besides the kind attributed to God or the neighborhood. She began to see that the half secret of her history was an easier burden to carry in Dublin, where babies emerged seven months after marriage with regularity, than here.

"I can't stay in this place all summer," she told Judie only hours before the boat incident with Emma. "I've got to get traveling."

Judie had something Rose should see before she left: "I can't touch them, go look in the desk drawer in the attic," she said. "They are yours. . . . The closest thing I can give you to understanding."

Rose read the lyrics, squinting through moist eyes. Judie's shame, she saw, wasn't about sex or even about Rose. It was about Judie's own parents and the agony they'd all caused each other.

~

She and Leroy rambled together, up and down the San Francisco hills, looking at the houses painted bright colors—so different from Dublin! Leroy stopped to snap pictures of her, methodical, making her move this and that way to catch the light just so, until the camera ran out of film. They ambled to the edge of Golden Gate Park and sat on a patch of grass near the entrance. There were some dirty old fellows watching them. ("Junkies," said Leroy. "Reagan.") They moved into a diner down the street. On sitting down, she became ravenous, and after he recommended that she order the cheese omelet and french fries, she came to see that they'd learned reams about each other in a short time, that she'd relayed her history in a manner that rendered it fearsome.

He hailed from Los Angeles but was due to enter his third semester at the University of California, Berkeley, studying to be an architect, as he'd loved building with blocks so much as a kid that he seldom stopped, not for one minute. The only Black student in his program, he had to work three times as hard, but he loved the work.

"Any school project that involved a diorama, that was my thing," he said with a laugh. "I'd love to design beautiful, affordable houses for people like my family. . . ."

"Was it drab?" she asked. "Dublin's dull as dirt."

She looked across the table at this man, about her age but a million years older.

"'Drab' is a nice word for it," he said.

She liked that he had a plan.

"It's good that you met your real mom," he said—she had already spilled the whole story, overemphasizing her political involvement and Mary's IRA fears—and she flinched at the word "real." "Now she's a person, not peering over you like some legend," he added.

"It was daft," said Rose. "I hate that she went along with my scheming— passed me off as a nanny. But the deceit started with my folks back home—no one wants to call things by their name."

"What name works?"

They were deep into a slice of cherry pie now, their knees touching and all of the rainbows and lightning bolts in the whole universe passing back and forth between them. Barry was dissolving into the mists of history.

Afternoon sunshine fell on them when they left the diner. This was heaven; why on earth would she have stayed in New Hampshire being nearly murdered by Emma, age eight?

She wondered what Mary would think of her eating dinner with a Black man she'd met on the corner or whether Judie would have a thing to say about it. Would either Mary or Judie pick up on the quality she'd loved in Barry, too—in any man who possessed it: the steady eyes, the follow-up questions, the interest in seeing her eat? She couldn't quite explain it, except to tell her girlfriends that "the quiet ones drive me mad." Neither Leroy nor Barry was quiet so much as soft-spoken. Nurturers.

Leroy left for his appointment but offered to meet her later for a drink where he tended bar—an Irish pub, of all places, about ten minutes from her hotel, comfortable and clean, a mind-your-own-business establishment, he called it. And when he got off from work, by which time she'd had some pints, they fell on each other, kissing for ten minutes without stopping.

Rose stayed in Leroy's apartment for a week, then two. At night, he tended bar. But they had mornings to take their small journeys up and along the hills where kite-flying children gamboled. Being near the ocean was like home and far away—the briny smell of it coming off the wind, the braying of the gulls, the slap of the water on the shore. It anchored her.

They flew their own kite on the Presidio, had dumplings in Chinatown, and took a boat out to Alcatraz. They bought more postcards to send back to New Hampshire, and nicer ones to send to Ireland. They visited the Fine Arts Museum, and when Rose wept at the beauty of Monet's waterlilies, he didn't find it strange. One afternoon they rented a car and drove out to see the redwoods, tall and lush. The air was more air-like than anywhere she'd ever been, and they walked to a spot where no one could see them.

When she craned her neck to look up at the treetops, he combed his hand through her hair and kissed her.

"You want to be an explorer when you grow up," he told her one day while they rested in the park.

"I'm not an explorer, I'm a *fighter*," she insisted, lying on the grass with her feet on his lap and giggling despite herself. "This is just a pause."

Evenings, at the bar, she watched him work so they could walk home together, singing a pop song. Sometimes she rambled alone or went to thrift stores and bought things that were passé: bell-bottom jeans and round sunglasses. And she drew. She doodled in a sketchbook, objects that caught her attention: signposts, old clocks, flowers, and boats and flags.

People were holding signs and petitions all over town, but with Leroy she rarely talked about politics or watched the evening news. He seldom mentioned the fact that by being together, they were, in a sense, being political.

When she tried to ask him about racism, he said, "One of the things I like about you is you're not hung up on this issue, like all American girls are, of any color—can we keep it that way?" She frowned—she'd even read *The Autobiography of Malcolm X* in Dublin.

"Do you just fancy me because I know nothing about America, then?" she asked.

"I like you because you're a sexy blonde with wild dark eyes," he said. "And you never know when to shut up. Besides, if you start telling me about the violence over *there* and I talk about what it's like here, you're gonna get mad, and so am I, and instead of feeling this nice breeze, we'll hear groans," he said.

"That's poetic," she said.

"I'm trying to tell you," he said. "It's not that I don't understand how deep and bad it goes. I know every second of every day. I try to let it live with me, so I can live with it."

"Grand," she said. She pulled three blades of grass out and tried to braid them, but they kept slipping out of whatever arrangement she tried.

"I can't trip myself up with rage if I want to be an architect," he explained again, frustration in his tone.

"Jews—race or religion?" she asked him once, causing him to cough and spit out his coffee. "My American family, they're Jewish. My dad—my real—my scientific—Eamon, studied with a rabbi. But Judie and her family didn't say a *thing* that seemed *Jewish* in New Hampshire. Do Black people and Jews have a similar—"

He took her two hands in his and said, "Rose, don't."

She pulled them away and said, "I'm not *trying* to be prejudiced, I'm bloody ignorant."

"Observe piece by piece," he said. "You're a quick study. Befriend people."

"I've befriended *you*." She offered him the big, dark eyes that drove the lads at home crazy.

She had expected going to America would propel her forward into a bigger life. Instead, this country had given her time to think and the seed of an idea, that she could explore and chronicle people and their ways. She preferred above all discovering Leroy, whose collarbones were perfect trapezoids. She and he called themselves two planets in space, drawn to each other by gravity.

"Showing you this city has made it feel more like mine," he said.

"I like myself here too," she said. "I feel so small. No one is watching me."

⌣

They packed up Leroy's things in August. He was due home for a few weeks before school started. He didn't invite her to LA; she didn't ask to go. Instead, Rose restarted her journey across the country, for real, on a Greyhound bus and on a train. She intended to see it all, or at least the major spots she'd yearned for from childhood—the Grand Canyon, Las Vegas, and Chicago and Florida and New York.

And then she was going to come back for him.

Before Leroy took her to the bus station, he gave her his phone number at the Berkeley dorms and reminded her to call him from Chicago.

"The phone at home gets shut off," he said, wincing. She counted down the days, collected dimes and nickels for the phone.

She rang at the appointed time. "His status has changed," the woman picking up the phone said. "We *do* have him on file, but he isn't enrolled this semester."

"Did he leave information?" she asked.

"That's confidential," the woman said kindly. "Where are you calling from? Scotland?"

"What about his mailing address at home?"

"Also confidential. Say, are you *Irish*?"

Rose pleaded, but the woman was firm. When Rose hung up the pay phone in the hotel lobby, stricken, an attendant approached and asked, was she all right?

Could you be all right when your uncle-father had died after a lingering illness, and your long-lost sister tried to drown you, and your real mother taught you to swim but let you run away on a bus to California, and you fell in love with someone who disappeared from this earth?

She could take a bus all the way back to San Francisco and go to the bar to ask Leroy's coworkers about him: but imagine showing up and telling them, "Hello, have you seen the man I was inseparable with for six weeks? He seems to have given me the slip!"

Maybe he hadn't loved her, or maybe this was what love *was* in America—a fling, like in the movies. He must have been lost and homesick when they met. And she provided a distraction.

"Ma'am?" The hotel attendant peered at her.

"Quite all right, thanks."

"Wow, that accent—*Where are you from?*" the attendant asked.

Darkness fell, violently, as a chill set in from the lake; September loomed, after all.

At a loss, Rose went to an Irish pub in the neighborhood—and before she'd drained a single pint, a thin-faced boy sat next to her. He had the teeth she associated with Barry.

"You're from Ireland!" he cried in a familiar lilt when he heard her order a second.

Around the fourth drink she invited him up to her room. His eyes lit up like a child's on Christmas, and she pulled him out the door and through the lobby of the hotel, not caring what the kindly attendant thought. Three years of true love till she slept with Barry, and now her second man in a summer, and unlike how it was with Leroy this was ugly—quick, unsatisfying.

She practically hopped back into her pants afterward. "You can go now," she said.

He pouted. "You have telly here," he said. "Can't we watch?"

~

What had she been trying to avenge with this foolishness? The condom they used was broken, she noticed as she put it in the rubbish bin with a dart of fear.

She moved on from Chicago. In Washington, DC, she walked among vast, cold American monuments. She booked a bus trip down to Florida. She sweated buckets in the sun and got a nasty burn on her shoulders. The air was so close it would flatten her into an oatcake. Florida must be close to hell.

On the bus ride back up north, she must have dry heaved fifty thousand times. In a state of near hysteria, she began to run over scenes from Eamon's deathbed that she'd pushed away: his coughs, the day they transferred him home, the contortions of pain that leapt across his thin face, Mary's crying at night, asking Rose, "What if he's not with Jesus?"

The sickroom smell, acid and sweet decay, the decision to sleep with Barry the night of Eamon's wake, pulling him into her room, shutting the door, and producing the condom she'd squirreled away for the occasion. How they'd pressed their limbs together, her tears mingling with the sweat and blood.

Months later, her small inheritance from Eamon made a chance to put her plan into action. Mary, at the airport, said, "Don't fly into her arms, she's not your real mother," and then, "What's wrong with me that I should be so small, I knew this day would come," as they embraced.

She rang Mary long-distance from Philadelphia. "I have the flu."

Her nausea continued. She had no fever, and her nose began to bleed; she could no longer ignore that her period was late. She stalled three days until she dialed Judie's number, which she'd written in marker inside her suitcase.

"I'm in Philadelphia and I need an . . . operation," she said when Judie got on the line. "I realize this is strange—" she gushed out. "Since I'm baptized Catholic and you chose not to abort me, but heaven help me, I *cannot* have a baby."

"Sylvia will help us," said Judie. "Tell me what bus you're taking."

"I haven't got my bus scheduled—" Rose began, faltered.

"I'll call the clinic at Bleecker Street. We'll take care of it."

"I don't know what—"

"*Rose*. We'll take care of it," said Judie.

During the final leg of her bus trip, "Route 95" played in her head. She was the opposite of Judie—defeated and sad, not hopeful or new. Rose disembarked at the Port Authority in a man's overcoat that she'd bought for ten dollars at a thrift store in Chicago and scanned the crowd for Sylvia, who was supposed to meet her by the moving sculpture with the "ball thingy in it" on the first floor. After a few panicked wrong turns, she saw her, cool in a black leather jacket, her hair in a dancer's bun—admirably constrained in the sea of perms around her. Her black pants brushed the tops of cowboy boots. She waved a businesslike hand and took Rose's elbow.

"The appointment is for tomorrow," she said. "Listen, I was scared of abortion before—before it was legal. But I've had two. It won't hurt, and it's not murder."

"I'm so—" Rose began to explain her mortification, and Sylvia shushed her.

"You ever had Jewish deli, Rose?" she asked. "Let's go." She steered Rose to the front of the Port Authority—looking up, Rose saw that the green sign said EIGHTH AVENUE—and stuck her hand in the air, queen of the city, ignoring the winding cab queue on the curb.

"Emergency," Sylvia shouted. They got into the cab, Sylvia hauling Rose's bag like a gunnysack.

"I sometimes *do* have a pastrami emergency," explained Sylvia with a wicked grin, and Rose felt a huge balloon of tension fly out of her mouth into the city sky as she guffawed at the joke. Sylvia, this half aunt of hers, was a blessing.

"I was gifted with a metabolism that gallops," she said. "I'm tall and my family are not. You're a beanpole too—take full advantage of it."

They alighted from the cab, Sylvia banging on the trunk for Rose's bag. She sidled right into a booth at the Second Avenue Deli, where the staff seemed to know her. She ordered for them both: chicken soup with something called matzo balls, a pastrami sandwich, coleslaw, pickles. For days, Rose had been nauseated, but she found herself famished—the strange, sour, salty food, the potato salad and coleslaw in small silver cups, oddly reminded her of home, and she began slurping and biting and spooning, until another wave of nausea hit and she ran to the bathroom and crouched over the toilet. Nothing came out, except retching and hot tears.

Sylvia didn't knock on the door.

Rose's own tired face in the dim bathroom mirror regarded her—was it different from how she had appeared arriving at the house in New Hampshire? How happy and how sinister it had been at the same time, like a gothic castle in *Jane Eyre*. A family that spoke its own language, consisting of music and aggressive verbal interplay. Quips were their currency, songs their frequency. Each day she had felt her initial resolve to conquer them drain by lunchtime, each day she'd felt more alien, convinced the idea she'd concocted to come here under false pretenses was madness.

The moment Emma pulled the boat away, her fear had been so brief and all-consuming. *I'm going to die*, she'd thought, shocked by the cold. *By my own kid sister's hand.* Her sputters and cries gave way to realization: I can *swim*. My mother taught me to swim.

She stopped flailing long enough to catch sight of a neighbor's canoe—how funny these American boats were. She'd homed in on the thin edge of the boat in the water and muttered to herself: "Swim, you calf. Swim." And she'd swum right over. Saved herself. And the thought crystallized: *I have to get out of here.*

Sylvia idly twirled a spoon in the soup, her back resting against the vinyl of the booth.

"Will I see my—will I see Judie soon?" Rose asked.

"Tomorrow," said Sylvia. "She's coming. She's with the kids tonight—Dave's at a shindig." She paused. "He's always at a *thing*. It's hard on Judie."

Rose spent the night at Sylvia's place, which was all the way east, by a river, with huge windows. Sylvia said the lights across the murky water were Queens, where Eamon had lived when he first immigrated.

"I want to be an anthropologist, or maybe a sociologist," Rose said after borrowing some toothpaste. She hovered in her pajamas, watching Sylvia smear white cream all over her face. "Someone I met this summer told me I had the mark of a social scientist."

"Someone special?" asked Sylvia, without judgment.

She assented, flushing.

"Someone, the person who did this?" Sylvia pointed to Rose's stomach.

"No, God, no." She flushed deeper.

"You should stay here in the States for college. It's better here. Judie would agree. She regrets not going. I got my BA."

"I have *nothing*—no visa, no nothing," said Rose. "I have to go back soon."

"Oh, as for that—" Sylvia said. "We know people."

~

How ironic, the briskness and kindness with which Sylvia and Judie handled her abortion. Because the next day was the most homelike thing she'd experienced since leaving Ireland, and yet it was an abortion—the last thing any good Irish girl was ever supposed to do.

Not that the doctor wasn't terrifying! A rosary even appeared before her eyes as she lay on the table, and her a nonbeliever (and a Jew!), touching its beads. But Judie and Sylvia talked to the doctor, jotted things down, exchanged looks, and took Rose home to an apartment well stocked with tea, maxi pads, and hot-water bottles for her cramping. They didn't ask about how she'd come to be in this position. Their kindness broke Rose more than her loneliness had. She craved Mary's hands, her low tones, even her horror and castigation. Surely the aching cramps in her abdomen were hunger pangs for Mary's touch.

The sisters had procured several movies for her to watch, too—old ones, black-and-white, with beautiful stars like Olivia de Havilland and Cary Grant.

"Rose wants to stay here to go to college," Sylvia said at some point, while they fussed over pillows and Rose was lying on the floor, trying to get comfortable.

Judie's eyes lit up. "College?" she said. "Could you call Pam? Do you think she'd help?"

Sylvia's old roommate had ended up a big shot at Wellesley, they explained. They listed names of people they knew—people at this office and that office, people who knew people in the government—a catechism. "Steve at the Boston office—Mom's old friend Henry."

"You'll follow through, Rose?" asked Judie, kneeling and looking at her with beseeching eyes. "You want to be an—an anthropologist, Sylvia said. Is that right?"

"Yes," said Rose, half delirious with pain and fatigue and loneliness. "College in America, *yes*. I want that. Anthropology, sure, or sociology. If you'll help me, yes, I'll do it. Why not?"

PART IV

EMMA

B y Emma's eighth month in LA, so isolated she'd started talking back to the TV, she got a call from an underling at her agency: an actor named Ben Felt wanted to go on a date with her.

Since his star-making turn in *Merry*, a teen retelling of *The Merry Wives of Windsor*, Ben's visage, pouting and big-eyed, was plastered on the bedroom walls of America's girls. His round eyes and heart-shaped lips gave him that androgynous look, which contrasted with his otherwise rugged features. He wasn't her type (she went for scruffy, bearded guys)—but he was objectively gorgeous.

Emma hadn't dated anyone since she broke up with her high school boyfriend after graduation. She'd grown spinsterish. She'd slept with people on the road—men and a few women—and occasionally felt a wild heart rush of infatuation for someone, a road crush, but nothing blossomed. Mae had accused her of having "intimacy issues," but in Emma's mind, a relationship would distract from her goal of stardom.

"He loves that video of you in the black dress," said the publicist. Emma winked at the receiver. *Everyone* loved that video.

"Flower," the lead single from her *Female Troubles (Female Singer)* album, hit number one on the charts a year after she recorded it, so ubiquitous that Emma herself began to hate hearing it even as she was chauffeured down the freeway to one event or another in LA.

As full tilt as the first part of her success had galloped, the second was faster. She had first come to LA to shoot the video for "Flower" in a glittery black dress, framed by peacock feathers, with black lipstick and electric-blue eye shadow, rendering her face ethereal. A week later, a *SPIN* reporter drove up to interview her for a short feature, and she languidly invited him to join her in the hammock, where they flirted and smoked and watched the sky.

"I'm in a hammock snuggled up with the stunning Emma Cantor, and we're looking at the clouds," he wrote. She *had* to stay out west after that. Emma was an It Girl. Parties and ceremony invites piled up; people gave her numbers for trainers and dietitians and smoothie guys. *Smoothie guys.* So in one sense, this Ben Felt request felt natural.

But inside, Emma was shrinking. Though the single slayed, the album itself wasn't selling as well as expected. Judie had sworn she'd sue but never sent word. Not about the songs or Rose. No phone calls or emails or postcards. Emma and Leon instant messaged, Dave emailed daily with weird articles about essential oils and the Beatles, and Sylvia checked in weekly on the phone. The only *actual* message she got from Judie was her mother's pointed refusal to comment when journalists tried to ask about the album. "I love my children and am proud of their work," she said in one canned statement or another—and that was it.

When those same reporters asked Emma about the two songs she credited to Judith Zingerman, with herself and Mae as secondary writers, she tried to be honest: "My mom isn't thrilled about my choices for these songs. But she's let me do my thing, and I'm so grateful." But her humble statements to the press didn't convince Judie to call.

She would go on the date, though she tried to play it cool with the publicist. "Can we go to Canter's?" she asked on the phone. "I'm starving. And homesick." Unsaid: *And more alone than ever.*

She'd had a blowup with Mae a few weeks back. They got high on excellent weed and watched *Don't Look Back*. Mae sided with Baez and Emma with Dylan because "no one in the universe wrote at that level and no one will again," and the stoned argument became a proxy war for all the pressures of fame already driving them apart. "Sometimes you have to make choices as an artist that hurt people," said Emma.

"You never sided with Dylan before that stupid black dress video went to your head," said Mae. "I don't even know why. It made you look like a generic brunette."

"I looked *hot*!"

Mae had been drumming on records around town and even been offered a producing gig or two, so she ended the fight by yelling, "I don't need you—you need me!" and slamming the door. But as a fellow New Yorker, she didn't drive freeways either, so they had to wait together in the kitchen, fuming, arms crossed, while the cab crawled over the hills to pick Mae up. They had emailed once since then, about a business thing.

Mae loved it out here, but Emma thought West Coast living sucked. She had been alone in the house for months, and shadows, breezes, made her jump. Were there intruders outside? Fans of her music asking for autographs like they did when she left restaurants?

⁓

That's a lot of meat you're eating," Ben said three days later, at their big dinner. "Wow. I love that. I would have thought you were vegetarian."

"Not by choice," she said. "It's too damn *healthy* out here. Smoothies as far as the eye can see! I needed a sandwich." She opened her mouth wide to dig in and he raised his eyebrows.

"So how do you stay skinny?" he demanded.

"I can't drive to the grocery store," she said. He laughed.

"I mean I have like, this *amazing* trainer and like, a green juice guy you should totally call!" she chirped.

"You're funny," he said. "Not as angry as on your songs. You seem pissed on that CD."

Emma paused, mid-Reuben, and smoldered at him.

"So why did you call?"

"You looked hot in your video," he said. "I mentioned that you were cute, and my publicist thought it would be a buzzy match—go out a few times, get our pics taken."

"You're being straight about your transactional approach," she said.

"People out here are both fake and full of themselves—and I'm *definitely* full of myself, and I can't change *that*. So I try at least not to be *fake* at the same time, you know?"

"Life here is contrived and vapid," she said before ordering a cream soda, not diet.

"Wow, good SAT words," he said. "Why stay?"

"I'm in a tight spot with my family," she said.

He touched her forearm with such kindness that she began to melt.

"Hey—before we split, you should check out your teeth in the mirror," Ben added after picking up the check. "You got some corned beef in there and there are paparazzi outside."

As if she'd sat on a scorpion, Emma got up and ran to the bathroom to floss the meat out with her fingernails, imagining Sylvia doing the same thing in New York.

Outside of the restaurant, a handful of flashes went off. Emma's face grew sweaty and she looked away, grabbing Ben's substantial arm for support. He patted her hand and helped her into a waiting car. A perfect shot.

"Nice touch with the arm," he said. "You're adorable. To be honest, less feminine than in the video—but I like your tomboy thing. And your vocabulary. What's your address?"

He looked right at her then, his eyes tunneling into her soul—and for half a second, she swooned like one of his teenage fans. How calming it might be to lean her head on his gym-enhanced chest and let him pretend to protect her.

"Look, I'm not about to get exclusive, but I had fun tonight," he said. "And I like your whole vibe, like I said. Want to take it back to your place for a bit?"

"I like you too, but I'm not that desperate."

She got home and brooded. She *was* that desperate.

⌣

A few days after the corned beef date with Ben, time she'd mostly spent contemplating whether to call him, her father came to visit. He came onstage at her Anaheim show.

"What a crowd!" he said, exuberant, as they arrived home around one in the morning. "Reminded me so much of my *Sweet* tour, when you were but a babe."

Emma moved Dave's scattered shoes and jacket into the closet. Dave required *managing*. Emma would try.

"Hungry, Emma-bear?" Dave asked her now, rummaging through her fridge. "Did I tell you? Rae and I get all our food at the farm store Sunday market. I know you enjoy a grilled cheese at night, but dairy is terrible for the voice. Are you exercising yours?"

"Trying," she said.

She sliced some cheese and layered it on a loaf of macrobiotic bread he had presented her at the airport, while he looked on.

"I eat *cashew* cheese now," he said. "Cashews are one of Mother Nature's most inventive foods."

His bread crumbled but did the trick. After the toaster dinged, Emma sat down and demolished the sandwich, then rummaged for beer.

"Dad, you seem too skinny," she said.

"I'm healthy," he insisted. "I can't outrun genetics—my dad was a sickly guy—but I'm trying."

She regarded her father again, in his green sweat suit. Her own circle-ringed eyes were worse than his, but he did seem wan. She shifted the conversation to her writer's block.

"Don't be like Mom," he advised. "Waiting for the muse to come down like lightning. Don't you know Calvin and Hobbes? Inspiration—you have to go out and chase it down, with a club?"

"That's Jack London, Pops," Emma said with a smile. "Calvin said it is *not* like a faucet—you *can't* turn it on. You *have* to be in the right mood. Calvin's more like Mom."

"Jack London is my guy, then," said Dave. "Screw Calvin."

Before they went to sleep, he wanted to see Emma's small but growing stash of guitars, her makeshift studio. Each chose one to play: a Fender Stratocaster, a Les Paul. Then they switched to acoustic, so they could sing.

At four in the morning they were still going. They'd avoided their own catalogs, grooving on old favorites: "Buffalo Gals," "Sixteen Tons," "Dink's Song," Dylan.

His guitar work had been undervalued, she always felt, because he'd had the fortune to top the charts with one corny song.

"Still got it, Pops," Emma said.

He held his hands out again, staring at them as if they had been sutured onto his arms. "You know that Mom had tremors before she quit performing, and I wasn't sympathetic."

She'd heard the story so many times: the shaking, the knee injury, the pills that made Judie act nuts. The babies that redeemed her, allegedly. Emma yawned and told Dave she was calling it a night.

A horrible grinding sound woke her the next morning.

"Dad?" she called down the stairs. It was noon.

"Making smoothies with this blender of yours!" he cried. "Too bad you don't have silken tofu, but I found some old spirulina powder."

She pulled on leggings and a T-shirt, splashed water on her face—her "team" would be shocked at her dearth of lotions, but she didn't feel like it today.

"What's the story with the Top Forty this year?" Dave asked her as they sat down at the table. "All these robotic layers between listener and song. These boy bands."

"The Beatles," Emma said, smiling, "were a boy band."

"Don't try to compare."

"What about Britney?" asked Emma, arching her voice. "Surely you can't resist that midriff and those pigtails?"

"She's a sexy pop star," he said. "The music's uninspiring."

Emma had the opposite sense—since she'd dropped off the charts, every song on the radio sounded like Handel's *Messiah*.

"I should call some people from before I came out here," she said to Dave. She ran her finger over a chapped lower lip. "I should really call Mae."

"You should call Judie," said Dave, his mustache now spirulina coated.

"Mom should call me."

"She is calling you. She sent me here. I am the telephone."

"Don't lie for her," said Emma. He held up his hands.

He handed her the smoothie in a mason jar. She tasted his concoction, made a face, but gamely kept drinking. Maybe it would help her look less haggard.

"It's not good, what we kept from you," he said. "But I'm mentioning my own dad because I never got right with him."

~

One afternoon, they took a hike in a canyon. That's what people did out here. Emma held Dave's elbow.

"I tried," he said. "To clean up. To be around for you. Now that you're famous too, you get what it's like to be me," he continued, and she rolled her eyes. Count on the ego to counteract the kinder impulses. He pointed down to a small ravine, at some animal tracks, and they reminisced about the raccoons they once saw fighting in New Hampshire.

"Have you written a song recently?" she said as they walked back.

"I have lyrics," he said. "I could use help rounding out the tunes."

Emma wasn't otherwise engaged. So from then on out they made music every day, even recorded it on demo tapes. Their whole time together, only one question she asked seemed to bother him: "How did you let Mom quit music?"

"I gave up," he said. "After a decade or so. For years I badgered her to write," he said. "Then I got used to things being a certain way." He paused. "I didn't lock her in a room and make her write songs. But would she have? She said that you and Leon were worth a thousand hit songs—"

"But she was unhappy."

"She was unhappy in the Singer Sisters, too. Some people are constitutionally discontent." He paused. "Maybe she's better now, without us around."

They squeezed each other's hands. They got Leon on the phone and he said he'd help them master an album in New York, with the songs from that week and more.

And then her father flew home, and Emma was alone again. She told her label guy that she was working on a stripped-down album of folk classics with her dad, and he cursed and hung up on her.

Stuck once again, she stashed the demos away in a shoulder bag Sylvia had given her before she came to LA and promised to explain it all to Dave in a few weeks.

"Call Ben for another date," her agent said. "Just to make them forget the acoustic dad album idea."

⌒

It took three nights for her to pour herself a Sylvia-sized gin and tonic and call Ben. "Does your offer still stand?" she asked.

"Come by anytime," he said.

They had athletic sex in several rooms of his bachelor pad—Ben liked showing off his arm strength by lifting Emma up and throwing her on the bed, then the couch, and she didn't mind being manhandled. His roughness told her: You exist.

In public, she symbolized an "empowered" woman, but in private, she pressed on the tender spots where Ben's hands had been and tried to exult over the millions of young girls who wanted to be in her place. She had won. She had won it all, and she hated it all.

One night at a benefit performance for a kids' music program, Emma had had too much to drink. "Women are everything!" someone yelled. She looked up.

"Okay, I don't know if women are *everything*—but we're a lot. We're a *lot*. And people joke about women in rock being man haters, but I do blame shit on men. I do. And I know it's not trendy to say this because whatever, but our president should have kept his dick in his pants. That girl was not much older than me, and he was her *boss*."

The crowd fell deathly silent. The only thing worse than ranting at a show was no one responding to your rant. Emma watched their stunned faces and remembered how she'd searched for her mother in crowds—now she sought out any friendly face at all.

The next day she got about twenty calls demanding comment.

Her new publicist, Alix, who looked exactly like Bitsy Calhoun, handled it with a statement: "Emma thinks the prosecution of the president is an outrageous miscarriage of justice. She stands firmly against impeachment but wants people to consider all angles."

Alix warned her that she had no more chances. She'd come across as "uptight" and she needed to loosen up.

Fortunately, sleeping with Ben became a standing affair. When they were done fucking, they often got into bed companionably with a bag of microwave popcorn—"Maid's coming tomorrow," Ben joked, because he had a maid every day.

Flipping through the channels a few weeks into their arrangement, they settled on *Saturday Night Live*, on which one of the new actresses played a character based on Emma, all pursed lips and whine and no sense of humor. She wore dark lipstick, a pair of short shorts, and Doc Martens, with a flowing peasant blouse.

When Irma first strode out onstage, Emma's eyes grew wide as Ben laughed and laughed, bringing his quilt up to his mouth he was laughing so hard.

"This is amazing!" he said, pulling one of her short curls. "You've made it! You'll have to do a guest appearance at Christmas mocking yourself."

Emma barked out a laugh. Her comments about Clinton had cemented her status as an angry chick. The Lilith Fair moment was over; a backlash was brewing.

Throughout the remainder of the season, the running gag was putting this character, "Irma Crushaman," in prosaic situations like a business seminar, a teacher's break room, or an office mailroom and having her fellow characters complain about their boss. Then Irma Crushaman would bust out her guitar and start howling about being mad at the boss for petty slights, ending up screaming, "Death to all them men!"

The sketch was facile, yet whenever it aired, Emma secretly hated it: not just for herself, but for all women in rock. She had no clue how to state her concern in public without reinforcing the angry stereotype from the show. Her own doubts prevented her from speaking up, too. What had she even been trying to do in those sessions back in Boston, with all the growling and the wailing? Express genuine fury or jump on a trend?

After the skit aired, the atmosphere around her changed. She walked into a party wearing one of her trademark black velvet dresses with burnout patterns and she heard a suppressed laugh. Thinking of Irma, no doubt.

Emma's paranoia compelled her to start dialing up her father and getting him to blather about fame and the abyss, which he did, but she found herself too jumpy to listen. She got her Valium prescription upped instead.

The label wanted her sophomore effort to be "poppy" and "polished," but the idea of going into a studio without Mae, now off recording with the Goo Goo Dolls, daunted her.

Live performances provided a salve. Stage work felt real, in its sweat and energy, in her communion with the girls in the front row—those same kinds of girls, wherever she was. She told her agent to book all the tour dates possible, no matter how far she had to fly.

⁓

During the season finale Emma agreed to go on *SNL* and poke fun of herself, and she wailed anti-male invective alongside the actress: always game, was Emma.

She triumphed. The audience roared. Pundits called her a good sport. Critics liked "Father Fascist" as the third single, one saying it was worth ten of Emma's own songs, and marveling at the "synthesis between this rudimen-tary song" and Emma's "intricate guitar work." But the world had moved on. There was a Christian fake cowboy running for president. The calls discussing a new image, a new sound, for her next album intensified—or maybe, people told her, she ought to explore acting, she'd been so funny on *SNL*.

She recorded an episode of *VH1 Storytellers* that featured a long, dramatic telling of the story of Flower—how she came to the house and frightened Emma. Judie's negligence figured prominently. Emma went back on tour, supporting P!nk, who was a new pop singer being marketed as hip-hop, and somehow the label thought they'd boost each other's fanbase.

Fortunately, Emma could perform for the crowd of young women who loved P!nk. The road was salvation: she played and played and shut her mouth about it because she didn't want Irma Crushaman to imitate her.

When she played New York, Sylvia and Leon sat backstage and played with her on a few songs, and they drank afterward for hours. She told them about Dave's visit, and they laughed.

Judie never showed.

An email from Leon admired his sister's full touring calendar, with a hint of admonition. "I met Rose and her baby, almost a toddler now, thought u should know," he wrote. "Mom is obsessed—wants to acknowledge them publicly."

"What did you think of them?" she began to type, and then thought better of it. Better to not get provoked into jealousy. She was busy being a rock star.

Judie wanted to acknowledge Rose? Fine, let her, let them, waltz into the sunset, the singer and her long-lost daughter. She, Emma, writer of a hit single (but her album was a disappointment), greeted thousands of fans each night (yes, she was an opener, but multiple concert reviews in multiple alt-weeklies had gone out of their way to mention how dynamic and strong her performance was *for* an opener).

The show at the KeyArena in Seattle reaped the dividends of her efforts onstage. Fans showed up even before Emma started, instead of trickling in. A solid group of a few hundred crowded on the floor up close to her and sang along. They shouted out requests and threw beach balls around. She honored them by covering Courtney Love's "Doll Parts" and doing the chorus as a sing-along, holding the mic out and watching their mouths turn into Os as they sang "You" and "Do." They wailed with the joy of anguish. She sweated, took a bow, mopped herself off with one of the big fluffy towels her dad had told her she had to put on her pre-tour rider. She pretended its softness was him.

Aunt Sylvia once called the stage her truest home.

~

They had a day off before they played Vancouver, and the sun came out, so the next day Emma drove out to Discovery Park with a group of backup singers, musicians, and roadies. The place was bleak and blustery, looking over icy-blue swaths of Puget Sound. You could see the jagged, clear peaks of the Olympic Mountains over the water.

"There are two kinds of people," said Marie, one of the singers, gesticulating with fingerless gloves, her other hand clutching a thermos of tea. "The people who look at mountains and the people who climb them."

"Which are you?" asked Emma.

"Oh, I'm already measuring crampons and shit in my mind—thinking about coming back here when we're done to try my hand at being a mountain woman. Just look at those pointy guys."

"That's nothing," said Robbie, a Seattle native. "Rainier popped." They turned around and took it in, white and alone, pasted onto the sky. A few people pulled out their throwaway souvenir cameras to snap shots.

"I once read a saying in this quote book," said Aileen, the only woman in the horn section. "It says, 'Climb the Mountains So You Can See the World, Not So the World Can See You.' So relevant to the biz."

"So like, it's saying it's not about your ego but your craft?" asked Robbie. "Deep."

"Tell that to any front woman," said Marie, to snorts.

"Ugh, singers," someone said. "That's how they're built." A general sniff of disapprobation passed through the group, and Emma pulled her hood up. *Singers.*

Was she climbing the mountain just so the world could see her? Not right now. She was hiding. But the aphorism taunted her on their van ride back to the pub.

In the dark, flattering light they ordered a round of local beers, strong, dark, and frothy, and sat close against each other with their coats in a friendly pile. Emma settled back, her body uncurling. She even teased Aileen, asking if she'd intended the message for *Emma*.

"No! No! It's for all of us," said Aileen, blushing.

People wanted to know if she and Ben were "exclusive," and she snickered and said, "It's not exactly the romance of the century, but I like him," but with a secret, smug smile that she'd perfected. In fact, Ben had floated the idea of flying up to see her that night, and she'd been tempted to say yes, but she didn't want to get excited and then come back to the hotel to find out that he'd canceled, as they both did so often. Maybe he'd surprise her—which would make her smile—but this way he couldn't disappoint her. She signaled for another beer.

"Hey," said a lighting guy named Joel, who had joined them at the pub, sliding in next to her. She had sensed for the past few weeks that he had a crush on her. Everyone had a tour crush.

Joel wore plaid shirts and had a beard and loved "rock" and "jamming" and weed—and was also the type who administered Sudafed to the roadies and knew about everyone's sick aunts and terrible landlords and new kittens but didn't make a show of it.

"A reporter from *New York* magazine called you at the hotel," he said, his voice rising to a squeak. "My, uh, name is also Canter, with an 'e,' so they transferred him to my room by mistake. They want your comment on a story. I told them you would be back tonight, but they seemed annoyed because of the time difference. A profile of your mom . . . and your sister," he said. "Sorry to pry, but you have a *sister*?"

Emma went rigid. She shouldn't be shocked—Leon said they were going public—but a teenage feeling hit her, as though hearing a whisper that her prom date kissed someone else.

"Half sister," she said automatically. "It's a long story. Magazine-worthy, long."

She finished her beer too soon. It sloshed in her empty stomach. She wasn't usually a stupid drinker like this, but all the fresh air had made her thirsty.

"I think I might be sick," she told Joel.

"Oh God, there's a bug going around with the roadies," he said.

"It might be that," she lied. "Can you drive me to the hotel? Or call me a cab?"

He jumped to her assistance.

Back at the hotel, Emma opened the minibar and grabbed a juice. But it seemed lonely, so she took out a gin, too. She went down the hall in her socks and filled her bucket with ice, then came back to her room, garnished her ice glass with gin, and took a big sip. Beer before liquor, never been sicker. Then she sat by the phone, holding the glass and staring at the ceiling. She still remembered an article from almost two years ago, when "Flower" was out, quoting her mother. She scrawled her mother's words on the hotel stationery and propped it in front of her.

"I love my children and I'm proud of their work," she jotted down. "Zingerman had no other comment."

The call came. Emma told the reporter she wasn't interested in talking. The reporter was undaunted, her voice high and excited despite the lateness of the hour. "I can't believe I'm talking to you! I heard the Seattle show was epic."

Emma chuckled. She had learned that a nonverbal reaction was a good way to establish the upper hand with the press.

"I understand your not wanting to talk. It must be so *hard*, though—having your world turned upside down that way. When exactly did you learn all this?"

Emma sat looking at the heavy hotel drapes. Diamonds dotted the fabric. One, two, three.

"Look, it's not for me to spill details," said Emma, preparing to say it repeatedly. "They chose to come forward. I don't want to make it about me."

"But *you're* the news hook," the reporter admitted. "Your mom is an icon, don't get me wrong, but you're the hot one. I mean, Ben Felt? *Hello.*"

"Yes," said Emma, dropping her professional tone. "None of this would be newsworthy if I hadn't made the decision to rerecord those old songs, would it?"

"Oh, that's good—can I use that?" she asked eagerly.

"No way," Emma said. "But you should *definitely* mention that I've made my mother's career relevant to a new generation. I've preserved her legacy."

"Do you have more stuff to say like that on the record?"

Emma paused. "It's distressing to feel—" She wanted to say "displaced," but just then there was a knock at the door.

"To feel what?"

"Look, enjoy your time with them. And remember, *No comment.*"

A sharp knock came from Joel at the door. "Emma," he said, "are you okay?"

She pulled him into the room.

"I did it," she said. "I said, 'No comment.' You saved my life." She kissed him, boozy.

"Is it true you're bisexual?" he asked, kissing back with ferocious lips, his hand around her waist.

"Sure," she said, pulling off her shirt. "If that turns you on?"

She pulled him onto the bed and they rolled around for a while.

This time, a clicking sound at the door. It opened.

Ben came in, sunglasses on, a suitcase in his hand, and on his mouth a round O of shock. The hotel staff, excited to see one half of the famous couple arrive to greet the other, had simply given him a key.

Emma shouted every curse she knew, took the ice bucket, and launched it against the wall, sending cubes scattering across the carpet. Then she tried to throw her glass.

Joel, fortunately still clothed, lunged at it, but it was too late. He and Ben began picking up the ice as she pulled her shirt back on. "Watch your knees, man," she heard Ben saying to Joel and, "Watch the piece over that way—clean break."

She smacked herself in the forehead, which throbbed even worse.

Joel fled.

Ben wasn't steaming mad—he didn't call her a whore. He sat on the bed stroking his chin and biting his lips.

She stumbled over words, trying to elaborate on the magazine story, her sense of crisis. He put his thick-wristed hand in the air and said, "Hey, man . . . I'm the dude who made it clear that I wanted to hang out but not be serious, so joke's on me."

"But still," she said. "That was shitty."

She lay down on the carpet, letting him sit alone on the white expanse of the bed. She stared at the same stupid curtains, ugly and crisscrossed with lines.

Her head pounded. Ben gave the best temple massages—and decent orgasms, which helped with headaches, too—but she had no right to ask him for either.

"I feel like an ass for thinking you wouldn't believe me, that you'd be more into me than I was to you," he said. He was literally scratching his head now. "You know, because you were a girl and I was more famous than you, no offense," he said.

She snorted.

"So I'm not enough for you?" he asked.

"Yes, I know. You're the object of every teen girl's showerhead masturbation fantasy."

He barely registered her words, too busy soliloquizing to the wall, shocked that any female would cheat on *him*.

"I thought you'd be thrilled to see me, but I should have known a girl like yourself would say, 'Okay, we're not exclusive, so I'm going to get my rocks off.'"

"I hoped you'd come," she began, "but I knew I'd be bummed if you didn't, so I put it in my pocket. And then this news about my mother and my sister . . . an article in a magazine."

She had come to sit on the foot of the bed. "My head hurts," she said. "I'm going to take a hot shower."

The water hit the back of her neck, hard, and she bowed her head for more. Ben came in, put the toilet lid down, and sat.

"What's the big deal with your sister? You've known for a while, right? You have a rock 'n' roll family. Can't you let it ride?"

"Well, my mom was mad at *me* first . . . ," she began, poking her head out into the steamy bathroom.

"Apologize, then," he said. "You take yourself too seriously." She could sense the hostility gathering force in his voice. "Just like Irma Crushaman."

"Between me and Judie," insisted Emma. "It's a woman thing."

"Literally none of that makes sense," he said.

She stepped out and he wrapped her in a white hotel robe, and gave her a vigorous dry, and surveyed her with a mixture of lust and pique as she got dressed.

"Hooking up with the *roadie*?" he said. "I was looking forward to having fun—I wanted to tie you to the bedposts." Ben's idea of fun generally revolved around tying Emma to various pieces of furniture.

"My head—" she began, flopping back on the bed.

"Forget it, it's not like I'd be up for that now. Here—this note is for you."

She let her head fall against the wall: bump, bump. It wouldn't end tonight.

He wouldn't dump her for this, now. But he would look at her through the prism of his own wounded ego and create some other reason to break up.

She held up the note that Joel had left on her bedside. She'd missed it before.

It said: "3 Missed calls from New York Mag. 1 missed call from Judith Z."

Emma tore it up, threw it in the trash, and left all her cash for housekeeping.

SYLVIA

VERMONT, 2001

F lower" came on the radio for the second time that day, the third on their trip. Sylvia frowned into the rearview mirror. Judie was being a bear, and this wouldn't improve matters—sure enough, on cue, her sister moaned, "The gods hate me."

"Flower" first hit the charts years ago, but in the back roads of New England on this late summer weekend, it still reigned, because time was mystically suspended here. Or maybe it hadn't been that long at all. Maybe it was still a new hit by today's standards! Sylvia had lost track of the number of times she'd pleaded, reasoned with Judie. Try calling her again. Just keep calling. Judie wasn't "respecting Emma's space"—she was withholding—and she knew it.

"If you went out there and just harangued each other, you wouldn't be so tormented, Mom," said Leon, twisting around from the passenger seat to address his mom and Ned in the back. "It's a perfect song, by the way, thanks to me. Emma's in deep shit. . . . Wait. Slow down, Sylvia . . . that's the swimming hole they mentioned at the motel."

Sylvia pulled over at a broad stretch of dirt alongside a river, and Leon was out of the car before she'd even turned the engine off. Emma and Leon were water babies, baptized by their early summers in New Hampshire.

They followed a small footpath beneath fir trees, leading to a spot where the water pooled into a deep brown expanse. The locals had augmented the natural pool, and some of them were working on it now, fitting rocks between other rocks—making a labyrinth for wading or swimming.

"When in Vermont," said Leon, stripping to his shorts and skimming the water with a toe. "Come on, Auntie Sylvia. Come on, Neddie."

Ned demurred, too elegant to swim in his clothes. He opted for wading.

Sylvia had a bathing suit in her car. She went to change into it, under her dress. Judie hopped back and forth on the bank. "Should I swim?" she asked. "I don't remember which bag my swimsuit is in. Am I too old? How are you so prepared? Can we make it quick—the party is at three?" Sylvia squeezed her eyes tight, blocking out the light and her sister's complaints.

This weekend had been Sylvia's plan. The clan, minus Emma and Dave, plus Ned and Angela, had driven westward to Bennington to play a clean water benefit at the college with some folk stalwarts, then woken up today to schlep to Massachusetts for Dolores's backyard party.

Sylvia tiptoed toward the water, her footing less sure than in her youth. Angela had gone home already (hitching a ride to Albany and taking the train). Tough and adventuresome as she was in every respect, including cold-water swimming, Angie would side-eye the white locals sitting here with beers and cigarettes. Sylvia felt protective of Leon and Ned, too, their tailored clothes and manicured hands, when she traveled out of the city with them.

"Come on." Leon's virtuoso fingers reached out to her, and Sylvia took them, grateful. He kissed her hand. Leaving Judie and Ned on the riverbank, Sylvia ventured across the rocks with her nephew. They sat down together on a big boulder and, at the count of three, slid in.

The river was icy, clear, and chest-deep. Eyes closed, Sylvia did the breaststroke against the current. She imagined she was swimming in snowmelt, in clouds. She imagined she was on the white sheets of her bed at home with Angela beside her.

Clear water. Clean water. Pete Seeger's cause had become all of theirs, all the aging folkies and their friends. Sylvia, too, had grown more political as she got older, thanks to Angela and to time itself. She worried less about herself and Judie and more about the planet, about women's rights and gay rights. About Leon and Emma and their futures.

Sylvia turned and swam toward Judie onshore until her knees slid against the slimy rocks, and she had to sit in the water. "Come in, sis!" she teased.

Judie pointed at her watch. "Dolores only turns five once."

But when they were dried off and prepared to leave again, the engine wouldn't turn on. They all piled out to look at the car.

"*Now* the gods hate us," Sylvia said with a sigh. Ned and Leon held up their hands as if to say, "Don't look at us." Fortunately, Leon had a mobile phone. He called Triple A and they put him on hold.

Judie paced next to the car, moaning. "This is the first birthday party DoDo will remember—we couldn't even get it together. I should have gone alone and missed the benefit."

"Mom, you're not helping," said Leon, his hand over the receiver.

Sylvia closed her eyes. At the benefit, as they played through their family catalog, it had been so clear that their songs circled around each other like water toward a drain—no, the earth around the sun, and the moon around the earth. Emma's "Flower" aimed at Judie—Judie's songs about Dave and Sylvia, Dave's early songs for Judie, their album of ditties for Emma and Leon. And Judie's song about Eamon, and Eamon's songs for Rose, and Judie's for Rose. And Rose giving Emma, in that envelope, Judie's songs about Anna and Hyman, and on and on it went. As they covered "Flower" and "Long-Legged Man" and "Little Brown Sparrow," she felt the deepest communion with Leon, the nephew with the gift, who shared her difference. As they played together, she swore they were discussing Rose and her saga, Judie and Dave's ups and downs, Emma's exile, and themselves: two souls who couldn't live without art, without love. She felt, sometimes, like he was hers.

The car baked in the sun. Ned, tall and blond and British and reserved, looped his arm around Judie now, whispering. Her expression fell under his shadow. Their shoes were coming off. Their feet traipsed the path toward the water. They put their feet in. Suddenly, Judie pulled off her dress, flung it on the beach, took a few halting steps, and then plunged in, her movements awkward but certain.

She popped up like a seal. Sylvia ran up to her.

"In his inimitable British way, Ned reminded me that standing by the car wouldn't summon help faster," she said to Sylvia. Sylvia pondered joining her sister there, but Judie had already exited and was being toweled off by Ned on the shore. Then two locals offered to give them a jump, curious about the back of Sylvia's van, which was stuffed, artfully, with guitars and keyboards.

"Are you famous musicians?" one asked Sylvia as they stretched out the cables. To her own surprise, Sylvia proudly told him about "Flower," about Emma being the writer and Leon the producer.

"I love that song," the Vermonter said excitedly. "That video—with the dress . . . my God. Is she still with the heartthrob? Did I read that there's trouble in paradise? You gotta get your girl in line!"

Questions about Emma's love life, a daily occurrence this summer, always elicited noncommittal laughs, which had a sort of terror underneath it, fear for Emma's exposure.

But the car was now humming away, and the miles of sunbaked asphalt spread out before them, so they tabled the question about Emma. Theirs was a satisfied silence of sun, cold water, a resolved struggle.

They arrived after cake, after singing, after all but two or three guests were gone. And they were sheepish, half-dry from river water, but with arms full of gifts—maple syrup and T-shirts from Vermont, Barbie dresses and a porcelain tea set from the city, hugs and wry comments.

Rose, tired, in a pair of wide-leg pants and Tevas, was everywhere: running after the remaining kids, trying to be a hostess, and annoyed that they were late but also thrilled that they had shown up. She looked older, softer-edged, no longer animated by that new-mother radiance that masked the exhaustion of the early years.

Dolores wanted nothing to do with them, even the presents.

"DoDo, please say thank you," said Rose, chasing her. Dolores stuck her tongue out at her mother, then fell as she ran away and began to holler.

Rose patted up a crying Dolores and stood, awkwardly, as their greetings and their gifts were presented to her daughter. Sylvia recognized the tears marshaling behind Rose's eyes.

"You're five now. It's not *okay* to be rude," she heard Rose say in a low, sharp voice. Sylvia came forward, thinking about herself, and Emma, and Judie, and Anna's expectations, and the way mothers teach girls to be in the world.

"You've had a big day, DoDo," she ventured. "How about you show me where the lemonade is, so we can get one for your tired, hot mama?"

DoDo took her hand.

In the house, Felix was washing dishes.

"Sylvia. She's so glad you came," he said. "The truth is, I think she's a little worried about the Emma thing in *Us Weekly*."

Sylvia felt her stomach drop. "Felix," she said, "show me the magazine."

EMMA

S lut!" The first time Emma heard it, she was at the grocery store buying a pint of low-calorie frozen yogurt, a twelve-pack of seltzer, and a
bottle—or should she get a case?—of white wine. The shout-whispered
epithet came from two preteen girls, spindly legs—younger than her fans.
Their doe eyes glared at her, then shrank away. And theirs were not the only
eyes on her. The longer she huddled, the more attention she sensed.

"Watch out, miss," said a stockist with pink hair and tattoos. "The paparazzi are outside."

A problem with being famous, Emma now realized, was that when you
screwed up, people found out. Millions of them.

The tabloids had got wind of her "dumping" by Ben. Her prediction had
been right: he'd broken up with her weeks after the Seattle debacle, not because of Joel, allegedly, but because "they didn't have much in common." *Us
Weekly* ran a picture of her in sweatpants, taking out trash, with the headline
SHE CHEATED? AND GOT DUMPED? The same agent who set up their initial
date had probably fed them a story, maybe the true one, and the world knew:
she had left America's teen heartthrob heartbroken. Ben's demographic despised her.

Crouched by the wall-to-ceiling freezers, Emma weighed her options.
She opted to buy so many protein bars she could survive for days, get them
delivered, and walk home after exiting the back way. It was only a mile, there
was a footpath by the highway, and nobody walked around here.

Emma had morphed from feminist icon to Hollywood whore. Small
comfort that the buxom pop stars whose songs clobbered hers on the charts
also got more space in the tabloids. She had to go underground.

Her label, this time, seemed to agree, telling her to wait a month or two to come in and record when the press around the breakup "died down."

Alix shipped her a monumental pair of sunglasses and a gaudy patterned scarf. Hiding behind this façade, Emma scooted up to hotel rooms. She avoided parties and hanging out with the crew after shows. Her crowds shrank in size and enthusiasm, and she went through the motions onstage. She counted down the days until her tour ended, trying to become one of those depressed women who couldn't eat but discovering a new desire for marble-frosted doughnuts at every airport. She crammed them into her mouth sitting in the wheelchair stalls of bathrooms.

Within weeks Ben was photographed at the Ivy with his slim, blond costar, and Emma had been reduced to a footnote in the *New York* article about her mother and sister, the one that had precipitated her downfall to begin with. Across the street from her hotel in Nashville, she found a strip mall Barnes & Noble, whose plush carpets and tall shelves shielded her from prying eyes.

The magazine was there.

The revelation of a Foley-Zingerman affair, and child, reveals a re-markable, secret chapter of music history. It's possible that the people who care about the comings and goings of a few semi-iconic folk mu-sicians are dwindling in number—but for anyone thinking about the story of two women—one a scared young woman in a dire situation, the other raised thousands of miles away without knowing the truth about her family, it remains deeply compelling.

When asked for comment, the third woman, Emma Cantor, is terse. "It's not my story," said Emma. "It's theirs." But Cantor looms large in the story: her decision to rework her mother's unpublished songs about Rose not only shone a spotlight on her mother's old secret, but revealed her own fascination with it. . . .

This story doesn't merely illuminate Emma Cantor's covers of her mother's unreleased "Father Fascist" and "Shame," it also throws light back on her mother and aunt's iconic debut album. The song "Rose of Winter," after all, could only be read as a story about Rose herself. And Eamon Foley's "Garden Bloom" is also thrown into a new light.

What Emma hated most was the way the writer set the scene.

Rose Foley Moore, her young daughter, Dolores, and Judith Zingerman Cantor sit easily on the rug of a sparsely furnished Greenwich
Village apartment, the place where Judie and her recently separated
husband of almost twenty years, David Cantor (aka seventies folk-
rock star Dave Canticle), raised Emma and Leon Cantor. It was a
happy if chaotic home, says Judie, with Judie serving as domestic chief
of staff while Dave hit the road year after year. But as the kids grew
up, the marriage frayed.

"It had simply run its course. We talk frequently and have stayed
close." Judie has plans to clear out the apartment and to put it on the
market next year and move somewhere "cozier"—but wherever she
goes, she wants room for her granddaughter.

Yes, her granddaughter. Rose and Dolores are playing with a toy
xylophone.

"I don't have musical training, but I appreciate it," Moore says. "It's
in my blood."

Only two glossy pages. Not nearly the eyeballs that SHE CHEATED? had
garnered, surely. But enough room for a photograph of Rose and Judie in
Riverside Park, wearing fall coats—the green leaves haloing their curls—and
in the light, Rose's sandy hair looked brown, like Judie's.

Emma folded the page of the magazine in on itself, creasing it with fas-
tidious care. Through the long weeks of publicity, the flashbulbs, and the
makeup calls of the last few years, she had desired one thing: to have a photo
shoot with her mother.

When she picked up her head from her knees in the aisle of the Barnes
& Noble, a bored security guard snapped that the store was closing, hadn't
she heard?

~

The tour ended, and Emma flew back to LA, muttering to the agent,
publicists, and label reps who called her that she was sick, and in a way,
she was. She'd been flattened by a cement truck. They told her she had to

pull herself together, avoid making any comments, warned her that the buzz around her was heading toward a disastrous nadir.

Emma didn't need to be told.

The brightness of the days—and they were blazing in LA—barely penetrated. Mornings began with packing a bowl of Ben's high-potency weed (he'd left an ounce in her bedside table). Then she lay on her hideous green carpet and listened to albums on repeat, ignoring the phone. CDs by her parents, her brother, Britney, Nirvana—all got a spin.

She looked up at the ceiling and saw the light from her pool reflecting onto it, shimmering like the New Hampshire lake. Her mother had been left by herself, hadn't she, as a pregnant teenager. Sylvia prattled on about how Judie had a *void*. Emma, swimming in the ripples on the ceiling, had a void, too.

Sylvia and Judie, when they aired complaints about "the industry," said *eat you alive*. Judie found it intolerable, while Sylvia had advice. But Emma had shut her ears to their music, to their warnings, to their efforts to help (controlling or not). She should have paid heed. She should have gone to college.

She wished she were poised, blonder, more feminine, and more natural for stardom. She wished she had told Mae the truth, that Joan Baez was right and Dylan wrong, that kindness mattered more than genius.

VH1 postponed the episode of *Storytellers* she had taped months earlier, citing "scheduling conflicts." The label had songwriters ready to meet with her, they said. *Pop* ones. They asked about her diet.

She waited to see what happened next, with almost morbid curiosity mixed with detachment, about her own fate.

Until the phone call from Sylvia, at her home number.

"Emma, I am with your mom. We're up at my place," Sylvia said, and by her tone, Emma knew something was terribly wrong. "Are you sitting down?"

Emma was lying down. She was always lying down.

"It's Dave. Emma, I don't know how to say this, but you need to book a flight home right away. Emma, he's gone."

Emma couldn't hold her phone up to hear more. She brought it to her chest and held it like a baby, while her aunt's voice echoed small and far away.

～

On her flight home, loaded up with Valium, imagining all the calls and emails and letters pouring into her turned-off cellular phone as the Rockies caused her to bump up and down, Emma flipped a coin, wondering what the answer would be, the cause of her father's cardiac arrest in the middle of Savasana.

Heads. Heart attacks are the leading killers of men over fifty. *Tails.* Aneurysms strike silently. *Heads.* He had overloaded on meds, stressed his heart. *Tails.* Heatstroke.

Not that it mattered. The tent where they'd been practicing yoga had been too hot, but "they" didn't think that was the cause per se. Maybe the trigger. What mattered was that he'd never answer a plaintive question Emma had with an anodyne Ram Dass quote again, never slice her a piece of tasteless macrobiotic bread again. He'd never step back in to sew up the hole in her universe he'd ripped by leaving it.

He was gone, and she hadn't called her mother back, as he'd begged her to. And she'd left the beautiful tapes they had made together in a bag in the corner of her apartment, simply because the label had yelled at her about it.

"You can't outplay genetics," he had said, sitting out on her deck. Warning her. She had worried about his health, then, a flash-quick premonition—but not enough to amend her behavior, to switch focus away from anger about Rose and her mother, the magazine article, and her own flopping career.

~

Dave was gone, and as her publicity team and agent had explained to her on the phone, while offering condolences, the narrative about Emma had overturned in an instant: from depraved whore to bereaved daughter, legendary offspring of a legendary guitarist, gone too soon.

"People love a tragic death even more than a sex scandal, and you can quote me on that," said Alix. "What do you think about us organizing a little shiva in LA? I'm sure Ben would come."

Emma didn't say much in response to these calls. She thought about the grass in Sheep Meadow, the downed kite, and her father's fingers around hers, teaching her chords. She tasted pickle brine.

She *did* thank trusty Alix for the big sunglasses, which helped hide eyes that had been weeping, keeping vigils, bloodshot and rubbed raw.

"It's nothing," said Alix. "I'm going to send you some cream for the dark circles, too."

The sunglasses had shielded her, since that first whispered "Slut!" in the grocery store. Now she wore them as she spoke on the phone with her family in the limo to the airport, as they agreed on a private graveside service that week, with a bigger memorial, maybe even a concert, to follow in time. Jewish custom demanded a quick burial, both relief and a torture.

They screened her as she spoke to Ben, on that same traffic-clogged ride to LAX. He said, Man, he loved that fuckin' song (she knew without asking it was "Wine," not "Sparrow"), and he was sorry about the tabloids, by the way, and she said, Uh-huh, okay, and for her next call, she told Alix to "tell everyone that Emma Cantor said, and you can quote me on that, 'My dad was a criminally underrated guitarist, technically speaking,'" and that "'Little Brown Sparrow' was a better song to remember him by than 'Sweet Camellia Wine,'" but the whole catalog was priceless. "Quote me on that," she said. *"Priceless."*

"You sound so, like, musical," said Alix. "Like you know stuff."

"He's my father, Alix," she said. "He taught me my chords. Quote me on that, too."

At the graveside, Emma trembled behind the sunglasses, flanked by her mother, her aunt, Rae, Leon. Rose mourned somewhere nearby, and Felix, but Emma barely registered them. She took the rabbi's hand and whispered thanks. She took her old principal's hand and whispered thanks. Then she walked away, head in hands, and she heard Sylvia say behind her, "Just let her go."

Behind the huge sunglasses Emma said the kaddish, by heart: *Yit-ga-dal ve yit-ga dash.* She shoveled dirt on the coffin; it thudded. She shuddered, the sound drumming in her mind.

"Dad," she whispered behind her sunglasses, prayer book. "I'm sorry. I'm so sorry, Dad."

Should we sing? Leon had asked her, and she said, Not yet, I don't have my voice.

~

Judie and Sylvia said it was an aneurysm. Judie and Sylvia didn't want her to go back to LA, but since when did she listen to them? Their words circled her like carousel horses. She flew back and turned her phone's ringer off for days. She smoked and smoked and wept while she watched TV, and had some wine, and fell asleep in her clothing, and smelled her own bad breath, and in between terror and sorrow, she loathed herself for the sliver of relief that the most awful thing that had ever happened to her had put a temporary (maybe permanent) stop to the gathering storm around her *slutitude.*

Mae left messages. Leon left messages. Ben called again. Alix called, said she knew a place where Emma could take the waters in the desert. The answering machine at home beeped and grew full. Her cell phone, too.

Emma tried to imagine picking up the receiver for everyone. But none of them were Dave. So she made tea, drank half of it, and left the bag in the cup until it hardened.

The air seemed drier than ever, the desert winds parching her skin. She burned through a six-pack of flavored lip balm Alix's assistant had sent her—cherry, vanilla, mint. Then booze, then cuticle cream, then Gatorade.

One morning, after tossing and turning until her body hurt, Emma finally fell asleep. In her dream, she was walking down a hallway and turned right into a room she'd never seen before, its walls covered with vivid murals.

Dream-Emma perused the art, which turned into a view, where mountains of purple and silver rose into a sunrise, and knew them to be New Hampshire, though they looked nothing like the lake house. She sought a doorway, and in the manner of dreams, she was now in the mountains, along a ridge, her footing precarious, in a mist so real she could feel the condensation on her arm. But then—in the valley below her, shrouded by pine trees, her mother's voice called her name amid a series of sharp bangs. *Judie was in danger.*

"I'm coming!" dream-Emma called. "I'm coming."

Judie needed her, so she ran. She ran, sending rocks skidding all around her, and then she was falling, falling, rolling down the hill.

She woke up, sweaty and cold. Someone was at the door, knocking furiously.

"Emma, open up," the voice through the door said. It was a gravelly contralto.

Emma made a keening sound, catching sight of her own smeary face in the tiny reflection of the peephole—like someone had taken the beautiful siren in the "Flower" video and rolled her in the dirt. Charitably speaking.

The house had taken on a classic post-bender appearance. Microwave pizza boxes and an empty case of wine. Bathrobes and sandals and ashtrays and smoke.

Again, the knocking.

"Mom?" asked Emma in a tiny voice. She realized that she hadn't spoken a word in a week, not even to herself. Judie had flown here for her.

"Thank God. Thank God you're okay," said Judie, breezing through the door, putting her bag down, and waving the smoke away with her hands as she began to open windows. "Mae called us. She was worried you'd overdosed."

"On what, *marijuana*?" asked Emma. But her mom was already on the way to the bathroom to inspect her prescription bottles, taking them down and reading labels.

"I'm not here for a big scene," said Judie over her shoulder as each prescription bottle, inspected and then shaken, was tossed into her own bag. "We need you, Emma."

"Need me?" asked Emma.

"Emma, your father and I never divorced. Everything is mine, yours, and Leon's. We have *a lot* to sort out. His music, the house, everything. It's time to come home."

Emma gaped. "You never divorced?" And then, through hot tears, "He begged me to call you, and I didn't."

Judie sat down on the couch and motioned to Emma: *Come here.*

"You need us, too—*obviously*." Judie gestured at the apartment. "My God, what a shithole."

NEW YORK CITY, NOVEMBER 2001

Already, at eight a.m., Judie and Sylvia were out doing errands. Emma, displaced from her room by her mother, had slept on the couch, which meant barely sleeping. After some fitful dozing, she slipped outside, sat on a bench in Riverside Park, and fiddled with Anna's ring.

That September, all of New York had gone into deep mourning, and shock, the doormen in gas masks and missing signs fluttering from poles. Judie was temporarily living uptown with her kids, all of them functioning by rote memory, all in a trance. Leon had been scoring a ballet in Denmark when Dave died, but he had stayed home after the funeral, too. As Emma's star had fallen, his had risen: the real genius of the family, people said on the music message boards online.

Emma kept meaning to book a hotel or find a high-end rental, but she secretly loved being stuffed in the same apartment as her family, hearing them wake up as she shifted out of her hard-won sleep on the couch.

Judie was supposed to meet her in an hour before they went downtown to reopen their apartment. How tall the trees reached up here. They'd witnessed a lot over the years, probably. The feuds of squirrels, and of New Yorkers. Anna's ring came off and Emma held it up and switched hands. Part of the enamel had chipped one night when she had been playing guitar and been too drunk to take it off. But only a sliver.

The years that had passed since that afternoon at Brown had brimmed with drama. She had a sense of a curtain falling on the era that had begun on that tour, that wild performance. It *should* be over. She was an anonymous woman with tattoos on a bench in a park, trying to conjure up her dead dad's voice, trying to make music with meaning.

Emma had come to New York City a week after her mother left, leaving the LA house as empty as she found it. As the plane took off and she popped a second Valium (she had renewed her prescription the minute Judie left), she muttered to LA: "Fuck you very much."

The anonymity of the city, even broken and ruined, soothed her gaping grief for Dave—the diners and dives and coffee shops where no one cared about you and you could sit with a coffee or beer for hours. She belonged with her people, her tribe, in their pain.

Judie wanted Emma's help figuring out the future of their family apartment and the house upstate. She wanted Rae to get something—but what? And Rae in her grief had gone frantic, insisting on doing sage ceremonies everywhere that Dave had been.

Judie arrived at the bench, and Emma demanded an embrace and was drawn in like a naughty child. Judie pushed her away after a few seconds, saying, "There, there, that's enough."

"You didn't talk to me for three years," said Emma. "The least you can do is let me hug you for a minute."

Emma took her big sunglasses and a floppy hat from her bag and put them on as they walked downstairs to the train.

"You've said things to me without saying them," said Judie with a sniff, and Emma, thinking of her "Father Fascist" video, which had featured a young actress playing a lonely game of jacks for three minutes while tears ran down her cheeks, clamped her mouth shut.

Emma wanted to embrace the grimy subway tiles, in shared grief. On new maps, certain stops near ground zero had been grayed out, and the sight riveted her.

No one here batted an eye or recognized her. After a final miserable week in LA, she had dyed her hair blond. She was letting it grow now, and the color was fading. So she looked like another mousy white woman in New York, trying to be a sleek Jennifer Aniston.

"Your hair looks interesting," observed Judie without a value judgment. Emma raised her eyebrow at her reflection in the moving subway window.

"I'm fine with it," she said.

"Then why ask?" said Judie.

"I didn't ask, Mom. *You* brought it up."

They exchanged a wry smile, a sign of their truce. Emma couldn't shout to the world that things had grown wonderful between them, but things *existed* between them—plans and sentences and hugs.

"It's good to have you in town," said Judie, sounding like Anna. "In the family circle." Emma asked if the circle included Rose. Judie complained that Rose was forever jetting off to Ireland to see Mary and Sean and Felix's folks out west.

"Denial is a river in—" Emma began, and Judie stopped her, bringing up the apartment, how Emma and Leon should have their share of the proceeds when and if they ever sold it.

New and intriguing, this woman-to-woman, let-me-catch-you-up way of speaking. When they got to the apartment, they flicked on light switch after light switch and found things undamaged, except for a coating of dust in some places. Judie wore a pair of corduroy overalls that did nothing for her figure but looked perfect anyway; her purple rag socks nestled into felt clogs; she was the essence of someone who had chosen comfort and wore it well—in contrast to Sylvia's svelte body, her black getups and silver shoes.

They scrubbed in companionable silence, but when they got to her bedroom door, Judie stopped.

"I can't go in there yet," she said. "I'll make tea."

If her mother harbored feelings for Dave, or at least for their years here, then Emma would rise to duty. She took a dustcloth and went to work on the surfaces. She hadn't cleaned like this since the days of the van tour. She swept across the bare top of her mother's dresser, which must be hiding sartorial treasures: scarves and bangles. But the sweeping stopped when she considered what might be under the bed, lying in wait.

Judie had encouraged Emma to stash precious papers under her own bed, after all. Maybe Judie's genius had been camping out down here for decades. She dropped to the floor, groped around until she found the box of notebooks, holding what looked like pages and pages of lyrics. A pause as she chided herself. Her eyes darted to the pages, anyway.

The books didn't hold lyrics. She found grocery lists and journal entries.

"Emma sassy today. In our bed for two hours after a nightmare—god I'm exhausted, need a drink to sleep." "So tired, don't even have a job," she wrote another time. "Emma singing Twinkle 30, 40 times. Leon can sing in a round and is trying to teach her, but she starts early."

This must be an old one. Where were the songs?

Emma felt the bed dig into her back as she flipped through pages, poring over words she could grasp: her name, Rose's, clues to Judie's mind and her own history.

December 11, 1988

I don't know if it's the cold winter—maybe one of the kids has gotten me sick—but I have the old feeling like someone has taken the stuffing out. . . .

I went to the Jefferson Market Library and stared at the stained glass, willing it to inspire me, but my head lolled back in my chair—why? I slept last night—why do I eternally exist in heightened frenzy or near hibernation? Like a bear.

Emma flipped a few pages—there was a blank one, a half-finished lyric about a rainy day that she remembered her mother singing when she was small ("A rainy day / is a lazy day / A rainy day / is a lazy day"), and ten pages of to-do lists, crossed off and arrows between items. Ten! Then more journaling.

December 17, 1988

Why am I worried about what Dave will make for dinner if we split? It stops me, but my loneliness stops me more, when the kids are at school and I pause the bustle of errands (Hanukkah gifts) and look around and want the person I know how to talk to.

Emma felt tears come to her eyes. *Dad*, she thought. Mom loved Dad. But she was thinking of splitting from him all the way back then!

1989

Sylvia called. Mom's not doing well. Leon and Emma both have strep, not even arguing over which bad sitcom to watch. When they are sick, especially at first, the rage drops away. Would give anything for my two brown-headed monsters to tear around and drive me nuts.

Light in the kitchen is out. . . . Writing this while waiting for superintendent.

Emma was lying face down on the floor now, digging under the bed. There were about a dozen journals, each going blank about ten pages before the end, as though finishing a project were such anathema to her mother that it couldn't be done, even informally.

Emma imagined those blank pages being scrawled with invisible ink, secrets. But she found the same: lists, reminders, phone numbers, folded-up receipts, and sometimes entire pages covered with Leon's and her scrawls, first big, open loops and later words and phrases, smiley faces and patterns.

There were big, block letters saying things like "CALL ABOUT TUES-DAY HAIRCUT." And in between all of this, Judie's notes to herself.

And finally, with one of them, a particularly weathered one, Emma found something of real interest.

December 1985

Can't leave Emma home alone—that aging flower child spooked her. She's sensitive. I spoke to Rose about giving her extra key to the guy at the corner store or the neighbor—it's what we did in the 60s. Also spoke to the nursing home about the medication issue.

Nothing to do when you fail them but try to fail a different way next time, I suppose.

With a mixture of care and abandon that might hide her tracks, Emma replaced the journals under the bed, and sneezed.

So. Judie had likely been gone that night because Rose was locked out of her apartment. She breathed through her lips. What had Rose said to her in New Hampshire—a family of liars? Rose, alone, scared out on the street at night. Emma, alone at home, a little too young for it. Poor Judie, dashing out and back, thinking it would be okay.

Pure speculation, of course. But it fit into the keyhole in her heart.

Emma had harbored rage for so long, but now she saw that she was just sad and always had been. She wanted mellow, late-life Dave to witness the idea she was contemplating here: Could she, might she, pick that anger up and simply put it aside?

She laid the diary down and looked up to see Judie at the door, watching her. And maybe Emma's wild imagination, mixed up with grief and her too-muchness, made her hallucinate it, but for one split second she saw her mother not as *Mom* or even as Judie Zingerman, frustrated folkie, but as just another woman, beaten down but not yet broken by life. And as Judie's coal-dark eyes, luminous and wet, looked right back, surely her mother saw her that way, too.

Emma slid the box along the floor toward Judie's socked feet.

"Old diaries. Keep, or burn?" she asked with a smile.

"There's not much there for future biographers," said Judie. "But it always helped me stay anchored in time."

Emma had been wrong. Ben, empty-headed, bright-eyed Ben, had been right. Yes, Rose distracted Judie, yes, the secret had damaged them all, but Emma had been mothered. The diaries proved it.

Judie threw her head back, letting her hair shake out, and then put it up in a bun.

"Diaries are not written to be read, you know," she said, her tone light. "They are a repository for random thoughts."

Emma shadowed her mother from room to room as Judie opened cupboards, pointed out flaws.

"We'll renovate the kitchen this winter so we can get a good price once downtown comes back," said Judie. Would Rose and Dolores get some of the money? Rae? Emma didn't ask.

At the doorway to the den, they paused. The room was almost empty and had been since Dave bought the Red House and moved the platinum record and awards and instruments there.

Judie rattled off a catalog of guitars and where they were: upstate, in storage. Her favorite three, it turned out, were at "the office"—Emma's old school, where Judie had her own locked closet.

Emma walked to the window and rapped out a drumbeat on it.

"When's the last time you wrote a song, Mom?"

"I cowrote the songs for the senior musical last year—with two of my advisees, you might have known them—no, I guess they were too young."

"I mean a song for *you*—on your own?" She put a hand on her mother's shoulder.

"There have been droughts," said Judie. "I didn't have the time, then I didn't have the urge."

Emma's own musical frustration hung on her like an anvil. And Judie, who had the most legitimate gift she'd known, casually said she didn't have the "urge."

"Don't you ever worry that you wasted your talent? That we smothered it?"

"Nonsense. I still have talent," said Judie. She sat down on the old leather couch and put her feet up.

"So what are you doing with it?" demanded Emma, standing over her mother.

"Oh honey," said Judie. Emma thought about the pages and pages of scribbles she'd read without a single functional song—the years her mother had made dinner and taken her temperature and tended to Dave's moods.

"I don't know what happened," Judie said. "I had you kids, then Rose came back, and time moved quickly." She began to cough from the dust.

Emma knelt on the rug and put her head in her mother's lap. Judie stroked Emma's hair. They sat that way for maybe six seconds, total, but long enough—the whole afternoon was enough—to begin to ice a bruise in Emma. Even when her mother said, "I'm sorry, but you are crying out for a haircut—Sylvia knows someone," Emma bristled, but not as she might have.

On the rug now, Emma stretched her legs out in front of her, while her mother remained on the couch. She leaned forward to touch her toes, felt three or four cracks in her back and shoulders, soreness flaring up the backs of her legs.

"Emma, your stretching reminds me of him. We need to plan the concert for Dave. And you need to go upstate and deal with the house."

Emma dug under her thumbnail bed and removed a thin layer of dirt. Only a few possessions remained in this old room. The photo of Emma's parents in New Hampshire, which she would take home today. Two bottles of whiskey from the Isle of Skye, where they'd gone when Emma was fifteen to celebrate Leon's acceptance into Juilliard.

Her mother took Emma's face in between her hands. "You have so much to do. You were his favorite."

JUDIE

Judie shoved a fifty-dollar bill into the front seat of the taxi before slamming the door. So much for cleverly putting wool socks under her clogs; her toes curled in with the frost.

The train ride had seemed enchanted, taking the pair of them most of the way to Dave's house along the snow-sprinkled Hudson. But her feet had slowly lost sensation. Emma, happily nestled in hiking boots, tugged their wheeled bag over the threshold.

Judie peeled off her gloves and shoes and began to rub her feet. The red ranch house was comfortable: a 1970s monstrosity Dave had furnished with generic oversize couches and dark rugs and a studio with every gadget imaginable.

"I wish I could hear him making a smoothie tomorrow morning," said Emma. Judie cleared her throat to keep herself from losing it in front of Emma, trying so hard to be mature and strong for once.

"I miss him too," she said.

Recently, Emma had played a tape of her and Dave's California demo sessions for Leon and Judie.

"This sounds like an album, right?" she said. "I got hours of us talking, but the songs work."

Leon strummed two chords, tapped his foot, and grinned. "I was thinking the same, Emma-bear." Her label came around on the idea; things had changed. The new, "serious" album could be her ticket to critical redemption: guitar-playing intricate, her voice raw and weathered. Besides, everyone was hungry for Dave Canticle music now.

At the Red House, Emma affixed white poster paper on the door to the studio and began to write down the names of songs for the record, crossing them out and moving them around with Judie's input. While Emma jumped with excitement, her hip hurt and she said, "I'm holding emotion in my hips," and then, "Oh God, I'm turning into a yoga person. Oh, Dad!"

Judie sent air whooshing from her lips. He had been absent so much, but it took this final absence to understand how present he had been, too, especially for Emma.

Judie would go home on Monday, while Emma settled in to sort out the house and polish the album in the studio. As the temporary mistress of Dave's home (Rae was already in India with the tidy lump sum they gave her from Dave's estate), Emma would have all kinds of new concerns: drywall and leaks, mold and mice. A mortgage, repair and maintenance people. Packing, deciding what to do with her father's things. Mixing and remixing her songs would preoccupy her, along with calls to Judie about Dave's concert.

Judie noted the spotty cell phone service here, the way the one computer with internet crawled. This would be so good for her daughter. The fresh air, the long walks, maybe sleeping without pills. She would spend hours in the studio every day, crafting an album that would be her gift to her father.

⌒

After all these years, Judie found leaving her kids elicited the same twisted cocktail of emotions: relief and desolation.

Back at home, in the downtown apartment that had fewer possessions, she put her dishes in the sink, ran water, lips moving in silent prayer, sending wishes into the air for her daughter's big meeting about the Red House album that afternoon. "Positive vibes," as Dave would say.

Whenever Emma called Judie to discuss the record, and to unload her never-ending grief, Judie was glad to play the role of mother again. And she noted with satisfaction that Emma had fallen in love with the area—hiking everywhere and making friends with the farmers Dave had known—and wasn't rushing to sell the house.

But that meant it fell to Judie to plan the concert. Sylvia and Angela were in postproduction on a documentary about lesbian AIDS activism they'd coproduced. Leon was working on a pop album for a Swedish singer.

That left Judie, perennially on hold with Town Hall, the receiver wearing a groove in her neck, loading dishes in the machine.

"Tell them *you're* dying," Emma suggested. "They'll get you a date right away."

One thing you could say about Emma and Leon, they had senses of humor. That, she and Dave had done right.

~

Judie in her fifties admitted that her life up to now looked like a stack of mistakes, bumbles, bungles, errors, grave misjudgments, screwups, and wild turns. Scurrying off to New York, getting knocked up in a hotel room, surrendering infant Rose, turning to Dave for security, keeping Rose secret from Emma and Leon, staying in music after her heart left it, staying away from music too long, being so furious at Emma that she shut the door between them.

She'd had reasons. Judie and Rose maintained their clandestine relationship the way they did because they had needed time to meet each other, to make it right.

But Judie had resisted squaring herself with Emma. She had pushed young Emma away out of guilt over Rose. Emma's eyes, her big dark eyes, were pools of reproach. And Emma, young and stunning, knew what to do with Judie's songs, with a canniness and sexiness that her mother had lost (or life had stolen from her). She had been, she admitted now, somewhat jealous.

The most obvious explanation was that Judie had cut Emma off to mirror the years apart from Rose, to even the score. Perhaps she was a stubborn, withholding jerk. The time she did call, the time she sent a message through Dave, Emma didn't answer. She should have kept calling and calling.

What a marvel to chitchat with Emma without the burden of hiding Rose. After all of her parenting calamities, she didn't deserve this renewal. Maybe she'd slide back to synagogue this year on Rosh Hashanah to keep things in balance.

Judie twisted the phone cord around her arm, as Sylvia used to do at the lake house. A calendar of psychedelic poster art Emma had toted home from upstate (as a half joke, maybe?) sat on the kitchen table. They had circled possible memorial concert dates. Emma had begged her mother to play music at the show.

Judie wanted to explain to Emma how it had kept getting pushed back, her music: one summer, when Emma was about to turn three (or was it four?), both kids seemed settled: potty-trained, obedient enough. Judie began to take a notebook to the kitchen table after breakfast: she doodled lyrics and even plans for a return to music.

Then Emma learned to climb out of her crib. She would vault onto the armchair where Judie nursed her, come into their room, and demand to *snuggle*. Every night for weeks. Dave would be gone or asleep, and so Judie would lead Emma back to the nursery, muttering, "I must go to Workbench and get her a new bed, I must," and lie on the carpet, and just when Emma seemed asleep, she'd shoot a pudgy hand out between the crib bars to make sure her mother was there.

No amount of coffee or cartoons the next morning sufficed to blast through the honeyed mess of Judie's brain: Will I nap, can I nap, will I be unable to nap if I drink more coffee, will Emma nap, can Emma nap?

One such night, Emma back asleep, Judie could not do the same. She tried chamomile tea, warm milk. She turned off the lights and turned up the fans. Each of these actions had the effect of waking her up further, until she howled with frustration, her face smothered in a pillow. Finally, she dozed into a recurring daydream, a romp through the house in New Hampshire, lavender ribbons streaming behind her. Up the stairs, past any reasonable number of floors, until she arrived at a room covered with Greek hieroglyphics.

At the far corner, an alcove with a window awaited her, and she rushed to the window, feeling it pull, knowing somehow her parents, death, eternity, all awaited her. But when she peered out the window, she saw children playing lawn games, so far below they were indiscernible.

You look for your parents but find your children. And even they are out of reach.

~

When Judie was heavy with Rose, Anna had come to her with hot-water bottles and warned her about children swallowing you alive. But she'd also softened the blow with statements like "Women have an impossible lot. The things we make are beautiful, anyway. You will start again."

Begin to begin.

Every morning, with eyes so tired they could barely open, she had to wake up and pack Leon's lunch (Who cared if it was usually deli sandwiches and chips?) and do the school-and-playground run, and wait for the babysitter, and tidy up. Each day might end up tedious but began fresh with the hope of her work waiting for her, although sometimes it hid itself for months.

～

L ittle Brown Sparrow,'" said the voice on the other line, a town hall guy who was waiting for his boss for confirmation. "Mrs. Cantor—I mean Miss, or is it Ms. Zingerman—is it true he wrote that about *you*?"

"Yes and no," said Judie. "There was another girl he loved, and I did too, named Valerie."

"Good stuff," he said. "I feel like *The New York Times* will cover this."

They put her on hold again. When she took on this task she had dreaded this part—the calls, being on hold.

But she found she didn't mind.

～

A t Emma's home studio, Dave had recounted to her his courtship of Judie, and Emma was folding snippets of those stories onto their album. She even asked Judie to "fact-check" them. Judie didn't deny Emma's requests. She'd learned her lesson.

It *had* been romantic, that day she saw him again, hurrying across Harvard Yard on the way to a teach-in about the war, looking up at a tree so yellow it burned against the October sky. Leaves crunching beneath her feet as she walked, but the grass still springy.

His voice calling to her from the library steps: "Judie! Judie Zingerman!"

Dave. She wished he could be there to plan his own memorial concert. She missed him deep beneath her flesh.

True, of course, that someone could be your shelter from the storm and also be the storm itself.

Judie paused, put down the dish she was washing, the phone on its side. Had she just written a new lyric, or was she stealing from Dylan? Funny that the question she once asked about her first attempts at songwriting—"Am I stealing from Dylan?"—haunted her still.

Did anyone feel haunted by her songs? Did Emma?

With slow, careful movements, she dried her hands. In the silver cabinet, she took out her notebook of lyrics—a school-issued one that Emma hadn't found. God knows when anyone had last looked *here*. She scribbled a note to herself. A new song was forming.

It had taken her five years to fill up half of the book, with work that lacked the sparkle of the stuff decomposing on the bottom of the lake.

But *these* songs hadn't dissolved in the mud. They'd endured.

~

I t's very important that we do this concert within a few months," Judie found herself saying on the phone, rushing back at the sound of a voice. "See if you can find a night next year, in early March."

"Will you be singing, too, Miss Zingerman?"

She was impatient now. "It depends on whether you give me a date I want."

Even if the world didn't see it, Judie had never stopped writing. Her songs wriggled to the surface: on *Chant and Sing*, on Sylvia's albums, in the corners of Leon's work, too, and—even against her will—keynoting Emma's album, a genuine hit.

During the silences, and the crises, the work waited for Judie. It waited for her to pick up her guitar, her pen.

And look what she had made in the meantime: her babies, and their lives, messy and jagged, but not unbeautiful either.

ROSE

2003

Rose ran smack into Leroy in the long hallway of a conference in an unremarkable American city. He was an urban planner, married like her, two kids, suit jacket. She was speaking on a panel about housing policy.

Holding identical manila envelopes, with plastic name tags dangling from their necks, they talked about spoon-feeding and babyproofing. She embarrassed herself by bragging about Dolores, whose teachers labeled her exceptionally bright and musically inclined.

The explanation for what happened that summer long ago was simple: his mother had a stroke, he withdrew from school. But he'd stopped by the old pub in San Francisco and told them to pass on his contact information if Rose came back.

"Oh," she said. "I see."

Her turn: she told him about how Judie had guided her to community college, then Sylvia pulled strings at Wellesley, how she'd excelled more each year until the postdoc at Brown, followed by the positions at UMass.

"I made it up with the family," Rose said. "They're having a concert next week and I'll be in the front row."

"I heard about the show," he said as her limbs weakened. "I read about you in *New York* magazine a few years back, too. Intense stuff."

"Sure," she said. But to her, *intense* was asking what would have been different if she'd gone back across the continent to that bar. Intense how your impulses at eighteen, twenty, twenty-two, set you on a path for your whole life, shutting doors you didn't know were doors.

"I should go," she said. "Session in hall C."

Rose had been overpowered by the urge to kiss him. She'd excused herself and gone to her room and called Felix to ask about Dolores, then knelt in the shower and let it spray her back (a trick she learned from Sylvia) as she tried to forget her nauseating bus ride to New York, the salty chicken soup, the imaginary rosary.

If only one could dissect one's heart, find embedded in the tissue the precise cause of an emotional freak-out at the sight of an ex-lover in the sterile hallways of a convention center, each of you holding tote bags with the word "Future" on them, the "F" shaped like an arrow.

Rose had pored through texts on adoption and trauma—it helped, but not as much as reading salacious tales about Jack Nicholson, who learned that his "sister" was his mother and his "mother" his grandma. This spoke to her: raised by loving blood relatives—and by half-truths. She and Jack Nicholson, and Leon and Emma. She talked to Mary on the phone for an hour every Sunday, after church (for Mary) and bagels (for her). And she thanked Mary for not trying to hide the truth about Eamon, for not holding on to it so tightly.

"Well, everyone on the street knew the whole business," said Mary. "If I'd wanted to keep a secret so, I would have moved back to London." Sometimes they argued, hung up, called each other back. That's how Rose knew Mary was her mother, even if Judie was, too. Their fights.

Free toiletries lined the marble-topped sink. Rose turned one over, unscrewing the silver lid and plopping it against her palm until a sea-green dollop emerged. Mechanically, she spread it on her upper arms, her wet, stubble-covered calves. A swipe across her stomach with its Dolores pouch, a smear on each thigh.

In only her underwear, her body slid under the starchy tight sheets. She had been conceived in a hotel room; she always recalled this whether in a curtained B&B or an air-conditioned cube. Her parents' rendezvous had not been in a soulless room like this, she hoped (the way her awful dalliance with the nameless Irish kid was), but they were all similar: bed emerging from the wall, dresser facing it, a row of windows.

Emma told her, at Thanksgiving, that the craziest rock-star shenanigan she'd pulled on tour was to chuck an entire ice bucket and glass against a hotel room wall.

"A life low," Emma said.

"You're young to be talking that way," Rose replied. Dave's place had been filled with city people visiting for the weekend, ogling the turning leaves and listening to a few tracks of Emma's new album. Emma had arranged the party, local caterers and all, and her eyes gleamed all night.

Emma told Rose it had been a rough few years in LA "without Mom." Rose remembered the conversation for the ice bucket anecdote, but mostly because of the way Emma had said "Mom"—without a possessive pronoun in front of the word.

Rose missed Emma's rise to stardom, the family battle over the album, because of the fog that descended with motherhood. Dolores's birth was "difficult"—a tame word for first-degree tearing, then searing pain while nursing. Mary had gone home after helping Rose through the beginning, where pain struck like lightning on the hour. But as she'd begun to physically recover, the baby grew fussy and colicky, screaming into the night, and Judie had arrived during the worst of it, night waking, weeping, daggers shooting from Rose's nipples down into her belly.

"I'm a terrible mother," she wailed. "I wasn't built to do this."

Judie had said what Rose needed to hear: "You need medication and rest." She had held Dolores against her chest while Rose went into the other room and slept for four straight hours and when she woke up told Rose to make an appointment with a doctor right away for pills, to stop being a martyr and let Felix give a bottle of formula now and then so she could sleep.

"I got that desperate feeling inside, too," she said to Rose. "After Emma. Also, after you, but . . ." She closed her lips.

Judie did laundry, rinsed dishes, ordered enough Chinese to last days. She even got behind the wheel of the car, once, to get "the best" sandwiches.

Once, as Dolores snoozed in the bassinet, Judie had asked Rose, whispered with confusion, "Rose, you . . . you gave Emma my old songs?"

"Have you heard her recent stuff?" asked Rose. "They were *made* for her voice."

Judie held up a tiny pair of pants and folded them. "But . . . I meant for those songs to be *yours*, dear."

Rose added the pants to a pile of similar ones. "Right. To do what I chose with."

"She stole them by recording them without asking," Judie said. "I said I'd sue her to stop her."

"Why?" said Rose, so loudly that Dolores stirred and whimpered. "But . . . why on earth would you sue your own child?"

Judie averted her eyes.

"I never do anything I say I will, anyway," she said. "Don't people know that by now?"

~

Rose arrived at Town Hall an hour before the show, wearing more lipstick than she'd put on since her dissertation defense and a crushed-velvet blouse she'd bought with Angela and Sylvia. "It's hip, but with quality fabric," said Sylvia. "Right in the Sylvia approval matrix."

"The lights in Town Hall are no joke," said Angela, holding up a sequined top. "I want to be a Christmas tree."

Angela was hipster royalty in NYC. Her long-delayed rock concept album, *High Street*, had been a hit in England, and she'd moved abroad. But the internet and word of mouth had slowly given it cult status everywhere. And sometime in the last few years, she and Sylvia had gone public, and they'd become doyennes to the young and sexually fluid scenesters of downtown.

Angela and Sylvia's bliss made Rose envious, although it had entered this phase only after years of hard and lonely living for both. They were blushingly in love—and in love with being open. Fingers brushing sleeves. Admiring glances across the room, checking in with each other for approval.

She compared their love with her steady union to Felix. He had called both Mary and Judie in for help after Dolores was born. They quietly took turns doing the school drop-off run, making sandwiches. Neither had published quite as much as they wanted or gotten quite as much recognition as they wanted. But they'd done good work. And how carefully they read each other's papers, talked through dilemmas about students.

And he put up with her family—both families, in fact.

When she and Sylvia and Angela were waiting to pay for their concert outfits, three warm, crystal-clear notes came on over the sound system. Eamon Foley's "The Rain on the Bay." Rose dropped one hanger on the floor, bent to pick it up, then dropped the other.

> *Your eyelashes*
> *Look out at the bay*
> *The wind stirs the ashes*
> *I know you won't stay*

She rearranged her bundles, and Sylvia gave her a knowing smile. "The Rain on the Bay" was unbearably sad. Eamon's music had been given a fresh airing a year ago, when a cover of "Golden-Haired Girl" played during the credits of *Minneapolis Love*, a quirky romantic comedy. Now it was common to hear one of his songs playing at a store or coffee shop.

"If this is how *one* Eamon Foley song makes you feel, you'll have to be institutionalized next week," said Sylvia. "Are you ready for the show?"

"I mean—"

"Do you need waterproof mascara?" Angela's elbow poked into her rib cage.

Rose loved Angela best. Angela, who as a fellow "church refugee" always sought God elsewhere, like Eamon. Angela, who had recently roped Rose into joining her for a lecture series on Jewish history, who was now making noise about a Hebrew class together. Angela, who wore glittery things because life "needed more sparkle."

They walked home with their shopping bags and speculated on whether Judie would perform. She had been coming to rehearsals but sitting on the side, murmuring to herself, and everyone was disappointed she wasn't playing.

But Rose, the only nonmusician, heard lots of little confidences from the family. And she knew something no one else did. Judie had new songs, including one for Dave.

"The thing about Judie," said Sylvia, resident expert, "is she never climbed out of the hole of her pain. I mean she did in a way, with the teaching, but . . ."

"She couldn't see how her songs mattered. Girls were *crazy* for her work," said Angela.

"Saving my sanity when I was going nuts with Dolores was a pretty major help," said Rose, even though she had been told by many a therapist she should stop compulsively defending the woman who had abandoned her at birth. "Letting Emma record her songs in the end. Taking Dave back after Miranda. Going to LA to get Emma."

"Touchy, touchy," snorted Sylvia. Rose felt anger throb in her throat but swallowed it down. To be part of this family was to lob and receive casual insults. Someday she'd adjust to it. Or Dolores would.

Rose had come to believe in the power of forbearance; maybe it justified her path, since she'd failed to cut a hugely distinguished figure, neither artist nor rebel. But through sheer womanly grit she had sutured her family back together—stuck it out and created a life, interesting and stable, and made Dolores, who had mended both her and Judie in different ways.

On the best days, sitting in her yard with Felix and Dolores, Rose thought what she had done was as remarkable as Judie or Emma, who created art from the things they broke. She *had* been broken, from birth. And she had created herself.

On good days she thought this, anyway.

Besides, Dolores was going to change the world—she was sure of it.

⌒

They arrived early, collected drink tickets. Dolores, her preschool chub long melted away, was wearing a fairy-tale-like turquoise dress with puffed sleeves, and Felix wore a new sweater Rose had gotten him, snug and professorial. In the hallway outside the bar on the second floor, Rose contemplated them in the mirror: her family, scrubbed up. They weren't a musical dynasty, but they were themselves and here and together.

As the bartender prepared Dolores a Shirley Temple, Emma swept up in a gold T-shirt and black leather pants, with high-heeled boots up to her knees. Her hair fell to her chin in soft curls. Rose noticed a single bright-red streak tucked behind her sister's ear.

Emma's focused face twisted into mirth. With Emma, you had to plow through.

"The *Red House Sessions* album is amazing," said Rose—always ready to load sycophantic bullshit on her sister. "Perfect for the moment."

"I hope what we do tonight makes you guys proud," Emma said. Then her eyes caught Dolores, who was sitting on the velvet carpet and playing with a Barbie.

"You let her play with Barbies?" she asked, and Rose felt herself tense up. "Good for you. You can't keep kids in a box." Pause. "But I mean, what do I know . . . about kids?"

Rose chuckled at Emma's prickliness. She was still so young, her sister. Dolores looked up, and Rose watched her eyes meet Emma's.

"She looks like Mom," said Emma. "With her hair that way."

Emma crouched down to Dolores.

"I like your shirt; it's sparkly," said Dolores.

"Thank you! You're wearing a lovely dress," said Emma. "Are you ready for the music?"

"I dance," said Dolores. "I like ballet, but Mommy doesn't—so I'm doing modern. I sing, too—but mostly dance."

Emma guffawed. "I never was much for dancing," she said. "Maybe you could teach me."

Dolores instructed Emma on how to move from first to second position, and Emma gamely complied in her platform boots. Rose watched, the voice of her own endless longing crying out *Yes!* while the self-protective voice within her asked, *Remember when she stomped on you in Providence? And at Dave's funeral?*

Emma didn't seem to have an agenda, though, except maybe to avoid talking further with Dolores's parents.

"It's been nice to catch up," said Emma. "I have to get mic'd up."

"Do you think she'll play?" asked Rose, looking at her sister's fourth earring, a stud right at the top of her ear.

Emma's headshake was minute but clear. She put a lacquered finger to the inner corner of an eye, and Rose felt her own eyes tingle with potential tears. But Emma couldn't smudge her mascara, not yet. She seemed to perform a ritual to avoid crying: she made a circle with her lips.

"She can't quite do it," she said. "She'll be backstage cheering us on."

She met Rose's gaze, then, her brown eyes wide.

"I'm sorry," she said. "I tried." Those first two words, evidently not Emma's favorites, came to Rose like an outstretched hand.

Emma walked away to warm up. Rose closed her eyes to the memory of the dirt hitting Dave's coffin and Emma flinching with each thud, not realizing how naked her sorrow was. Rose had so wanted to embrace her—but to do so would have been taking advantage of a wraith. Thank God Judie had gone out West to rescue her.

Rose's own family found their seats. The lights went down. "It's starting!" whispered Dolores, excited. "Shh, Mommy."

Silence spread out to the wings, the balconies, a soft cloud filling the room. A rustle of paper, a cough.

Rose stretched her feet out toward the stage—under sensible clogs, Dolores had insisted on her mom donning gold-threaded socks. They shimmered in the light.

Emma and Leon strode out together, holding hands. The crowd roared to see them. This family had fans. Her family had *fans*.

"Well, hello—this concert is for our dad," Leon said as Emma beamed at him. "But it's also for all the people whose music has been part of our lives, and his life, and your lives. It's a celebration of the life of Dave Canticle: the man, the miracle, the mensch." Leon winked, and two guitars materialized, carried by guys in black.

"This night's for you, Daddy," said Emma, sniffing back tears. "I spent some time with Dad and we kind of ended up recording an album"—hoots and whoops—"and when we were talking, I learned this song was inspired by my mom, by words she said on a street corner a few miles from here. Which leads us to ask . . . where her royalties are. Anyway, it's a beautiful day, let's keep it going."

The siblings launched into an acoustic duet on "Summer Rain"—"Summer rain / it washes us clean"—and parlayed it into "Early Morning Rain."

The velvet curtain flew up and revealed the band. Rose recognized the drummer—the short-haired, tattooed woman who had played with Emma at Brown. She had pink hair now. The drummer smirked as if she found the whole thing silly but was pleased to be a part of it. A bassist and a few backup singers in blue velvet vests completed the backing group. A whisper behind her: "They got Tomi Tiptree to sing backup? Wow." She recognized the name. A gender-bending downtown cabaret star.

Leon and Emma knew everyone.

Angela arrived onstage in the glittery top Rose had helped choose, sashaying close to Sylvia in trademark silver sandals and long black dress. They took up instruments and began to play, crescendoing until they launched into "Sweet Camellia Wine." Getting the biggest hit out of the way first—even Rose saw this as a bold move. With the whole gang, except Judie.

Rose sat on her hands as the concert rolled on, her breath caught in her throat. Sylvia paired up with Angela on four of Dave's children's songs, then the Judie Zingerman–penned classic "Saucy Cat," and the crowd clapped in time to the beat, sang on the choruses.

Rose couldn't think of the summer those songs were recorded, the summer of lies, and Emma on the lake, and Leroy, without blushing so deep her internal organs were blushing, too.

Fortunately, Dolores reveled in this section, and even Felix, who tended to think Rose's interest in her family's musical catalog was pathological, swayed to these songs.

Next, Emma raucously sang lead on "Like a Rolling Stone," and Leon led them on his own song, the beloved album cut "Adonis." They did a section of folk standards—"Michael, Row the Boat Ashore," "Dink's Song," "This Land Is Your Land."

Then they got serious.

"Our president is making noise about another war," said Leon. "Dave stood against unnecessary war from the first. We want to say to you, our friends here tonight—don't give up. Keep marching, keep singing, write letters. We *shall* overcome."

This family's commitment to politics ran no deeper than anyone else's in their social circles, Rose had known since New Hampshire. One couldn't accuse them of apathy. They *cared*—but after they cared about music and themselves.

Angela and Sylvia stepped to the front now and, holding hands, began a rendition of "Down by the Riverside." They closed their eyes and made their voices fly up to the chandeliers. Rose let her mind run away, to the ideals that drew her to student meetings with Barry, despite Mary's fear. Her inner walls crumbled. Leon and Emma sang a Hebrew song, "Hineh Ma Tov," then a funky "Give Peace a Chance," and they all joined together to sing "Where Have All the Flowers Gone?"

A silly act—to play protest songs for a well-heeled crowd in a climate-controlled theater. But as the group plowed enthusiastically through a series of songs "dedicated" to President Bush, Rose's sense was of a thunder that first rumbles farther away and then comes closer, and closer still, until the rain is lashing you. It entered her, in a place beyond the cynic in her, beyond her doubts about family, about politics, about Judie, who admitted early feminist meetings made her "want to die," who began her folk career declaring she wanted to win freedom for others but couldn't even claim it for herself.

All these things were true—but so was the music. Oh, Rose knew the power of songs. They reached you in the back pocket beyond your thinking self, the place where colors and feelings and vectors of light leapt around, entered, and left you, changed you from the person you were the day before, and at least temporarily stopped the questions that pounded you at night.

"Aren't you going to sing, Mommy?" asked Dolores, who was studiously clapping. Rose glanced at Felix, whom she'd met, after all, at a No Nukes rally, and lifted her own voice: "When will they ever learn? / When will they ever learn?" She sang and sang and sang, straining her untrained voice (she could carry a tune beautifully—genes), and closed her eyes, and when she opened them, Dolores was tapping her frantically. "It's DeeDee!" said Dolores, and Rose looked around the seats near them to see where Judie had come to sit.

"No, not here—on the stage, singing!"

~

Sylvia had told her all about the spats and disagreements leading up to the show; Judie had said she was not going to play, while Emma and Leon had squabbled over billing, orchestration, and set order. But here they were, and their mother, too.

Emma stepped to the microphone.

"Dad was proud to be her collaborator for years—and we are proud of the job she did raising us and my sister, Rose, out in the audience with her beautiful family." She paused. "Dad would have done *anything* to be here and let Mom show us her stuff . . . I wish he could have seen you join in."

"Judie, you took us on a ride. We didn't know if you'd play tonight. I'm in danger of rambling . . . ," Leon said, his voice thick with tears.

"Ladies and gentlemen," Emma said, "the one and only Judie Zingerman of the Singer Sisters. Back onstage after thirty *long* years."

One of the black-clad magicians materialized with a stool, and a microphone next to it, and Judie stepped forward and sat down on it, with her guitar.

"This is a new one," she said. "Though the whole catalog is new if you haven't played for thirty years."

Judie took a deep breath, strummed her guitar with stiff fingers and looked out, panic in her eyes. Rose covered her mouth. But Dolores waved softly. "Hi, DeeDee!" Dolores whispered from the front row. She knelt on her chair to get into Judie's sightline.

"Hi, DoDo," said Judie, smiling. Holding up a finger to the audience, she flitted to the edge of the stage and reached an arm down for Dolores and brought her beside her. Dolores sat with her legs crossed.

"This is my granddaughter, the antidote to my well-documented stage fright," Judie said, her voice low but clear. "Now I'm steady."

She began to play.

I had three feathers and one fluttered away
I had two feathers and I promised I would stay
But the wind swept in, and the snow stumbled down
And my darling feathers were nowhere to be found

I once put all my feathers in my hair
I told my papa I didn't care
I swore that no one cried for me,
but I carried myself, I began to see

I had one feather, and she flew across the deep
I had two feathers, they woke me from my sleep
I had three feathers and promises to keep
But the sun burned hot and the rain fell down
And my darling feathers were nowhere to be found

But I found you, I found you waiting for me
Forgive me, I found you waiting for me

The performance felt halting, even slow, and she stumbled over a word or two. But Judie Zingerman was singing a new song onstage in front of hundreds.

Dolores sat respectfully at Judie's feet while she played. And then Judie coughed . . . and Dolores looked out to the audience and registered where she was, and her face crumpled. Rose's little girl was about to have a meltdown in front of hundreds of people.

Rose tensed up and leaned forward, wondering what to do, but before she could make a move, Emma swept onstage, took Dolores's hand, whispered, and prodded her to the edge, where Rose was waiting to receive her.

"My God, that was quick," whispered Rose, taking her daughter in her arms.

Emma settled herself on the ground near Judie, where Dolores had been.

Another black-clad helper arrived, with a microphone lowered so Emma could reach it while kneeling.

"He wrote this for you," said Judie. And she began to sang Eamon Foley's "Follow the Line."

> Let the line stray, young one
> All over the land
> Follow the line from your heart
> And you'll understand

Who was the "you"? *Herself*, Rose, right? Or was it someone else out in the audience who needed to hear it? One had to simply close one's eyes and listen, after all, to feel like Judie's conversation partner when she played this way.

The song finished, and Rose heard Judie breathe heavily through the mic, fighting back some sort of great wave of feeling.

"Well, this one is for my Dave," said Judie, almost inaudible. And she began to sing a song that drew tears out of her audience like an ancient magic trick. "We miss him so much."

> You were my shelter, and you were the rain
> Babe, you were the comfort and the pain
> You were my refuge and my tempest too
> So how do I go on now, now that I've lost you?

"Well," said Leon, coming back onstage, his face red and his wrist swiping at his eye. "That was worth waiting for. Do you have one last song in you, Judie?"

~

At the party afterward, the crowd was flushed. Champagne bubbled up and out of bottles. Rose had too much, especially after Felix took Dolores home.

Judie was radiant, glowing in the corner while well-wishers lined up in droves, but there was a melancholy current undercutting the joy. Even Rose felt it, the sense that Dave should have been onstage himself, his mustache twitching and eyes moist as Judie finally sang.

Emma ambled up to Rose at one of the tall, round cocktail tables, chewing on a maraschino cherry. She tossed the stem back in her glass and waited for Rose to speak.

"Her new songs," said Rose.

"They're gold," said Emma with a frown. "I'll never have what she has as a writer."

"You were so . . ." And Rose thought about Felix, who told her to stop gushing over Emma like a besotted fan. "You're so *versatile*," she settled on.

Emma's face went dark, the way it had the night they met when she turned around and slammed the door, but now she closed her eyes and put her cocktail glass down.

"I guess I am."

"You're the best live performer in your family," said Rose. "You know you are. Leon has the rawest musicality, Dave had a specific charm, and our mother has the catalog. See, I know—I can break it all down."

Emma's brown eyes, like Rose's eyes, like cartoon-cat eyes, turned round.

"You have us nailed," she said.

"Why didn't you play 'Flower'?" asked Rose.

"Timing," said Emma. "It's still—honestly, it's such a massive hit compared to even 'Sweet Camellia Wine' that it didn't fit."

"Wow."

"I know. I'm a one-hit wonder."

"I have so much I want to ask you," said Rose. "But it's never the right time."

But time will unfold eventually. Someday, Rose, drunk on Manischewitz, will finally ask Emma if she wishes she'd never been born, not for her own sake, not to snuff out her own small life, but so Judie's existence could have been different. *Bigger.*

And Emma will laugh and put her silver-streaked, close-cropped head of curls against Rose's blond one and say, "I used to wish that *you* had never been born, to be honest, but if you had never been born, I would never have been born, so maybe we both shouldn't have been born—or maybe we're her greatest creation, in the end."

One day, after they've shared even more pain, they'll truly be sisters.

But before that, before the years can dance onward—before Emma and Rose talk at the after-party, before Dolores shoots up like a flower and discovers her own gift for writing, before Emma falls in love with an upstate artist, before Judie gets the nerve to sit down and record "Feathers"—this concert for Dave, this velvety, tearstained night, must find a way to finish.

—

And it does. When the singers seem like they can sing no more, the Zingerman-Cantor family and all their friends step back out in front of the red plush curtain for a final curtain call.

"Sing 'Flower'!" someone starts shouting. Emma considers it but shakes her head.

Instead, they add more Dave Canticle songs, piling it on like they are building a ladder to heaven: "Morning Crickets" and "Little Brown Sparrow." And then, when the cheers die down to an ember, Judie steps up to the microphone.

She looks right at Rose and calls Rose and Dolores and Felix to the stage, and they are pulled up by someone's hands and standing in a line with the group, and Judie is singing the opening notes of "Route 95," and they are joining her.

"I had to make a change / So I left the life I know," they sing, and Rose hears everyone's voice distinctly, even as they harmonize into one bouquet of sound: Leon's flourishing baritone, Emma's growl, Angela's rich alto, Sylvia's perfect soprano, and her own family—her Felix, her DoDo—singing along together, their voices amateur but rich.

A person's life has so many new beginnings. The launching pads and the false starts, where you say, "This time, I will strike out for freedom," and fail, and repeat old patterns. But you try again. To Rose, whose life has been many lives, this song is both prayer and answer.

The audience claps in time to the chorus. Under the hot glare of the lights, Rose spies dozens of women who'd been preparing to leave and board their subways and hail their cabs and lament their blotchy skin, their lives made up of pregnancy tests and late babysitters and tired spouses and demanding bosses, all of them turning around. Filing back down the aisle, standing up, swaying, and singing every damn word of the song like an incantation, some with tears in their eyes that shine in the lights.

Hands wave back and forth, reaching for the chandeliers, worshippers at the altar of Judie's songs. Cell phones light up. Bodies, eyes, locked on to the stage, on Judie Zingerman, who cradles her guitar like an infant she's holding captive with a lullaby.

Rose's warble bursts forth unafraid. She knows something true, and the people onstage are proof of it: in Leon's arrangements, in Dave's best tunes, in Emma's chart-toppers and Angela's perfect album, in Sylvia's endurance, the same thread sparkles: Judie's songs. Judie's music, and Judie's love, twisted though it may be.

All the women are welcoming Judie back after her absence, her silence; they missed her, they needed her voice. They are welcoming Judie back, but Judie has always been with them.

ACKNOWLEDGMENTS

To my superb agent Susanna Einstein, I am so lucky you ended up loving these singers and their *mishegas* and found them a perfect stage at Flatiron with the perfect editor, Megan Lynch, who knew just what to do with them. Susanna and Megan, thank you beyond words for being on Judie, Emma, Sylvia, and Rose's team, and on mine.

Thank you to the Flatiron team, especially Kukuwa Ashun, for your sharp eye and care throughout the entire process. I'm so lucky to have the brilliant Katherine Turro and Marlena Bittner helping this book reach readers, and the ace production team of Emily Walters, Jeremy Pink, Vincent Stanley, Donna Noetzel, Jen Edwards, and Sona Vogel. David Litman designed a stunning cover that belongs in bookstores and on merch tables alike.

Thank you to Yona Zeldis McDonough, the literary mentor of my dreams, for changing my life twice. Thanks to the early champions of this book, including Robin MacArthur, Elizabeth Graver, Adelle Waldman, Elisa Albert, Rob Sheffield, Bethany Ball, and Jessica Gross.

Much appreciation to readers from the "before" times: Naomi Zeveloff, Erin Blakemore, Ben Woodard, Sarah Levitt, Emily Arnason Casey, and Sarah Twombly. A huge shoutout goes to Heather Aimee O'Neill and Julia Fierro of Sackett Street, and to my manuscript class, especially Mary Ann Casavant, Kelsey Miller, and Amritha Kasturirangan. Thanks also to Caroline Woods and Kate Racculia at Grub Street.

Thank you to Kristen Gwynne, the only person not bound to me by blood who both shaped the manuscript *and* watched my kids so I could write it. Lauren Kelley, Bryce Covert, and Emily Douglas, thanks for those tequila shots and all they signify. Zach Seward, Mike Grynbaum, Doug Lieb, Anita LaScala, Kate Lee, Abby Kornfield, Kate Schmier, and MJ Knefel—thanks for the texts and LOLs during the dark years and beyond.

At *Lilith Magazine*, I thank Naomi Danis, Lindsay Barnett, Rebecca Katz, Susan Weidman Schneider, Arielle Silver-Willner, and our writers and interns for their cheer and understanding.

At Vermont College of Fine Arts, I learned the craft from Connie May Fowler, Ellen Lesser, Abby Frucht, Jess Row, and Dominic Stansberry. To Chanel Dubofsky, Kate Senecal, Brendan Todt, Liz Young, Mahtem Shifferaw, and Sarah Braud, I am grateful for *you*. Thanks to Louise Crowley and the VCFA staff, and to the resilient city of Montpelier, Vermont.

It's my debut novel, so I acknowledge teachers, editors, and colleagues who guided my writing trajectory: the late Tom LaFarge, Claude Catapano, Geraldine Woods, Caroline Bartels, Kyoko Mori, D. A. Powell, the late Ehud Havazelet, Judy Berman, Eric Messinger, Gabrielle Birkner, Jason Diamond, and Andi Zeisler.

So much gratitude to the people who helped our household function while I hustled, wrote, and revised: Greta Longville, Patricia Evo, the staff of Children's Learning Center, and Paige Wills.

Julia Pollak, thank you for a lifetime of best friendship.

Thanks to Molly Vozick-Levinson and Debbie Theodore—my ridiculously cool and brilliant sisters-in-law—and Tina Vozick and Paul Levinson, bestowers of Cape Cod pep talks, publishing insights, and so much more. Thanks to Lyla and Artie Seltzer, for being so darn cute.

Thanks to my hilarious, wise, and endlessly giving parents, Ann Lewis Seltzer and Richard Seltzer, for making it a feat of imagination to conjure up family dysfunction. Mom and Dad, you introduced me to the things that matter in life: music, books, art, and deli food—and supported my winding path unconditionally. To my beloved twin Dan Seltzer, I won the lottery by being your wombmate, friend, fellow parent, and Springsteen concertgoing companion. You make every day better.

Mikey and Julian: Thanks for giving my life new purpose and so much sweetness. It's the joy of my life to be your mom, your best buddy, and your bedtime storyteller.

Simon Vozick-Levinson: my forever partner in life, art, and conversation and the driving force behind this book making it to shelves (in fact, you are out with the kids right now so I can finish copy edits). You proofread until late, troubleshot plot holes, and drew that chart in my planner detailing two paths: submitting the book vs. letting it languish. Thanks for pushing me to choose the right one. On a deeper level, you kept my enjoyment of music alive when I might have let it fade—and took me as your plus-one to the concerts and films that planted the seeds for this book. Thanks to you, I have dual sources of eternal joy: music and love.

CHRONOLOGY

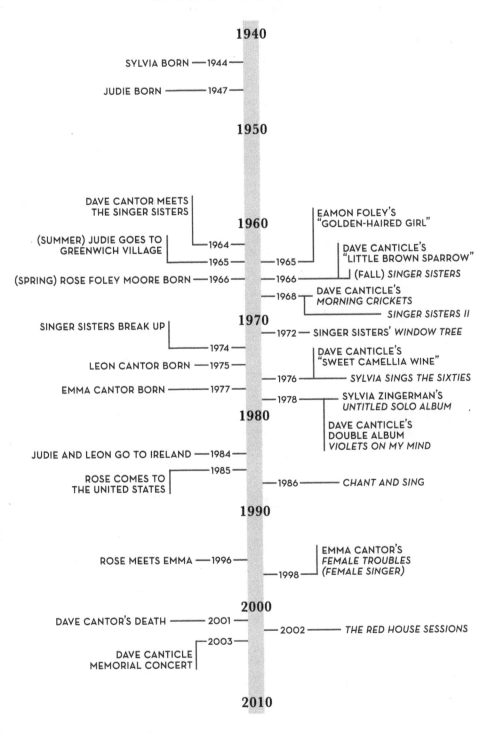

1940

SYLVIA BORN —1944—

JUDIE BORN ———— 1947—

1950

DAVE CANTOR MEETS
THE SINGER SISTERS

EAMON FOLEY'S
"GOLDEN-HAIRED GIRL"

1960

(SUMMER) JUDIE GOES TO ——1964—
GREENWICH VILLAGE

—1965— —1965— DAVE CANTICLE'S
"LITTLE BROWN SPARROW"

—1966— (FALL) *SINGER SISTERS*

(SPRING) ROSE FOLEY MOORE BORN —1966—

—1968— DAVE CANTICLE'S
MORNING CRICKETS

——— *SINGER SISTERS II*

1970

SINGER SISTERS BREAK UP

—1972— SINGER SISTERS' *WINDOW TREE*

—1974—

DAVE CANTICLE'S
"SWEET CAMELLIA WINE"

LEON CANTOR BORN —1975—

—1976—— *SYLVIA SINGS THE SIXTIES*

EMMA CANTOR BORN ———— 1977—

—1978— SYLVIA ZINGERMAN'S
UNTITLED SOLO ALBUM

1980

DAVE CANTICLE'S
DOUBLE ALBUM
VIOLETS ON MY MIND

JUDIE AND LEON GO TO IRELAND —1984—

—1985—

ROSE COMES TO
THE UNITED STATES

—1986——— *CHANT AND SING*

1990

ROSE MEETS EMMA —1996—

EMMA CANTOR'S
FEMALE TROUBLES
—1998— *(FEMALE SINGER)*

2000

DAVE CANTOR'S DEATH ——— 2001—

—2002——— *THE RED HOUSE SESSIONS*

—2003—

DAVE CANTICLE
MEMORIAL CONCERT

2010